HOLLYWOOD REDEMPTION: LUKE AND ALEX

FAIRLANE #1

HARLOW LAYNE

"I'M SO GLAD YOU FINALLY MADE IT BACK OUT HERE." ANNA smiled genuinely from the seat beside me at the restaurant's table.

Anna and I had become good friends over the last several months. First, by talking on the phone and texting, and then one day she informed me that she and Colt were coming to visit Colt's family in Fairlane for the weekend and wanted us to meet up for lunch or dinner. To say I was shocked would be an understatement. We had only met once at Becca Matthews party and after hearing about my wreck from Becca, Anna called to ask if there was anything she could do.

I had a feeling that her husband, Colt, felt somewhat responsible since he'd brought Matt to Fairlane and chose our table to sit at that fateful night. I didn't blame him for any of it. It had been my decision to continue seeing Matt after that night.

A couple of months ago, Mason and I had gone for the weekend to hang out with Anna in Chicago where she was shooting a movie. We'd never been and, being the great host that she was, Anna showed us around like the tourists we were and as if she'd lived there her entire life. It was a fun weekend visiting the Shedd Aquarium, the Art Institute of Chicago, Adler Planetarium, and of course, we took in a baseball game too. Mason had a blast and wore himself out every day. He could barely finish his dinner every night before he'd pass out, leaving Anna and I in our hotel room giggling and gossiping like a bunch of schoolgirls.

Almost a year ago, I went out with a friend for a girl's night out to celebrate the one-year anniversary of my divorce. That may sound strange to most, but I needed it after dealing with my ex-husband's verbal abuse for over a decade and then all the bullshit he'd put me through after I left him. During my night out, I met *the* Colton Patrick, a big movie star from my hometown, and his friend Matt Ryan. Matt and I ended up dating for a hot minute, until he freaked out on me in the car on the way to the airport and we got in a wreck. That's when Anna, Hollywood's sweetheart, became my friend.

"You know not wanting to come to LA had nothing to do with you and more to do with what happened the last time I was here, right?" I exhaled as I twirled a piece of food with my fork.

"I know, and I don't blame you. You got a shit deal when you were here." Shaking her head, Anna looked down at her lap as she twisted her napkin. "I still can't believe Matt freaked out and, caused you to wreck, and then for him to cheat on you! Colton still won't answer his messages, he's so mad. I think he feels responsible in a way."

Shaking my head, I gave her a sad smile. I didn't like to

think about that weekend often, and what could've happened. This was the first time since her initial phone call after the accident that Anna had said Matt's name. In fact, no one mentioned it around me, as if I'd break down or have steam come out of my ears. From what I knew, none of them talked to him after I got out of the hospital. Jenner had stopped talking to Matt and had blocked his number after sending him a message saying that he didn't want to have anything to do with a man who would cheat on a woman and then blame her because of his guilty conscience.

Reeves Jenner was another person that I'd met through Matt, and we'd become good friends after he drove me back to Fairlane from LA. I'd had a concussion and a broken arm and was advised against flying immediately after getting out of the hospital. All I had cared about was getting back to my son, Mason, and Jenner had made that a reality.

Jenner and I bonded on our trip and the subsequent week that he spent with us. After he got back home to LA, we talked a lot about his wife Poppy and what she was up to all the times she disappeared. I'd yet to meet her since she had been MIA the night I met Jenner, but I wasn't a fan of hers since she was always distressing Jenner in some way or another.

Over the months, Jenner and I had stopped trying to figure out where and what Poppy was up to. Lately, she did seem to be around more. Luckily for me, she wasn't around last night when we were hanging out. I wasn't sure I could hold my tongue knowing how much Jenner worried and loved her. I had no evidence that Poppy had been, or was, cheating on Jenner, but from everything he'd told me and the look that passed between Becca and Matt the night I'd met them, I had a pretty good suspicion she was.

Anna was having a little Fourth of July party and invited me out to LA once she found out I would be alone for the holiday, since Mason had gone on vacation for two weeks with Decker, my ex-husband, and his parents. At first I didn't want to, as the memories of the wreck came back, and how upset Mason had been and how long it affected him. I didn't want to risk a repeat, but I also knew I wouldn't be putting myself in that type of situation again.

If I thought Anna and Colt's house in Fairlane was the most beautiful I'd ever seen, their home in Beverly Hills was breathtaking. It was a three-story Spanish-style house with a courtyard in the front and a large backyard with an infinity pool that looked out over LA. During the day it was beautiful, and at night the sight was miraculous. It was even equipped with an outdoor kitchen/barbecue area. There were small colorful lanterns hung from the trees, and seating areas that were almost like little cabanas. In keeping with the Spanish design, the interior of the home was gorgeous, filled with vibrant colors and very welcoming. I'd immediately felt at home.

After the party the night before, we were a little slow to get around that morning and decided to have a girl's lunch out with a few of Anna's friends. At first, when I found out that she was inviting Ruby Price, Grace Anderson, and Cyndi Hanson to lunch with us, I almost had a mild heart attack. They were all big-name actresses that I had grown up watching. It was one thing to see them at the party last night, but a whole other to be sitting around a table with them. The girls were Anna's Hollywood best friends, and I was highly intimidated by them the night before as they eyed me throughout the night. I hoped they didn't think I'd befriended Anna only to use her. The public had either been on my side or the glaring opposite with Matt comma from what Taylor had told me. I stayed away from the gossip, but Taylor ate it up. From what she'd read there were many who thought it was my fault that Matt cheated and wrecked the car. They also thought that I'd used him to try to become famous. Hearing what they'd said was what made me stay away from the gossip.

"Luke," Cyndi waved excitedly to an extremely tall and attractive man who was walking by our table. "Hey, what are you doing here?" She asked as she stood and kissed him on the cheek.

"I'm just here for an interview before I head back out of town in a couple of days." His deep accented voice was smooth like velvet.

I couldn't help but ogle him as I took in the man that stood before me. Not only was he remarkably tall at well above six feet, but his shoulders and chest were broad, and his well-defined biceps flexed as he gave her a small hug. This Luke guy was the epitome of sexy with his tight black t-shirt clinging to his upper body in the best possible way. It took all my self-control not to drool as I continued my appraisal that only got better and better with each inch I took in. His waist tapered down, and I knew that if he took off his shirt he'd have one of those delicious V's that I'd only seen in magazines and movies. You know, the ones where you want to get up close and personal with each line leading down to the pleasure zone, while following them with your tongue. He was wearing dark jeans that I was sure would hug his ass because that's what I would do if I were those jeans on that body. My gaze made its way back up his body to his face. I was sure that if I hadn't been sitting in that moment I would have made a complete ass of myself as my legs gave out. Even seated, I could feel they were weak. Luke was perfection. His hair was a light blondish-brown from what I could see peeking out from underneath his black baseball hat, but it was his eyes that captivated me. They were unlike any color I'd ever seen before on a person. In one instance they looked blue and in the next green. They reminded me of Caribbean waters, that beautiful island color I was a sucker for. Lowering my gaze, I took in his full pink lips and the dimple in his chin. I wanted to nibble on that lip and then bite and kiss that dimple until the end of my days.

Dear God, what was this man doing to me?

I couldn't remember the last time I'd ever had such a reaction to a man, but then again, I'd never meet anyone as gorgeous as Luke.

"Please, join us. We have too much estrogen at this table. We need your hotness to balance us out," Cyndi joked, laughing with a twinkle in her eye before extending her arm out to the table. There were a couple of seats available and I thought for sure that he'd pick the one closest to Cyndi, but instead he started for the seat directly in front of me.

This wouldn't be good. I wasn't sure if I could keep my cool while he was across from me. I didn't want to stare, but how could I not, and I sure as hell didn't want to ignore him. This was my one and only chance to be in the presence of perfection.

"Are you sure?" he asked, eying us as if we all might attack him the second he sat down.

Ding, ding, ding.

He was right to feel a little wary because I wanted to pounce.

Again, what was wrong with me?

"Yeah, yeah, we're all a friendly bunch. Aren't we ladies?" Cyndi smiled almost evilly as she took her seat. I hoped he knew that Cindy was mostly harmless.

We all smiled, and a few waved from the other end of the table as Luke took his seat, a hesitant smile on his face. Surely if Luke was in the restaurant to do an interview he must be in the entertainment business. I couldn't be sure because I didn't recognize him. Although that wasn't surprising, since I didn't watch too much TV or have time to go to the movies.

Looking at me from across the table, Luke smiled in a friendly way, looking as if he was going to speak at any moment. I wasn't sure if I was ready for talking to the hottie sitting directly across from me. Never in my life had I been so attracted to a man, and it scared the shit out of me. He stole my breath as his gaze locked with mine.

My phone rang, saving me from staring and possibly hyperventilating like an idiot. Once I saw it was Mason calling, I jumped from the table to take it.

"Hey, honey. Is everything okay?" Mason had called me first thing in the morning and right before bed since he'd been gone and while he seemed to be having fun, I missed him more and more every day.

"Yep." Mason replied brightly into the phone. "I just saw the Grand Canyon. It's so big! Have you seen it, mommy?"

I answered as I walked toward the bathroom, wishing it was me that Mason was with when he got to see all the amazing places on his vacation. "I have. My grandpa took me when I was a little older than you."

"Was it big then?"

"It was." I smiled, thinking back to my trip with my grandparents. "I remember standing right at the edge against the hand rails, looking over, and my grandma freaked out because she was afraid of heights, but my grandpa was right beside me, looking out over the vastness. It was amazing."

"Awesome."

"It *was* awesome. What are you doing now?"

"Waiting for dad to get back from the bathroom so I asked grandma and grandpa if I could call you."

"I'm glad you did. I miss you." My last word was a croak as I tried not to cry. I could hear his grandparents tell him that he was going to have to get off the phone soon, making matters worse. Instead on dwelling over how much I missed him, I finished washing my hands and made my way back to the table. I'd need the distraction once I got off the phone.

"Mama, I have to get off the phone now. Dad's on his way back and he'll be mad if I'm on the phone." There was no hiding the sadness in his voice at having to get off the phone. At least his grandparents were with them and I knew they loved Mason.

"I know, baby. I'll talk to you tonight. Okay?"

"Okay," Mason sniffed.

"I love you and have lots of fun." Pulling out my chair, I kept my eyes down and away from everyone.

"I love you, too. Bye."

"Bye," I said even though he had already disconnected.

Pasting on my best smile, I took my seat before grabbing my mimosa and draining the last half. Anna gave me a quick side hug before going back to whatever discussion everyone else was having.

Looking around for a waiter to get another refill, I was startled to hear Luke's deep and slightly accented voice ask, "Your husband?"

Instead of answering a laugh bubbled out of me. Luke probably thought I was crazy because he'd said nothing to cause my outburst. Looking over at him, I saw a 'what the fuck is wrong with her look' and quickly settled down.

"I'm sorry, I promise I'm not crazy or anything. At least I don't think so." God, I was a mess.

"Nothing wrong with a little crazy." His eyes sparkled with mischief along with his smirk.

"I guess not, but for now I'm happy with boring and normal."

One lone eyebrow rose on his handsome face. "Is your husband boring?"

"My ex-husband is nowhere near boring. More of an asshole than anything else, but that wasn't him. That was my son who's with his asshole father."

"And you're not happy he's with his father?" Luke asked scratching his cheek.

"No, but I don't really have any say on the matter so what can I do?"

Luke cocked his head to the side and gave me a sad smile making me feel guilty. I didn't want his pity and it was obvious I wasn't hiding how upset I was from my phone call.

Letting out a deep sigh, I tried to smile back at him. "I'm sorry. I shouldn't bother you with my problems."

He chuckled and gave me a crooked smile that for one moment made me forget all my troubles. "I don't mind. Sometimes it's nice to hear someone else's problems and forget our own."

"True." I agreed. "Do you want to tell me yours, so I can forget mine?"

Shrugging he started to run a hand through his hair but came into contact with his baseball hat instead. His cheeks flushed as he looked away. Somehow knowing that he was embarrassed made him even more attractive. I wanted to roll my eyes at myself and my hormones. The poor guy's embarrassment shouldn't make me want to jump him.

"I don't have any exes causing me problems or anything like that, but I do miss my family. It's been a long time since I've seen them and with my hours it's hard to find a good time to talk to them on the phone." He gave a grimace of a smile and glanced away again.

It was strange that I had only just met this man, but the sadness in his voice spoke to me and caused my heart to ache. I felt an instant connection to Luke and his pain. The backs of my eyes burned with tears that I fought away.

"Do you want to talk about it or will that just make it worse?"

"No, but thank you." He shook his head, his eyes sad.

"I understand." Turning back to the rest of the group I listened until a hand covered my own. My head whipped around so fast, I almost got whiplash only to see Luke's retreating hand.

He flinched. "Sorry."

"You have nothing to be sorry for." My brows drew together wondering what Luke thought he had to be sorry for.

"For touching you and for not wanting to talk," he explained as if he could read my thoughts.

I shook by head hastily, hating myself for making this hot guy think I hated his touch. "The touching is all me. It may seem weird, but I'm not really used to being touched very much, and it took me by surprise. As for the other, I truly do understand about not wanting to talk about your problems. First, you don't know me and not everyone wants to talk to a stranger. Second, no reason to dampen this," my arm indicated the table and people around it. "Third, I assume you are some sort of celebrity if you know Cyndi and as such, you have to be careful about who you talk to so that whatever you say doesn't get leaked to the press."

Letting out a small laugh, Luke studied me for a minute. "I swear I'm not saying this to be conceited or because I have a huge ego because I don't, but you really don't recognize me?"

"No," I replied, shaking my head and giving him another once over. How in the world would I ever forget that face if I'd seen it before? "I'm sorry. I don't watch a lot of TV or movies."

"To tell you the truth neither do I."

Feeling bad for not knowing who he was I asked. "What should I know you from?"

Luke made a low hum in the back of his throat. "I've done two shows for the H@T network. One was a mini-series about drug addicts and the other is in its second season, about vampires that are taking over the world. I also did a movie last summer that was out in theaters a couple of months ago."

"Wait, a minute. I watched a show on H@T about addicts. Were you on Fix?"

"Yeah," Luke answered uneasily as if he was afraid I was going to go all fangirl on him.

"And you're on another show on H@T that has vampires in it?" His only answer was to nod his head. I was probably scaring him with the way I had perked up as I tried to figure this out. I didn't watch much TV, but I did normally watch H@T's Sunday night shows because they were always good and never disappointed. "Are you on Night Shadows?"

"Yeah." He answered again only this time with a little chuckle.

I watched and knew both those shows, but I couldn't place the Luke who was sitting across from me on either one.

"I'm sorry for staring, but I've watched both those shows. I actually love them, but I can't place you."

"Don't worry about it."

"It's going to drive me crazy!" My eyes traced over his face one last time and slowly my synapsis started firing, connecting the dots on who Luke was on both shows. He didn't look like either character as he sat across from me. On Fix, Luke's character, John Connelly, had short, black hair, and he was so skinny he looked emaciated. "Wow," I exclaimed a little too loudly for inside the restaurant and smiling what probably looked like a Joker smile. "You were John Connelly. I never would've guessed that was you."

"Yeah, the dark hair and the weight I lost throws people." His shoulder lifted in a half-shrug while his cheeks turned a light shade of pink. It seemed Luke was a little shy talking about his roles for some reason.

"I'm a few episodes behind on Night Shadows, but I can't place you." My head shook as I tried to figure out who he was on the show.

"Hmmm, I wasn't on the first episode of this season and in the first season I wore a wig."

Laughing, I couldn't believe I still didn't know who he was. "Are you going to make me beg for you to tell me your character's name?"

His mouth curved into a wicked smile and his eyes glinted in the light. "Maybe."

Was he flirting with me? No. There was no way on this Earth that this fine specimen of a man was flirting with me.

Instead of thinking about how Luke would never find me attractive, I mentally went through all the characters I remembered from Night Shadows. The one problem with H@T was that once the season was over you had to wait another year for it to be on and within that year and having only seen one episode of the new season, I had forgotten many of the characters and what they looked like.

"Oh my God! You're Nikolai! I can't believe I didn't see it sooner. My mind can't wrap around the fact that both John and Nikolai are the same person, and it's you. The hair really threw me." My words came out too quick with excitement.

Luke only smiled at me and I hoped that I hadn't made him uncomfortable, but I had to figure out who he was on the shows that I loved.

"I'm sorry. It was really driving me crazy that I couldn't figure it out. We don't have to talk about it if you don't want to."

"I'm glad you figured it out. I know what it's like when

you know you're supposed to know or remember something it can drive you crazy, but yeah if we could talk about something else that would be great. All I've been doing for the last two months in my spare time is talk about myself and my projects. I'd rather hear about you."

"Is that how you met Cyndi, or did you know her before?"

He moved his head from side to side. "We met once before when I went on her show, but I was a secondary guest then and we didn't really talk much. When my movie came out, I did her show again," he shrugged his shoulders. "We seemed to hit it off, but I think she usually does with all her guests. So, when she asked me to join you ladies I said yes."

I had a feeling there might be other reasons as to why Luke joined us, but either way I was happy. "Well, I'm glad you did."

"Me, too. Now that you know what I do for a living, what do you do?"

I rolled my eyes at my boring profession. "I'm a web designer. It's not exciting in the least."

"I don't know. I think it's pretty cool. I mean, I have no clue how to do anything like that."

"It can be cool, but normally I get boring jobs."

"I'm sorry. Here we've been talking, and I don't even know your name," Luke gave me a lop-sided smile.

"Oh my gosh, how rude of me. I'm sorry. I heard Cyndi call you Luke, so I already knew your name, and I don't know where my head was. I'm Alexandra Sloane, but my friends call me Alex."

"It's nice to meet you, Alex. I'm Lukas Sandström, but everyone calls me Luke."

Luke and I continued to talk as if we were the only two people in the restaurant. Once I got over his hotness, he was easy to talk to. It wasn't until Anna put a hand on my arm that I realized that I'd been ignoring everyone else at the table. From the look on her face Anna didn't mind, in fact she looked amused.

"Honey, we're getting ready to leave."

"Oh!" I looked around the table for my bill but found nothing but an empty plate and glass. "Has the waiter came by? I haven't paid yet."

Anna smiled, lighting up her whole face. "Don't worry about it. I already took care of it."

"I can't let you do that." I hadn't come for her to pay my way.

"Hey! It was my idea for you to come out here, and you wouldn't let me pay for your plane ticket, so it's the least I can do. The girls are all going their separate ways and I think I'm going to go home. What do you want to do?" Her eyes darted toward Luke as she smiled.

"Um, I guess I'll go home with you. I don't really have any plans except hang out with you and catch my plane tomorrow."

"If it's okay with both of you, I can bring her home later," Luke piped in looking a little unsure.

Anna beamed as she looked back and forth between us. "Of course, I don't mind. Go and have fun!"

I couldn't help but laugh. It was like she was my mom giving me permission to go out on a date. The irony was that I'd never once been asked out on a date and my mother hadn't been in the picture since I was around three.

"Is that okay with you, Alex?" Luke asked, tugging on his shirt collar nervously.

It was sort of like he was asking me out and there was no way in hell that I was going to say no.

"I would love to." I answered quietly before turning to Anna. "I guess I'll see you later tonight."

When her only response was another beaming smile, I bit my bottom lip until I caught what I had done and realized how unattractive it probably made me. Releasing my lip, I licking them and watched as Luke's eyes followed the movement of my tongue.

2

With Luke's hand resting on the small of my back, we slipped out the back of the restaurant unnoticed, and he guided me to his car. My body tingled at the contact. Why was he affecting me in a way no one ever had before?

All my life my friends panted after men and went gaga for them, but I'd never felt that way until this moment. After all those years, I'd thought there was something wrong with me, but now I knew I just needed to meet the right man. I only hoped I didn't make a total fool out of myself because all I wanted to do was stare at him.

Luke was perfection.

Clearing his throat, Luke's lips tipped up slightly in what seemed to be a nervous smile. "So, I know of this park that's pretty isolated, and I thought we could hang out there for a while. If that's okay with you?"

"That sounds perfect."

There was no way I was turning down being somewhere isolated with him.

Once we arrived at the park, we sat on a jacket that Luke had in his car. Well, mostly I sat on it so that my bare legs wouldn't be on the itchy grass.

Leaning back on his elbows, Luke looked up at the sky. "This is going to sound so cliché, but where are you from? Not to be rude, but you don't seem like you're from around here."

I couldn't help but laugh. "In no way do I think you're rude. I'm actually from Fairlane, Missouri."

His brows furrowed, deep in thought. "Never heard of it. How'd you meet Anna Jenson?"

I wasn't surprised that he'd never heard of my hometown. Only diehard Colton Patrick fans knew of it outside of the Midwest.

"I actually met her at a Halloween party that Becca Matthews was throwing." Wringing my hands together, I looked out at the green grass and the trees swaying in the wind.

"I sense there's a story there."

I snapped my fingers and pointed at him. "You'd be right."

His lips twitched, but he said nothing waiting for me to continue.

"A girl who used to be a friend of mine, and I won't go into that because that's a whole other story, convinced me that I needed to get out and have some fun after the one-year anniversary of my divorce rolled around."

Luke had sat up and turned to face me as I told my story to how this all came about. I told him of how I met Colt and Matt in a club and how I sort of started dating Matt after that. The two trips I made out to LA to visit him, and Becca's Halloween party we went to where I seemed to have met every A-list celebrity in Hollywood, and my last trip, where we got in a wreck when Matt lost control both literally and figuratively, and I found out that he'd been cheating on me.

"So, between my ex-husband and him, I haven't had very good luck with men." A flush swept across my cheeks at all I'd told him. Luke was practically a stranger, even though it felt as if I'd known him for years. It was strange. Taylor was the only other person I'd ever felt an instant connection to, but this felt like more. I had to remind myself not to let him in because after today I'd likely never see him again.

"Maybe you haven't met the right man yet." He countered, after his cerulean blue eyes sparked at their examination of me.

I ran my sweaty palms down my legs and shrugged. "I don't know. Maybe I'll stay single and turn into a crazy cat lady."

"Did you know that a cat will eat you if it's trapped inside with you and you're dead?" he screwed his face up in disgust.

My nose scrunched. "Ugh. That's gross. Okay, how about I become a crazy dog lady?"

We laughed until it died down into a companionable silence. I watched as a father pushed what looked like his three-year-old daughter on a swing. She laughed or smiled with every push.

Out of the corner of my eye, I caught Luke look over at me. Breaking the silence, he spoke with conviction. "One day you'll find a man that'll redeem what they did to you. Not all men are like that. I promise."

Unfortunately, no matter how much I was drawn to him, Luke wouldn't be that man.

Luke's eyes darted around the park before he quickly stood up. "I hate to cut this short, but it seems we've been spotted."

Jumping to my feet, I spotted a man with a camera aimed right at us. Keeping my head down, I made my way to the passenger side of his car and hastily got in.

Luke tapped his fingers on the steering wheel as he listened to the directions my phone gave on the way to Anna's. "I'm sorry about that. If the house I was staying at wasn't packed, I would've taken you back there." He smiled over at me sheepishly.

"You don't need to explain yourself to me."

"I feel like I do. I'd like to see you again."

Really?

"Unfortunately, I'm leaving tomorrow." I hoped he didn't hear my sadness that our time was almost over.

"What time's your flight? Maybe we could do breakfast or lunch?"

"It's at 1:20 so I could do probably do breakfast if Anna doesn't mind me skipping out on her."

"After you talk to her let me know. I can also take you to the airport afterward."

"Oh, I don't want to put you out. I know driving to the airport here is a real pain in the ass."

"It's not a problem." He shrugged while keeping his eyes on the road. "Just let me know."

When we finally pulled up in front of Anna and Colt's place, Anna stood outside waiting for me. My mother had never been around, but if she had, I would've expected something like this when I came home from a date. Even from the car you could see her eyes sparkling with happiness.

"Do you think she's been waiting there since the guard called up?" His mouth twitched as we watched her look at some flowers as if she wasn't waiting for me.

"Probably. I feel like a teenage girl coming home from a date." I slapped my hand over my mouth. Quickly I tried to rectify the situation. "Not that this was a date."

"No, worries." His knee bounced up and down nervously as he looked from Anna to me. "Give me your phone and I'll put my number in it."

In awe I handed over my phone in a daze and watched as the most gorgeous man in the world put his phone number in my phone.

"Call me later." He called as I stepped out of the car.

I leaned down, holding the door. "I will. I hope to see you tomorrow."

Halfway to the door, I turned back to wave and could have sworn that Luke had been staring at my ass.

The second his car left the driveway, Anna pounced on me. "I want every single detail." She pulled me inside by the arm. "I've got margaritas and guacamole waiting out back."

"There's not much to tell."

"Oh please. First, you were gone for three hours and second, you guys totally ignored the rest of us from the moment he sat down."

"He did ask to see me again tomorrow before I leave. I told him I had to talk to you to make sure you didn't mind and that I'd call him later."

Her eyes went wide, and a smile stretched across her face. "What are you waiting for? Go call him!"

3

LUKE'S CAR SPED ALONG THE 405 AS I WATCHED LA AND THE traffic out my window. We'd left a little over three hours before I was supposed to catch my one o'clock flight. We knew that we'd be fighting traffic so after saying goodbye to Anna who was practically jumping with joy; we took off.

Inside his car was coffee and chocolate croissants that were still somehow warm in the bag. Even with the wonderful smells coming from the food, Luke's unique scent of sandalwood and ocean lingered.

"I'm sorry we couldn't make breakfast work, but these are some of the best croissants in all of LA so at least there's that." I nibbled on mine as he drove.

"I've never had chocolate before, but I have to agree they're the best I've had."

This time as I left LA, I was happy and obviously not hurt. My trip had been great and the only way it could've gone better was if I'd spent more time with Jenner or got down and dirty with Luke the night before.

My phone chirped from inside my purse and I took a quick look at it before putting it back in its pocket.

"Are you not going to answer back?" Luke asked from beside me with a curious look.

"I will when I get to the airport. I can't type while in the car for even the shortest of distances without getting car sick, and I definitely don't want to be sick before my flight."

"Do you get sick on planes?" he glanced at me from the corner of his eye.

"Luckily, no, but I don't want to chance it. Do you get sick on planes?"

"No," he answered with a laugh. "That would be horrible in my line of work and with how far away my family is."

"I never got around to asking you yesterday. Where are you from?"

"I grew up in Visby, Sweden."

So that's where that sexy little accent came from.

"Sweden." I turned in my seat to see him better. "That's so interesting. That's where that little accent comes from. Does your family all still live in Visby?"

He smirked and shook his head in amusement. "No, everyone's moved away and most now live in Stockholm. My brother Leo, we're the closest in age, lives in England."

"That must be hard. How long is the flight to Sweden?"

"Hmmm," he hummed as he thought about it. "If I can get a nonstop flight then about eleven hours, but that doesn't happen very often. Otherwise, flights normally are between fourteen to sixteen hours depending on the layover from LA."

"I can't imagine being on a plane for that long. Do you get bored or are you normally too excited to see your family?"

Instead of answering, Luke only smiled.

Fidgeting in my seat, my hand made its way to my earring where I absentmindedly twirled it around. "What?"

His smile only grew, lighting up the profile of his face. "You're cute."

My cheeks flushed from embarrassment. "Why do I feel like you're making fun of me?"

Luke shook his head while staring out the windshield, his knuckles noticeably going white as his grip increased. I could only stare at him from my side of the car, wondering what was going on in that head of his. "I promise you I'm not making fun of you. I don't know you well enough *yet*. You misinterpreted my smile and comment; it's because normally I try to get as much sleep as possible on the plane before I get to Sweden. Typically, I only get to visit about once a year, so the time change is brutal and once I'm there, I'm too busy visiting with family and friends."

Biting my lower lip for feeling so silly, I nibbled on it before asking. "How many hours difference is there?"

"From LA it's eight, and New York five hours."

"Wow." My mouth formed an 'O' as I thought about the time difference. "I can't imagine trying to get used to that. I have no problem adapting to LA's time change from my own when I get there, but for some reason it's much harder once I get home. Maybe I'm not meant to live in the Central time zone."

Glancing over with curiosity, Luke asked. "Where would you live?"

"I don't know. I love California and the people, but there's something about Florida and its beaches. I haven't traveled much out of the country, or in the country for that matter, so I'm sure there are plenty beaches that are much better than Florida's, but for some reason I've always felt a kinship when I've been there. I think it's the pretty color of the Gulf and its warm water. Plus, right now my best friend lives in Florida and I miss her like crazy. If she hadn't been on vacation, I think I probably would've ended up there this weekend."

"Then I'm glad that she was on vacation otherwise I wouldn't have gotten to meet you."

Could he be for real?

"Me, too," I murmured not believing my luck.

Luke chuckled from beside me. "What was *that* look for?"

Had I made a look? Obviously, I had and now I was getting called out on it. Shaking my head in disbelief, I answered. "This," I indicated the car, and the both of us. "It's all surreal and I don't know how I ended up in your car with you taking me to the airport. Why you want to get to know me and seem to be happy to have met me this weekend?"

"I wouldn't use the word surreal. I'd say…" Luke hummed in the back of his throat as he thought of the word he wanted to use and then muttered something that I couldn't understand.

"Um," I laughed. "I have no idea what you just said."

"Sometimes I can't find a good English word for what I want to say."

"Is it hard to speak English? What language are your thoughts in?"

In my limited upbringing, I'd never met anyone who spoke another language fluently.

"It's not hard. I've been speaking English since I was young, but I think in Swedish."

"Are you constantly interpreting what needs to be said from Swedish to English?"

"No," he shook his head. "But that may be because I've been doing it for so long. I do remember when I came here as a child I struggled to speak English correctly."

"Do you speak any other languages?"

Please say no. Please say no. Please say no.

"Italian and Spanish."

My shoulders slumped. "Are you fucking kidding me?" I felt like a huge failure only knowing one language.

Luke let out a booming laugh that echoed through the car. "It's common to learn multiple languages where I come from. Most of Europe knows how to speak at least two languages."

"You must think I'm dumb only knowing English and a little bit of Spanish and that's after taking it all through high school."

"American schools have different priorities, but you shouldn't feel bad. Plus, it's never too late to learn if you really want to learn another language or two."

"Two?" I squawked out. There was no way in hell that was ever going to happen. I didn't have the time or the brain capacity.

"Or not. Regardless, I don't think you're dumb."

"Do you use the other languages very often?" I asked getting off the subject of my intelligence.

"Not really. Sometimes when I travel for work or vacation, I get to use them, but if you don't know their language then typically they know English."

"So, I'm good. I only need to know English."

"You're good," Luke agreed with a smile.

The airport was on the horizon and we were both quiet as Luke's car inched its way toward dropping me off.

Clearing his throat, Luke spoke. "So, I guess I should warn you now that I don't really text much. If I'm on a computer, then I'll iMessage or email, but if it's just me and my phone I go without."

"Okay," I drawled out the word. Never had I had anyone tell me that they didn't text. "May I ask why?"

He shrugged from his broad shoulders. "I constantly hit the wrong keys which frustrates me."

"Understandable. Have you tried voice-to-text?"

Luke let out a bitter laugh. "Yes, and for some reason it doesn't like me. My damn phone hardly gets one word right."

"It's probably the accent."

This seemed like the brush off. Hey, guess what? I can't text you and don't have time to talk on the phone.

"I just wanted to let you know because when I get back to New York I'll be busy and if you send me a text, I might not answer back in a timely fashion. Unless it's something I can answer with a simple yes or no."

"You don't have to explain yourself to me. I get it. Don't worry."

"What do you get? Because from over here it seems like you don't."

Exasperated, I huffed out. "I get that this is the blow off. You're done with me and have come to your senses."

"Alex," Luke sighed, keeping his eyes on the road. "I know you said your ex-husband was an asshole and it seems like he did a real number on you. But listen, I'm telling you the truth, and it's fine if you don't believe me right now, but I'm going to prove it to you. You'll have to wait and see."

"I guess we'll see who's right."

"How about we make a bet?"

My eyes narrowed as I took in the smirk that slowly grew on his face. "On if you'll call, or text me, or whatever? Sure, why not?" Inwardly I rolled my eyes.

What did I have to lose?

"Yes, if I call you within the next few days - and the few days of allowance are because I'm leaving for New York tomorrow and have to get some sleep before I'm back on set and the first day back is always busy- then you have to come visit me in New York sometime while I'm filming." Luke had a devilish smile on his face and his eyes gleamed knowingly. "Don't worry about airfare or your hotel room. I'll take care of all of it."

Luke's reasoning wasn't very solid with this bet. "That sounds like what I'd get if I won a bet, but okay. What do you win if you don't call? Me out of your life? If you don't call, there's really no point in a bet. Are you going to make me send you money or something?"

"Or something, but it doesn't matter because I *am* going to call."

"Your bet seems backwards. I win if you do what you say you're going to do. I'm not following your logic, but whatever floats your boat."

Clearing his throat nervously, Luke asked. "Do you want to come see me in New York?"

I gave him a soft smile before I could even answer. From

what I knew of Luke he was unlike any man I'd ever met. He seemed perfect with his tall frame, muscular body, and gorgeous face, but that was on the outside. On the inside, Luke was a sweet and funny guy, and I wanted to get to know him more. I wanted to know everything about him and if I got the opportunity to run my tongue all over his body, well, that was just icing on the cake. But truthfully, I wasn't sure if I'd get the chance.

Narrowing my eyes at him, I lifted my chin. "I do, so you better call."

"I promise," Luke answered before crossing his heart like I'd done as a child. Cross my heart and hope to die.

Pulling his car up to the curb, Luke jumped out and grabbed my luggage out of the back.

Grabbing my suitcase once Luke sat it on the sidewalk, I fiddled with the handle. "If I don't ever see you again, I wanted to tell you that your car is awesome, and it was nice meeting you."

His face softened at my words before his lips tipped up at the ends. "The pleasure was all mine and I'm glad you approve. I got her the last time I was in LA and haven't driven her all that much."

Men and their cars.

Although it really was a hot car. It had an all-black matte finish and was the sexiest thing I'd ever sat my ass in. The only thing I knew was that it was an Audi, because it had the little circles on the steering wheel and hood.

"Her?" At his proud nod, I asked her name.

"No name. Not yet." Luke smiled with his cute lop-sided smile.

"Sir." A big, burly man with a belly almost as big as he was tall came striding toward us. "You've got to move on. This is a loading and unloading area only."

"You've got to go," I said as I pushed him toward his car and started for the door. "I hope I get that phone call."

"Alex," Luke called.

Looking back over my shoulder, he was striding toward me with purpose and a serious look on his face.

Once we were toe-to-toe, I started to ask if everything was okay, but instead Luke dipped down until his lips brushed mine in a feather like a caress. Pulling back to look me in the eye, he whispered. "I'll talk to you soon."

A loud throat being cleared broke us apart. A stern look from the same man who'd already told him to move had Luke jogging back to his car and slipping inside.

Instead of walking inside, I stood as still as a statue while I watched Luke's car disappear. Only after I couldn't see his taillights did I move with a smile on my face that I couldn't contain, my fingertips touching my lips as I remembered the soft brush of his mouth against mine.

4

WORKING ON AN UPDATE FOR A CLIENT'S WEBSITE, I WAS STARTLED when my doorbell rang. Everyone knew to always let me know when or if they were going to drop by. The only person who was rude enough to not let me know was my ex-husband. I wasn't in the mood for his bullshit today or any day for that matter, but today was definitely not a good day.

For starters, I was PMSing so bad that I was scared of myself. Mason had woken up with a raging cold and had been beyond cranky all day. He'd been taking a nap, but I was sure the doorbell had woken him up. Also, it had been three days since I had been home from LA and I hadn't gotten one phone call or text from Luke. He'd gotten my hopes up and now I wanted to kick him in the shin for making me believe that he could've possibly been interested.

Instead of finding my ex-husband at the door, I found Prue, my next-door neighbor. A much better option – if I had to deal with his bullshit today, I probably would have ended up in jail for assault and battery.

I swung my front door open. "Hey, Prue."

"Hi, Alex." Prue's eyes darted over to her house and then back again.

"Is everything alright? You seem a little nervous."

Normally when I saw Prue, she exuded calmness. It was strange because she never seemed what I would call happy, but I always got a strange sense of calm from her. She'd lived in her house all her life and was the first person I met when we moved in.

"I need to run to the pharmacy to pick up some medicine for my dad and I was wondering if you could come over to make sure he's okay while I'm gone." Her eyes once again darted back to her house and then to me.

We didn't get to talk much because I was always working or with Mason, but I did know that Prue's father had cancer and she was taking care of him. I knew she wouldn't be asking if she didn't really need to make a run to the pharmacy.

A deep sigh escaped me as I looked over my shoulder and back into my house. I didn't want to leave Mason here by himself especially when he was sick, but there was no way I was going to take him over to Prue's house and risk either of them catching his cold.

"Mason's home sick right now. Let me go and check on him really quick to make sure he's okay. He was taking a nap and I wouldn't feel comfortable taking him over to your house. I'd hate it if you or your dad got sick," I explained.

"Oh," she said peering over my shoulder. "Maybe I can find someone else. I don't want Mason to be left alone."

"I know you wouldn't be here if you didn't need to, so let me go check on him and I'll be right back. You can come in if you want, but I understand if you don't." I wrinkled my nose at her and my germy house.

Mason was still sound asleep when I went to check on him, so I followed Prue over to her house, sat on her old green couch as I waited for her return. Prue had promised it would only be ten to fifteen minutes maximum. The prescription was ready, and the pharmacy was only a mile and a half away from our houses, but we both knew that it could be awhile waiting in line.

My knee bounced as I sat there nervously, afraid that Mason would wake up and go looking for me. I had a monitor so that I could hear him, but I didn't want to leave Prue's house until she arrived home. If it had been anyone but Prue, I wouldn't have left. She never asked for help; we were a lot alike in that way.

I could hear her car as she passed my house and turned into her driveway. I stood and watched as she jumped out of her little beat-up old car with her purse and the white pharmacy bag in her hand. I think we both held a face of relief as we looked in each other's eyes and realized neither of our worlds had burned down and we could go on as normal.

"Thank you so much, Alex. I won't forget this. If you ever need anything just ask." Prue rushed into the kitchen to fill up a glass with water from the fridge and shook out a couple of pills from their bottles.

"I'm always right next door if you need me. Even if it's just to talk or drink a beer, a glass of wine, or whatever, you know where to find me. I'd better get back before Mason wakes up and wonders where I'm at," I replied as I walked to her front door.

"Thank you again."

A light buzzing sound escaped my hand causing me to look down. I hadn't realized my phone was in my hand instead of the back pocket of my jeans. Turning it over, I checked to see who it was, afraid it might be Mason. To my surprise it was Luke's name that flashed on my screen.

"You better get that." I could hear the humor in Prue's voice, but I didn't look up from my phone. Instead I waved at her over my shoulder as I stepped outside.

"Hello?"

Yeah, I was acting as if I didn't know who was on the other end of the line because I was mad that I'd got my hopes up and that I had let Luke not calling get to me.

"Alex." My name was said in a caress. It was smooth with his slight accent, and it evaporated every bad thought I'd had since I last saw him at the airport.

"Luke."

His chuckle traveled through the phone and straight to my toes. I had to stop walking across my yard for a moment to let the feeling settle in.

"It's good to hear your voice. I've been counting down the minutes until I could talk to you. Did you give up on me?"

"Maybe," I answered, but I was sure he could hear the smile in my voice all the way across the country.

"I promised I'd call and I don't break my promises." The conviction was easy to hear in his voice and it seemed important to him that I knew he'd never break a promise. My eyes closed as I took in his words and let them settle deep down in my soul. Time would tell, but I had a feeling Luke was a man of his word.

My eyes stung as I said, "Thank you." Those two words were all I could get out.

"What have you been up to?" he asked, as I heard a rustling in the background.

"Working and taking care of Mason. He got home yesterday from his trip with his dad and grandparents and woke up sick today. Not the way I wanted to spend time with him, but it's better than nothing."

"You're a good mom."

"How do you know?"

"I knew from the moment you sat back down at our table after talking to him."

"Thank you." I smiled. It made me happy to know that he could see my love for Mason so clearly. Not that it was hard to tell because I was a crazy, overprotective momma bear with anything that had to do with Mason.

"When are you coming to New York?" Luke asked with humor, but I sensed he also really wanted to know.

"Mama," Mason cried from his room. It was a sad and sickly cry that broke my heart to hear.

"Luke, I'm sorry, but I've got to go. Mason needs me. Can I talk to you later?" My feet sped down the hall toward Mason's room while I held the phone to my ear.

"Yeah, I'm sorry it took me so long to call. I'll try to find some sort of schedule and email it to you, so you have some sort of idea how little free time I have and when I can talk." The disappointment was evident in his voice, but I couldn't help it. I needed to be with Mason.

"I'm sorry I have to go. I hope you understand."

"I do. I'll keep my laptop with me, so we can message

when you get a chance. Bye, Alex. It was good to hear your voice."

"Bye, Luke." I'd only known Luke a few days, but even with Mason sick and needing me, I was sad that I had to get off the phone with him. I only hoped it wouldn't take a few more days before we got to talk again.

10:28 p.m. **Alex: Hey! You around?**

02:59 a.m. **Luke: Sorry I'm just now getting back to you. It was a long day on set. Are you awake?**

03:00 a.m. **Luke: Shit, I probably woke you up. I'll try you tomorrow.**

12:47 p.m. **Luke: Please tell me you're available. I have a whole twenty minutes until I have to be back on set.**

12:50 p.m. **Alex: You're in luck. I'm sitting at my desk working. You weren't kidding when you said you're a busy man.**

12:51 p.m. **Luke: I love my job but it makes it hard to have friends or a girlfriend.**

12:52 p.m. **Alex: When was the last time you had a girlfriend?**

12:55 p.m. **Luke: Almost a year and a half ago. How long have you been divorced?**

12:57 p.m. **Alex: Almost 2 years.**

12:57 p.m. **Alex: Did you love her?**

12:58 p.m. **Luke: No. Have you dated anyone since that one guy?**

01:00 p.m. **Alex: No. He definitely put me off dating for a long while.**

01:02 p.m. **Luke: Definitely not the way you want to get** back into the dating world. You told me he freaked out, but not why, and how long were you married?

01:03 p.m. **Alex: I was married for 11 years.**

01:04 p.m. **Alex: Matt freaked out because he thought I cheated on him when it was actually him.**

01:05 p.m. **Luke: Why did he think that?**

01:06 p.m. **Alex: First of all, I'm not a cheater. Never have been and never will be. He thought that because I'd been texting a guy friend of his. We're now really good friends because of the whole ordeal. He drove me home from LA since I couldn't fly.**

01:08 p.m. **Luke: Why couldn't you fly?**

01:08 p.m. **Luke: It happened in LA?!**

01:10 p.m. **Alex: I had a concussion and a broken arm. The doctor advised against it so Jenner drove me home from LA.**

01:12 p.m. **Luke: That must have been horrible.**

01:13 p.m. **Alex: It was and when I got back home Mason was a mess. I don't ever want to do that to him again. When you met me was the first time I'd been back to LA since the wreck.**

01:14 p.m. **Luke: I'm glad you were there.**

01:15 p.m. **Luke: SHIT! I'm late. I'll try to call as soon as I can or message you. Gotta go!**

01:16 p.m. **Alex: Bye. I hope you didn't get in any trouble.**

ANNA HAD BEEN ON A BREAK FROM FILMING WHEN SHE FIRST started calling me and when she went back to work she was busy, but it had never really registered how little free time she had and if it was anything like Luke's then she'd used a good portion of it on me. Knowing that it made me appreciate her friendship even more.

The same went for Jenner. He managed for quite some time to find time every day to call or message me once he got back to LA and while filming his latest movie which had taken him to Quebec. But we never really talked for too long.

Looking back on it, meeting Matt wasn't so bad when I considered all the people I'd met and had come into my life. I still hadn't figured out what Luke wanted from me and it was going to take forever for us to get to know one another with the pace we were going.

It didn't matter if Luke only wanted to be friends or not. I was happy he was in my life and maybe getting to know each other with him across the country would help me the next time I saw him instead, of being an idiot who acted like I'd never been in the presence of anyone who was good looking.

The truth was I'd never been around anyone in all my life who affected me quite like Luke. If he was a mind reader, I was sure he'd want nothing to do with me after all my inappropriate lustful thoughts. Don't even get me started on the dreams that Luke had started to appear in. It hadn't even been a week since I met Luke and there wasn't a night that went by where I didn't have to grab my Hitachi out of my nightstand and finish myself off. I imagined this was what a pubescent teenage boy went through and here I was, thirty. I could barely make it through a day without picturing Luke - either from when I had met him or in my memories of all the dirty things he'd done to me in my dreams the night before - without my sex clenching and my cheeks becoming flushed.

Hopefully the time we took to get to know one another would set my brain straight and I would treat him like I did any of my other male friends. Maybe his hotness would be gone or diminish the more I got to know him. I had to hope so, because otherwise it was going to be hard to be his friend when all I wanted to do was jump him.

5

One Week Later

11:01 p.m. **Luke: I'm done early. Are you still up?**

11:05 p.m. **Alex: I'm still up! I've been trying to get this website to look exactly like what the client wants but they keep changing their minds. I might be up all night trying at this rate.**

11:08 p.m. **Luke: I hope you're not doing all these changes for free.**

11:10 p.m. **Alex: It's in my contract that they only get so many changes included and they've been changing everything each time I show them the update. So, they're paying me hourly now for all these changes they want made.**

11:12 p.m. **Alex: How was your day? I'm glad you're done early.**

11:15 p.m. **Luke: It was good but long. I don't know what it is**

about this set. Hey, can I call you, this would be so much easier?

INSTEAD OF ANSWERING BACK, I HIT THE CALL BUTTON AND waited for him to answer.

"Hey!" Luke answered in high spirits.

"Hey," I answered, leaning back in my chair. "What were you saying about your set?"

"Normally everyone is easy to get along with, but for some reason hardly anyone talks to me. There's no one to make small talk with while I'm standing around. The only person who talks to me is the makeup artist."

"Poor baby."

"I know I shouldn't be whining because I love my job and the character I'm playing, but it gets lonely when there's no one to talk to, and I see others talking all the time. That's not how it is on Night Shadows." Luke let out a deep breath that sounded as if he'd been holding it in for a very long time. I had a feeling that the situation had been weighing on him for awhile.

"I wish there was something I could do to help you. I'd talk to you if I was there."

"You could come and see me soon."

"Luke, I don't know. I can't just up and leave. I would love to visit you, but…"

"I understand," Luke said interrupting me, unable to hide the sadness in his voice.

"I'll see what I can do, but it may be awhile. How long are you going to be in New York?"

I couldn't let Decker know that I was going to go out of

town while he had Mason, or he'd cancel with some bullshit excuse.

"Until the middle of October," Luke answered with his accent slightly stronger, making me smile.

"I'm sure I can come before then. Let me look at my calendar tomorrow and see if I can find a time that will work for the both of us. You have some weekends off, right?"

"There are a few between now and then that I have off." I could feel his excitement through the phone and I'd do everything in my power not to disappoint him.

"What time do you have to be on set in the morning," I asked.

Luke groaned into the phone and then there was a rustling sound. "4:15."

"I don't want to get off the phone with you, but it's almost one o'clock your time. You need to get some sleep."

"I know, but it's so nice talking to you. I'd rather lose sleep than miss hearing your voice."

"Oh, Luke. If you keep saying such sweet things to me I'm going to fall in love with you."

Clapping my hand over my mouth, I realized my mistake immediately. Going by the radio silence on the other end of the line I was sure Luke was done talking to me.

Clearing my throat, I said the only thing I could in that moment. "I'll talk to you soon." Or not, I muttered as I hung up.

∽

Since I couldn't concentrate on anything but Luke the next day, and was getting no work done, I decided to call my friend and see if he could help me with the male perspective.

Answering on the fourth ring, Reeves immediately asked if everything was okay. I hated that his mind went directly toward worry, but I couldn't help that I secretly loved all the new people in my life and how much they had brought into it.

Letting out a long sigh, I answered. "I'm fine. Well, not exactly fine, but... okay, I'm not fine. Jenner, I think I messed up with Luke." I couldn't help the sniffle that came out after the words left my mouth.

"Want to tell me what happened? Did you guys get in a fight?"

"No, we haven't fought. We've barely gotten to speak to one another. I seriously don't know how you have time to talk to me because Luke sure as hell doesn't."

Jenner guffawed into the phone. "Please don't take this the wrong way because I'm not trying to toot my own horn, but I've been in a few major movies and I don't have to prove myself any longer. I'm not saying I'm not busy when I'm filming because I am, and it is tiring, don't get me wrong. Luke hasn't had any big break through movie roles yet and sometimes directors are hard on actors that come from TV series. I'm not saying it's fair, but it's what I've seen, and I'm definitely not saying that Luke is a shit actor because he isn't. From what I know about him and his career, Luke doesn't want to be stereotyped and I totally get that. He's done a little bit of everything, but with each new thing he tries, he has to prove himself. That's my two cents and I could be very wrong about what's going on with him or he could be lying to you.

Sorry," Jenner added the last in a sad tone that said he didn't want to have to tell me this, but it was possible.

"You could be right, and I may never know because I think he's done talking to me."

"Why do you say that?"

"Because I said the 'L' word."

"What?" Jenner sputtered out. He sounded as if he was choking.

Even though it sounded bad, I couldn't help but laugh. What was with men and the 'L' word?

"I didn't tell him I loved him. Jeez, we barely know each other."

"Then what did you say about love?" Jenner coughed again. I found this strange since surely, he had to love his wife to still be with her and give her the benefit of the doubt.

"He said something that I thought was sweet, which isn't something I'm used to from guys, and I told him that if he wasn't careful and kept saying things like that, I would fall in love with him. Afterwards he said nothing, and I haven't heard from him since."

"Ouch." I could imagine Jenner flinching on the other side of the phone.

"Ouch is right. I didn't realize until after radio silence just how much I like him and now I think he's done with me."

"I don't think he's done with you. If it went down as you say it did then maybe he was a little taken aback by your comment, but I would give him time." Jenner cleared his throat a couple of times before he spoke. "What's going on between you two?"

Shaking my head, I let out a sad sigh. "Truthfully, I have no clue what's going on. I think he's lonely and just wants a friend. Why he'd choose me is anyone's guess. Why else would he want to be around me?"

"But you want more?"

"I don't know what I want except that I don't want to get my hopes up. Maybe I'm not dating material. If he ever calls again, I'll happily be his friend."

"Has Luke ever said he just wants to be friends?"

"No, he's never said anything about what's going on between us. Isn't that the definition of being in the friend zone?"

"Not necessarily, I think he wants to get to know you a little better before he puts himself out there. It's hard in this business to know if the people that surround you are around you for you, or if they're using you. I would think in your case it would be pretty obvious. He met you when you were with some top-notch celebrities and yet you don't care about that. You just see them as your friends. I mean I could tell right away that you didn't care about my fame or if it died the next day."

"Wow! You got all of that from the little amount of time you've known me?"

"Yeah, you're easy to read in that sense."

"Are you saying I'm not always easy to read?"

"That's exactly what I'm saying, and that's fine because like you and Luke, we are getting to know each other. I didn't expect you to tell me your life story."

"But you do now?" I joked. It was true that I kept some things to myself. I'd learned from Decker not to be open about my feelings or give any information about myself, and it was going to be a hard habit to break.

"I hope that as time goes on, you won't hide yourself from your friends, me included. I know you have your reasons."

"Thanks. It's a hard habit to break when you've done it for so long. And I want you to know that if your career died tomorrow I would care, but only because you're my friend and I know how much it would hurt you."

"Yeah, thanks," Jenner said sadly.

"How's it going with Poppy?"

"Funny you should ask that because when you called I was driving around trying to find her. She said she was going to yoga with some friends and that they might go shopping, but that was hours ago."

"You know…"

Jenner interrupted me. "I know that women can shop for hours upon hours, but…" he breathed heavily into the phone.

"But what, Reeves? Are you still driving?" I asked concerned. I hated that he was going through this.

"No, I'm home now." Even with over eighteen hundred miles between us I could almost feel his sadness. I wanted nothing more than to be able to reach through the phone and hug him.

"Is everything okay?" I asked tentatively.

"No," he answered with a bitter cry. "I don't think I can keep lying to myself about what Poppy is doing when she disappears."

"What do you think she's doing?" She was either cheating on Reeves or she was doing drugs. Or both.

"I think she's having an affair." Jenner all but sobbed out.

"Oh, honey!" My eyes welled with tears. I knew how much he hated to admit it and how much pain he had to be in. "I'm so sorry. Here I'm calling you with my silly problem when you've got much more going on. Is there anything I can do for you?"

"Treat me like you've always treated me and don't walk on eggshells around me. I… It's been a long time coming. Now I just want to figure out who she's been with."

"Well, if I've learned anything from reading books and watching TV, I'd say you need to hire a private investigator. It would be a lot easier for someone else to follow her and find out. What happens if what you think she's doing is confirmed?"

"I'm going to divorce her ass that's what I'm going to do," Jenner answered angrily.

"Do you have a prenup?" I would really hate it for her to take him to the cleaners when she's been the one fucking around.

"Is there anyone who gets married in Hollywood anymore without one?"

"Surely there's a few," I mumbled. I mean, there were idiots who got married in Vegas who couldn't possibly have a prenup.

"Shit! I gotta go. She's home. Let me know how things go with you and Luke. Just give him a few days. Bye."

Before I could even say my own goodbyes, Jenner had hung up.

～

BEING MARRIED TO AN ASSHOLE FOR OVER A DECADE, I WAS USED to being told I messed up a lot. Nothing was ever Decker's fault. It didn't matter if there was no one around for miles, it would always somehow be someone else's fault. Logically, back then I knew the things that I was blamed for weren't my fault, but after you hear it long enough, it starts to bring you down. That was one of the main reasons for me filing for divorce. I was no longer myself and felt as if I had to walk on eggshells whenever he was around.

This time around, I knew that it was my fault that I hadn't talked to Luke, and I was more depressed than I would like to admit for having known him a short period of time. Needing a pep talk, I called Taylor, but she couldn't talk until later in the day. Even though I knew Taylor would call me back when she had some free time, I needed to talk to someone about what I was feeling or else I was going to eat every bit of chocolate that Fairlane had in its stores. My talk with Jenner a couple of days ago had done nothing for my mental well-being.

"Hey," Anna answered after a couple of rings in her bright, chipper voice.

"Hi." I replied with zero enthusiasm.

"Uh-oh, what happened? It isn't Matt is it?" Her worry echoed through the phone line and once again made me glad that Anna had been brought into my life, no matter what I'd gone through for it to happen.

"No, not Matt. I haven't heard a peep from him and I really hope that I don't. Who causes a wreck like that and then doesn't say anything? He didn't even apologize. Instead he just up and disappeared."

"From what I know, he hasn't been talking to any of his friends and only hanging out with... never mind."

"The Victoria's Secret model." I filled in for her.

"Yeah, I didn't want to say." Anna exhaled softly into the phone. "I've been cheated on and I know how much it sucks and the thoughts that go through your head. No one wants that reminder. If that's not what's got you down then what is it, sweetie?"

"It's Luke." I was glad that Anna couldn't see me through the phone because I looked ridiculous with my mouth in a full-on pout while my hair was in a mess on the top of my head, and still wearing my pajamas from last night.

"Already? What happened?"

"My big mouth is what happened."

"I doubt that. What could you have possibly said?"

"Well, we've been getting to know one another, and Luke's been really busy filming his project. We've had a few minutes here and there, but not much. Luke was done early and sent me a text. I was still up, and we started texting until he asked if he could call me because it would be a hell of a lot easier. So, I called him, and it was all going well. He was telling me how he felt left out because no one on the cast or crew talks to him and that's a first for him."

"Oh, that's so sad. I can't imagine why. How long has he been on the film?"

"At least a month. Probably going on two. I'm not really sure since we barely talk."

"Wow, that's a long time for them to not be talking to him."

"That's what I thought and from what I know of him, Luke's so nice and easy to talk to, so I don't understand. I said that I wished there was something I could do, and he asked me to come visit him. At first, I told him I couldn't come because, you know, I can't just pick up and go to New York, but then I asked him how long he was going to be there and told him that I thought I could make it there before he was done film-ing." I sighed deeply and closed my eyes. "Then I asked him what time he had to be on set and he said 4:15 a.m. It was getting really late. It was almost 1:00 in the morning so I said that we should probably get off the phone, so he could get some sleep. Luke said he'd rather lose sleep than miss the sound of my voice."

"Awe," Anna said into the phone.

"I know," I cried. "It was so sweet, and I haven't had sweet in a very long time. So, I was stupid and said that if he kept saying sweet things to me, then I was going to fall in love with him. After that he said nothing. I couldn't even hear him breathing on the phone. I knew I'd made a mistake and said I'd talk to him later. And now nothing, I haven't heard from him yet. I hate that I messed up whatever is going on between us."

"I don't think you messed anything up. You did say he was busy, and it's only been a few days. Give it a little more time before you think he's brushed you off, because I really don't think that's what this is. When you two met, there was instant chemistry between you and I hope that it doesn't get thrown away over something so small. I don't really know Luke, but he doesn't seem like the type of guy who'd get freaked out by the word, love. I could maybe see it if you'd said that you were in love with him." Anna paused making a tapping noise on the other end of the line. "How long ago was his last girlfriend?"

Pulling the hair tie out of my hair, I shook my hair out realizing that I was in desperate need of a shower. "About two years ago, but I don't think he's hung up on her."

"How can you be so sure?"

"I'm not sure. Hell, I'm not sure about anything having to do with Luke, but I asked him if he loved her and his reply was no." Looking at myself in the monitor on my desk, I still looked sad, but inside Anna had given me a small glimpse of hope. "Do you really think he's not freaked out?"

"I really don't. Cyndi and I talked the other day, and even she mentioned that she thought there was a little something, something going on between you two. She said she was shocked that the both of you didn't know each other before with how well you got along at the restaurant, and then hanging out with him afterward."

"She doesn't think anything happened between us, does she?" I didn't want the rumor mill to start up with that I was after the men of Hollywood. Not that I thought Cyndi would think that.

"No, she didn't mention anything, but what would it matter? I can't remember the last time I saw an instant connection like that. It's like something out of a fairytale or romance novel."

"Ha, ha. The girl hears from the guy again and he doesn't freak out about the word love."

"What romance novels are you reading? Guys freak out all the time about love and commitment, but I really don't think that's the case with Luke."

"I hope you're right because I really like him. I was hoping that getting to know him would make it so that I didn't want to jump him if I ever saw him again and now I might not ever get the chance."

"You'll get your chance." Anna's conviction gave me a little more hope and the thought that maybe I should try to message Luke even though I had no idea what I might say. 'Oh, don't worry about what I said the other day. I don't love you.' Right, that would go over well.

"How obvious was it that I was about ready to drool all over the restaurant every time I laid eyes on him?"

Anna laughed hard into the phone. At one point, I thought I heard her snort. It must have been obvious going by her reaction.

"Great," I grumbled. "That's so embarrassing!"

"It was cute and sweet, not embarrassing. I wouldn't say that Luke was about ready to drool, but you definitely did a number on him too."

I couldn't help but shake my head. "I think you're wrong."

"Why? It was obvious from where I was sitting *and* when he took you to the airport. Why do you think I was so happy?"

"I have no clue. I'm pretty sure I'm hopeless in the world of men and dating. Not that we're dating. I think he just wanted to be friends and now he's done with me."

"He's not done with you by a long shot."

My phone beeped letting me know that I had another call.

"Hang on a second there's someone on the other line. Let me look really quick." Pulling my phone away from my ear, I saw Luke's name and my heart soared. I must have made some sort of noise because I could hear Anna laughing. "It's Luke," I squealed. "Can I let you go?"

Anna continued to laugh even as she spoke. "I assumed by

the squeal. I'll talk to you soon. Remember, I'm always here if you need me."

"I know. And thank you, Anna. You made me feel a lot better."

"No, Luke calling you made you feel better. Now hurry up and click over before he hangs up!"

I wasted no time in following her orders. Hitting to accept his call, and answering in a breathy hello, I started to pace from room to room in a frenzy.

"Did I catch you at a bad time?"

"No, I just didn't want you to hang up." I paused for a moment to shore up my conviction. I could do this. "I'm sorry, Luke. I wasn't thinking about what I was saying the other night, and I never meant to make you uncomfortable."

"There's nothing to be sorry about. You hung up before I could say anything, and I didn't think you were proclaiming your love for me or anything like that. I should've sent you a message right away."

"So, we're all good. Friends?" I asked, relieved that Luke hadn't thought I loved him.

"Yeah, friends." Something was different in his voice. It was off, but I couldn't identify what it was.

"Anything new?" I still felt awkward, but I figured if I kept talking to him, I'd talk myself out of the feeling. Or at least that was the hope.

Luke laughed. "No, my life is pretty boring while on set. Actually, it's normally pretty boring. Except I do try to go on one adventure during my downtime between shooting Night Shadows and movies."

"Try living in the Midwest and then you'll think your life is far from boring. Do you already have your next adventure planned out? When do you start shooting Night Shadows again?"

"I'm glad you're back," Luke laughed into the phone. I could feel the awkwardness melt away from both sides, causing me to smile. "We start back around the middle of January and I do in fact already have my next adventure planned. A few friends and I are going to Iceland at the beginning of November for a week."

"Iceland? I've seen pictures and from what I can tell it's beautiful. I hope to visit one day. Have you ever been?"

"Maybe one day we can go together and to answer your question, yes, I've been before and it's even more beautiful than it is in pictures. I can't wait to rough it."

"Rough it? Are you staying outdoors? It may look beautiful, but it always looks cold."

"Coming from Sweden, I like the cold so when I go on vacations I try to get away from the LA heat."

I couldn't help but laugh. We were the exact opposite.

Luke chuckled along with me. "What's so funny?"

"We're so opposite. If I go on vacation, I try to go anywhere where it's warm and with a beach. I shy away from the cold."

"Well, you know what they say, right? Opposites attract. Have you *ever* vacationed somewhere cold? Maybe to go skiing?"

"I've never been skiing in my life. There's no skiing where I live and growing up the only vacationing we did was go camping. My dad had me freaking out about water skiing, so I never even tried that."

"You don't know what you're missing. Maybe someday I

can talk you into it. I think you'd enjoy it if you knew it was for a very short period of time."

"Maybe," I grumbled. I didn't believe I'd like it no matter how short of time I'd be there, knowing I could be on a beach somewhere listening to the tide come in and enjoying the beautiful water.

"How did your dad freak you out about water skiing? I have to admit I've never tried skiing, but I have been tubing."

I closed my eyes and leaned back on my bed where I had finally sat down. I loved hearing Luke's voice and accent. I was pretty sure I could listen to him talk all day and if he was in front of me doing it where I could ogle him, would only make it better.

"My dad was as blind as a bat without glasses and from the time I could remember he always shied away from skiing. One day, when I was probably six or seven, we were at some company barbecue and he went skiing. Don't ask me why because I have no clue. I don't know if the boat took off from where the barbecue was being held or what, but I remember standing on the shoreline and watching my dad ski. What I remember most was watching him fall and freaking out. The reason my dad didn't ski was because he wore glasses and if he took them off, he couldn't see anything within a few inches in front of him. It's embedded into my brain to not ski even though I have perfect vision."

"I'm sorry that happened to you. It's amazing how an experience can shape the outcome of our lives and you never know which ones it will be."

Something about what Luke said was nagging at me and I

wanted to ask what he meant by it, but I didn't want to scare him away again.

"Are things any better on set?" I asked, to change the subject and because I was hoping someone else had befriended him.

"Actually, one of the actresses I'm working with did talk to me yesterday. We talked about our parts and how our characters are supposed to become involved."

White hot jealousy consumed me. Even though I wanted there to be someone to talk to Luke because no one wanted to feel like an outcast, I didn't like the fact it was an actress that he was going to have to do more than I wanted to think about with her. Why couldn't it be some fat, hairy man?

"Involved?" I heard myself say. Why had I said that? Obviously, I hadn't been tortured enough these last couple of days with the thoughts that Luke was finished with me.

"They have a small relationship. It's pretty volatile and hot. I was surprised that she was nervous about the sex scenes and being naked on set."

Kill me now! Luke was going to see her naked.

"Who's your costar?" I asked because I couldn't help myself and I needed to torture myself more by knowing who the actress was.

"Lindsey Sterling. Do you know who she is?" Luke asked innocently. I was sure that he had no idea that the woman on the other end of the phone was losing her mind with jealousy and hate.

Okay, hate was a strong word, but he was going to see Lindsey Sterling naked. Lindsey was tall at around five feet ten inches if I had to guess, and all beautiful long legs and a graceful silhouette that most women would die for. Her hair was so blonde it looked white and fell to her ass in a beautiful white wave. I'd never seen a picture where she didn't look perfect. Even the few times she'd been spotted without makeup she was gorgeous. Lindsey Sterling had curves in all the right places and the rest of her was tan and toned. I'd listened to Ryan go on and on about her one night, about how she was every man's fantasy.

And now my fantasy was going to see her naked.

"Will there be nudity for you too?" I asked casually.

"Yeah, but I don't mind. It always makes me laugh at how conservative you Americans are. You're taught to be embarrassed or ashamed by your body at such a young age, but in Europe we embrace our bodies and sexuality."

I wanted to yell at him to stop talking because the more Luke said, the worse it became.

"Mmhmm," I agreed because I needed to say something.

Luke was going to fall in love with this woman before I ever got a chance and why wouldn't he fall for her? Nothing bad was ever said about her and now she was talking to Luke on set. Maybe if I was lucky she had a boyfriend, but I didn't think luck was going to be on my side for this one.

"Are you okay, Alex? You've gotten awfully quiet on me."

"Yeah, I'm fine. I'm happy that things are looking up for you on set."

Maybe that was why I hadn't heard back from him until today because Luke and Lindsey were getting to know each other.

Ugh. I wanted to scream. Damn Luke for being so sweet and attractive.

I mean I couldn't blame any woman for being interested in him because Luke was HOT. It didn't even matter if he wasn't your type, you'd think he was hot. I wasn't sure how he was still single with his smoking hot looks and how sweet and funny he was.

The longer I thought about it the more depressed I got. I'd never have a chance with Luke with all the Lindsey Sterling's out there in the world.

"I bet you're tired. I should probably let you go. I'll try to talk to you soon. The next couple of days are long ones. Maybe I'll send you an email that way I can write it when I have a chance and you can answer me back when you're awake and have time. How does that sound?" Luke asked as if he hadn't just crushed my heart.

To be fair, Luke didn't know my internal struggle and hopefully he'd never find out.

"Sounds good. I hope you have a great couple of days." I prayed he couldn't hear the sadness in my voice or ask about it.

"Send me a text with your email so I'll have it, okay?" It was evident from Luke's tone that he knew something was wrong, but he wasn't going to call me out on it. He probably thought it had to do with him not talking to me for the last few days, but that couldn't be further from the truth.

"I'll send it now," I replied as I typed in my email address for him.

"Good night, Alex."

"Goodbye, Luke."

6

HAVING MOST OF YOUR FRIENDS LIVE THOUSANDS OF MILES AWAY was depressing. I was in serious need of a girlfriend where I could cry on her shoulder. Luke had been sending me emails every day and most of them were before I even woke up. In some he would tell me about the day before and how *nice* it was that Lindsey was now talking to him and including him. Don't get me wrong, I didn't want Luke to feel left out of the group and I wanted him to have friends on set, but why, oh why did it have to be Lindsey Sterling?

The emails that were about his budding friendship with his beautiful costar were the hardest to reply back to, but I did manage to not sound like the jealous bitch that I was. In his other emails I could tell that Luke had written them throughout the day as he thought up questions that he wanted to ask me. Some were generic, and others were deeply personal. It reminded me of when I was in elementary school and we had to write to our pen pals. We were getting to know each other better than we had through our brief phone calls and iMessages because we had all the time in the world to think up what we wanted to know and answer back.

Without talking on the phone in almost two weeks, Luke was getting irritated with me. Every time he'd called I let voicemail answer. I knew it was stupid and immature, but I knew I wouldn't be able to hide my jealousy over the phone. More than once Luke had asked if everything was okay with me and us.

Desperately I wanted to ask him what he wanted from me, but I was afraid of his answer. The more I got to know him through our emails the more I cared, and I didn't want to lose what we had. With each passing day and email that went by it was getting a little bit easier to think of Luke as only a friend. I knew I couldn't keep dodging his phone calls that were placed when he knew I was at home alone working so I vowed that the next time he called I would pull up my big girl panties and answer the phone. I had no idea that when I made that decision I wouldn't hear from Luke for another five days.

Over the last five days I had emailed and called more times than was healthy. I wouldn't have been surprised if Luke hadn't put a restraining order out on me. If he was done with me the least he could do was have the decency to pick up the phone and tell me. At the very least, he could've answered one of the twenty some emails I'd sent him.

My pride had died on the second day I hadn't heard from Luke. By the third day I had spent the majority of the day berating myself for being so stupid. If I wanted any type of relationship with Luke, then I had to start acting like an adult and not a three-year-old. Instead all of my friends were now worried about me as I sent all their calls to voicemails as well and then sent a message saying that I was busy, and I'd talk to them later. I would've turned off my phone to wallow in my own misery if I wasn't afraid that on some off-chance Luke might call.

I'd become what I hated to read about in books. I was the stupid girl that had a good thing and then let her insecurities rule her life until she lost the very thing she'd wanted.

During those days I tried to hide my pain from Mason, but he still picked up on it and tried his best to make me feel better. We sat snuggled up on the couch watching all the Marvel movies that he owned, eating popcorn, and other junk food. While I was with Mason, I could forget my sadness, but once he went to bed, it seemed to double.

Logically I knew I could call any one of my friends and tell them what happened, but I knew this was my fault and nothing they would say could make me or the situation better. I'd dismissed many of their calls and had even not answered the door when Ryan had come by to check up on me. He'd sent me a message saying he was worried and going to stop by. After he left, I sent him a message saying that I was sorry I hadn't answered the door, but I wasn't feeling well. I truly wasn't because I had been crying since the moment I dropped Mason off at school and by then I had a horrible headache and a stuffed-up nose. At least that was what I told myself at the time. I would really need to make up my absence with my friends. The only one not on my case was Taylor, and that was because I'd sent her a text telling her that I messed up with Luke but was not ready to talk about it. If her whole family hadn't been sick with a horrible summer cold, I knew she would have been all over me. A summer cold was bad enough but being pregnant while having one, and not being able to take any medicine, I knew she was miserable. Each day, she would give me an update on how they were all feeling and if she didn't start to get better soon, I was afraid she'd have to go the hospital. Of course, Taylor being Taylor, each day she would ask if I was ready to talk. Even if she wasn't up for it.

Worrying about my best friend who was hundreds of miles away only added to my depression. I couldn't help her, or her family and she wasn't here for me to cry to. More than once I thought about packing up and heading to Florida. I wasn't sure if it was more for me or her, but each time I talked myself out of it. But just barely. I knew if much more time went by with Taylor sick and no word from Luke, Mason and I would be hitting the road.

One night while I tossed and turned in bed, I vowed that if Luke ever talked to me again that I would answer every single phone call, email, or any other form of communication from him even if it killed me. A little dramatic, yes, but I was desperate.

On the fifth day, I was sound asleep when my phone rang, waking me up. Not looking at who was calling me before the sun had even risen for the day, I answered with a croaked, hello.

"Alex?" A hoarse voice asked before giving into a coughing fit.

"Yes? Who's this?" When there was no answer, but a continued bark of a cough, I looked at my phone to see who had called. To my utter surprise it was Luke. Sitting up in bed, I brushed my hair out of my face and looked again to make sure my eyes weren't deceiving me.

"Luke? Are you there?" With no answer I started to worry. Finally, I heard a hacking cough coming closer to the speaker. "Luke?"

"Yeah, I'm sorry. Give me a minute." He choked out. His voice sounded strained and weak.

"Take all the time you need. Are you okay?"

His only reply was something that came out as a half-laugh, half-cough.

While I tried to be patient, I knew I wasn't going back to sleep so I headed into the kitchen to make a pot of coffee. I had a feeling I would need it as I checked the time on the microwave and it read a little after four in the morning.

When I heard Luke was back on the phone, I scrambled to pick it up and take it off speaker. I'd sat it down, so I could rinse out my coffee pot and filter.

"Alex?" he asked weakly.

"I'm here, Luke. I'm here."

"I thought you might hang up it took me so long."

"I could never hang up on you," I said casually even though to myself it was a promise. A vow to not fuck up my relationship with Luke.

"Never say never," he joked before coughing again. "As you can tell I'm as sick as a dog. I'm sorry it took me so long to get back to you, but I haven't left my bed until this morning. The studio even called a doctor in to come see me."

"What did the doctor say?" It couldn't be good whatever it was because his voice sounded horrible, he could barely stop coughing, and he sounded weak.

"I've got bronchitis, and it's kicking my ass. I can't remember the last time I was sick and then this hit me. I can't go back on set until my cough subsides. Luckily there are plenty of scenes they can film that I'm not in so I'm not delaying production."

"I'm so sorry. You don't sound like you feel well at all."

A hacking cough filtered through the phone before Luke asked. "Is that you telling me I sound like shit?"

"You don't sound good," I answered with a slight laugh. It was hard to feel good when he obviously was still pretty ill and then there was the thing when I thought he was done with me.

"The cough and my voice sound bad, but I'm feeling better. I'm finally out of bed. I'd left my phone in the living area of my suite and when I found it this morning, it was dead. Once it finally charged up enough to turn on I saw all your missed calls and messages. I'm sorry if I worried you."

"I was worried for a different reason than thinking you were sick. I thought you were done with having me in your life." I admitted and then held my breath for his reaction.

"Nah, I wouldn't do that. I'm still waiting for you to come visit me."

Okay not the reaction I was thinking he'd have.

"I wish I was there now so that I could take care of you."

"That would be nice," Luke replied with a sleepy yawn.

"I was looking to see when I could come to visit you although that might not work now that you've missed so many days of shooting."

"Really? That's great. Hang on and let me start up my laptop to look at my calendar to see if we can make it work." His words sounded as if he was excited for me to come, but there was no enthusiasm in his tone. I couldn't tell if it was because he was sick, or he was just placating me and would then say that none of the dates I gave him would work.

"You still want me to come?" I asked unsure if I wanted his answer or not.

"Why wouldn't I?" he asked absentmindedly as I heard the clack of his fingers typing on the keyboard.

"Because I'm stupid." I replied bluntly. Was there any other word to use for what I'd done when I ignored his phone calls just because I was afraid to hear him tell me that he was falling for another woman? Well, any nice ones that is.

"Don't be so hard on yourself. You're not stupid." His tone was distracted almost as if he didn't know what he was saying and maybe he didn't or maybe it was that he was too sick to remember that I'd shut him out, and when he was feeling better he'd remember.

"Do you know one of the dates you had in mind? When is the soonest you could come?" Excitement filled his hoarse voice.

"Shit. Hang on. I should've got my planner out when I was waiting on you. Instead I've just been standing in my kitchen drinking coffee like a zombie."

"No worries, I've got all the time in the world now that I'm not going to work for the next couple of days," Luke said before he started to cough again.

"Although I'm beyond happy to talk to you finally, I'm not going to keep you on the phone for long because you need your rest so that you can get better."

"I promise you that I'll rest while I talk to you. As soon as you give me some dates and we decide when's the best time for you to come then I'll get back into bed, but don't get off the phone. I want to talk to you."

"Fine even if I don't think it's what's best for you," I huffed out, even though I was smiling. "Okay, let me see when the earliest I could come is… how about… Mason is going to be with his dad next weekend for a long weekend before school starts. I could come on that Friday if the plane tickets aren't too expensive."

Luke cleared his throat in annoyance or from his cold, I couldn't tell which. "If you don't remember, I said that I was paying for your plane ticket and hotel so don't worry about the cost. Do you have an airport in your town or do you have to drive elsewhere?"

"Luke, I don't feel comfortable with you buying my ticket and paying for my hotel room. Let me look…"

"No," Luke cut me off with a stern voice. "I won the bet fair and square, and the agreement was for me to pay. I want you to stay at the same hotel that I'm at and it might be a little out of your price range. I'd hate for you to waste your money when I want to do this for you."

"Ugh, why do I give into you?"

Luke let out a shaky laugh. "Because I'm so charming."

"That must be it. Maybe I should pick another time since the ticket will be so much more expensive this close to the date."

"No," he called out. "No, I want you to come next Friday. It'll be perfect."

"Why do you want me to come so badly next Friday? I promise I'll come and visit you when we have more time to plan it and it'll be cheaper."

"No," Luke said so quietly I could barely hear him. "Next Friday is my birthday. You coming is the perfect gift."

"It's your birthday? Why didn't you say so?" Knowing it was going to be his birthday and that he'd most probably be alone otherwise, I couldn't say no. Not that I wanted to.

"I don't know. It never came up. When's your birthday?" Maybe it was the sickness, but Luke seemed a little vulnerable that morning.

"My birthday isn't until May. It's the twenty-fifth. How old will you be?"

"Thirty," Luke yawned out.

"We'll be the same age. If you're tired, I can let you go. Did you lay down yet?"

"Not yet," Luke yawned again. "I'm looking at airline tickets. It doesn't look like you get a non-stop flight and your layover would be in Chicago. I think your layover is going to be longer than the flight. Would you rather fly in the morning, afternoon, or early evening?"

"Well, if I'm coming in on your birthday then I want to be able to spend time with you and not get there when it's almost over. Do they have any late morning flights? I need to get Mason over to his grandparents and it'll seem strange if I do that too early."

"Okay, so no flights at six in the morning." He let out a laugh that then led to coughing. "There's one that's around eleven, would that work?"

"Probably, I should boot up my computer and be looking at these with you instead of you telling me every flight. That would make this much easier on you."

Luke was silent except for a couple of coughs as I went into my office and started up my computer. If I was going to see Luke next week, then I was really going to need to get a lot of work done since I'd been utterly useless on the work front for the last few days.

Once I got my computer started and a site up that would show me all the flights from here to New York, I relaxed against my office chair.

"There aren't a lot of options which is what I expected. There aren't many non-stop flights from Fairlane to anywhere. Do you know if you have to work that Friday?" To say that I was a little nervous about flying into LaGuardia was an understatement. I'd flown more in the last year than in my entire life but landing in big cities was nerve wracking for me. Fairlane was a small town that was just big enough to have what I needed and always wish for a few of the stores that were in the bigger cities like St. Louis and Kansas City.

"I have a half day… let me look through my email and see if they've sent the schedule for next week and when I'll have to be on set. The latest is at six and we have such long days that a half day won't matter too much."

"It's okay. We'll work something out. Don't worry about it. Right now, you need to think about you and getting better. My trip won't be any fun if you're still sick or run down."

Luke laughed down the line. "You are so a mom."

"I am. Sorry, it's hard to turn it off sometimes. I was at lunch with a friend one time and unwrapped her gum for her. It's engrained into my brain after all these years."

"It's not a bad thing, except for making me homesick. Normally if I'm not shooting a movie, I go home for my birthday and it's been almost a year since I've seen my family."

"What about them coming to visit you? Is that at all possible?" I wondered if Luke's family knew how much he missed them and how homesick he was.

"Not this year. I guess you could say that none of us planned our year very well because everyone is too busy to make it. Maybe one of my brothers can come visit me in LA when I'm shooting Night Shadows, but it's hard to spend quality time when I'm working so much."

"I don't think the public realizes how hard actors work when making movies and TV shows. I know I've learned quite a bit since meeting you, Anna, and Jenner. It makes me respect what you do so much more."

"Thank you, I feel like I'm constantly complaining about my work to you, but this set is nothing like any other I've been on. You'll see a difference when I'm filming Night Shadows, I promise."

Night Shadows would start filming in January and Luke planned for me to be around for the filming. I was one part astonished that he saw me being around that long and the other part giddy with the thought.

"Did you find out what time you have to be on set next Friday? You really need to get into bed and rest."

Rustling was in the background before Luke coughed and grunted. "I brought my laptop to bed with me, but you're right I do need to rest. I'm already getting tired. Now, let's see. Next week's schedule says I have to be on set by four, but since it's a half day for me, I should be done around one. That would be perfect if you took the 10:45 flight. You would get in around three so even if I was held up some I could still come meet you at the airport."

"You don't have to meet me at the airport if you're busy. I can take a taxi to the hotel it's no problem."

"Let's plan on me meeting you at the airport and if something comes up, I'll message you and let you know. I'll also have your room ready at the hotel so that all you'll have to do is get your room key."

"Thank you, Luke. This is all very sweet, but it makes me feel bad because it's going to be your birthday and you're going to all this trouble."

"I'm doing it because I want to. Don't feel bad. What day would you need to head back to Fairlane? Do you want an early morning flight then?

"I need to come back on Monday and an early morning flight would be great that way it won't be too late when I pick up Mason."

"Are you going to tell Mason where you're going?" Luke asked in a strange tone.

"Yes, I'll tell him and my friends where I'm going, but I don't want my ex to know otherwise he'll come up with some excuse to cancel or to make me come home just to ruin my trip. He's been even worse about me going anywhere when Mason is with him after the wreck I was in. Not that it's any of his business, but he likes to make my life a living hell as much as he possibly can."

"He does sound like an asshole. Do you think he'll ever leave you alone?"

"Probably not and the only way that would happen is if he

met someone and I don't think anyone is stupid enough to get involved with him."

Luke hummed thoughtfully. "Okay, I bought your ticket, and I sent you the information so that you can print out what you need to take to the airport. Although I hate to let you go, I feel like I could fall asleep at any moment. Can I call you later?"

"Of course, you can. I've got a lot of work to finish before I come visit you, but if you call, email, or text I promise I'll answer."

"Okay," Luke yawned. "Goodnight."

"Goodnight, Luke."

AFTER GETTING ONE OF THREE PROJECTS DONE THAT DAY, I TOOK A break and started calling all the friends that I had blown off the last few days. Anna and Taylor were both busy but promised to call me back later. Luckily, Jenner had been busy and had no clue that I'd stopped talking to everyone, so I didn't have to explain anything to him. Ryan on the other hand was another matter.

"Finally decided to see me, huh," Ryan answered his door in his dusty work clothes. The annoyance in his tone told me that I'd hurt his feelings.

"Actually yes, I wasn't in a good place and I knew that if I talked to you that I'd be a crying mess and you know how much I hate to cry in front of anyone."

"That bad huh," he grunted out, leading me into his living room.

"Sort of," I laughed nervously as I took a seat. "I guess you'd call it a misunderstanding."

"You don't know? What happened? Wait! Do I need to sit down for this?"

"Doubtful, but does it matter since you're already sitting down?" I laughed, eyeing him in his recliner. "Anyway, you know how I told you that I met a guy the last time I was in LA and we've been getting to know each other?"

Ryan narrowed his eyes. "Yeah, did he already fuck things up?"

"Would you believe it was me?" My laugh was bitter as it escaped.

"You? No, I don't believe that." His smile told me he was joking.

"Well, you're obviously biased because twice now I have almost fucked things up with Luke."

"What's going on with you and this Luke?" Ryan asked, his voice tight.

"I have no idea and I'm too afraid to ask him." This time my laugh came easier.

"That doesn't sound like you."

"Well it is me, and I'm so afraid I'm going to continue to fuck things up. I need to be honest with him and let him know what I'm feeling, but what if he feels the opposite and finds it too awkward to be around me after I tell him?"

"How are you feeling about him? It hasn't been that long since Matt."

"You don't have to remind me of Matt. Luke is nothing like him. I don't know what's going on. It's hard to explain, even to myself. First, I've never been more attracted to a man in my life. I swear I acted like a total idiot when we met because all I wanted to do was drool and stare at him. Well, I wanted to do more than that, but we won't go into all that I wanted to do to him." My cheeks pinked up at the thought of what I'd imagined doing to Luke since the day I'd met him. "We've been getting to know each other for the last month through phone calls, messages, and emails, and with each one I learn a little bit more about him and he seems perfect. I know he's not, but everything about him is what I want in a man, and the complete opposite of Decker."

"Maybe that's why you're so hung up on him, and I don't blame you, but no one is perfect."

"I know no one's perfect, but maybe he's my perfect. Maybe Luke's the one. My fairytale."

Ryan let out a frustrated breath and put his hands on his knees, "And maybe he isn't. I don't want to see you get hurt again."

"That's not fair. Matt didn't hurt me emotionally. I got hurt because he was an asshole who took out his problems on me." Maybe Ryan wasn't the person I should talk to about this, but he had asked and was one of my best friends.

"Would you rather me not tell you how I feel?" I asked confused.

"I want to know how you feel, but… it's strange hearing you talk about a guy like this."

"To be honest, it's strange feeling like this about a man, but I can't help it. It probably won't matter anyway because I seem hell bent on fucking it up."

Ryan ran a hand through his short blond hair. "You need to remember that Luke's not Decker or Matt, or anyone else. You shouldn't take out your past on him or any future man in your life. I know that I don't know him, but if you're messing things up, it's probably because of Decker."

"You're probably right, but the way I feel about him is so profound for how long we've known each other."

"It sounds like you've got to know him pretty well. Do you want to tell me how you almost messed it up?"

"I got jealous," I cried out, flustered with myself. "Me." I covered my face with my hands. "You know me and that I don't get jealous, but when Luke told me that Lindsey Sinclair started talking to him on set, I lost my mind."

"Lindsey Sinclair?" he asked, sitting straighter in his chair.

"Yeah, the Lindsey Sinclair that you think is so fucking hot. If Luke could have her then why the hell would he want me?"

Ryan sat in silence his mouth slightly hanging open.

Even Ryan, who'd known me for sixteen years couldn't come up with a reason as to why Luke would want me over her.

"So, you got jealous and then what happened?"

I went on to tell Ryan everything from how I had first messed up to how I stopped answering Luke's phone calls.

"Sounds like you went off the deep end."

Looking down, I nodded. "I was a mess and I'm really sorry that I wouldn't talk to you or anyone else."

"And now you're going to go visit him? Do you plan to tell him how you feel?"

Letting out a frustrated sigh, I answered. "I'm not sure what I'm going to do. I've only been in his proximity the one weekend, so I figured I'd see how I feel when I see him again and try to figure out what page Luke is on."

"You really think he could be the one?"

"I think he could be the one for me, but I might not be the one for him."

"Don't be ridiculous, Alex. You deserve to be happy and he'd be lucky to have you."

"You think?" I asked. Insecurities were going to eat away at me if I didn't get myself under control.

"I know." Ryan answered with a reassuring smile.

7

MY FLIGHT LANDED AT LAGUARDIA OVER AN HOUR LATE. I WAS IN a panic once we touched down to check my messages to see if there were anything from Luke or Mason.

Mason didn't have a cell phone, but his grandparents let him use theirs to keep in contact with me when he was staying with them.

Luke was supposed to let me know if he was going to meet me at the airport or if I'd have to catch a cab. In all honesty, I wanted him to meet me because I was as excited as I was nervous about being in New York City.

Turning my phone on, I waited impatiently for it to boot up as I exited the plane and made my way to baggage claim. I knew I should've tried to pack everything in my carryon, but I wanted to be prepared for whatever might come my way. Once the little apple disappeared on my phone, it immediately started to ping with several missed texts. All of them were from Luke putting my mind at ease.

02:15 p.m. **Luke: You should be here soon and I'm on my way to meet you at the airport.**

03:05 p.m. **Luke: Your flight is delayed which you obviously know. I'm waiting inside by the entrance.**

03:59 p.m. **Luke: Text me when you get here.**

04:36 p.m. **Alex: I'm here and headed to baggage claim. See you soon!**

WHEN I SAW LUKE LEANING AGAINST THE WALL AT BAGGAGE claim, I didn't think twice about rushing over to him and giving him a big hug.

"Happy Birthday!" I whisper-yelled as I tipped my head up to meet his eyes.

"Thank you." Luke smiled before kissing me on the cheek. "Let's get your bag and get out of here. What color is your suitcase?"

I couldn't help but laugh. "You'll know when you see it."

Obviously being greeted at the airport was the way to go because once we turned around it seemed to only take a few minutes for my suitcase to show up on the conveyer belt.

Luke laughed, "Yeah, I see what you mean. Not very many hot pink suitcases with a big 'A' on the side of them."

"Nope, it makes it easy to spot. I'm sorry you've been here for so long waiting for me and on your birthday." I went in to grab the handle of my suitcase.

"Don't even think about it," Luke said while stepping in front of me and easily lifting my luggage as if it was as light as a feather. I knew it wasn't since I'd had to pay because it was over the limit for the airline.

"Thank you for everything, Luke. I'm really glad I'm here and in case I don't tell you before I leave - I had a really great time with you this weekend."

Luke stared down at me with an odd look on his face. "You may have just jinxed us. What if we get into a huge fight while you're here? You'll be sorry you said that."

I highly doubted that we were going to get into any fights and I asked him as we made our way out of the airport and slipped into a town car that was waiting for us. "Do you often get into fights with your friends?"

"Rarely. I'm a pretty easy-going guy, or at least I think so," Luke answered.

"I think so too." Looking around the town car as we sat in the back and the driver sped off toward the city, I was surprised we hadn't taken a cab. "You hired a car to pick me up?"

"Nothing but the best for you on your first visit to New York City." He winked and then leaned back in the seat like this was a normal occurrence for him, and it probably was. The only time I had someone drive me around was when it was one of my friends and that wasn't very often because I easily got car sick. Something I wouldn't think of now, in the hopes that I wouldn't feel ill in front of Luke. It might be nice to be driven around if you were assured that you weren't going to puke on yourself or passengers.

"I feel kind of bad that you had to plan everything, but I wouldn't have known what to do or where to go. I'm so excited to see you though!" I clapped my hands and jumped around in my seat causing Luke to throw his head back and laugh.

Still laughing, he said, "I'm happy to see you too. You have no idea."

"Oh." I gave him a side hug with a worried look I couldn't hide. "How's the set been since you've been back? We've barely gotten to talk with how busy we've both been."

Luke looked over at me, his eyes flickered with sadness. "Back to the way it was before. Lindsey barely talks to me now. It's like everyone thinks I have the plague."

"Well, you were pretty sick. I'm just glad that you're all better and we can have fun while I'm in town."

"I would've made sure you had fun no matter how sick I was, I can promise you that." Luke smiled wickedly for a moment before his smile slid off his face. "There's something I wanted to talk to you about before we get to the hotel and are seen together."

That didn't sound ominous or anything. I gave him my best fake smile. "Okay."

"You probably already know this, but when we're out together in public, we need to keep a safe distance otherwise the paparazzi will be relentless trying to take our picture. They're always trying to get the money shot and any woman I'm pictured with is automatically my girlfriend."

My heart sank as my hopes for what Luke and I could've been were dashed with his words. He didn't want me to be seen as his girlfriend.

"I understand. I know how the media likes to portray things even if they aren't true. Don't worry I'll try to stay an appropriate distance away from you, but can you..." I bit on my lip worried about getting separated in a big city as we tried to play off that we didn't know each other.

Luke placed his hand on my shoulder. "Can I what? You can ask me anything, Alex."

Wringing my hands, I answered. "I'm worried about getting separated and lost. The amount of people on the streets is astounding."

"Hey," Luke gently said, his warm voice soothed me. Wrapping his hand around mine, Luke gave it a short squeeze. "I won't let us get separated. We don't have to walk everywhere if you don't want to, we can use this car for the entire time. It's up to you what you want your first New York experience to be."

Giving his hand a squeeze back, I replied with a grateful smile. "That makes me feel a lot better."

"Did you grab anything to eat for lunch or are you hungry?"

"What do you have planned?"

"I thought that you'd probably like to go to the hotel and get cleaned up before we went out to eat. I have a reservation for 7:30 and then I thought I'd show you Times Square at night. I didn't have a lot planned for tonight because I wasn't sure how tired you'd be, and I wanted to see what you wanted to do. I did get information for some places I thought you might want to see. I'll give them to you and let you decide what we do for the rest of the weekend."

"Sounds good to me. If you could tell me how I should dress, then that would be a big help. Hopefully I brought clothes good enough for where you have planned. If you can't tell," I indicated the simple pair of shorts and t-shirt I had on. "My style is not…"

Looking me over, Luke said. "Your style is you. Embrace it. Did you bring a dress? It doesn't have to be fancy."

"There might be a dress or two in my arsenal for the weekend. I brought way too much for the little amount of time I'll be here, but I wanted to be prepared. It happened to me once and ever since I always way over pack for any trip I take. I don't want to embarrass you if my clothes aren't nice enough."

Shaking his head, Luke laughed before pulling the end of his shirt up. For a moment, my brain short circuited hoping that he would lift it a little higher and I would get to see the six pack that I knew he was rocking underneath that shirt.

The sound of Luke clearing his throat, brought my gaze up to his. When I saw the knowing look on his face, I couldn't help but blush.

"I'm sorry. What were you saying?" Instead of meeting his eyes, I watched his Adam's apple bob while he softly laughed from beside me.

"I wanted you to take a good look at the shirt I'm wearing. This is what I normally wear. Do I have some *fancy* clothes? Yes, but I don't like to wear them."

I let my eyes wander as I took in his attire. "Guys can get away with wearing a t-shirt and jeans while women are supposed to be all glammed up. I'm so not the glam girl. Are you going to wear that to dinner tonight?"

Shrugging his shoulders, Luke answered. "I hadn't really thought about it, but I'll probably wear a button-down shirt with jeans."

Pursing my lips, I thought about the two dresses I'd

brought. One I had already owned, but the other I bought online after talking to Anna about what to wear. She'd helped me look online and find what I hoped to be the perfect dress.

"Whatever you wear will be fine. Don't worry about it. It's just me and you going out for my birthday."

Laughter burst out of me with no chance of holding it inside. "It's not just me and you. There's a possibility that hundreds or even thousands of people could see what I wear tonight. You're the one that mentioned the paparazzi. For me that's a lot of pressure."

"Forget the paparazzi and enjoy New York. If you let them, they can ruin the simplest of things. Does it bother you that we might get our picture taken together?"

What? Wasn't it only about ten minutes before when he asked that we keep our distance because the media would assume that I was his girlfriend and now he was asking if it would bother me if there was a picture of us together?

"No." My forehead scrunched up, confused. "I don't mind being photographed with you. What I don't want is the world to criticize what I wear when I'm with you."

Even though Anna had helped me pick out an amazing dress, I knew that if there were pictures of us together there would be people out there who would say negative things about how I looked and no, I wasn't sure if I was ready for that. I'd already had enough negative media attention because of Matt and I didn't want more.

"Sadly, there's always going to be people out there who are going to say negative things about you. You can't take it to heart because they don't know you. They only see what's on the outside and while the exterior may be beautiful, it's your interior that really shines."

There was no holding back the tears that welled in my eyes after what Luke had said to me. He was giving me so many mixed signals - from telling me we needed to keep our distance, to stating that he thought I was beautiful. I knew that sometime during the weekend I was going to have to open up to him about my feelings and lay it all out on the line. I only hoped I got up the nerve to say what I needed to say.

8

LESS THAN AN HOUR LATER I WAS LEAVING THE BEAUTIFUL ROOM Luke had arranged for me as we headed downstairs to the waiting town car. When I had walked into my room, there was no way for me to hide my shock. It was more than I could have imagined.

The walls were a warm yellow that made the room feel cozy and homey with large windows that overlooked the Hudson. The bed was covered in a gorgeous sea-green quilt that I couldn't wait to wrap myself up in. All the furniture was a warm light-brown that was modern, but still made the space feel inviting.

It was the view of the water and the Statue of Liberty that took my breath away as I gazed out my window from the thirty-fifth floor. Lady Liberty was standing tall off in the distance, while boats zipped by without a care in the world.

Calling it a room was an understatement. What I stayed in for the weekend was a suite that was almost the size of my house back in Fairlane. It was safe to say that until that point in my life the hotel that Luke had lived in for months was the nicest hotel I'd ever stayed in.

Placing his hand on the small of my back, Luke guided me out to the car until we hit a crowd and he put distance between us. His face held a secret smile that drove me mad wondering what he was thinking.

Turning in his seat, Luke looked me over with appreciation. "You look beautiful. Thank you for being here to celebrate with me."

One tan leg crossed over the other, making my already short dress ride up higher on my thigh. It was revealing, but worth it with the way Luke couldn't take his eyes off me. I'd never owned a mini dress, but Anna was right. It fit me in all the right places, and with one of my new bras the sexy V-neck showed just enough cleavage. The gold dress was sparkly with crystal beading making me feel more girly and sexy. I only had one nice pair of heels and they were the ones that Matt had bought for me to wear with my Halloween costume. I didn't want to wear them with Luke, but there was no way that I could afford to buy another pair.

Smoothing out my dress the best that I could in the back of the car, I couldn't help but thank Luke again for setting up my trip to New York.

"You don't need to thank me. I like doing things for my friends and it's for my own selfish reasons."

"I guess it's hard for me because if my ex-husband ever did anything nice for me, he expected something in return and rarely was it something I wanted to give. Accepting gifts or good deeds isn't easy for me even when I know that your intentions are good." Shaking my head, my shoulders fell.

"I'm sorry. It's something I need to work on. For a long time, I didn't realize how much I'd changed until there was so very little left of me."

"I promise you that I'll never expect anything of you because I gave you a gift, made you dinner, or a trip. Only give me what you want and if I ever make you feel uncomfortable, then talk to me like you just did, and I'll understand. We all have baggage, and some is just a little harder to see than others."

"You would be running for the hills if you could see all of my baggage," I stated with a bitter laugh.

By the time we pulled up to the restaurant I was starving. I hadn't eaten much since my breakfast with Mason and as I took in the high ceilings, huge windows, hanging pendant lights and all the chairs and booths upholstered in a deep blue velvet, I became nervous. It was elegant and romantic; by far it was the fanciest restaurant I'd ever laid eyes on let alone been in. I wanted to pig out, not eat the amazing food that looked like art at I saw on the tables nearby. At least it looked like I'd have no problem finding something I wanted to eat. If anything, it was going to be hard to choose only one.

After Luke gave our name to the hostess, we were escorted to a secluded table by the far back corner. Luke waited and then pushed my chair in for me once I sat. There was a simple ease to his effort that made it apparent that Luke wasn't doing it for brownie points or because he thought that was what he should do. No, Luke Sandström seemed to be one of the few gentlemen left on the planet.

"Would you like some wine or a cocktail?" Luke asked as I looked over the menu. It was fine dining at its best. I almost choked on the prices when I realized that our dinner would be well over four hundred dollars.

"No, thank you," I choked out. Looking back at my menu, I tried to hide that I was looking for the cheapest food they had to offer.

"Alex," Luke called gently. "Are you okay? Do you not like the restaurant?"

"The restaurant is spectacular."

"But?" Somehow, he knew there was more I wanted to say. I obviously wasn't good at hiding my thoughts or feelings tonight.

"This place is out of my league. I could never afford to eat here, and I feel like whatever I eat will be a waste of money."

Tilting his head to the side, Luke sat his menu down. "Does nothing appeal to you? If that's the case, we can go elsewhere."

"Everything looks lovely, but the prices are astronomical. We could feed a small village for the price of what our dinner will cost." I didn't mention how much I hated when he insisted he pay for dinner tonight. "Do you eat here often?"

Until now, Luke seemed laid back and not the type who would shell out over five hundred dollars for a meal. Luke already seemed out of my league with his good looks and movie star status, but with everything else we had in common and how easily I found talking to him, it made me feel better about our differences. Now I wasn't so sure.

Shaking his head, he looked around the restaurant. "Never been here in my life, but I asked around and it's one of the nicest restaurants in New York. It was never my intention to make you uncomfortable. Like I said before if you want we can leave and eat elsewhere if that would be better."

"No, I'm sorry. I'm being ungrateful. The prices took me off guard and I thought that if this is the type of place you usually eat at then…" To stop myself from finishing, I pressed my lips together.

"Then what?" Luke questioned, leaning forward in his chair, elbows on the table.

Luckily, I didn't have to answer. I was saved by a waiter who'd come to take our drink order. I was tempted to only order water, but one look from Luke had me ordering a cocktail. From then on, I decided to not look at the prices and find me something that sounded good and hopefully plentiful.

"What are you thinking about ordering?"

"I'm not sure. When I saw all the food on the tables, I thought I'd have a hard time narrowing it down because everything looked so good, but after looking through the menu there are a lot of things that I don't eat."

"Really? You never said you have food allergies." Luke glanced at the menu, his brows furrowed, as if there would be a clue on it as to what he thought I was allergic to.

"I'm not allergic to any foods that I know of, but I have a thing about not eating any animals that are cute."

"You don't eat animals that are cute?" he laughed. "Let me see if I can guess what you won't eat." A silly smile tipped his lips as he glanced over the menu again. "You do know that you're cutting out all the best foods the restaurant has to offer, right?"

"I wouldn't know because I've never tried any of them. I

know it sounds crazy, but I hate the idea of eating cute little animals."

"Are you sure you're not a vegetarian?"

"Positive. I thought you were going to guess," I joked.

"Okay, tell me if I get one wrong. Rabbit, lamb, and veal. Did I miss any?"

"Only one that I noticed. The duck. I don't eat sausage because I don't like it. Although there are some cute pigs."

Luke rubbed his eyebrow before tapping the tip of his finger against his lip. "Do you eat regular cows?"

"Do I eat regular cows? I'm not sure what a regular cow is, but I do eat them." I couldn't help but laugh. "Although I do think they're cute with those big eyes, but I was already eating them before I had a chance to form an opinion on what I would and wouldn't eat."

"So, if you had tried any of the animals that you won't eat before you, might eat them now?" Luke asked with raised brows.

"Possibly, but we'll never know. Although now that I think about it, when I was a child I had rabbit and I remember liking it, but I haven't eaten it since I was a small child."

"Oh, Alex," Luke laughed until tears shone in his eyes. "This is why I like you so much. I never know what you're going to say."

We ordered, and I tried to ignore that Luke was going to eat lamb in front of me. When our drinks came, we sipped them leisurely until our food came.

"Is it going to bother you that I'm eating lamb?"

"No, I've been around others when they've had it. I don't

expect others to follow my belief. It's not really a belief, but it is what it is."

Luke nodded as he sipped his beer.

Dinner was easy, we ate, drank and talked just as we had done on the phone since we met. What I didn't do was let on how I pretended that we were on a date and not a friendly dinner for his birthday. Once the weekend was over, I would have to figure out how I was going to stay friends with Luke while I was falling for him.

Luke told me more about his two brothers, Liam and Leo, and his sister, Stella. They were all extremely close, and it was easy to see how much he missed his family, especially on his birthday. His youngest brother, Leo, was still in college and his other brother Liam, was in England filming a TV series. He showed me pictures of the last time they were all together, making me wish I had a family for both me and Mason.

"Is there somewhere I can take you for a piece of birthday cake? Everyone should have cake on their birthday." It seemed wrong that he was taking me out to an expensive dinner on his birthday. I wanted to try to make his birthday a little special even if it was by a little piece of cake.

"Maybe we'll find a place for dessert as we walk Times Square. You don't want to miss it at night." He answered with warm eyes and a lopsided smile.

WE WALKED DOWN THE SIDEWALK WITH LUKE A FEW FEET BEHIND me. At first, I felt silly walking down the busy sidewalk in a flashy gold mini-dress by myself, but it didn't take me long to get lost in the lights and atmosphere of New York. It was everything I thought it would be and more. Sharing it with Luke would always make it special even if we had to do it with a few feet between us.

I was sure I looked like an idiot with my mouth parted and my headed slightly tilted back so that I wouldn't miss anything.

As luck would have it, the heel of my shoe got caught in a crack causing me to almost land on my face. My arms scrambled out to catch me, but instead Luke's strong arms wrapped around me before setting me back to rights. I was embarrassed for almost falling and the attention we seemed to be drawing. Looking to my right, I saw we were right in front of a little cafe that served coffee and pastries. Without thinking, I dragged Luke inside with me and up to the counter.

"Are you okay?" he asked as he took me in from tip to toe. "I don't know how you walk in those shoes."

"Believe me I don't know either. It must be the magic of New York. The last time I wore heels was almost a year ago, and it was a struggle. Now," I said moving closer to him so that he could hear me as I whispered. "What would you like for your birthday cake? Do you think they have a candle we could buy?" My hand patted him on his firm chest. "It's my treat, birthday boy."

Stepping back, I waited for him to choose. Luke looked like a kid in a candy store as he perused the two display cases in front of us. Everything from the oatmeal raisin cookies to the dark chocolate five-layer cake looked amazing. It might have had something to do with the fact that dinner wasn't the most filling after not eating for most of the day and I was ready to fill my stomach with flour and sugar.

"Are you going to get something? Maybe we can share because I can't decide." Luke eyed the desserts hungrily as if he hadn't had one in years.

Taking matters into my own hands, I pointed to the five-layer cake, a couple of different types of brownies (my favorite), about five different cookies, and some sort of cherry tart. I'd paid close attention to Luke as his eyes kept going back to some of the desserts more than once.

"Are you ready to head back to the hotel?" he asked as he took the bags of goodies from me, phone in hand.

It was more than obvious that Luke was ready to be back at the hotel and I couldn't blame him. It had been a long day for the both of us. Still, I was disappointed that my time with Luke would be over once the desserts were consumed.

The bright side to heading back to the hotel was that I'd be able to talk to Luke instead of acting like I had no clue who he was. I'd never realized how lonely the life of a celebrity could be if you wanted your life to be private.

Luke had been stopped twice for a selfie with a couple of women who'd stopped and asked, and I saw quite a few people with their phones out to take his picture as they watched him walk down the busy sidewalk. It was a good thing the windows of the town car were tinted otherwise he probably would have made me take a separate car.

Again, we were quiet as we made our way toward our hotel. I felt like a kid with her face plastered to the window as I took in everything that went by. It was exciting to see the city, but at the same time a little disappointing when I couldn't point and talk to Luke about what I'd seen. I might as well have been by myself at least, then it wouldn't have been as depressing.

When we stepped into the elevator, Luke hit the button to his floor before wrapping his arm around my shoulders. When I glanced up at him, Luke's face mirrored what I'd been feeling. His eyes were sad with disappointment shining in them. He'd felt as alone as I had out there on the street.

"I'm sorry. I didn't think this through. What's the point of you being here if I have to act as if I've never seen you before? We'll regroup tomorrow and figure out how to enjoy your time here without the paparazzi intruding. There's so much I want to show you." He paused, looking down at his shoes. "Did you go through the pamphlets left in your room?"

"Luke," I said, turning so that we would be face to face. "Take a deep breath and slow down. Don't worry about tonight. Let's enjoy the rest of your birthday with all these yummy desserts."

The elevator pinged on the thirty-eighth floor. One down from the top. Now that I was so close to being able to take off my shoes, I would admit they were not the shoes to walk any amount of distance in. I had little doubt it wouldn't matter if it was the hundredth or second time I'd worn them. My feet were not made to wear heels unless I could sit there and look pretty.

Luke hung his head as he held the door open and we walked into his room, "I feel like I let you down."

"You didn't let me down," I replied from beside the door where I promptly took off the offending heels. "Times Square was a small portion of our night. Yes," I continued as I started to put all our desserts on the table. I hoped he didn't mind, but I was ready to get as comfortable as I could in this dress. "It would have been nice to talk to you and walk by you, but I do understand."

Once Luke sat beside me and took a good look at all the sugar that was on the table, he seemed to have forgotten everything, but what was right in front of him. He still couldn't choose.

"Why don't we split everything in two except for the cake and share. Whatever I don't eat you can have."

His head whipped toward me with a huge, lopsided grin. "Are you sure?"

"Absolutely. Are you still hungry from dinner? The last time I saw that look on someone's face was on Mason last year on Halloween. We'd gone to every house in our neighborhood before he then went trick-or-treating in his grandparent's neighborhood. His bag was so heavy he could barely carry it and when all his candy was spread out all over our dining room table, he looked like you right now."

"I'm that bad?" Luke asked with a laugh and I wasn't sure, but I thought I saw his cheeks pink up before he leaned forward and scooped up the container with the cake in it.

"A little," I admitted. "I didn't eat lunch and although dinner was the best meal I've ever had, it wasn't enough."

"I limit my sugar," he said quickly before placing a giant bite of cake in his mouth and chewing. "I can't gain any weight for my role as Nikolai on Night Shadows. None of us can. It's in our contracts and it can be torture sometimes. I generally eat pretty healthy but abstaining from sugar is almost as bad as not having any sex."

A piece of cookie flew out of my mouth as I choked and coughed on his answer. I'd not been expecting that.

"Sorry," Luke said, but it was obvious he didn't mean it since he was silently shaking with laughter. After giving my back a couple of hard pats, he sat back and started eating his cake again without another word.

"It's okay. I wasn't expecting our conversation to go there when we were talking about desserts. I have to say, I wouldn't really know because I went without sex for over two years and before that…"

"Yeah, you said it wasn't good. What kind of man doesn't at least finish off his woman?"

"Ones that are all about themselves. When was the last time you had sex?" I asked as if the answer made no difference to me at all.

"It had been about a month before the last time I saw Sophia, so it's been almost two years."

"No, one-night stands or little flings for you since then?" I was shocked because Luke could have any woman he wanted, and if he wanted to get laid there would be women lined up around the block.

He shook his head as he chewed his last bite of cake. Luke's eyes were already eyeing the rest of the sweet treats lined up in front of us.

"Been there, done that and it's not worth it. Now that I'm older I want to find a woman to love, who'll love me for me and not my status, someone to have a family with. I'm not going to find that fucking a different woman every night."

I wanted to raise my hand in the air and yell, "Me! Pick me!

I'll take the job!" Instead, I continued to eat my half of a salted caramel brownie.

"Do you want to find love again?" Luke asked from his corner of the couch.

"Do I want to? Yes, but I don't know if it's in the stars for me."

"I think it is. You were just looking in all the wrong places."

Luke leaned into me and gently tucked a few loose strands of hair behind my ear as if he'd been doing it all his life. It was so natural for him to do it.

"What's with the look?" he asked puzzled once he sat back eying me.

"It's going to sound stupid and girly," I responded, heat touched my cheeks and burned the tip of my ears.

"Whatever it is isn't stupid. You can tell me."

That was the wonderful thing about Luke, I knew I could tell him what I had been thinking and he wouldn't ridicule me like Decker always had.

"No one's ever done that to me before and I swear that in almost every romance book I've read the hero in the story tucks the heroine's hair behind her ear. I always thought it was kind of silly until now."

"How do you feel now?" he asked softly with an unknown emotion in his voice.

Taking in a deep breath, I slowly let in out while closing my eyes to gather my strength. I could do this. I could tell Luke, who'd become a good friend and who I trusted with what I was feeling and not mess up what we had. Right?

Opening my eyes, I took in the man in, before me. By the

look in his eyes I could tell that he genuinely cared what I thought and how I was feeling.

"It felt wonderful. In that small moment, I felt cherished, safe and…"

"What?" Luke voice came out lower than ever with a sexy husky mix.

"Beautiful," I whispered before looking away. Had I messed up what we had between us? I hadn't planned on telling Luke my feelings tonight. I wanted to visit my friend for his birthday because he'd become to mean so much to me and I wanted him to have a friend to celebrate with since he was on location and hadn't formed a tight bond with anyone here. It had nothing to do with a lost bet that he'd rigged to win.

"Alex," Luke said moving closer to me on the couch until our knees brushed and I felt the heat of his body start to seep into me. "I wish you could see yourself the way I and the rest of the world see you. Your ex-husband really did a number on you, messing with your head." Cupping my face with his large, warm hand, Luke smiled, and lit up the room with it. Once again, he was giving me something so simple and yet so complex that I'd never had. "You. Are. Beautiful. Don't ever doubt it again." He punctuated each word with a sharp head nod.

"I'll try," I murmured as his thumb stroked my cheek. "You're going to have to stop doing that. Stop giving me these firsts."

"More firsts? I'm honored. What else did I unknowingly do?" I couldn't deny him, or his voice that made me want to tell him all my secrets, and I'd told him just about everything these past couple months because of that soothing voice with the slight accent and how easy it was to talk to him.

"Cupping my cheek and stroking it." I would have looked away if he hadn't been holding me in place. "I'm pathetic."

"You're not pathetic. You fell for the wrong guy and he took his unhappiness out on you. I hate what you went through and that he didn't treat you right, but I'm happy that I can give you these firsts. Now, why do you want me to stop?" His voice was deeper, more gravelly than ever, burrowing deep inside me as I took him in.

"You're making me feel things that I shouldn't feel and I'm afraid that if you keep doing all these things that are so sweet and romantic I'm not going to be able to handle what I'm feeling."

Luke moved closer until his chest brushed against my shoulder. There wasn't any place else for him to go on that couch, but in my lap and that would have been awkward. Although I wouldn't have cared. For only a tiny moment, I thought his eyes dropped down to my mouth as I bit my bottom lip with nervous energy.

"How are you feeling?"

I took the cowardly way out and answered. "I like you."

"I like you too," he replied back with a sly smile.

"I didn't mean for this to happen. I'm sorry. Maybe I should go back to my room."

I tried to get up, but the hand Luke still had against my cheek moved around to the back of my head to cup my neck, keeping me in place.

"Don't run. Stay and talk to me. Please," Luke implored, his blue-green eyes holding me hostage.

"I'm scared. I don't want to ruin what we have. You've become important to me and I don't want to lose you."

His hand, somehow without me even feeling or knowing it happened, was back to cupping my cheek, his thumb caressed me as he spoke. "You'll never lose me, and do you want to know how I know this?"

"Yes," I answered quickly. My head nodded in an almost frantic manner.

"When I met you, I had an immediate pull toward you and I think you felt the same."

Yes, I did, but I thought it was just me.

"Did you ever wonder why, out of all the people at that table, I sat down by you? As you've come to learn, I'm a very private person and I definitely don't hand out my phone number to just anyone I meet. I wasn't sure how you'd fit into my life, but I knew that I wanted to get to know you and I'd have time to figure the rest out later. Right here, right now, is later and we've gotten to know each other over our emails and phone calls where you probably know me better than almost anyone. I wasn't sure what would become of us when you said you were going to come visit me, but the instant I saw you, I knew what I wanted."

"What do you want? You're going to have to spell it out for me here Luke. I can't risk taking anything the wrong way. I hope you understand." I was desperate to hear what he had to say and utterly terrified at the same time.

"This," he rumbled, his voice like gravel before sweeping his full, soft lips against mine.

My eyes closed in happiness and longing, only opening once he pulled back, much too quickly. I wanted to tug him back to me. I already missed his lips and the heat of his body.

"Tell me this is what you want." His eyes were heavily lidded as he gazed at me from under his long lashes.

I had no words for how much I wanted Luke to kiss me in that moment, so I answered him the only way I knew how. My lips crashed against his and when he moaned his pleasure, I slipped my tongue inside only to meet his in the best kiss of my life.

Soft, full lips against mine kissed across my jaw and down my neck as I pressed my chest to his. I wanted to climb in his lap, but I couldn't help thinking this was only the second time I'd been with Luke and I was about ready to jump him. Had I turned into a slut? First, sleeping with Matt the night I met him and now this?

"Stop thinking," Luke murmured as his mouth trailed wet kisses across my collarbone.

"Do you think I'm a slut?" I blurted out. Luke told me to stop thinking, not to ruin the moment, so of course I had to say something.

His mouth left my skin, and I immediately wanted to take back my words.

Taking my hand in his, he asked. "Why would you think that?"

"Because even though we've been getting to know each other we've only been in each other's company in LA and today. When you think of it like that, it seems fast."

"Don't think of it that way. Yes, it's true we haven't spent much time together, but we've been getting to know each other and what I've gotten to know, I really like. Do you want to fight the pull we feel toward each other?"

"No, but I don't want you to think less of me tomorrow either."

A sad smile crossed his face before Luke leaned in and brushed his already swollen lips against mine. "You don't have to worry about that with me. I'll never think less of you for anything you will or won't do, sexually or otherwise. I wish you'd been raised in Sweden or anywhere in Europe. Your views on sex and your body would be so different, but mostly I blame your ex-husband. It wasn't right to want one thing sexually from you and then make fun of you afterwards for giving it to him. I can see how that would shame you into repressing yourself. I want to bring out your sexuality in a positive way. Show you what a man is supposed to give his woman, in and out of bed. Will you let me?"

How could I say no? I wanted to give all of myself to Luke, but I knew it would take time. I couldn't get over the way I had been taught to think overnight.

Instead of speaking, I stood and pulled the zipper down at the back of my dress and then shimmied out of it leaving me in only my barely there black lace bra and panties.

Reaching out, Luke brushed up and down the outside of my thighs, pulling me closer and skimming a little higher each time, until his fingers grazed underneath my breasts.

Looking up at me, his eyes were heavy and full of lust, and I knew mine mirrored his. Never had I wanted a man so badly in my life. Stepping in between his legs, I skimmed my hands down and then up his shirt, feeling the ridges of each muscle as they tensed at my touch. The muscles I'd been dreaming about since I met him. Slowly I unbuttoned his shirt starting from the top, leaning in to kiss each new inch of skin revealed to me.

Once his shirt was off I straddled his lap, bringing us skin to skin. Our overheated bodies slid against each other as I ground down on his rigid cock.

With his mouth on mine, Luke stood from the couch and made his way to the bedroom, my legs wrapped around his trim waist. Lowering me onto the bed, Luke traced the tip of his finger from the arch of my foot slowly up, until he reached the seam of my lace panties. Leaning down, he placed an open mouth kiss right where I wanted him before he pulled back and traced the other leg. I couldn't help but writhe in his bed as he took his time torturing me.

"I'm going to show you what you've been missing. Your body's mine and I'm going to worship at its alter."

I couldn't help the shiver of pleasure that traveled through my body as I leaned up and cupped the back of his head, bringing his mouth to mine. Our tongues danced as we learned each other's taste, my teeth grazed his bottom lip before sucking hard.

Luke moaned, setting my body on fire, arching up to meet his. He cupped my breast through my bra, brought his mouth down and sucked my nipple into his hot mouth. The fabric was wet and rough, a striking contrast to his mouth causing it to stiffen and ache with want.

My fingers brushed across his chest, feeling the light smattering of hair, and his rippling abs. Going lower, my hands found his belt and frantically tried to undo the clasp.

"Slow down. We've got all night," Luke said before taking

my other breast in his hand, pulling down the cup to lightly bite and then gently soothe the ache with his tongue.

With his pants off, I ran my hands around to squeeze his firm ass. My hand slid around to find him hard and long as I stroked his velvety length. Luke growled against my breast before he licked, sucked, and nibbled his way back to my mouth, eliciting another moan from me.

Luke dipped two fingers inside and, finding me ready, pumped them in and out while his thumb circled my clit. Crying out his name, I lost myself to him. My body clenched, arching up into him as my orgasm seized me. Shaking in his arms, I chanted his name over and over with each new wave of pleasure until I was a puddle of sated bliss underneath him.

In the dim light coming through the window, Luke seemed content as we stayed on our sides while I caught my breath. He ran his fingertips up and down my back, down my arm to my fingers and back again. The pattern repeated itself over and over as I came down from the haze of my orgasm. With only his fingers, Luke had given me the best orgasm of my life and I couldn't wait to find out what he could do with his tongue and cock.

My traitorous mind fought against my body's blissed out state while my heart pounded a furious beat in my chest. I wanted to bask in the moment of feeling sexually fulfilled and the fact that Luke wanted me, but inside my mind, my past kept screaming at me that pleasure wasn't about me it was about the man. Luke would get tired of me if I didn't satisfy him.

Kissing my temple, Luke spoke softly into the dark. "Are you okay? You're thinking so hard I can feel it."

I chuckled darkly. "That bad, huh?"

"I would like to think that I know you pretty well, even when I can't see your face. It's strange because most of the time you're as easy to read as an open book and other times, I feel like I couldn't make a guess even if I were psychic."

"I sound like a pain in the ass." My head burrowed deeper into the crook of his arms. "To answer your question, I'm perfect and not as the same time if that makes any sense. Internally I'm battling bullshit that's so engrained in me I wonder if I'll ever be over it, but I don't want to darken your doorstep with my silly problems especially since it's your day."

Long arms wrapped around me pulling me tight against Luke's warm body. "If you don't want to talk about whatever's bothering you, I'm not going to make you. I only want the answer to one question. Can you give me that?"

"Yes, what do you want to know?" There was very little I wouldn't give Luke in that moment.

Burying his face in my hair, Luke squeezed me tighter. He seemed nervous, but I couldn't imagine why until he asked. "Do you regret what we did?"

Without thought, I answered with conviction, "Never." It was the truth. No matter how long Luke and I were together I would never regret a moment of being with him.

My arms had been pinned between us and now that my lust induced haze was gone, I realized how cold I must have seemed as I laid beside him like a limp noodle. I wiggled one arm out of Luke's hold so that I could rub his back. It wasn't sexual in nature, it was to put both of us at ease. We were quiet for a long while, our fingers and hands stroking and caressing the others back.

"When I was young, my grandfather used to always rub my back. For me it's always been a soothing gesture. Platonic, I guess you would call it."

Brushing the hair away from my neck, Luke moved onto rubbing my scalp and running his fingers through my hair. I wanted to fall asleep in his arms and stay there forever, or until I had to go back home on Monday. The voice in the back of my head still said I needed to please Luke even though I had no clue how to make that move. I was out of practice and worried that I wouldn't please him the way that he'd pleased me.

"Platonic? Why do you say that?"

A cough of laughter escaped, but it did seem like a strange choice in words. "Decker, he thought that if he rubbed my back, it should always lead to sex. It was payment for providing something I liked. At first, he would ask if I wanted a massage and why wouldn't I want a massage, so I said yes. It didn't get me in the mood. In fact, it probably hindered me from getting horny. I associated it with my grandpa and that's just gross. It didn't seem to matter to him when I told him. He knew I liked it and used it against me."

"I can see how that the association would be a turn off. If you think I'm rubbing your back and head because I want sex that's not the case. There are no strings attached to my touch. It's pure affection because you're finally in my arms and we only have a short time together."

I wasn't sure whether Luke meant we'd only be together this once or that our time was short, but we'd see each other again and continue this. In that instance, I decided I would worry about it another day, like when I got back home and could over analyze everything.

"If I ever meet your ex, I'm going to punch him in the face and kick him in the balls. The things that he put you through." I could feel him shake his head against the bed. "What he still puts you through with your son."

"Thank you, and I just might take you up on it. I worry about Mason so much when he's with his dad, and how this is going to affect his life and who he'll become."

"From what you've told me, I don't think you have anything to worry about. Mason sounds like a great kid that can see through his father's bullshit. You've done an amazing job with him and I know it hasn't been easy."

"Luke," I choked out. "Don't say such sweet things to me if you don't want me to fall in love with you. I'm not used to nice words."

My lips clamped shut when I realized what I'd said. The last time I mentioned the 'L' word it hadn't gone so well. I decided to quickly change the subject.

"I wanted you to know because I enjoy your touch immensely and it makes me want to fall asleep in your arms, and…"

"I understand," Luke cut me off. I wasn't sure he did, but I would take him at his word. "I take no offense. I want to learn these things about you and for you to feel like you can tell me anything without consequence."

"There's something about you Luke that makes it easy for me to talk and open up to you. It's refreshing not to feel as if I have to bottle up my feelings so that I won't have to feel the wrath of expressing myself."

Rolling me to my back, Luke held himself above me with his weight on his forearms. Peering up, I could see the smile on his face even in the darkness. I'd put that smile there, and I wanted to continue to do so. Running his nose along mine, one of Luke's hands spanned my ribcage and trailed down.

"What if I were to caress other parts of your body such as your legs, stomach, or breasts? Would you still feel the same way as when I rub your back?"

What he wanted to know was did any touch turn me on and I didn't blame him for wanting to know.

"I wouldn't feel the same way if you were to caress *other* parts of my body."

Nuzzling my neck, he replied huskily. "I'm glad we cleared that up."

9

SETTLING DOWN FURTHER BETWEEN MY LEGS, I COULD FEEL LUKE'S hard length press against my thigh. Knowing he wanted me made my body arch up and feel him against every inch of my overheated skin.

My hands roamed over his bulging biceps and around his shoulders before trailing down. As my nails lightly scratched over his nipples he moaned, spurring me on to let loose and give both of us what we wanted. I knew that Luke would never make fun of me for what I wanted to do to his body.

"This bra needs to go," Luke rasped out as he slid the strap off first one shoulder and then the other. I couldn't agree more. "Are you on birth control? I don't want anything between us. I want this to be special."

"I'm on the shot. The last one was a month ago," I answered as my lips trailed the contour of his jaw.

"I've never had sex without a condom. I'm clean." His voice was gravely from lust. His teeth grazed my collarbone down to my nipple taking my aching flesh into his mouth and sucking until I felt it down to my core.

"I'm clean. I got tested even though we used a condom every time."

"If you're uncomfortable, I'll use one, but I want to feel every inch of you inside and out."

"I want that too," I moaned into his mouth.

Luke slid down my body, nudging my legs wider with his broad shoulders, his large hands followed until they spread my sex open wide. I was open bare for him and before I could feel uncomfortable, his hot tongue swept through my folds and he moaned. With Luke, all my inhibitions were forgotten as he claimed me and made me feel alive for the first time in my life. He made me feel beautiful and unashamed of my body. A body that was far from perfect after having a child.

Pulling me further down the bed and deeper onto his face, Luke plunged his tongue inside of me, penetrating me in one swift movement.

"Fuck me, you taste divine," Luke growled.

My hips rocked lazily at first, feeling his mouth devour me, his thumb rubbed my clit as we both moaned. Luke into my sex, and me into the night.

I clenched around his tongue, my legs shaking against his shoulders, my body vibrated with my second orgasm of the night. My fingers pulled Luke's hair as I threw my head back and screamed his name.

Before I could catch my breath, Luke had his mouth on mine in a desperate kiss. It was hard and frantic as he bruised my lips with his. Twirling his tongue with mine, I tasted the sweet tang of my juices.

Reaching down, Luke stroked his cock a couple of times before gliding it through my folds and hitting my already sensitized bundle of nerves. My body automatically lifted to him. I needed him in me like I needed my next breath. When his tip reached my opening, Luke slid into me inch by glorious inch.

It was safe to say that Luke had the largest penis that had ever graced my body. When I thought all of him was in, he would keep going as my insides stretched to accommodate him. For a moment, I was scared. I wasn't sure all of him would fit.

"Oh, God, you're so tight," Luke moaned from above me as he watched where we were connected. His movements were slow as he watched me stretch and suck him in with each thrust. "We fit perfectly together," Luke grunted as he drove back inside of me. "Do you feel it?"

"Yes," I panted. My hips moved up and down in tandem to meet his in a sensual rhythm. Lost in sensation, my body moved without thought. I let myself go, throwing my head back as Luke continued to slide in and out of me in a luxurious tempo. There was no hurry as we felt each other's bodies for the first time.

"Yes," I moaned as he hit a place inside me that made fireworks light up behind my eyes. "Right there. Keep doing that."

My hand snaked down between us, rubbing my clit faster as my impending orgasm hurled toward me. I moaned and cried out, noises I'd never made before during sex, and with each one that came out of my mouth, the freer I became.

"Luke," I cried out, scratching down his back as my whole

body clenched around him, shaking and shuttering with the most powerful climax of my life. Luke swallowed my cry with his mouth, his tongue following the same rhythm as his hips. A few more thrusts before he stilled, buried deep inside of me. He groaned out foreign words and bit against the skin of my neck, his body collapsing on top of mine.

After a few minutes, Luke slid off me, rolling onto his back, pulling me along with him. Our legs were tangled together, and I could hear his heartbeat slowing down from its frantic pace only moments ago.

With my cheek to his chest, I could feel Luke's silent laughter.

"What's so funny?" My eyes were still closed; a smile on my face. I was beyond sated. I wasn't even sure if I'd be able to walk later since my legs still felt like jelly and I hadn't even moved yet.

"I thought you were going to be timid our first time, from the stories you've told me about your ex-husband. Instead you blossomed right in front of me. It was spectacular."

"Yes, it was." I agreed, as I snuggled deeper into his embrace. A shiver ran through my body as my heated skin cooled.

"Would you like to take a bath with me? Warm up and…"

"And?" I laughed, lifting up on an arm and looking down at him. I couldn't see much in the dark with only a sliver of light coming through the windows. His body was big and broad, tan and smooth. Luke was gorgeous, even in the dark, and somehow we fit together perfectly.

"You might be a little sore in the morning. If you soak now, it might help."

Luke was right that I might be sore tomorrow, and I didn't want it to ruin our day out and about in the city. I'd never taken a bath with a man before and it sounded lovely.

"Is the tub big enough for the both of us?"

"Not very many places have bathtubs big enough for me to enjoy; I got lucky with this room. Stay here and I'll come get you when it's ready."

I watched Luke from behind and grinned at his sculpted ass when the lights came on in the bathroom. My core clenched, surprising me. Luke brought out my inner vixen and I couldn't get enough of him. Never had I been so sated and lustful at the same time. I already wanted to jump him again after three of the best climaxes of my life.

Enveloped in his scent and the warmth of the bed, I yawned, my eyes dipping closed as I waited.

My body jumped when I felt the bed dip. I guess I'd fallen asleep. Three orgasms will do that to a girl.

"The bath's ready if you're still up for it," Luke said softly as he rubbed up and down my arm.

"Sounds heavenly." I felt like I was living out one of the many romance books I'd read and when I stepped into the bathroom and saw a few candles lit around the bathtub with steam rising from its depths, I knew I found my fairytale.

Spinning around, I looked up at Luke in shock. "When did you do this?"

He smiled, and his eyes twinkled. Luke knew that he'd pleased me. "You fell asleep for a few minutes. I came out to get you and took advantage that the hotel had a few candles throughout the suite."

"I'm glad you did." It was romantic, and my heart

swooned. "Will you help me step in?" All I needed was to fall and smack my head on one of the best nights of my life.

"Anything," he replied holding out his hand for me to take.

Slowly I lowered myself into the water before scooting up to the front so that Luke could step in behind me. Once Luke had stretched his long legs out beside me, he wrapped an arm around my middle and pulled me flush against his chest.

His cock was hard and hot as it pressed against my lower back. I had the urge to turn around and stroke it, but the water and the feel of Luke all around me was too perfect to get me to move.

We were quiet for long minutes as we soaked our overused muscles. Luke cupped water and ran it over my arms, stomach and breasts before lacing his fingers through mine and humming to himself. It was bliss.

"I've never taken a bath with a man before," I murmured, turning my head to kiss his chest.

"Another first," His lips brushed against my ear. I could feel his smile. "But you've taken a bath with someone before?"

"I have with Mason, lots of times. When he was young, he loved baths. I miss those days. Not that he isn't a great kid now, but when he was a baby, he would look up at me with his big blue eyes like I was his everything."

Wrapping his arms around me, Luke asked. "Would you ever have more kids?"

"It's a possibility," I shrugged in his hold. "I don't want to say never, but if I decide to have more kids, the man would need to be special. My body's not meant to stay pregnant, so every pregnancy is high risk and it felt like I was a single parent because Decker never did anything to help. I don't want that again."

"Hmmm," Luke hummed taking in the information I'd given him. "Why are all your pregnancies high risk? I know nothing about pregnancy and never thought there'd be trouble, although I do know that's not always the case."

I wiggled closer into his arms and Luke tightened his hold as if he knew what I was about to say would be difficult. "The reason I married Decker was because I got pregnant right after my senior year in high school. Our parents made us get married; they had everything all planned out. We moved out and found our own place and I guess we were supposed to live happily ever after. Nothing worked out like anyone planned. We got married when I was three months along and I had a miscarriage only a few weeks later.

"I think at that point I would've been happy to get a divorce and stay at home, but I didn't want to disappoint my family. My grandfather was a very religious man, and he meant the world to me. I didn't want to shame him anymore than I already had by becoming pregnant. Instead I went to college in a town not far from Fairlane and Decker landed a job as an exterminator at a company which he eventually took over and bought.

"Six years later I was even more miserable and wanted a divorce. The moment we moved in together Decker changed. He was no longer the person I met in high school. He turned cold and mean overnight. I'd been sick and not getting any better, so I went to the doctor and found out I was pregnant. You can imagine it was not the news I wanted to hear, but in the end, it was a blessing. Since I had a miscarriage before my

OB-GYN told me that they would watch me carefully and do a few extra tests to make sure my pregnancy went smoothly. At twenty-six weeks, I started to have contractions and had to be put on bed rest where I stayed until I had Mason when I was thirty-six weeks along."

"I'm sorry," Luke said softly from the top of my head. "With your history of pregnancy and your ex, I understand why you'd want to make sure the man you created a child with was worth the risk."

"I'm already a single parent, I don't need to do it again. Do you want kids?" I asked as I rubbed my hands up and down his long, muscular legs that encased mine.

Resting his head against the top of mine, he murmured. "I would like a family one day, but I'm open to many ways of attaining the family I want."

"Really? Like what?" Most men who wanted families in my experience wanted their children to be theirs by blood.

"Besides the traditional way of having kids, I would be open to adoption, surrogacy, or finding a woman who already has a child or children."

Could Luke be talking about me? I wasn't sure what to think about if Luke wanted a family with me. I was dumbfounded at the prospect, but I knew that I needed to take it one step at a time and not get ahead of myself.

"You've really put some thought into it." I was glad that Luke couldn't see how wide my eyes were. I was more than a little shocked he'd put so much thought into how he might have children in the future.

"I think it's important to know your priorities. I'm thirty years old and my career has taken off." His fingertips brushed the bottom of my breast back and forth. "I've been asked on numerous occasions in interviews if I want a family and it made me think about if I wanted to have a family and what that would entail."

"You mean being away while you work?"

"I wouldn't want to be away from my family much, so I would hope at first they could travel with me to wherever I was shooting and then eventually I would have to slow down or perhaps stop altogether."

"You would give up your career for a family?" I couldn't hide the shock in my voice.

Wrapping his arms around me with his cheek resting on the top of my head, Luke replied. "I would give up just about anything for love and family."

"I think that's the way it should be if you really love someone."

The moment had gotten too heavy. We'd talked about things that were way beyond wherever we were in our relationship. I was confused because it felt too soon, but it also didn't at the same time. Through emails and talks on the phone we had gotten to know each other more than we would've in a normal situation. I knew there were things I still needed to know about him, just as there were things I needed to tell him about me.

Silence echoed through the room. In any other circumstance it would've been uncomfortable, but not with Luke. No matter what we did together I was always comfortable with him.

Slowly one of his hands splayed out across my ribcage and started to slide down until it disappeared into the water. He only stopped once he met my already swollen nub, where two of his fingers caressed and pinched. His other hand massaged my aching breast, rolling my nipple before moving over to repeat the process on my other. My body arched against his chest, my head thrown back onto his shoulder.

Biting my bottom lip, I chanted his name over and over again until I cried out, shaking and sloshing water all over the floor.

Once again Luke had blown my mind with another incredible orgasm. Where had he been all my life?

A low rumble came from Luke's chest, his voice was pure sex when he spoke. "Sweden."

Oh my God! "Did I just say that out loud?"

"You did." His amusement was evident in his tone.

"You've scrambled my brain and given me more orgasms in one night than I've ever had in one month. Probably more."

Pressing a kiss to my temple, Luke spoke. "More firsts."

"Are you trying to give me every experience I've never had in one day?" Seriously, Luke was knocking them off the list faster than I could name them.

"No," he answered, turning my now limp body in his arms until we were chest to chest. My cheek rested on his shoulder. "I plan to give you many more firsts for a very long time."

"Sexually you can give me a lot, because Decker was very vanilla in bed and you already know about him not giving me any orgasms. It might take time before I'm ready to explore some things, but I'm open to just about anything."

"Do you think I'm some BDSM Dom?" he asked with laughter in his voice, pulling back to see my face.

"The thought never crossed my mind, but I wanted to warn

you that although I want to try new things, there might be a few that will take some time before I'm comfortable doing them."

"Alex," Luke said my name with such tenderness my heart instantly swelled. "I will never make you do anything you're uncomfortable with. Don't feel like you can't speak up if that's ever the case. Okay?"

"Okay," I answered. "Seriously, you're too good to be true. Everything feels like a dream. How did a girl from Missouri find a tall, gorgeous, sweet, caring man from Sweden?" Ducking his head, Luke flushed, but I wanted him to know what I said was truly how I felt. "It's all true. I could keep going if you want."

"Maybe later," he answered before his voice lowered and his eyes filling with lust. "Right now, I'd rather do something different if you're up to it."

"Something or should I say *someone* is up." My hand snaked down between us to stroke his cock that had been hard the entire time we'd been in the tub. It was time to reward him for his patience.

"Alex," Luke groaned. Licking up my neck. "I want you to ride me."

I rose up on my knees ready to take Luke in when he pulled me down on him in one hard motion. Buried to the root, we both moaned as my sex clenched around him.

"Oh God, Alex, you feel so good. I can't get enough of you. Fuck," he growled out. "Ride me."

His wish was my command. I wanted to be able to make Luke feel half as good as he'd made me feel that night. With one hand on his shoulder and the other on the side of the tub, I slammed down hard on his cock until I could feel him hit my cervix.

The noises Luke made spurred me on, driving me to go faster and harder. Water splashed out onto the floor with each wave our bodies created.

"Can you come again? I need you to come one more time for me. Come on, Alex." His talented fingers rubbed my clit in slow circles as I continued to ride him.

"I'm going to come." I panted. With my fingers threaded through his hair, I tucked my face into his neck and rode out the fireworks that ignited inside me.

Strong hands grasped my hips, continuing to move me up and down once, twice, and on the third time he stilled and dug into my soft flesh. Luke let out a low moan before enveloping me in his arms. We lazed in the cooling water, touching, rubbing, and kissing where we could reach. After a few moments, he stood with me in his arms as if I were as light as a feather and strode into the bedroom where he placed us both in bed, chest to chest, our legs tangled, and in each other's arms.

"When I buy a house, I'm going to make sure it has a bathtub big enough for the both of us or put a new one in."

"You're ruining me," I murmured sleepily, my cheek resting on his chest. "I know I keep saying it but thank you for tonight and all the amazing experiences you've given me."

Tucking a wet lock of hair behind my ear, Luke smiled lazily. "You said that I was the first to tuck your hair behind your ear."

"You are." I smiled just thinking about it. "I became like one of the women in the romance books I read who swoon after the hero over the most ridiculous of things. I never thought having it happen to me could make me feel so special. It makes me feel silly." My face flushed, and I was silently happy Luke couldn't see it.

"There's no reason for you to feel that way. I think it's sweet. I hope to be able to keep giving you what you've missed out on all these years, and that I continue to make you swoon."

I couldn't help but laugh. "If swooning equals sex like that, then I agree. I'm not sure I'm going to be able to walk tomorrow. You may have put my body out of commission."

Pulling my body up higher on his chest, I was splayed against Luke's naked form when he looked me in the eyes. "It doesn't have anything to do with sex. Yes, the sex was amazing and hot, and I want to do it again. Many more times, in fact. But I want to be that man for you. The one who makes you swoon, the one who gives you many firsts even at the age of thirty, the one who treats you the way you've always deserved to be treated. I want to be that man for you. I want to be the redemption for your past."

Tears welled, and my heart swelled from happiness. How could this be my life? There was no way I was the lucky one that Luke wanted to give all the experiences that I'd missed out on all these years and be in a relationship with.

"I want that too. You have no idea how happy you've made me. It's your birthday yet you're the one giving me all the gifts tonight."

"You're my gift, Alex. It might take some time before it sinks in, but one day soon you'll realize what you brought to my life. Now sleep, beautiful girl."

Rolling to the side, I slid my leg in between Luke's as he settled his over mine. His hand came to my chin, tilting it back before his soft but firm lips found mine. It was only a caress. A goodnight kiss. But in that moment, I realized that Luke Sandström was the greatest kisser of my life, and I was falling for him with no turning back.

10

Waking up in Luke's arms was what dreams were made of. I actually had to pinch myself to make sure that I wasn't still dreaming. Never did I think this could be my life. No man had ever held me in his arms like Luke had last night. Even with our height difference, we fit perfectly together, as if we were made for each other.

The way Luke held me told me a lot about him. I could tell that he would always be there to hold me and give me the strength to endure anything that came at me. He made me feel safe and cherished and, most of all, beautiful. Luke's embrace said everything we couldn't yet say to each other.

Still snuggled against his long, warm body I scooted my head back on the pillow to take him in better. Luke was still asleep and very naked. His long blond lashes fanned out on his cheeks, eyes moving behind his lids, his full lips parted with soft puffs of air coming out. Stubble covered his jaw making him even more handsome in the morning light.

The bedding had fallen to his waist, so I wasted no time taking in his muscular chest and chiseled abs. His body was perfection. Without any control, my fingers traced the sparse, short hairs on his pecs. Last night it was too dark to see him properly and now that I wouldn't be caught ogling him, I couldn't get enough. I could take in every glorious inch of him.

My hand dipped down running across each ridge of his six pack where a trail of hair disappeared under the sheet. I was surprised at how little hair Luke had on his body and what little he did have was most probably kept trimmed. On anyone else it would have seemed pretentious, but he knew what looked good on his body and I fully appreciated everything he had to offer. Especially the delicious 'V' that led down to what I wanted to see the most.

Sliding down the bed, my tongue sought out the smooth skin of that wonderful 'V', trailing it until I needed to push the sheet down past the promise land. I was going to wake Luke up and thank him for all the orgasms he'd given me yesterday the best way I knew how.

My eyes feasted on every inch of his body as I ran my hands along his muscular thighs and up to his shaft where I froze.

Luke was large and thick, and already hard. His penis was begging to make my acquaintance once again. I wanted to make him happy, but I had no clue how to do that. Luke was uncut, and I'd never seen a cock look like that, let alone knew what to do with it.

"Are you just going to stare at it or..." Luke's voice broke the spell his uncircumcised cock had put me in and I jumped almost falling off the bed. "Shit!" Strong arms pulled me over him until I was safely away from the edge of the bed where I promptly buried my head in embarrassment. "I didn't mean to scare you."

"I know. I was transfixed by your penis." My hand slapped over my mouth. "Oh God, I can't believe I said that."

"I think it's pretty great if I do say so myself. If you need more time to…" Luke pointed at his still hard shaft.

"Well, I… I'm not sure how to say this." I sucked in my lips in an effort to not say the wrong thing. "I'm not very worldly and I…"

"What does that have to do with my cock?" His eyebrows furrowed as he looked from me to his penis that was now laying against his stomach, slowly softening.

"I haven't been with very many men in my life. You're lucky number five." He smiled as if honored to be my fifth. "What I'm trying to say is that I've never seen, let alone handled anyone uncircumcised. It caught me off guard."

"I can see that."

There was nothing on his face to give him away, Luke's face was blank as he silently looked at me. The worst part about the whole situation was that I had a feeling that I'd hurt his feelings. Had I made him feel as if I was disgusted by him?

"Luke." The one word was filled with sadness and regret. "I didn't mean to hurt you. I'm the ignorant one here. I never thought about the fact that you would most likely not be circumcised. I wanted to wake you up in a pleasurable way, but when I saw you, I had no idea what to do. Am I supposed to leave it alone, pull the skin back, or hell, I don't know.

Ugh!" I covered my face with my hands. "I'm just digging myself a bigger hole. I've messed this all up. I'm sorry."

I slipped off the bed and raced to where my dress was in the other room. I needed to get out of there before I started to cry. Once I got to my room, I would let the tears flow.

"Stop." Luke grabbed me by the shoulders and then led me over to the couch where he pulled me down along with him.

"I'm sorry, Luke." I stated as I looked over his shoulder. I couldn't look him in the eye and see the hurt that I'd put there. "I was taken aback because I have no experience with an uncut man or blowjobs in general."

Kissing my forehead, Luke pulled me tighter against him and leaned back fully on the couch. He blew out a deep breath that he seemed to have been holding in for some time. "I'm not ashamed of my penis despite my reaction, but I've had American women react badly to it. When I thought you were rejecting me…"

"I promise you I wasn't. I only wanted to do the right thing. The way that Decker made me feel when I gave him blowjobs has had a very negative effect on my view for a long time. It wasn't until I talked to Taylor and read in books how common it was and how uncommon his ridicule of me was…"

"He should never had made you feel dirty or made fun of you." Luke shook his head, his eyes sad. "One thing I can promise you is that I will never make you feel ashamed for anything we do or do not do sexually."

"Thank you." I kissed his bare shoulder and worked my way up his neck until I reached his soft, full lips. "Will you show me what to do?"

"If it's what you want to do and not what you feel you have to do. I can wait."

If I wanted to wait, I knew Luke wouldn't pressure me, but the strange thing was I didn't want to wait. I wanted to drive him wild with my mouth and tongue. To show him I was more than ready, I got down between his legs running my hands up the coarse hair and hard muscle. My nipples grazed his stomach as I placed open mouth kisses from the dimple in his chin down to his chest starting with his nipple.

Lightly biting his nipple caused Luke to moan while his hands on my breast did wonderful things. I soothed my bite with my tongue, slowly swirling away the pain.

As I made my way down, I licked down one side of his 'V' that needed to be worshipped and then the other. I wanted him to know that I appreciated whatever he did to have his amazing body and I would show him one lick at a time until I'd tasted each inch of him.

My hand wrapped around his shaft stroking up and down and I watched as the foreskin moved along with the movement. My gaze darted back to his face to make sure I was doing it correctly.

"Put your mouth on me," Luke said as my finger slid over the tip that was peeking out. I followed his directions, licking from base to tip and swirling my tongue on his slit. "Just like that. Pull the skin back when you suck my head. Oh, God just like that." Luke groaned as I followed his directions, his fingers tightening in my hair. He pulled it out of the way so that he could watch.

With the noises and the way his cock jumped, I figured I

must have been doing something right. I continued to suck and swirl my tongue around his tip paying special attention to the underside as my hands pumped the rest. My tongue followed the thick vein down his cock until I reached his balls where I traced them with my tongue and massaged with one hand.

"Fuck, baby! Give me your beautiful mouth. I'm so close. Just a little bit more, but I want to finish inside you."

"You had nothing to worry about." Luke smoothed the hair away from my face. Tilting my head up, I looked at him questioningly. His lips slowly tipped up into a wicked grin. "You give good head."

I let out a laugh. "Good to know."

Dipping down he moved his warm, full lips across my own. It was soft, sweet and too short for my liking. "As much as I would love to stay in with you all day we really should get ready so that I can show you around New York."

My bottom lip stuck out in a pout. Staying in bed all day with Luke sounded like heaven, but I wasn't sure when or if ever I would be coming back to the Big Apple and I couldn't waste the opportunity.

"You're right," I agreed. "Do you want me to let you know when I'll be ready? I have to take a shower, so it will probably take me close to an hour to get ready. With the heat and humidity, I have to do something with my hair or it will be a frizzy mess the second we walk outside. Normally, I get ready pretty quickly unless I have to shower, and blow dry my hair, but I'm sure you don't care about all that. I just wanted to give you a general idea on how long it would take me."

A genuine smile was on his face once I was done rambling. Decker would've been scowling or stopped listening, but Luke seemed to be genuinely interested in what I had to say.

"I don't mind. I like getting to know these things about you. They're what makes you, *you*." Luke scratched his head and looked around the room. "Why don't you... would you like to move your stuff to my room and stay here for the remainder of your trip? I could help you go get your stuff and then you could get ready here."

"Are you sure that's a good idea? You didn't want us spotted together, and I'd hate it if some maid or something gave the information out."

Moving into his hotel room for the rest of the weekend was a big deal. Wasn't it?

"Once you're moved up here, I'll tell the front desk that you checked out if that'll make you more comfortable. That way no one will expect your room to looked lived in."

"That's not what I'm worried about," I replied, pacing the floor beside the bed. "I'm worried about people finding out and you being unhappy."

"I'll be happy if you move your things to my room. Unless you want to have some time alone."

Walking over to Luke, I wrapped my arms around his middle and gave him a small hug. It was strange because even though we had sex and kissed, the act of hugging him was intimidating until he wrapped his own arms around me and squeezed. I noticed that the top of my head barely reached his chin without shoes. I personally loved a man to be taller than me and after Matt's cheating fiasco that Taylor and I had boiled down to a short man complex, I was sticking to men who were tall. Even if that was my preference I wasn't sure what Luke liked. Maybe he wanted a woman who was taller or many of the other things that I was not.

As we walked from his room to the elevator, I couldn't stop thinking about what Luke wanted in a woman. Would he get frustrated every time he had to lean down to kiss me? Even on my tippy toes, I couldn't reach his lips without some help. Even though it would only take a moment for the elevator to reach my floor, I had to say something.

"Does our height difference bother you?"

Luke turned and gave me a confused look. I was sure he was wondering what brought that question on. For a moment, he only shook his head and didn't speak until we were walking to my room.

"No, I think we fit together perfectly. Does it bother you?"

"Me?" I asked with a laugh. "No, I've always preferred tall men." Luke sat in a chair while I gathered my things and put them in my suitcase. "Do you have a type?"

He'd been looking at his phone, but at my question he stood and placed it back in his pocket. "Not really. There are multiple things I look for in a woman. I want her to be funny, someone who loves to laugh with me, and not high maintenance. As for physical qualities," he shrugged. "Most women are quite a bit shorter than I am so that doesn't really bother me unless she's extremely short."

"I'm a lot shorter than you. How tall are you?"

"Six foot, five."

"And you don't think you being over a foot taller than me is a big difference?"

"Do you want it to be?" he asked with an eyebrow raised.

"No, of course not. I guess I just don't want it to become a problem. I'm being stupidly cautious."

"Stupidly cautious," Luke laughed with an indulgent smile. "Last night and this morning we proved that our bodies mesh together flawlessly. If you really want me to give you one physical preference, I guess you could say that I like blondes. Most of the women I've dated throughout the years have been blonde."

Zipping up my suitcase, my response was a short, tight thanks. Even though I did want to know Luke's preference in women, I guess I didn't really want to either. My stomach sank at the thought of him with anyone other than me, even though I knew he had girlfriends in the past.

Luke took my suitcase and left my keycard on the countertop in the little kitchen area. "Besides being tall, do you look for more in a man?"

"Not particularly. The last time I was in the market for a man or boyfriend, I was in high school. I do know what I'm attracted to and what my ideal man would look like."

His eyes lit up, and a smile spread. "Do tell."

"It's kind of embarrassing. I'm not sure I want to tell you."

His eyes gleamed. "Now I must know. Don't worry you have nothing to be embarrassed about. I would never make fun of you. I said I want someone to laugh with, not laugh at."

"I know and that's not what I was insinuating. My ideal man would be tall, at least six-foot, blond, blue or green eyes, and muscular."

"Really?" he asked, his smile widening.

"I kid you not. You literally check off everything I look for physically in a man. If you don't believe me than you can ask Taylor when you meet her."

It was endearing to see how happy I'd made Luke by pretty much describing him to a T. It's not that he didn't know that he was good looking. He had to know from all the women who drooled at the sight of him and the way the general female population reacted.

"What about the non-physical? What are you looking for?" Luke asked as we made our way back onto the elevator.

"I also want a man with a sense of humor and someone who will laugh with me. A man who is secure in himself and doesn't mind doing the mundane with me. I want a man who can sit and read with me or watch TV just as easily as going out to a bar, club, or dinner. A man not afraid to love me and my son."

"All good qualities," Luke murmured into my ear as we parted ways to get ready.

Several hours later, Luke had taken me to Central Park where we walked closely together, but not too close. It was beautiful and the only thing that would've made it better would've been with Luke by my side and holding my hand. We looked out from the top of the Empire State Building, went to the Museum of Modern Art where I could have spent the entire day looking at all the amazing art, and had some of the best pizza I'd ever had. There wasn't enough time to do everything that New York offered in my short weekend there, but Luke promised that we'd visit again and next time we'd check off more of the places I wanted to see.

For the rest of the weekend we stayed inside his hotel room, ordered room service and christened almost every surface of his suite. It was one of the best weekends of my life until I had to leave and go back home. Even with Mason waiting for me, I was sad to leave New York and Luke behind.

11

A FEW MONTHS HAD PASSED BY WITH NOTHING BUT PHONE CALLS, emails, and FaceTime with Luke. He was done shooting his movie in New York and was back in LA where he was auditioning for movies to shoot during his next hiatus, which would be next summer, and working out in preparation for when Night Shadows started shooting in January.

When he was done for the day, Luke was set to call me, and I was going to ask him to join Mason and I for Thanksgiving in Fairlane and to join me on a trip for New Year's Eve.

Although Luke and Mason hadn't met in person, they'd talked to each other a few times with FaceTime. Luke was amazing with Mason. They didn't talk for long periods of time, but he always asked about him when we talked and found out what interested him so that when they talked Mason was engaged. Talking to a seven-year-old boy on the phone was a challenge at the best of times and Luke rose to the challenge each and every time. It warmed my heart when they talked and as I watched Mason's eyes light up about Luke's super-hero knowledge.

Mason had gone to bed a couple of hours ago and I was working on my computer, which wasn't unusual when I had free time. I was either working or reading if Mason wasn't with me. Earlier in the night, we'd gone to a Halloween Super-store to buy him a costume. Instead of buying one, Mason ended up with three of his favorite superheroes. He couldn't decide and had outgrown the ones that he currently owned so I knew they he would get a lot of use out of them. Costumes in our house were not meant for only Halloween, they were worn year-round.

When my phone rang a little after ten o'clock, I couldn't stop the smile that spread across my face. My heart raced knowing that I was going to talk to Luke and get to see his handsome face.

"Hey!" I answered holding my phone up so that Luke would be able to see me.

"Hello, beautiful. How was your day?" His phone moved around as Luke got settled most probably on his bed. My tongue peeked out and wet my lips knowing that we would be having phone sex. My body was in need of a real visit from Luke soon. Me and my toys were not as good as what Luke could do to my body.

"It was good, but much better now that I'm talking to you. How did your day of auditioning go?" Moving away from my computer to get comfortable, I left my office and went into my bedroom.

"I had two. Both of them have good scripts and have great

promise. Now, I just have to wait and see." He shrugged his shoulders as if it didn't make any difference. I knew he wanted one or both roles depending on the shooting schedule. Luke was used to the rejection, but I wasn't. I wanted him to get every part he wanted. He'd already heard back from one audition where he didn't get the part and I think I took the news worse than him.

"Did you get Mason a costume today?" The phone jostled as he leaned back on a bed showing blank walls and not much else.

"I did. He got three. I'm such a sucker." I laughed. It was true, I gave Mason almost everything that he asked for because he rarely asked for anything.

His brow rose. "Three, huh? Is he going to be doing multiple wardrobe changes throughout the night?"

I couldn't help but laugh. That was such a diva or actor thing to think. "He'll pick one and stick to it. He recently had a growth spurt and can't fit into any of the ones he has. He already wore one all night until it was bedtime. They'll get good use."

It took at least twenty minutes for me to tell Luke all about the Halloween Superstore with their decorations and all the costumes. Halloween was one of our favorite times to decorate and I'd found a fun witch to put up at our front door. We went a little crazy decorating now that it was just me and Mason. Luke listened intently like he did every time I talked making me fall for him more each time. He didn't only listen but engaged in the conversation and asked questions. To most this might not seem like a big deal, but I had years where I was ignored or told to shut up if what I wanted to talk about didn't interest Decker.

Tapping my toes on the bed to try to work out some of my nerves, I took the plunge. "I don't know a lot about Sweden, but I do know that you don't celebrate Thanksgiving."

With a small smile, he tilted his head to the side. "We don't celebrate Thanksgiving, but I do know what it is since I've lived in the States for the last four years."

"That's good. I… um, don't know your plans, but I was wondering if you'd want to come here for Thanksgiving." I bit my lip with nervous anticipation. To ask Luke into my home for a holiday where he'd meet Mason in person was a big deal.

"I think I can do that," he answered. Luke looked perplexed for a moment before he asked. "It's the third Thursday in November, right?"

"It is. If you don't want to or you're busy, I'll understand."

"Are you kidding me? You can't keep me away now." Luke grinned causing me to smile too. "When do you want me there?"

It was easy to see that Luke was excited to come for a visit. Had he thought I was never going to have him here? He'd been busy, and I wanted to make sure he was going to stay a part of my life before he met Mason. It was one thing to break my heart, but a whole other if you hurt my son.

"Can you come Tuesday or Wednesday? Mason doesn't have school Wednesday through Friday so if we want some alone time it would have to be on Tuesday while he's at school or at night while he's asleep. Whatever you can manage I'll be happy with."

Once again Luke's phone shook as he moved. Sometimes I thought he forgot about it. I watched the ceiling until he settled back down. I wanted to laugh but didn't want him to stop Face Timing me, so I only smiled and waited until his face was back on the screen.

"What were you doing?"

"Grabbing my laptop to look at flights." Luke sat his phone against something so that I could still see him while he typed.

"Hey! I'm not going to change my mind. You don't have to book a flight right now."

He only shook his head with a silly smile on his face as he scanned the screen in front of him.

"Well, while you're looking at flights." Luke's gazed came back to me intrigued. "Are you free to go to Mexico with me for a few days after Christmas?"

"You're going to Mexico?"

"Hopefully you are too. I want you to come with me. Anna asked me earlier, and I told her I'd have to see what you're doing. There's a group of people going, and she needs to know how many of us are going for some reason. I'm not sure why since she and Colton are renting a couple of villas that sound bigger than my house, but I didn't ask questions. I was honored that she asked me."

"The holidays are pretty slow around here and you know that I don't start shooting until the middle of January. The only thing I have to be conscience of is that I don't get a tan. It's a bitch to cover up with makeup."

"Does that mean you'll go?" I asked, excited.

"I know how much you love the beach and ocean. There's

no way I would deny you. What about Mason? Where will he be?"

I loved that he thought of Mason. I couldn't contain my smile as I answered. "I get him for Thanksgiving and his dad will have him from the day after Christmas until a couple of days before he goes back to school."

"Are you okay with that?"

Tears filled my eyes. "I don't really have much say. It's in the custody agreement and I don't have enough money to fight to get what I want."

There was silence for a few moments when neither of us knew what to say next. My situation sucked but I tried not to dwell on it, and had learned to make the most of it by reading while Mason was gone or hanging out with Ryan. The holidays were the hardest though even if Mason would be with me for Christmas Day, it still hurt that he would be gone for his break.

"Do you have any other information about Mexico? Do you know where?"

"Playa Del Carmen. She told me they planned to fly there on the twenty-sixth and come back January second. Since I'm going to be in LA, I'd like to come a day or two early so that I can see Jenner and give him his Christmas present before heading to Mexico."

Luke's eyes widened. "Are you already Christmas shopping?"

"Oh no! I don't even have any ideas about what to get anyone especially you, Anna, and Jenner. Anna seems to literally have everything so what could I possibly get her."

"Something from the heart," Luke answered, sincerely.

"I need to start thinking about it now, so I have enough time to figure it out."

"Don't stress out about it. I think she'll be happy to spend time with you. She won't need a gift. For now, let's deal with booking some tickets."

I would worry about what I was going to get Anna, Jenner and especially Luke, but I'd try to keep it to myself. In the meantime, I was happy to stare at him through my phone as he found a flight that would bring him to me in one month's time.

"I think Tuesday will work better for arrival. Mason has to go back to school on Monday and you'll need to work, right?"

"Right." I felt like I always needed to work, but I was saving up to buy us a better house and the only way to do that was to work my ass off.

"Okay." Luke drew out the word. "I don't want to overstay my welcome so why don't you tell me when I should book my flight back home."

If the weekend went well, I had a feeling that I'd never want Luke to leave. "Is Sunday good for you? I don't want to keep you if you have work to do."

"I would tell you if I had to work and the only thing I need to do is keep a somewhat decent diet and workout. There's no need to worry. I have most of November cleared for when I go to Iceland, and after the beginning of the month, I won't have any more auditions until I've finished shooting the season of Night Shadows."

Smiling, a high-pitched squeal erupted. I couldn't contain my excitement over Luke being here. "I'm so excited!"

"I can tell," he chuckled. His eyes twinkling. "What's a good hotel that's close to you?"

A hotel? No, way in hell was Luke not staying with me.

"I thought you'd stay with me. It'll be a little cramped with Taylor and her family here too, but…"

"Hey." Luke soothed me with only one word and his gentle tone. "I wasn't sure you were ready to take it to that level yet with Mason. If you want me there, I have no problem staying with you and I can even sleep on the couch."

A burst of laughter escaped. There was no way that Luke could sleep on my couch and actually get any sleep. He was much too large for that.

"Is someone else sleeping on the couch?"

"Not that I know of. There's no way you would be comfortable on my couch. It's not made for Vikings to sleep on."

"Viking, huh?" His brows quirked up along with his smile. "If I can sleep in your bed, I am down for that although it will make it harder once I leave to sleep without you."

"Long distance sucks." I pouted.

"It does, but I think we can make it work."

"I do too, but life is so much better when I can wake up with you beside me."

"I have to agree, which brings us to going to Mexico."

Luke went over all the flights that were available on the dates that we would be coming and going and the days that I'd be flying to and from LA. I'd still need to get the resort information from Anna and make sure that Jenner would be available for me to visit him while I was there.

After multiple yawns that I tried to cover up because I

didn't want to let Luke go (orgasms will do that to you), Luke convinced me to go to bed.

"Think of me there with you and soon enough I'll be lying next to you, holding you in my arms."

"I can't wait." Another yawn escaped, preventing me from saying anything more that was much too soon to say.

"Good night, beautiful."

"Good night, handsome."

12

WAS IT POSSIBLE TO BE ON CLOUD NINE AND BE A NERVOUS WRECK at the same time? I could barely contain my excitement as I waited for Luke's plane to land. We'd only have a couple of hours to ourselves before I had to go get Mason from school and then introduced them.

Mason knew that Luke was coming, but I wasn't sure how he was going to react to his mom having a boyfriend. He even knew that Luke was staying at our house, but he also knew that his friend Ben was coming with his family and that they'd also be staying with us. To Mason it was just one big happy slumber party. That was unless he freaked out when there was another man in my bed besides his dad. I didn't know what I'd do if for some reason they didn't hit it off or Mason hated Luke.

Ten minutes before his plane was set to land, I parked my car in the short-term parking lot and made my way inside. Our airport was extremely small compared to LAX, and I knew that Luke would have no trouble finding me at the curb, but I wanted to greet him the same way he greeted me in New York. I'd even made a sign with his name on it to hold up. It was cheesy, but also fun. Or at least I thought so.

Luke Sandström was not hard to miss in a crowd. Even if he wasn't a movie and TV star, his height and looks would naturally draw attention. He towered over almost everyone as they made their way to baggage claim. Heads turned, and whispers were uttered with pointed fingers. It made sense that Luke valued his privacy with all the attention he received from the media to the everyday common folk like me. In the small amount of time I was with him in New York, Luke was always gracious to anyone who came up and asked for an autograph or for him to take a selfie with them. He explained how he never gave out personal information to anyone who wasn't a close friend or family in fear that it would get out and create a media frenzy.

I knew the second he spotted me. Luke's pace quickened, and a large smile broke out on his handsome face. I wiggled the sign I was holding before I couldn't stand still any longer.

After Luke said that we needed to keep a certain distance when out in public, I wasn't sure how he'd greet me once he was here. There was no reason to worry. The moment we were close, Luke wrapped his arms around me, lifting me up and kissing me. The kiss was what one would expect when alone, not when there were dozens or more people watching with a great possibility that they might take pictures and post them to social media. Never once had Luke expressed that anything would change when we were out in public.

Setting me down on my feet, I swayed a little before Luke's hands gripped my hips, causing my world to right itself. My eyes feasted as I took him in. Per his standard wardrobe, Luke was in dark, tight jeans that fit him perfectly. I knew that if I turned him around his jeans would be cupping his delectable ass. He had on black boots along with a tight black t-shirt that hugged his biceps, sunglasses on top of the bill of his baseball cap, and a jacket hanging over the bag he had slung over his shoulder.

I wanted to devour him right then and there, and the only thing that got me through the next thirty minutes was the thought of the very small amount of time we'd have together before Mason got home.

Clasping my hand in his, Luke placed his sunglasses over his eyes as we started to move through the airport. When I turned to head to baggage claim, he stopped me and informed me that he only had the one bag.

"If I can I prefer not to have to check any baggage. That way I can get in and out of the airport as quickly as possible. In big airports, most especially LAX, it can get pretty crazy once the paparazzi spots you. Having to wait for a suitcase while getting swarmed is not ideal."

"I can imagine, but as you can see there's no paparazzi here in Fairlane. People may take pictures from far away, but no one is going to attack you or at least I don't think they will. I've lived here all my life and until last year I'd never seen Colton Patrick here." I shrugged because for me I knew there was a possibility that a celebrity could be in town because for some strange reason there were quite a few from around here. I knew that if I saw one, I'd never bother them, but maybe take a picture and send it to Taylor to let her know who I saw.

Luke smiled down at me as we passed through the doors and out into the chilly air. In Missouri you never knew what the weather was going to be from one day to the next. Only two days ago it had been close to seventy degrees and now as we walked out to my car I could see our breath. It was supposed to stay cold the entire time Luke and Taylor were in Fairlane. I was jealous that they'd leave and go back to warm weather while I'd be stuck in the cold until I left for Mexico.

"This is me." I pointed to my maroon Camry and popped the trunk. "It's not an Audi, but it's dependable and gets me where I need to go."

Luke stopped me with a hand to my shoulder. "Are you embarrassed of your car?" I shrugged as I used the remote to unlock the doors while he threw his bag in the trunk. "If you saw the car I was driving around before I got the Audi you'd think this is a luxury vehicle. Don't be embarrassed. You may have wealthy friends, but you don't need to compete. It wasn't that long ago that I was a struggling actor. In fact, I still live the exact same now as I did when I first moved to LA. If anyone should be ashamed it should be me. After four years I should stop mooching off my friends and find my own place, but what's the point when I'd barely be there?"

"You make a good point. Are you going to show me all the pictures you took in Iceland? I've been dying to see them." I asked as I pulled out of the parking lot.

"Of course, but I still plan to take you there one day. Even if it's cold, you'll think it's beautiful."

"I look forward to going with you. From what I've seen in pictures its stunning."

Several minutes later we were on our way to my house when my phone rang. The number that displayed on my dashboard was one I didn't recognize, but I answered anyway.

"Hello?"

"Alex?" A stranger questioned.

"Yes, who's this?"

"Hey, it's Brad Thomas."

"Oh, hey, Brad. How are you?" The last time I'd talked to Brad had been when we graduated high school.

"Not so great. I'm calling in case you didn't know that Bill Miller died, and his funeral is on Friday. I called Decker, and he informed me that you two are no longer together."

Tears instantly trailed down my cheeks. I couldn't believe that Bill had died. We grew up together, and I'd had the biggest crush on him when he moved to Fairlane. The last time I saw him was at a gas station eight years ago. He'd changed so much that I'd barely recognized him.

I hadn't realized that Luke had taken the wheel and pulled us over onto the shoulder until his voice broke through.

"Brad is it?"

"Yeah, who's this?"

"I'm Luke, Alex's boyfriend. We're in the car and… well we had to pull over. I think Alex is too upset to talk right now. If you could give me the information for the funeral, I'll make sure we're there."

"Is she going to be okay?"

"Yeah, it's obvious that Bill meant something to her and I

think she'd like the chance to say goodbye. Do you know if Decker is going to be there?"

"I couldn't say. He got pissed off when I asked him about Alex."

"Yeah, they don't get along but hopefully for the sake of your friend he'll be cool."

Luke ended the call and helped me out of the car and into the passenger seat.

"Baby," Luke called. His concerned face dipped into my vision. "I think I should drive. Can you type your address into my phone's GPS?"

Without a word, I entered my address before handing Luke back his phone. He laced our fingers together and placed them on his thigh as he drove and gave me time to come to terms that my friend had died.

Staring out the window my vision blurred with tears. I saw nothing, but my past with my old friend. Bill was thirty-one and way too young to die. It broke my heart that I lost contact with him, after being friends with him since the moment he stepped into my second-grade class room, and that I'd never get to talk to him again.

I hadn't even noticed that we were in my neighborhood until I saw Luke's hand reach up and hit my garage door opener. He pulled into the garage and shut off the car before coming around to help me out of the car.

My tears had stopped at some point, but I was a walking zombie as I made my way into the house. Luke followed behind, his hand on the small of my back for comfort until we hit my bedroom. Once there, he sat me down on the side of the bed and took off my shoes placing them neatly by my nightstand and then curled himself around me. No words were spoken, but none were needed. Luke gave me exactly what I needed by holding me close to his body and not letting go.

Earlier when I'd set my alarm, it was intended to give me time to clean up before picking up Mason. I thought I would've been having amazing sex with Luke, not crying on his shoulder the whole time. I hoped that this wasn't going to be indicative of his trip here.

"Is it time to get Mason?" Luke asked from behind me, his arms giving me a small squeeze.

"Yeah," I breathed out. "I'm sorry, Luke. This isn't how I planned your welcome to Fairlane party to start."

"I know, but that's life. It's unpredictable, and I'm happy that I can be here for you when you need me instead of across the country and not being able to do anything about it. I hate that you lost your friend. I'll do whatever you need me to do while I'm here even if it's only to hold you in my arms."

My voice broke and my chin quivered as I turned in his arms and whispered his name. "Can you go to the funeral with me?" The thought of seeing Bill in his casket caused me physical pain every time I thought about it, and the added thought that I might encounter Decker while at Bill's funeral was too much to bear.

"Anything you want. Why don't you go wash your face before you pick Mason up so that he doesn't see how upset you've been?"

I must have looked a wreck. I'd put on makeup and wore mascara to pick up Luke and with all my crying it had to be all over my face. My hands covered my eyes in the insane hope that he could forget the mess that I surely was.

"Hey," Luke called softly as he peeled my hands away one finger at a time. He smiled down at me with warm eyes. Kissing my forehead, he gave me one last hug before helping me off the bed.

Looking in the mirror, my face wasn't as bad as I thought it would be. There were streaks running through my makeup, but my mascara had miraculously stayed on. Instead of trying to fix my makeup, I washed my face and placed a cold washcloth over my eyes for a few minutes to try to alleviate my red, swollen eyes. The washcloth helped a little, but not enough to fool Mason. The only way he might overlook what I looked like was his excitement over meeting Luke.

Noise filtered down the hall as I made my way out of my bathroom. Luke was making himself feel at home which caused me to smile a little. I was happy that he felt comfortable in my house. I should've been helping him instead of breaking down, but I knew that he understood.

"Hey," I called when I spotted him in the kitchen leaning against the counter drinking a glass of water. "Can I get you something else?"

"Water's good," he replied, patting his toned stomach.

"Do you want to stay here while I go get Mason or come with me? His school is pretty close, so it should only take about ten minutes."

Striding over to me, Luke pulled me into a hug. "I'll leave that up to you. Would it be better if Mason met me in the car or once he got home?"

"Truthfully, I don't know. It's not like I've ever done this before. The only other man I've brought around him is my friend, Ryan. I'm in uncharted waters here with you." I rested my head against his chest and breathed in the smell of the ocean and sandalwood. I'd missed how good he smelled. I loved being in his arms and that was a scary feeling. I'd always been an independent person from the time I was a little girl, and now I was desperate to be by his side every moment that I could.

Luke looked down at me, his concern etched on his face. I had a feeling that if I hadn't lived the hell that Decker had put me through, the little things that Luke did wouldn't mean as much to me as they did. Maybe it meant I wasn't ready to start something with him or anyone for that matter, or perhaps it meant that I found the exact right person to be in my life.

"How about I stay here that way you and Mason can have a few minutes by yourselves before he gets home. With everyone that's going to be here in the next few days it's going to be pretty crazy. I think you need those few minutes with him."

"Thank you for knowing what I need even when I don't. I feel like I'm ruining your trip."

"Why? Because I didn't fuck you in your kitchen or against the wall? I didn't come for sex, Alex. I came to be with you and to meet the people who matter the most to you."

My heart swelled at his words. He was my real-life book boyfriend who made me swoon with only words.

"How are you even real?" I laughed. I felt like a crazy person. One minute I wanted to jump him and the next I wanted to cry. "It's been months since we had sex."

"We can have sex tonight if you're comfortable doing that with Mason in the house. I'm not sure if you can be quiet though."

My hands flicked out dismissively before I pressed my chest to his. "He won't wake up and I'm sure you can be creative enough to keep me quiet."

Strong hands slid down my waist and cupped each ass cheek. Luke placed a series of soft and sweet kisses to my forehead, each eye, my nose, and the corners of my mouth. His lips lingered as he breathed, "Challenge accepted."

Not long after, I was pulling away from the curb of Mason's school with him in the backseat looking disappointed.

"How was school?" I asked as I left the parking lot.

Mason answered gloomily. "Fine. I made a turkey for you."

I peered at him through the rearview mirror. "If school was fine why the long face?"

"I thought Luke was coming."

"He is. Actually, he's already here and at the house waiting for us."

"Really?" Mason asked, clapping his hands in excitement.

"Really. He thought it would be nice if we had a few minutes to ourselves before everyone shows up tomorrow and Thursday."

"That was nice of him." Mason mused. "He seems like a really nice guy, Mama. He even likes the same superheroes I do."

I couldn't help but smile. "That's not hard to do because superheroes are awesome."

"When's Ben going to get here tomorrow?"

"Around five o'clock. Just in time for dinner." It had been too long since he'd last seen his best friend. For seven-year-olds, talking on the phone didn't seem to work. Not that it worked for my age either. I only knew I didn't have any other options until they moved back.

"Are we picking him up at the airport?" His face brightened. Mason loved to watch the airplanes come in and take off.

"No, they're going to rent a car for when they go visit some other friends while they're here."

"Oh." His little face dropped.

"But we'll have to take Luke to the airport on Sunday and I'll bet you'll be able to see a bunch of planes while we're there."

"Cool!" He answered back excitedly. I loved how easily it was to please him.

For the rest of the ride home, we sang along to the radio and Mason kicked his feet to the beat in his booster seat. The moment the car stopped in the garage, he quickly unbuckled his seatbelt and slipped out of the car and into the house.

Even though I wanted to see Mason's reaction to meeting Luke in person, I took my time grabbing his backpack out of the backseat and making my way inside. I didn't want either one of them to feel pressure from me. I wanted their reactions to be organic. Maybe I was making too big of a deal about it, but for me, Mason meeting Luke, the man I was falling for, was a big deal, and I desperately wanted it to go well.

I shouldn't have been worried. All the times they talked on the phone, Luke and Mason always got along and when I walked into the living room, Mason was talking animatedly about the new movie I'd bought him.

"Do you want to watch it with me? Me and Mama normally watch movies after dinner snuggled up on the couch." Mason's big blue eyes were so eager, and innocent as he looked up to a kneeling Luke who still towered over him.

"I'd love to watch it with the both of you. I haven't watched change to seen it yet."

Mason's mouth dropped open as if Luke had just dropped a bomb. I wanted to laugh. For Mason, not watching his beloved superhero movies when they came out was the ultimate sin.

"You haven't? Then we have to watch it tonight!"

Luke laughed and looked over Mason's shoulder at me and winked.

Mason either didn't notice or didn't care because he continued on asking if Luke had watched each movie in order, while I made him a snack in the kitchen, with a smile.

SOFT LIPS TRACED A PATH DOWN MY NECK, STOPPING TO NIBBLE along my shoulders before continuing all the way down to my tailbone. Luke's strong hands gripped my hips, pushing them skyward. His warm tongue licked from front to back. I let out a strangled moan before burying my face in a pillow.

Hands caressed the backs of my thighs and cheeks, two fingers dipped leisurely in and out before Luke replaced them with his thick, long cock. It had been too long since he last touched me, and I wasn't going to last long, especially if he kept hitting me in the right spot over and over again. Fire blazed down my tailbone straight to my toes as fireworks went off behind my eyelids. My walls clenched against his pulsing cock, pulling him in deeper with every spasm until I collapsed on the bed in a heap of sweaty limbs.

Luke lithely slipped down beside me, pulling me into his body. His long arm wrapped around my front until his hand cupped my shoulder. Every time I was in his arms I felt younger, alive, and safe. Everything about Luke was intoxicating, from his unique scent, the way he listened to everything Mason and I said, to the way he made my body feel. I was falling hard and fast and I hoped when I landed he would be there to catch me.

13

EVEN THOUGH RYAN KNEW ALL ABOUT LUKE EXCEPT FOR THE SEX, because we'd agreed not to tell each other about our sexcapades, he kept giving Luke the stink eye from across the table. I wasn't sure what his problem was because I'd never uttered a single bad thing about Luke to him.

I sat at the head of the table with Luke at the other end. It felt right him being there, but I wanted him beside me and not so far away, especially with Ryan acting so weird toward him. Mason and Ben were Luke's new buddies and insisted that they sit on either side of him where they chatted about none other than all the Marvel movies they'd watched since he'd arrived. Once Ben got here, he joined in on the movie marathon, giving Luke and I very little time together. Taylor and I enjoyed being able to talk without constant interruption and baked the entire day yesterday. We may have gone overboard, but we didn't care. Everyone's favorites had been made, and we even attempted making a couple of Swedish desserts that we weren't sure were successful.

Next to the boys sat Taylor and Jack with Ryan beside Taylor and me. On my other side was an empty seat. Ryan was supposed to bring the woman he was seeing but for some reason she wasn't able to make it. Maybe that was why he kept giving the evil eye to Luke, but that didn't make any sense. I wanted to say something, but at the dinner table wasn't the right place with so many witnesses and innocent ears.

Taylor clinked her water glass with a knife causing all eyes to fall on her. "Before we dig in why don't we each say what we're thankful for. I'll go first." She smiled and cleared her throat. "I'm thankful to be back in Missouri and with our good friends. Mason do you want to go next?"

Mason straightened in his seat, squaring his shoulders on his tiny frame. "I'm thankful my mom met Luke, and he's nice to her."

I had to bite my lips to contain the sob that wanted to break out, but there was no hiding the tears in my eyes. Taking a deep breath in through my nose, I calmed enough to give a watery smile to an expecting Mason. "Me too, sweetie."

Luke cleared his throat as he looked down the table at me with an unknown emotion in his eyes. "I'm thankful to have met our amazing hostess and feel lucky that she brought me into her life and family." Before he said 'family', Luke looked at each person around the table.

Ben stood, excited for his turn. "I'm thankful to spend Thanksgiving with my friend, Mason."

Jack smiled across the table at his wife, he'd been in my office working for most of the time they'd been here. "I'm thankful for Alex letting us into her home and cooking this amazing dinner for us today. Also, that my case will soon be over and then we'll be able to move back to Fairlane and close to our friends."

It was my turn, and I had no idea what I wanted to say. I was thankful for so many things. I blinked back the tears that still lingered from Mason's little speech and smiled at each person that sat around my table. "I'm thankful for each and every one of you. You're all my family and mean so much to me. I'm blessed to have you in my life and that we are all happy and healthy. Thank you all for being here."

Last was Ryan who took a long sip of his beer before he spoke. "I'm thankful for Alex opening her home to all of us today and cooking this amazing meal in front of us."

"Can we eat now?" Mason asked, a big scoop of mashed potatoes on his fork halfway to his mouth.

"Dig in everyone." I called, cutting into a piece of turkey.

Instead of eating, I watched the family I had made for myself and Luke who'd become to mean so much to me in such a short period of time. They were what mattered the most in my world.

Dinner had taken a little longer than planned to cook so by the time it was done we were all pretty ravenous to the point that no one spoke until their first helping of food had been gobbled down and needed seconds. After that we all spoke easily except for Ryan who seemed to be fuming the entire time he ate. I loved him, but he was ruining the vibe. At least for me and I planned to nip it in the bud.

Standing I turned to Ryan and looked down at him, my eyes slightly narrowed. "Would you please help me bring in the desserts?"

"I'll help." Taylor broke in ready to be of assistance like always.

"You did most of it. If anything, it should be you that sits, and we bring in the desserts." Taylor hadn't witnessed the looks and sour note emanating from Ryan through the whole meal. I would have to tell her about it later once I found out what the hell was up his ass.

"Nope, Ryan and I will get them."

Instead of waiting for Taylor or Ryan to say anything, I left the room and stood in the kitchen hoping I wouldn't have to drag Ryan outside and kick his ass. Luckily, I didn't have to wait long for him to stomp into the kitchen with more attitude than I'd ever witnessed from him in all the years I'd known him.

He stood on the other side of the kitchen with his arms crossed over his chest. "What do you want me to take?"

"Do you really think I asked you in here to help take desserts?" When he didn't answer and only stood there I continued. "What the hell is wrong with you? Is this because your girlfriend or whoever the hell she is, couldn't come?"

"You cannot be serious. I don't give a shit if she's here or not."

"Then what's up your ass? You've had an attitude and been giving Luke the stink eye since the moment you walked in."

Angry lines marred his face. "Did you ever think that maybe my problem has to do with him?"

Spinning around in a circle, I tried to calm down. Ryan was making no sense. He had no reason to have a problem with Luke or anyone at the table for that matter. "No, the thought never crossed my mind because Luke has never done anything to you." My index finger poked him in the chest and for a brief moment I wanted to hit him. He was ruining my Thanksgiving. "Whenever we've talked about Luke, you've never had a bad thing to say about him, so I don't understand why all of a sudden you're acting like he's wronged me in some way. Luke's probably one of the best things that has ever happened to me and if you ruin it for me, I'll never talk to you again."

Grabbing the pumpkin pie, I started to make my way out of the kitchen when Ryan grabbed me by my elbow. "I'm not trying to ruin anything for you but think about it. What would it say if because I didn't kiss your boy toys ass, he dumped you?"

A deep, unhappy voice rumbled from the entry of the kitchen. "Is there a problem in here?"

"That's what I'm trying to figure out," I cried out, confused. "I don't know what his problem is with you."

Walking over with a serious determination on his face, Luke wrapped a hand around my hip and pulled me close before placing a kiss on my cheek. "Not everyone has to like me."

My hand slipped around his waist, my finger hooked into one of his belt loops. "He has no reason not to like you. Ryan doesn't even know you." I turned to Ryan with narrowed eyes. "You tell me right now what your fucking problem is, or you can leave. Either one is fine with me."

"Alex..." he glanced over at Luke. "Can we please discuss this in private?" Ryan's eyes begged me to give in, but he had his chance to speak.

Shaking my head, I replied. "No, I'm sorry. You had your chance, so if you want to talk you can say whatever you have to say with Luke in the room and whoever else decides to walk in."

"You want to know what my fucking problem is then I'll tell you what my problem is. Ever since you told me about Luke, I started to follow him online. I setup a Google alert when anything new came up on him and after you went to New York to visit him things started to pop up."

My front turned until it was pressed to Luke's side, looking up at him, I asked. "Do you have any idea what he's talking about?"

Luke shrugged looking confused. "Anything can pop up. If I'm seen on the street and someone takes my picture and posts it on social media, it'll pop up on an alert depending on how the alert is set up. As to what your friend is talking about, I have no clue. We talked about that there were some pictures of us while we were out and of course there was speculation, but I haven't heard of anything else from my publicist."

I looked to Ryan wondering what else there could be. "That's all we know about."

Ryan rolled his eyes, his lips set in a firm line. "Because your precious Luke would never lie to you."

My arms spread wide, I yelled. "He has no reason to lie to me."

"To get in your pants," Ryan yelled back.

"You have got to be fucking kidding me. It's endearing that you think I have a magical pussy, but Luke could literally have any woman he wants."

"Well, it looks like he's been having at least one other woman. First, she posted pictures of him in New York and then there were pictures of him in LA."

"Okay," I said drawing out the word. "Was she in bed with him? Were they kissing? What were they doing?"

Looking away, Ryan murmured with tight lips. "Nothing."

"They were doing nothing? So obviously Luke's cheating on me." I shook my head in sadness. "Ryan, you know I love you, but it seems like you're grasping at straws to find something wrong with Luke."

"In the pictures they were doing nothing. Luke was the only one in the pictures, but it was what the captions said."

"Let me get this straight. Okay?" At Ryan's nod, I continued trying to keep my calm, but it had left the building the minute I walked into the kitchen and I wasn't sure it would ever come back. "Some woman posted pictures of Luke and he wasn't with any women in these pictures, but," I said, my eyes narrowed. "This woman, whatever her fucking name is, said some shit that made you think Luke's cheating on me."

"Yes," he shouted back before taking in a deep breath. "She said they started dating back in June and wanted to keep it private then she would give updates on what they'd done that day or weekend with pictures of Luke."

Stepping forward, Luke towered over Ryan's six-foot frame. "Show me." His voice was like granite causing Ryan to take a step back.

Pulling out his phone, Ryan scrolled through looking for something to prove that Luke had been lying to me. I believed both of them. Luke hadn't cheated, and Ryan had seen those posts. The person who was lying was this woman, and I wanted to know why.

Luke stood watching Ryan, his mouth grim. Once he looked back at me with sad eyes. Our holiday hadn't gone according to plan. First, Bill had died and now Ryan with his cheating accusations.

"Here," Ryan said with too much glee in his voice, his finger pointed at his screen.

Standing by Ryan's side, I looked down at his phone. A picture of Luke was posted on Instagram. He was standing at a counter in a crowded coffee shop looking down at his phone. The captioning read: Up all night #myboyfriendcandoevery-thingbetter #myboyfriendisahottie #longnight #needcoffee @ashlynjade

"This proves nothing. She could be talking about her boyfriend and saying they were getting coffee while also posting a picture of Luke."

"How do you explain the four other pictures she posted of Luke with similar captions? She was in LA and New York with him. I can show you more if you want. Why don't you try to explain, Luke?" Ryan aimed a hateful look at Luke.

"It's all going to sound like excuses and bullshit." Wrapping my hand in his, Luke placed them on his chest. I could feel his heartbeat, it was steady and true. "Once before, I met this Ashlyn Jade when I was at a gala. We were introduced, and that was it until she bumped into me when I was getting dinner one night after you left New York. She introduced herself again and reminded me where we met before. I talked to her for maybe two minutes, if that, before my food was ready and I left to head back to the hotel."

Not once did Luke hesitate nor did his heart speed up. I didn't think he was lying to begin with but trying to convince Ryan of this would be a problem.

Turning to Ryan, I pinned him with my disbelief. This was

one of my best friends and he was trying to rip apart what Luke and I had. "It's been months since I was in New York and you kept this to yourself this whole time? Why?"

Looking chagrined, Ryan answered. "I didn't think you'd ever see him again and didn't want to hurt your feelings."

"Show me the others," Luke demanded.

"Luke," I softly called his name, wrapping my hand around his wrist. "I believe you."

"Did you brainwash her with your dick?" Ryan growled out.

"Oh, my God! First, it's my magical pussy and now it's his dick."

"Is everything okay in here?" Taylor asked as she walked in looking startled. I was sure that everyone could hear most of what we'd been saying.

"No, it's not okay. Did you know about this?" Ryan asked flashing his phone screen in her direction.

"Know about what?" Taylor looked at his phone for a few seconds before shoving it back in his hand. "I didn't, but it doesn't matter because it's all bullshit." Taylor said, her last word a whisper for the children's sake and then kept whispering this time looking in my direction. "That lady is bat-shit crazy! You do not want to get in her sights, Luke."

"Too late." I shook my head as Luke stared down at Ryan's phone, his jaw ticking more and more with each new picture he looked at. Giving his arm a squeeze, I picked the pumpkin pie back up. "Can you guys help me take in all the desserts and give Luke a few minutes to himself?"

Ryan hesitated for only a moment before he picked up one of the almond caramel cakes (one of the Swedish desserts) we'd made and another pie and followed us to the dining room.

Since Mason and I'd moved in, we hadn't used the dining room once and it was strange to see it filled with people and food. It made me want to do this more often minus the accusations that my boyfriend (If that was what he was. We hadn't discussed it.) was cheating on me.

By the time everyone had tried most of the desserts and cleaned up the mess, it was time for the boys to go to bed. They were so tired that they didn't even protest. Mason kissed me good night and gave everyone else hugs.

Even though Ryan gave me and Taylor a hug goodbye nothing had been resolved between us, or him and Luke. I decided I'd wait and talk to him next week when we'd both cooled off and everyone was gone. I wasn't sure how I could convince him that Luke hadn't cheated. I had a feeling the more I tried to talk to him about it the worse it would get. Ryan would think I was gullible and desperate and, it seemed, willing to believe anything because a man was nice to me.

14

ALL EYES WERE ALREADY RED RIMMED, AND A FEW INCLUDING myself were swollen, by the time we stepped foot into Bill's funeral, Friday morning. There wasn't a great deal of people, but I knew each and every one of them. Some it took a little longer to recognize, but little by little their names popped into my head. It was amazing how badly some of my classmates had let themselves go over the years. Over half of the men were heavyset and nearly bald, but the majority of the women looked better than they had in high school.

Luke's warm hand held mine as we made our way to find a seat. He must have felt when I spotted Decker, who was seated in the front. My whole body tensed as I kept walking. I'd hoped that my ex-husband wouldn't be there. It was almost impossible for us to be in the same room without some sort of drama and Bill's funeral was no place for our bullshit. I only hoped that Decker would be as keen to the situation as I was. Lacing his fingers through mine, Luke squeezed my hand before stepping into an aisle to sit.

Pulling out a pack of tissues, I watched as Brad moved away from Decker and made his way toward Luke and me. He stopped a few times to say hello to friends but kept his focus on me. He was a man on a mission. Instead of doing what I expected him to do, Brad sat down next to me and took my hand in his. Out of all the guys that I'd been friends with I knew Brad the least and was a little uncomfortable until I saw the tears in his eyes. It didn't matter that we hadn't been the best of friends back in the day, Brad had been the one to make sure that I knew of Bill's funeral. For that I was thankful, so instead of just trying to get my hand loose from his, I released Luke's hand and got out another pack of tissues, handing it over to Brad.

"Thanks," Brad said with a watery smile, taking the tissues.

"No problem. Let me know if you need more. I stuffed my purse full of them."

Looking around me, he held out a hand to Luke. "Hey, I'm Brad."

"Luke."

Instead of taking my hand again, most likely sensing that I'd be in need of it, Luke wrapped his arm around me, giving my shoulder a hug.

Eyes back on me, Brad shifted closer. "Afterward, I think we're all going to Blue's to eat and catch up. Would you guys like to join us?"

My vision shifted to look at Decker. Yes, I'd like to catch up, but I knew that would be a slim possibility if he was anywhere near.

"As far as I know no one has told him about lunch. If you can't make it maybe we can figure something else out. I know a few of the guys are going to stay in town for the weekend. Either way, it would be nice to catch up. Think about it and let me know."

I'd expected for him to get up and leave, but instead he turned his attention to the family that sat in front of us.

"Hey," Chris Reynolds said sadly after he turned and faced us. He was with who I assumed was his wife and daughter. Leaning forward both Brad and I said our hellos.

I'd tried to avoid catching a look at Bill's body in the casket but was unsuccessful when the minister stood before the room and started to speak. Even though Bill looked nothing like he once had, I knew it was him and couldn't stop my eyes from welling up. If I'd run into him on the street, I would have walked right by without ever knowing who he was. How had I let so much time go by without at least reaching out? I knew how. Decker. It killed me to know that I'd never speak to Bill again.

Sensing my unraveling, Luke pulled me closer and kissed the top of my head. I listened as person after person stood up in front and told how their life was affected by Bill or a funny story. With each new thing I learned about my dear friend, I cried more and more as discreetly as possible. I thought about saying something, but I knew that I'd break down if I had to talk in front of all these people. Friends or not. From the time I could remember, I'd always hated crying in front of people. I couldn't believe that Luke had witnessed it twice now.

I couldn't imagine going to a funeral to someone you didn't know, but Luke hadn't made it seem like a big deal. More than once he'd told me that he wanted to be there for me and I couldn't thank him enough.

After the last person talked about what a great and quiet man Bill had been, we all bowed our heads in prayer one last time. Sniffing and wiping my eyes, we made our way out of the building and successfully avoided any encounters with Decker.

I should've known that he wouldn't make it that easy on me. Luke and I had only been seated for a couple of minutes at Blue's when Decker walked in. I tried not to make eye contact like the chicken I was that day, and continued to talk to Josh, one of my high school friends. In essence the lunch after the funeral was like a mini reunion. The only people that were there were the old crowd I used to hang out with. Most of them I'd met in junior high or high school, the only ones that I knew from elementary had been Bill and Jack. Everyone went around the table and introduced their spouses, girlfriends and boyfriends.

Decker was at the end of the table and therefore the last to go and of course was pissed off. I wasn't sure if he was mad because he didn't have anyone with him, because he was last, or the combination of the two. It was always hard to tell what exactly set him off and luckily, I didn't need to worry about it every day like I had when we were married.

Giving me a seething look, Decker introduced himself in true Decker fashion. "You all know who the hell I am and that bitch down there at the other end of the table is my ex-wife."

Luke gripped my leg from underneath the table and many of the women gasped in shock. Ignoring his comment, I did nothing. I wanted to laugh or shake my head, but I knew that would only get a rise out of him. In all honesty it didn't matter what I did - everything would piss him off. You couldn't confront him nor ignore him. Surprisingly, all the guys that had once been friends with Decker back in high school gave him bad looks, and Chris Reynolds, who I'd never liked back in the day, told him to stop or he'd have to leave. I couldn't hear what else Chris said to Decker as he turned away from the rest of the table and gave Decker his full attention.

My blood boiled with anger and embarrassment and I hoped that my face wasn't as red as it felt. I didn't want to give him the satisfaction of knowing that he'd affected me once again. What was the most confusing thing about Decker was that his entire family were extremely nice. I wasn't sure what had gone wrong, all I knew was that I was never going to be the one to change him.

Kissing the top of my head, Luke stood to his full height and within three steps he was in front of Decker. Everything about Luke in that moment was menacing, and I was in complete and utter shock. My Luke was gone and in his place was his character Nikolai from Night Shadows.

Looking down at Decker, his eyes filled with disdain. "Your time here is done. I will not have you spewing your bullshit about Alex or disrespecting her in any way. Say your goodbyes and leave."

Instead of really paying attention to what Luke had said to my ex, I was turned on by him defending me and the fact that his accent had become more pronounced because he was upset. I wasn't sure if it would be good or bad for our future if every time his accent got stronger I wanted to jump him.

Decker being the stupid man that he was, stood and tried to get into Luke's face. Both were tall men, but Luke had a little over three inches on him and where Decker was wider and heavier from letting himself go over the years, Luke was lean with muscle. My money was on Luke, but Decker would never give in that easily and that scared me. I wasn't sure if anyone at Blue's knew who Luke was, but it would not be good if anyone took pictures or video of him physically assaulting Decker. I had a feeling that Decker would goad him into trying to hit him just so he could call the cops on my boyfriend for assault, and then try to get Mason taken away from me.

My body was already up and out of my seat before I realized I'd started to move. Putting myself in between my future and past, I turned my back on Decker and looked up at Luke. Even in heels, he was still a great deal taller than I was, so I had to crane my neck to lock eyes with him.

"Luke," I spoke softly, but I hoped with enough caution in my voice that he'd back off.

I wasn't used to a man paying that much attention to me or even caring, so I was more than surprised when Luke's eyes immediately met mine.

Shaking my head, the entire time, I cautioned. "He's not worth it. He'll do what he does best and push you until you do something you'll regret."

Scowling, Luke continued to look at me while keeping an eye on Decker. "I would never regret defending you."

Gently, I tried to clarify what I wanted to say without giving anything away. Knowing another language, namely Swedish would have come in handy in that moment. "Maybe regret is the wrong word but trust me when I tell you *he* is not worth it. Please, come back with me and let's eat lunch."

Softly, Luke conceded when it was obvious that he didn't

want to. "I do trust you." It was clear to see that he did trust me but was confused as to why I wanted him to back down.

"Thank you. I promise to explain later."

"Yes, *later*." His emphasis on later made it clear that what had just happened would not be forgotten. Luke knew how Decker had treated me in the past and still tried to rule my life even now that we were divorced.

When I started to step back to where we were seated, Luke spoke one last time to Decker in a growl. "Do not fuck with me. You need to leave."

A few of the guys stood as we made our way back to our seats and walked Decker out into the parking lot. At first I wasn't sure if it was because they thought it was wrong that he was being kicked out, or because they were making sure he'd leave. Once they walked back into the room we were using, it was obvious they were on my side. It was safe to say that I was a little shocked. I thought their loyalty to Decker would supersede what they thought about how he'd treated me. I was sure that if Decker had talked to them about me that he hadn't painted me in the best light, but it seemed they remembered the girl that I was in high school.

By then we had attracted some attention with the workers and patrons in the restaurant. Luke sat and acted as if nothing had happened. Instead he signaled a waitress and ordered a beer. Okay, maybe ordering a beer at eleven o'clock in the morning was an indication that something had occurred, but otherwise you wouldn't know by looking at him.

"Thank you," I whispered as I kissed his cheek. "I was afraid he'd goad you into hitting him, or some other compromising situation, and then call the cops on you."

One eyebrow raised, he asked. "Really?"

"I wouldn't put anything passed him to try to make my life worse and give him a reason to take me to court to get Mason taken away from me."

Vehemently, Luke declared. "I would never let that happen, but never did I think he'd do something like that." He looked at the table to find all eyes on us. "Let's finish this later. I want you to visit with your friends."

Not long after everyone had ordered their food, Jason, an old friend and sort of boyfriend from high school, came to sit by us.

"So, I guess it's safe to say that things didn't work out well between you and Decker." Jason noted.

I couldn't help but let out a small laugh. That would be the understatement of the year, but I wasn't going to air out all of my dirty laundry to people I hadn't seen in over ten years. "It's pretty safe to say that."

"Is he bitter because you've got a boyfriend?" Josh asked, looking Luke over.

"No, he's bitter because I couldn't stand to stay married to him any longer. Having a boyfriend, I'm sure doesn't help matters."

Jason's body shook silently with laughter. "You could say that. Dude, don't you remember how Decker warned everyone away from Alex and, fuck, if he caught you looking at her, he'd practically threaten to kill you."

My eyes widened in shock. "I had no idea it was that bad. I remember Josh telling me that Decker had told him to stay away from me after he found out about us," I indicated Jason and I, "he wanted to start something again after we'd been broken up. I should've seen the signs then."

"Yeah, you had no chance in hell dating anyone at our school once he set his sights on you," Jason joked.

Wrapping an arm around my shoulder, Luke drew me to his side. "Do you think he could be dangerous?"

"That I couldn't say. I haven't talked to him in years and he seems to be a little unhinged. I mean, come on, how often do high school romances last, especially when you're a total dick?" Jason replied.

"Let's not worry about it for now. You just need to remember not to let him get to you and trust me, I know how hard that is to do. I wouldn't put it past him to get it all caught on video." And once Decker found out who Luke was I had a feeling he'd be even more of a problem.

Luke looked down at me and swore under his breath. "I have a right to be worried when most days I'm almost two thousand miles away and there's nothing I can do to protect you."

"No, I know, and I understand how you feel. We'll talk about it *later*." My head tilted to the side to indicate the audience we'd attained. Usually Luke was more aware of his surroundings than he was then.

"Where do you live man?" Josh asked taking a swig of his beer. After Luke ordered one just about everyone else soon followed and a couple of the guys were on their second.

Luke followed suit and tipped back his beer finishing it off in one big swallow. "LA."

Josh's brows rose in surprise. "Really? Cool. I've never made it out that way. How'd you meet Alex if you live in LA?"

"We met there while she was having lunch with some friends."

Jason coughed. "Shit, Alex, why are you still living here?"

"Because there's no way in hell that Decker is going to let me leave the state with our son. If that were the case, I would have left long ago."

"What the fuck happened to him?" Jack asked from down the table. "Decker used to be so chill."

"Your guess is as good as mine," I replied. "It's like one day a switch got flipped, and he totally changed."

"How long were you two together?" Mark Fisher asked from a couple of seats down. I hadn't talked to him yet, afraid that if I looked at him I wouldn't stop staring. Mark was the one who'd changed the most out of everyone. His hair had gone fully white, and he had a beard to match. He looked like a skinny Santa Claus.

"Too long. We've been divorced for almost two years now. But hey, let's not spend all of our time talking about Decker. He's an asshole. End of story. What have all of you been up to since I last saw you? It's been forever, and I've missed all of you." Over the years, I hadn't thought a great deal about the people who surrounded me then, but being around them again made me realize how much I missed them from my life.

"How about we all go around the table and say where we live and what we do, if we are married and have kids? I'll go first." Brad was a little too eager, so it was obvious that he was proud of whatever job he had. "I'm still in Fairlane and married with two girls. I'm a financial advisor."

"Can everyone also state your name so that Luke will know your names in case he or anyone else missed it earlier?"

I interjected. I had a feeling that most everyone knew each other's spouses that had come with them, but it would be weird to learn about someone and what they were doing with their life and not know their name.

"No problem, I'm Brad."

"I'm Mark Fisher, and I live in Chesterfield with my wife and four kids." All the guys hooted and hollered, a couple even wolf whistled. Mark took it good naturedly, shaking his head and chuckling. "I'm a lawyer for a firm in St. Louis."

"I'm Cory Willis and I live in Fairlane with my wife and son. I'm actually the football coach for our old high school. Both my wife and I teach history there."

Around the table everyone took their turn like it was the first day of school and we had to introduce ourselves. It was kind of comical. They were all married or had girlfriends and had good jobs, which made me happy that they'd all done well for themselves throughout the years.

All eyes were on Luke when it came to his turn. "I'm Luke and I live in LA where I'm an actor. Alex is my girlfriend."

Once he was done, Luke took a big bite out of his cheese-burger, paying no mind to the jaws that had dropped open at his announcement of being an actor. One of the things I loved about Luke was that he was so humble about his acting and even though I knew other actors, and none of them had big heads about it, especially Anna and Colton, there was something different about it with Luke. I think it had a lot to do with his upbringing.

Whoa! Had I just thought about Luke and love in the same sentence? I wasn't ready to go there yet. It was too early, right?

It didn't take long for the guys to go back to being their

176 | HOLLYWOOD REDEMPTION: LUKE AND ALEX

usual selves and talking to me and Luke. I wasn't sure if they knew of his shows or movies and if they did, I wasn't able to tell. Maybe they were as unfazed about it as I was because even though we didn't personally know the celebrities who came from our town like Colton, we were used to it. I wasn't sure, but I was happy they continued to treat him the same way as they had before.

Chris and I were catching up when I overheard Josh ask Luke after they had been talking for a while. "When are you headed back to LA?"

Giving me a sad smile, Luke answered. "Sunday."

"That sucks, man. Do you have any plans for coming back anytime soon?"

"I don't know when I'll be back. My show starts filming in January and doesn't end until around May. I haven't seen a schedule yet to know."

I hadn't thought about when I'd see Luke again after our trip for New Year's Eve. I knew that he'd be filming soon after that but from the beginning of January to May was a very long time not to see your boyfriend.

"That's gotta suck," Josh said with a sad smile.

"Yeah," I answered trying to keep the heartbreak out of my voice. It was going to suck.

"We'll figure something out, and we always have FaceTime."

Yes, because FaceTime was just like being in the same room with the person. *Not.* But I would take what I could get.

"I may never let you leave the room when we're in Mexico." I whispered into his ear and ran my hand up his thigh.

"You won't hear me complain." Moving closer, he brushed

his lips against the shell of my ear causing a full body shiver. I could hear the smile in his voice. "If you want to visit with your friends, you should probably move your hand."

Even though I'd love to go home with Luke and let him do wicked things to my body, I knew we wouldn't be there alone. We'd have to wait until tonight when everyone was asleep. So instead I took my hand from his leg and laced my fingers through his.

My plan had been to catch up with everyone, but I couldn't stop thinking about how I wouldn't get to see Luke for months next year and how busy he'd be. The only upside to the day had been when Luke called me his girlfriend. It was official or at least in my book it was.

I wasn't sure how long I'd zoned out for, but it was enough for the surrounding people to notice especially Luke.

We said our goodbyes, and I gave out a few hugs, promising that we'd keep in contact.

After a few moments of silence as Luke drove us back to my house, he broke the quiet. "Hey, I meant it. Don't worry. As soon as I know my schedule we'll try to find a way to see each other." Luke frowned, looking out the windshield. He swallowed heavy, his Adam apple bobbed. "It can be difficult, and I'll understand if it's too much."

"It's not too much, I just know that I'm going to be spoiled after getting to spend this week with you and then next month. I'll miss you, that's all. I didn't realize how long it might be that I wouldn't get to see you. I'll try to come to see you as much as I can, but with Mason being in school, and Decker, it won't be easy."

"I know it won't."

"Maybe Mason and I could come during his spring break. That would be longer than a weekend. That'll be sometime in March. It's better than nothing." I said trying to find the bright side of only seeing him for one week during a four-month period.

"I would love for both of you to come out then, and we *will* see each other before then, but you're right that it will probably only be for a weekend, and with flying back and forth that really only leaves us with one full day."

"Wow, you're really selling it." I gave a sarcastic chuckle.

"I don't want to disillusion you. You deserve to know how it's going to be if you're in a relationship with me. You've already been living it, but the more time we spend together the harder it'll be to say goodbye and be apart. I'll need to keep in mind that more projects mean more time away from you. My contract for Night Shadows has another three years unless it's canceled."

"Which it won't be. It's one of the hottest shows on the air." Now that we were back at my house and parked, I turned to face Luke. "Do you want it to be canceled?"

"It's not that I want it to be canceled. I am so grateful for H@T giving me my big break." Luke looked conflicted and torn as he opened and closed his mouth a couple times searching for the right words. "When I first signed on to do Night Shadows, I had no idea the time commitment that it would require, and you do have a right to be sad about the amount of time I'll be busy filming. Even though I know we'll be fine, it's a lot of time a part. I want you to know I'm all in and I'll do whatever I can to make this as easy for you as possible."

"What you won't do is not accept jobs that you want, just for me." I couldn't let Luke give up something he wanted to appease me when I was weak. "I won't let you damage what you've worked so hard for just because I'll miss you." I stopped myself, unsure how much I wanted to divulge. The hesitation must've been clear on my face for Luke to read.

My Camry wasn't the ideal car for a man of Luke's height to drive, but he managed and hadn't complained once about the cramped quarters. It didn't look easy, but Luke turned in the seat, twisting his torso and head to face me better. "You don't have to hide your feelings from me. Finish what you were going to say. I'll never make fun of you for expressing yourself."

"I know you're not Decker. You're far from it, actually. I've learned not to express my feelings, but for you I'm going to try. You just need to be a little patient with me. Can you do that?"

"Of course, I'd do anything for you, but no more stalling. We're going to have to go in soon or the cavalry are going to stop looking through the window and come out to the car."

The curtain moved back into place when I looked to see if anyone was indeed watching us. I couldn't see anyone at the window but someone had been watching, meaning we didn't have much more time alone.

"From a very young age I became independent. It's possible that sometimes I'm too independent, to the point that I won't take help when I need it, and I think Decker hated that I didn't rely on him like he wanted. The more I get to know you the more dependent I become on you in so many aspects of my life. It's not something I'm used to, and I don't like the way it makes me feel sometimes."

Reaching across the console, Luke took my hand, pulled me to him and rested his forehead against mine. "It makes you feel vulnerable." Nose kiss. "I understand why you wouldn't like it." Eye kiss. "I've become dependent on you too." Other eye kiss. "Give it some time." Kiss to the corner of my mouth. "I promise I won't disappoint you." Kiss to the other corner of my mouth.

"I only hope that I don't disappoint you." Lips pressed against his, my tongue swept across his lower lip. When his mouth opened for me, I wanted to dive in and taste him. Instead a knock on my window jolted me, causing me to jump, twirling around to see who was interrupting.

I wanted to be mad when I saw it was Mason, but his big innocent eyes looked too excited to see us. He'd waited as long as possible and it was sweet to see how much he liked Luke. I had a feeling that once again I'd be losing Luke to Mason and Ben until later that night.

Luke murmured something I didn't understand, possibly in Swedish. Pressing one last kiss to my lips before getting out of the car, it was hard and short.

Much too short for my liking.

"Until tonight."

15

HE WAS LATE AND NOT JUST A LITTLE BIT LATE, BUT ALMOST AN hour late. I'd already got my suitcase and had been waiting for nearly forty-five minutes. When I wasn't looking around the airport which was crazy, busy, huge and intimidating, I was calling and texting Luke to ask him where the hell he was. Instead of answering each time his phone went immediately to voicemail. That meant he either turned off his phone or it was dead. I was really hoping it was the latter because I didn't want to think about the alternative.

I was only staying in LA for two days before we headed to Playa del Carmen for New Year's with Anna and a few of her friends. Before we left for Mexico, Luke and I were to have dinner with Jenner. With him home for the holidays and me being in LA, we were not going to pass up the opportunity to hang out.

Maybe I should have asked Jenner to pick me up at the airport, so we could have spent more time together, but I wanted Luke to be the first person I saw when I arrived. I'd asked him if it would be easier if I took a cab or if I should book a room at a hotel since he was staying at a friend's house and Rob would be home. Luke had been a little evasive about the whole thing and told me he'd take care of it and pick me up.

Not knowing what else to do, I decided to get a taxi and a hotel room and then figure out what had happened to Luke. Activating my screen, I started to walk toward where I knew I could catch a cab. Only a couple more minutes and Luke would be an hour late. Even though I knew no one in the airport knew my situation, I felt like all eyes were on me and that they knew I'd been stood up. Tears stung at the back of my eyes, but I refused to cry. I couldn't imagine if someone got a picture of me crying at LAX. It was irrational, but for the moment I was choosing to go with my crazy thoughts instead of thinking the worst and all the horrific things that could've happened to Luke.

Strong arms wrapped around me, pulling me off my feet and into a solid chest. Before I could scream or kick my way out of the arms of my attacker, heavy breaths echoed in my ear. Whoever had ahold of me was breathing so heavily that my body was moving with each deep inhale and exhale.

Squirming I opened my mouth to scream for help when my attacker spoke.

"Hey beautiful, it's me, relax."

My body stilled as I took in his words. Realizing that the man that was holding me against him wasn't trying to restrain me, but to hug me, I turned my head to make sure I wasn't hallucinating.

Luke looked frazzled with his hair sticking up this way and

that, his shirt wrinkled, and he looked exhausted, but still gorgeous. Even with talking to him on FaceTime almost every day, I forgot the effect he had on me in person. When he gave me his lopsided smile, my body melted and would have slipped to the floor if Luke hadn't been holding me up.

Feeling my body go loose, Luke's brows knit in concern and he turned me in his arms until I was facing him. It had only been a month since I was last in his arms, but that was thirty days too long. The smell of sandalwood and ocean filled my senses making me hazy with lust.

"I'm sorry I'm so late. Are you okay?" Pulling me out of my fog, I nodded before I slipped my arms around his neck. I wasn't sure of the touching protocol in LA or what it would be in Mexico. When Luke had been in Fairlane, he didn't care if we were seen together and had held my hand out in public. There was no crazy PDA, but enough to show we were definitely not friends.

"Yeah, I'm fine. Are you? I didn't think that you were going to show up."

"I know and again I'm sorry. Some beast at the gym stepped on my phone and broke it and I knew with the crazy traffic I wouldn't have time to replace it before I needed to meet you. And I was still late." He made a disgruntled noise that sounded like some foreign swear word.

"It's okay." My mouth brushed his scruffy cheek. Our arms tightened around the other. "You're here now and that's all that matters. I got worried that something had happened to you when I kept calling your phone and it went straight to voicemail."

"Fuck." He grumbled under his breath. "This whole day

has been a total clusterfuck. Up until the moment I saw you, of course."

"Of course." I mimicked him with a huge smile on my face. Cupping his cheek rough with stubble, I looked up at Luke. "I missed you so much it's ridiculous. How is that even possible when I just talked to you last night?"

Luke grinned his endearing lopsided smile that never failed to make everyone around him smile too. "I don't know how, but I missed you too." Something caught his attention over my shoulder causing his lips to thin into a firm line. "Let's get out of here. I've got a surprise for you."

"Really?" I asked as I started to grab for my suitcase handle before Luke shook his head and started for the exit. "What kind of surprise?"

Turning to look back at me, Luke had a wry smile on his face. "Hopefully the good kind."

With how fast Luke was walking, I almost had to run to keep up with him. Luckily, we didn't have far to go. I understood the need to get away from the airport as fast as possible when a group of photographers were lined up just outside of the doors.

"Remember to keep your head down or their flashes will blind you." Luke's hand found mine and gripped it tightly. "Are you ready?"

"Ready." I huffed out.

If I had thought ahead of time, I would have had my sunglasses on or ready to put on, but I was out of sorts with Luke being late to pick me up, his surprise, and the alarming amount of paparazzi that were waiting to get a shot of any celebrity to pass through LAX on any given day.

Walking quickly hand in hand, I kept my head down and let Luke lead me to where we needed to go. My little legs didn't stop until the matte black of Luke's Audi came into view. There were only a couple of paparazzi that had followed us to the car, still I kept my head down until we were out of the parking lot.

"It's clear." The gruff tone in his voice made it obvious that Luke was not a fan of his lack of privacy.

Slipping on my sunglasses, I looked around, and didn't recognize where we were, not that I knew my way around LA. "Where are we going?"

Patting my knee in reassurance, Luke kept driving. "To your surprise."

Where were we going? We had been heading out of town for at least a good thirty minutes. "I'm not sure I like surprises."

He laughed a big booming laugh that filled the car with his happiness and made me smile. "You'll like this one."

"If you're so sure why not tell me what it is?"

"That's not going to work on me." Luke shook his head with a knowing smile. "It won't be much longer and then you'll see for yourself. Trust me."

"I do trust you, but I'm impatient to get you somewhere so I can strip you naked."

Luke groaned and adjusted himself. "You're killing me." Clearing his throat, he looked over at me. "I promise to rip the clothes off your body in no more than five minutes after we arrive."

"Five minutes you say?" I tapped my watch, smiling over at him. "You better keep your word."

"Oh, Alex, you have no idea." His deep, sexy voice was full of promise.

Oh, I had some idea of what he wanted to do to me if all the phone sex we had over the last month was any indication. I couldn't count all the times that Luke had made me blush and turned me on with all the dirty things he said to me.

"Stop thinking all those dirty thoughts over there, you're driving me mad," Luke growled.

"Did you become a mind reader since I last saw you?"

"Funny, but no." His right hand grasped my leg and slid up until he met the juncture of my jean clad pussy. "You keep rubbing your legs together like you're trying to alleviate something only I can fix."

His hand didn't move from between my legs. I wasn't sure if he was trying to torture me by leaving his hand there, but I couldn't stop moving around in my seat as I thought about what I wanted him to do to me.

"Baby, you've got to stop. We'll be there in a couple of minutes."

Baby? No man had ever called me baby and when I read it in books I normally thought it was generic. It wasn't his usual 'beautiful' that he called me but coming from Luke I liked it.

A few minutes later, Luke parked his car in the driveway of a gorgeous modern house that was a combination of what looked like dark gray concrete and wood. I loved the house immediately and wondered who lived in it. Was this where Luke had been staying?

There was a door to the right of the garage that led into a small courtyard that was filled with lush green trees and flowers of every color. I could imagine a hammock strung between two of the trees, relaxing and reading while enjoying the outdoors. I was definitely looking forward to being in the warmer weather of LA and Mexico for a few days. Los Angeles was a lot nicer in December then Fairlane. When I'd left Missouri, the temperature was in the low thirties and about to dip lower and it had already snowed once. Nothing like the balmy seventy something it was in LA.

"Alex, let's go inside." Luke tugged my hand, my body crashing into his.

Turning to look back over at the entrance, I asked. "Whose house is this? It's amazing."

"What would you say if I told you it was mine?" he asked, guiding me to the front door.

"I would say that you don't own a house, but I would fully support you having one like this. I love everything about it, even the decor. I love all the windows and greenery surrounding the house." The house was something straight out of a magazine and exactly what you would expect a Hollywood movie star to live in. All the trees that surrounded the property made it feel exotic and private. "Now please tell me whose house this is because you promised me that I would be stripped down in less than five minutes and I hate to remind you, but the clock is ticking."

"I'm fully aware of what I promised." We looked around the living room, dining room and kitchen area. I was in total awe and hoped that this was where we would be staying for the short time I was in LA. Luke was taking it in with an appraising eye. "Do you really like it?" Luke stepped further into the room until we were underneath a set of stairs.

Looking up to meet his eyes, I wrapped my arms around

his neck and started to pull him down. I wanted his lips on mine. "I absolutely love it."

Pushing me back until I was flush against the wall, Luke smiled at me mischievously. His hands traced up my thighs and under my shirt where he proceeded to take it off hastily. His lips crashed against mine in a desperate and fiery kiss.

"It's been too long. Fuck I can't wait to get you naked and take you against this wall. Tell me you want the same thing." Luke growled into my ear, biting down on the shell.

"I do," I moaned into his neck. "But what if someone walks in?"

"No one's going to walk in. I promise you." Flicking open the button to my jeans, Luke made quick work of getting them down my legs. My fingers fumbled at first trying to work his pants off, I was so eager to get him naked and inside of me.

Wrapping my legs around his waist, I rubbed my center up and down his hard shaft coating him with my already wet pussy.

"I need you inside of me." Arching my back, I positioned myself until I could feel his tip at my opening and let myself drop down until I felt him kiss my cervix.

Gripping my ass cheeks, Luke's fingers dug in deep. There would probably be bruises tomorrow, but I didn't care. My body missed him too much. "Fuck, Alex you're going to kill me. You feel so fucking good."

Luke took over, angling his hips to thrust up in long, swift movements as his tongue plunged into my waiting mouth, their thrusts matching move for move.

One hand held onto his shoulder while my other hand

found purchase tangled in his disheveled hair as Luke continued to hit me in just the right spot over and over again.

My head fell back when hot tingles trailed down my spine as my orgasm drew closer. I dug the heels of my feet into Luke's ass causing him to drive deeper and harder. Hot breath fanned my face and neck with rough kisses. Taking my nipple into his mouth, Luke sucked hard sending me over the edge. Toes curled, back arched, I held on for dear life as I quaked against the wall and in Luke's arms.

"Alex," Luke groaned against my collarbone as his hips jerked uncontrollably.

Luke stood with his forehead against my shoulder as his breath somewhat evened out before he wrapped his arms around me and started up the stairs.

My head lazed against his with my eyes closed until I felt him go down on one knee and start to lean down. Eyes open, I looked around to see we were in a bedroom on a huge white bed. Once again, the greenery filled almost every inch of the windows of the room except for the gorgeous overlook of LA from one wall.

"Luke," I murmured as he placed me on the bed before his long, lean body laid out beside mine, and pulled me flush against him. "We can't be on someone else's bed. Especially when I've got your cum dripping out of me."

Humming, Luke shoved his leg between mine. "I like the sound of that. It's fucking hot."

"Me leaking on someone's bed?"

"Just the thought of you leaking my cum makes me want to fuck you again and again, filling you with more."

"The fucking was hot. I don't think I've ever done it against a wall before and I have to say it's definitely a favorite."

Pulling back to look down at me, his eyes full of concern, Luke asked. "I wasn't too rough?"

"Rough in all the right ways, but not too rough. Don't think just because you've dazzled me and I'm in a sexual haze, I haven't realized you've been avoiding my question. What's going on? Whose house are we at?"

Blowing out a breath that ruffled the hair on the top of my head, Luke pulled me tighter into his body. My eyes closed, being with him again made it feel as if I could melt into him and I never wanted to move.

"You know how I've been busier than normal these last few weeks since I got back after Thanksgiving?" I nodded my head that was against his chest and kept listening to his rumbling voice. "I was looking at houses to buy so that I could finally have a house to call my own and so that when you were here, we weren't staying at my friends or a hotel. A place to call home."

Pulling away, I sat up on an elbow. "You bought this house?"

"Yeah," he answered looking sheepish.

"Are you embarrassed? Because I can't understand why! This house is stunning. From what I've seen I love everything about it. You should be proud to be the owner of this house."

"You don't think it was impulsive?"

"No," I drew out the word as I sat up and faced him slinging one leg over his hip. "You've lived here for four years and I understand why you stayed with friends when you were gone most of the time, but it has to be nice to have a place that's all your own."

Looking pensive, Luke bit his bottom lip making him look adorable. I was sure that there was nothing he could do that would make him look bad, but it troubled me that he was unsure whether he should tell me something. I wanted him to be able to tell me anything.

"Luke," I said softly, but unable to hide the hurt in my voice.

Something flashed in his eyes, they changed from a beautiful Caribbean blue into a stormy sea, but before I could identify what it was, it was gone.

Pulling my hand up to his mouth, Luke kissed my knuckles and kept his eyes on our linked fingers. "I'm afraid you're going to think I'm moving too fast and freak out on me."

"Why would I freak out? I love the house and…"

"And what?" he asked, eyes bright.

There was no way I was going to answer him with what was about to come out of my mouth. My feelings for Luke had been steadily getting closer and closer to the 'L' word, but I didn't want to say it after sex. I would hate for him to think it was only because of the sex that I told him I loved him. It wasn't as if Luke had said he loved me yet either. I did know that he cared for me a great deal, but love and caring are not the same thing.

I lied only a little bit. "I'm happy you bought it."

"What if I told you I bought it for you?"

"I'd say you're crazy. You did *not* buy this house for me,

did you?" My mind spun, and I couldn't think one coherent thought. There was just no way.

"Well, it's not in your name or anything like that, but I bought it for you and me. I was hoping that you'd be able to come and stay here some this summer and when you come back for Spring Break with Mason. Living in hotel rooms gets old fast and it'll be more comfortable for you and Mason to have a place that's permanent."

My heart melted at the thought that Luke had done all of this for Mason and me, but I was afraid he'd done it for the wrong reasons. "That's amazingly sweet, Luke, but I feel like I made you spend a lot of money," I said as I looked around the room and out the windows. "For something that you wouldn't have done otherwise."

"I want this, and I want you and Mason in my life. I needed to step up and be an adult, not a mooch on my friends. Are you telling me you would rather stay at a hotel or someplace else while you're here?"

"That's not what I'm saying, but it's a lot. You spent god knows how much for a place that you'll barely be at, just so Mason and I can stay here when we visit."

"Maybe I'm doing and saying this all wrong." He shook his head and then stared back at me with so much emotion in his eyes that I wanted to reach out and shut them. It was beautiful and sad all at the same time. I wanted to kiss him all over and yet cry at what I saw in his eyes. It was true what they said about being able to see a person's soul through their eyes.

"I've already told you that I'm all in, and maybe you're not ready to accept that yet. I understand why after all that you've been through, but this is me showing you that I want a life with you. That I'm planning a life with you and that I'm not going anywhere." He pulled me back down on the bed and then rolled on top of me, resting his weight on his elbows while he nestled the rest of his body between my legs. "Right now, me and you, it's easy. If you thought it was hard not to see me in person for one month, wait until I start shooting in January. I'm not going to lie to you and say you're not going to feel deprived of me because you will, but this is the life that I live, and I desperately want you in it. I want you to have a place to come to whenever you want. A place to make your own and for you to be comfortable in."

I couldn't stop the tears that welled in my eyes at what Luke had said. It was everything that I wanted to hear but didn't know it until that moment. The only thing that would've made it better was if he told me he loved me. I was all in. I had been since I went to visit him for his birthday and gave myself to him.

Pulling Luke down until we were chest to chest, I buried my face into his shoulder.

"Hey," Luke said softly with surprise in his voice. "What's going on? I didn't mean to upset you. If anything, I thought you'd be happy."

Instead of talking I pushed Luke off me and forced him onto his back. If I wasn't so close to crying, I would've laughed at the look of shock on his face. Luke probably thought I was crazy for the way I acted, but he'd already seen me cry too many times.

Laying my body over his, I wrapped my arms and legs around him as best as I could, and once again snuggled into the crook of his neck and shoulder. With a sniff, I murmured against his skin. "Hold me."

Luke didn't question my request. Instead he wrapped me tightly in his arms as if he was afraid I would fly away at any moment, and waited until I was ready to explain.

After a few minutes I had calmed down enough, I thought I could talk without crying. I wiggled enough for Luke to loosen his hold. Once I could move, I rested my head on his shoulder at an angle so that we could see each other.

Luke seemed unhappy with our position as he slid me onto my side, rolled over, and wrapped me back into his body's cocoon. He looked down at me with concern but said nothing. Giving me the time I needed, and I loved him more for it.

"I don't want you to misinterpret my reaction. I *am* happy. So happy with everything you said. It's what every girl wants to hear especially me, but I didn't want you to see me cry. It's stupid, but I hate for people to see me cry. I never know what's going to set me off. Sometimes it's a hug or if a person talks to me. I know my reaction had to come off opposite of how I'm feeling so I'm trying to explain, but as I'm explaining it sounds so bad and crazy. The more I care about someone the more I don't want them to see me cry."

Luke frowned down at me while a look of sympathy crossed his face. "Some time," he started softly. "When you think you can talk about it without crying, I'd like for you to tell me about it. I won't pressure you, but I want to under-stand. Here I am spilling my heart out to you and…"

"And I ruined the moment because I was so happy I wanted to cry. You probably thought I wanted to break up with you or something as equally insane."

"Something like that. One moment you're smiling and the next... I thought you were going to break my heart." Tucking a wayward strand of hair behind my ear, Luke leaned down, his lips glided over my cheek and left little kisses on each eye.

"I'm sorry." My voice caught, and I had to take a deep breath. I couldn't hurt Luke because I had some weird aversion to crying in front of people. "I never want to break your heart or hurt you in any way."

God it would be so much easier if I told Luke I loved him. He had to love me back, right? Why else would he buy this house and tell me he wanted a life with me? I knew I wouldn't be able to hold it in much longer.

16

WITH FINGERS TAPPING AGAINST THE STEERING WHEEL, LUKE WAS quiet as we sat in the LA traffic. If I thought it was bad normally after Christmas was brutal.

I couldn't help but comment on his actions. "Are you nervous?"

Luke shrugged his shoulders but stayed quiet.

"You have nothing to be nervous about. Jenner already likes you."

He looked at me from the corner of his eye. "How do you know?"

"Because I know. You've made me happy, and he told me that he's seen a huge change in me since we met. Do you think he might not like you and I'd dump you or something?"

If Luke thought that, he was being ridiculous. Even if Taylor told me she hated Luke, I wasn't sure I'd be able to break up with him. The only thing I could think that would change my mind about him was if he started to act like Decker or cheated on me.

When there was nothing but silence from him, I started to get a little worried. I hoped that my little freak out earlier hadn't put any doubts in Luke's mind. I thought I'd put his worries to rest, but maybe I hadn't been as successful as I thought. Nothing had been amiss since Luke had left Fairlane and went back to LA. We still talked every day and normally ended the night with FaceTime. It wasn't perfect, but it was important to the both of us to talk for at least five minutes every day, and to know what was going on in each other's lives. He'd been extra busy, but that was explained earlier with Luke surprising me with the house that he'd bought.

"I can promise you that there's nothing that Jenner could say that would make me end things with you. Is there someone in your life that could tell you to dump me and you'd listen?"

Turning his head, Luke gave me a strange look. "I would listen to the concerns of my family, but they've never interfered in my love life before."

"Well, who's saying that they won't start now? I mean you're dating a woman from the Midwest who's a single mom. Someone who's already been married before. They're probably going to think I'm with you for your money and tell you to dump me the second you tell them about me."

"Are you finished?" Luke laughed. Interlacing our fingers, he placed our joined hands on his thigh.

"Everything I said is what people are going to think when they find out we're together and you know it's true. What I don't want is your family thinking those things about me. If the shoe was on the other foot, wouldn't you hate it if my family thought badly about you?"

"I've told everyone in my family about you and no one said a negative thing. In fact, they're excited that I've finally met a woman I'm serious about. They can't wait to meet you. My little brother, Leo was begging to talk to you while you're here."

"Really?" I asked astonished. I couldn't believe that he'd told his family about me and I was beyond relieved that they weren't questioning his judgement on dating me.

Luke nodded his head with a soft smile and I couldn't help but lean over and kiss his cheek.

"I was worried about what they'd think."

"Anyone who knows you would never doubt why you're with me, and you can't worry about the media. They'll write whatever they want. You could be an actress and they could say that you're with me to ride my coattails to the top. It doesn't matter who or where you're from they're always going to have something negative to say about us. That's why I wanted us to stay apart in New York. I didn't need you getting skittish when the paparazzi started to follow us. Even the public will try to get photos, but at least they won't be making up stories about us when they post on social media."

"You've thought a lot about this."

"So, have you," he shot back with a wry smile.

"Actually, not so much. Everything with you is so easy it almost feels like a dream. Half the time I think I've imagined you, and one day I'm going to wake up and you'll be gone."

Pulling our joined hands to his mouth, Luke kissed the back of my hand. "Not going to happen. You'll never be rid of me and I can assure you that this is not a dream." He said the last on a laugh as he switched lanes.

"Are you closest to Leo? It seems like you talk to him the most out of your siblings."

He shrugged and kept his eyes on the road. "I guess you could say that. I moved out when he was so young, so I felt it was important to still try to keep contact. Liam and Stella are busy with their own lives. While Leo is in college, he still makes time to talk to me multiple times a week, where the others have schedules like I do. We're really busy for a great deal of time and then are free for long stretches."

"I'm sorry you couldn't be with them for Christmas. I feel guilty that I kept you from them asking you to go to Mexico with me."

"While I would have loved to have seen my family for the holidays, I'm used to not seeing them. They would have come here if they had the time. You shouldn't feel guilty." Luke squeezed my fingers. "If I was spending this time with my family, it wouldn't be until March when we saw each other again and that would be far too long."

"I hope you get to see them soon."

"Me too. I think Leo is going to come here sometime next year. I'd love for you to meet him. All of them, but I think Leo is the most excited about you."

"I'd love to meet him. You'll have to show me pictures of your family. When you tried to show me from your phone it was too hard to see through the computer to phone."

"You are one of a kind," Luke laughed. "If you wanted to know what they look like you could Google them."

"Where's the fun in that? Anyone could find those pictures. I want your pictures and the stories that go along with them."

The smile on his face was indication enough that Luke

liked that I had waited for him to show me pictures of his family, but when he pulled up to a red light and crushed his lips to mine, I knew how much it meant to him. It was hot and wet and way too short like most of his kisses.

~

PULLING LUKE UP TO JENNER'S FRONT DOOR, I COULDN'T HELP but laugh at his nerves. It was as if he was meeting my father. Which he would never do, but it was sweet and endearing all the same. "He's going to love you."

"I'm no longer worried about if he'll like me or not, but if I'll like him. He's turned into a good friend and I'd hate to put a rift between the two of you like I have you and Ryan."

"Ryan is being stupid, and I don't know why he won't see reason."

"He's looking out for his friend and it doesn't look good when your friend's boyfriend has some woman posting pictures on social media claiming that they are dating. I'm grateful that you believe me and aren't buying into her craziness."

"I probably shouldn't believe you, but you're not a liar and from all accounts Ashlyn Jade's a crazy woman." I rang the doorbell and turned back to him. "Is your publicist still keeping a record of everything that's being posted?"

"Yeah," Luke answered right before the door was thrown open and Jenner picked me up in a big bear hug.

Holding me by the arms, Jenner looked me up and down. "Look at you."

"Look at you! You look great and so happy."

"Of course, I'm happy. You're here!"

Wrapping my arm through Luke's, I introduced them. "Jenner, I want you to meet Luke Sandström. Luke, this is Reeves Jenner."

After exchanging greetings and doing all their silly male posturing, we went inside where Jenner had a buffet of Chinese food containers waiting for us on his kitchen counter.

Jenner swept his arm out indicating the smorgasbord that awaited us. "I wasn't sure what you guys would want, so I ordered one of everything."

"I hope you like leftovers because there's no way in hell we can eat all of that. There has to be at least forty containers here."

Luke's eyes twinkled as he looked down at me. "I don't know. I'm pretty hungry after exerting so much energy earlier."

My eyes widened. I couldn't believe he'd just said that.

"Dig in," Jenner called with a plate already in his hand.

WE ATE AS IF WE'D BEEN DEPRIVED OF FOOD FOR THE LAST WEEK. I don't think I'd ever ate so much in my life.

"Oh my God, I think I'm going to bust. I shouldn't have eaten that last thing of noodles. You may have to carry me out of here."

"Normally I'd say that wouldn't be a problem, but I'm about to go into a food coma over here. It's like Thanksgiving all over again."

Jenner laughed and then slumped over onto the couch

closing his eyes for a brief second. "Yeah, I heard about dinner and the wrath of Ryan."

Running a hand through his hair, Luke let out a deep sigh. I had a feeling the way Ryan treated him bothered him more than he let on.

"Everyone had been so open and fun that when I met Ryan, he took me by surprise. At first, I thought I was imagining all the looks he was giving me until I heard Alex and him arguing in the kitchen. I get it though." He shook his head. "He's looking out for Alex and if I was in his shoes, I'd be skeptical too."

"Have you talked to him lately?" Jenner asked me.

"Not really. I tried, but every time he asks if I'm still seeing Luke and I tell him nothing's changed, he hangs up. Every time that crazy bitch posts something Ryan sends it to me. I have no clue how to prove to him that Luke isn't cheating on me and I think that it will only get worse the more time we're apart, especially if she keeps spewing her lies." I let out a weary sigh. "It's fucking ridiculous. You believe Luke isn't cheating, right?"

"He wouldn't be in my house if I thought for one-second he's going behind your back. Especially after what happened with Matt. It helps that I've heard all the rumors about Ashlyn and they all come from very credible sources. I can't believe there's nothing that can be done to stop her. I'd say to address her, but I have a feeling that would only make it worse. She just might be certifiable."

After Luke found out about Ashlyn Jade's posts, he talked to his lawyer and publicist to see what they had to say and what he should do about her making up these stories about them being together. Sadly, there wasn't anything he could do unless she slandered him in some way and then Luke would be able to sue her, but for now all anyone could do was take a record of each post she made about him. It was a little creepy that she seemed to be able to find him wherever he was and take a picture of him in the background. Luke had even started to look around for her when he went out hoping to catch her, but he hadn't spotted her once.

"I don't know what to do about either situation. I'm not sure Ryan will ever believe that Luke isn't or didn't cheat and without taking a hit out on that crazy bitch there's not much we can do.

"Not having Ryan in my life sucks. We've been friends since high school and even stayed friends after we broke up. We lost track of each other for a time, but when we reunited it was as if no time had passed, and I had missed him being in my life. I'm not saying things have been perfect between us though. It wasn't that long ago that I found out some information that changed our friendship. He kept at me to forgive him and I eventually did. Maybe I'm a bad friend because I'm not trying harder to get him to listen to me, but right now I don't care."

"Don't think that," Jenner cut in. "I don't know Ryan from a hole in the wall, but from what you've told me it's got me thinking that maybe Ryan's feelings for you are more than platonic. Have you ever thought about that?"

"No," I shook my head vehemently. "Not since high school has it ever crossed my mind and I'm not sure it ever crossed my mind back then. Ryan was my first *everything*. I was so fucking naïve back then and to think a boy was interested in me was unfathomable. I'm sure he thought I'd be an easy lay or something, knowing what I know now. I don't know what he was thinking. But fuck Ryan and his suspicions. I'm with two of my favorite guys and I don't want him ruining our night." I stopped to lean over and give Luke a light kiss. He'd been quiet and taking all of this in about Ryan which I'm sure wasn't too fun for him.

Pulling back our eyes met. "Are you good?"

"It's all good," Luke answered, then pursed his lips. "I don't like that I've come between you and your friend."

"If I had to choose who I want in my life, I'd choose you over Ryan." Shrugging my shoulders, I continued. "Maybe he knows that."

"He knows," Jenner interjected. "He's repeatedly told you that your boyfriend is cheating on you and you're telling him to fuck off." Chuckling to himself, Jenner finished, "That's what I think your buddy is thinking. That and he lost his chance with you."

There was no way that Ryan was interested in me like that. If he had been, wouldn't he have tried to convey that sometime between my divorce and now? Unless he knew that, I didn't feel the same way. It didn't matter now. I had Luke in my life and I wasn't going to let go just because my friend was being stubborn and still might be interested in me after all these years.

"Either way it doesn't matter. As of right now, we aren't talking to each other and I don't want to keep talking about him. I'm on vacation and I don't want to be dragged down by his bullshit." Shaking my head, I turned to look at Jenner. "Let's talk about your bullshit."

"Mine? No, I don't think so. Let's not, and say we did. Doesn't Luke have some shit we can talk about? He can be in the hot seat."

Luke chuckled and scrubbed his hand across his stubble. "We already talked about mine. Remember?"

"Jade? Yeah, I'm sure you've got more than that going on."

"Shouldn't the night be light-hearted instead of us all talking about our problems?" I asked, saving Luke.

Jenner narrowed his eyes but left it alone. "What do you want to talk about?"

I didn't know, but nothing that was going to stress anyone out.

"I know," I exclaimed. "Luke surprised me after picking me up at the airport by taking me to his new house. He bought a house, and it's awesome! I love everything about it, or at least what I've seen, but I doubt there's anything there that could change my mind."

"Congratulations you're an adult now," Jenner sneered.

"Hey! Don't be an asshole." With my brows set, I huffed and shook my head at him. He needed to play nice. "Don't judge."

"You're right and I'm sorry. I'm in a bad place right now as you can probably tell. Poppy and I had a huge fight earlier and I'm taking it out on the two of you."

"Shit. I'm sorry, Jenner. Do you want to talk about it?" I scooted over and gave him a side hug.

I wasn't sure when he was going to wake up and smell the coffee that his wife wasn't good for him. I was ninety-nine-point nine percent positive that she was cheating on him, and that was why he felt the way he did about cheaters. Yes, Jenner was there for me after I was in my wreck with Matt, all because he freaked out about our newfound friendship and because he felt guilty for cheating on me, but I felt he used that as an excuse instead of admitting to himself that his wife had been cheating on him for who knows how long. Not only did I think she was cheating, I was pretty sure that she was doing drugs and might be an addict.

I tried to give Jenner every opportunity to talk about it if he wanted, but he wasn't ready. There were a few times when he'd opened up to me, but he seemed to be back in denial or he didn't wish to talk about it in front of Luke.

"No, like you said tonight should be cheerful and I know just what the doctor ordered."

"What's that?" I asked intrigued.

"Christmas presents. Let me go grab yours and I'll be right back. Don't think I didn't notice you dropping your package underneath my empty tree."

"I wasn't trying to hide it. What would be the point? I told you I had a present for you."

"I'll be right back," Jenner called as he rushed from the room. Now he was excited, and it was good to see the smile back on his face.

"Baby, he's not ready," Luke said softly so that Jenner couldn't hear. "He wants to help you with your problems as a way to detach himself from his own. Let him live in denial a little while longer. At least until the holidays are over."

"I know, but I hate seeing and hearing how much she hurts him. I swear if she was here tonight I probably would've punched her in the face. Maybe the boob too just for good measure. She's like the female Decker. I hate her."

Using his finger in a come-hither motion, Luke patted his leg with his other hand. "Come here."

Yes, please! I scrambled over the couch cushions to crawl onto his lap as graceful as possible. With the quiet laughter that was shaking his body, I obviously wasn't successful. It didn't matter though because Luke hugged me to his body and kissed my temple.

"You're a good friend. Be patient and he'll come to you. It's got to be hard to accept that the woman you love and pledged your life to is going behind your back."

I ran my fingers through his silky hair. "I hate to see him hurting this way."

"Ugh," Jenner moaned as he walked into the room. "Really guys, I was gone for all of a minute and you're already all over each other."

Sliding off Luke's lap, I kissed the dimple in his chin and then gave my attention to Jenner. I was happy he hadn't heard us talking about him and gotten upset.

"I hate shopping, so you should be happy that I actually went out myself and got you your present."

"Pfft." I dismissed him. "It's nothing like trying to shop for people who have everything and can buy themselves anything they want, while living in a town with a tiny mall. Yes, men hate shopping but guess what, I'm not too crazy about it either so stop tooting your own horn."

"You're feisty tonight. Okay, how about Merry Christmas?"

"Perfect. Merry Christmas to you too! Now open your present." Shoving his present at him, I chewed on my lip. I wasn't sure if he'd like it or not.

"And bossy too." Jenner laughed as he unwrapped his present.

"I had no clue what to get you because you've never said you wanted anything." I said nervously. I wasn't kidding about trying to figure out gifts for people who could literally buy almost anything they wanted.

Jenner's grin grew as he pulled out a dark blue cashmere scarf that I'd knitted him. Once I figured out that I'd make him a scarf, I scoured the Internet for patterns that caught my eye. Of course, I found one that was more complex than anything I'd ever made, but I was determined to make it for him. I may or may not have had to start over a couple of times from messing it up.

"I know it doesn't get super cold here, but I figured you can use it when you travel or when you're on set. I hope you like the color because I stood in the yarn aisle for forever trying to decide a color for you."

"Wait!" Jenner's jaw dropped open. "Did you make this?" Jenner asked, wrapping the scarf around his neck.

"I did. I know it's not as awesome as some that you can buy in the store. I'm not that great of a knitter."

"The fuck you are. This *is* awesome. I can't believe you made this. Did you know she could knit?"

"Yeah, but only because she told me she was making you a scarf. She did an amazing job. I know there's no way in hell I could knit anything."

"Sure, you could," I said to Luke. "If I can, anyone can."

"There's something else in there." I told Jenner indicating the box he'd placed to the side as he examined his scarf.

"A hat to match?" He placed his knitted cap on his head. "Hell yeah! I'm going to rock this all over town."

"Oh my!" I laughed. "You don't need to go overboard. I'm just glad you like it."

"Like it? I love it. This is a gift from the heart. What more could I ask for? I kind of feel bad about my gift now that I know that you made mine and went to so much trouble."

I couldn't help but laugh. Obviously to these two knitting was extremely hard. I wasn't saying it was easy, but I felt that I'd taken the easy way out even if I'd bought expensive yarn to do it with. "I didn't go to that much trouble. I mean I didn't have to donate a kidney or anything to buy the yarn."

"Whatever. It's time for you to open yours. Have you guys exchanged gifts yet?" He asked eying Luke.

"Not yet. I haven't been in town for that long and Luke surprised me with his house. I'm kind of sad that we're leaving tomorrow night, and I won't have more time to spend in it."

"It's not going anywhere. When you come back in March, you'll have plenty of time."

"Yes, because I want to wait over three months. I want it now," I laughed. I was a big believer of instant gratification and three months was way too long. It was a real possibility that I would make him take me for a tour during one of our FaceTime chats.

"Fight about it later," Jenner said good naturedly. "Right now, it's time for you to open up your present."

Excitedly, I tore the gold wrapping paper off the small box. It wasn't crazy small making me think it was jewelry. Inside was a smaller box that would be used for gift cards. I gave him a big smile as I pulled out a gift card to the nicest spa in the town next to mine.

"Jenner, this is great! How did you know that this is the best place in town?" I held the gift card up for Luke to see. I'd only been once, and that was right before Taylor had moved. We enjoyed a spa day, relaxing in their lounge room, massages, using the sauna and arctic rooms, and got our nails done.

"By reading lots and lots of reviews. I wanted to get you something that I knew you'd use and would never buy for yourself. Now every month for a year you can get a massage."

My eyes widened. *A whole year?* That would cost a serious chunk of change and all I did was knit him a scarf and hat.

"Stop being so shocked and give me a hug," Jenner said elbowing me in the side.

Giving him the hug that he deserved, I wrapped my arms around Jenner and squeezed tight. "Thank you." His arms tightened around me for a few moments before he patted me on the back and let me go. "Really, Jenner, thank you. You're right that I wouldn't spend the money, but I do appreciate it and will totally use it. I love getting massages."

"Good to hear. I hate to say it, but I'm going to have to kick you guys out, so I can go to bed. I've got to head to the airport at four so that I can catch my flight."

"Did the studio book your flight?" Luke asked as he stood up and then helped me to my feet.

Jenner laughed without humor. "Those assholes always find the worst times to fly. It's good to know that I'm not the only one."

"It's because they're the cheapest flights. We should get going anyway so we can get up early."

Jenner gave Luke a weird manly back-pat-hug thing. "It was good to meet you, man. You know I have to say it so let's just get it out of the way, shall we?"

Luke laughed, wrapping his arm around my waist. "Have at it."

"Don't hurt my girl, or I'll have to hurt you."

"I expect nothing less from a friend, and it was good to meet you too."

"Have fun in the sun and send me lots of pictures. I'm going to be in Canada freezing my balls off for the next three months."

"Poor baby," I said, patting his cheek. "Have a safe trip."

"You too," Jenner answered with a hug. "See you on the other side."

17

"YOU CAN SIT HERE WHILE MR. SANDSTRÖM GETS INTO WARDROBE and makeup. We'll come get you when he's done." A tiny girl who was all of twenty sneered at me, pointing to a chair that I'd been assigned.

"No," Luke argued. "She's with me."

"But." She started, but quickly closed her mouth at the flash in Luke's eyes when she tried to deny him. "Yes, sir. If you'll both follow me."

"I can stay here." I whispered as we followed the girl back to hair and makeup. "I don't want to be a problem."

"What would be the point of you coming? I want you to see the whole process of what it takes to make a commercial, not sit in a room and wait for me."

The tiny girl we'd been following looked over her shoulder at Luke with worry etched on her face. I was sure she was worried that Luke was going to cause a commotion about her trying to get me to stay behind.

Indicating the door with the words Hair and Makeup on it,

she opened it and looked down at her feet. "Right here, Mr. Sandström."

Luke nodded, but said nothing. It seemed she'd put him in a bit of a grumpy mood. I hoped that didn't follow him throughout the day.

"Mr. Sandström, please take a seat and I'll be right with you." A woman with beautiful purple hair said as she looked through what looked like a toolbox filled with makeup. "If you'd like to take a seat too that should be fine. I've already finished with Lana."

"Thank you," I murmured as I looked around the small room that was brightly lit, and sat in the seat next to Luke's. "Is it always so bright in the rooms?"

"Yeah and it makes it hard to sleep when you have a lot of makeup that has to be done early in the morning."

Turning in my chair, I faced Luke. I was ready to watch what she did to him. "I can see that. I can't imagine trying to sleep with this much light."

"Eventually you get used it and take the time to get a much-needed nap. Especially on the set of Night Shadows, they have to put makeup on any skin that shows. That can be a lengthy process depending on the scenes being shot that day."

"Really?" I asked waggling my eyebrows up and down. "I'd like to be there for that."

Luke shook his head at me and chuckled. "One day you will be."

"Okay Mr. Sandström, today won't take nearly as long as you're used to so lean back and I'll get this over as quickly as I can. By the way, my name is Elise."

"Nice to meet you, Elise. You can call me Luke and this beautiful woman is my girlfriend, Alex."

Even a month later my heart sped up each time Luke introduced me as his girlfriend.

Luke sat with his eyes closed, as comfortable as could be, while I watched in fascination as Elise put a heavy foundation all over Luke's face, and then contoured it until he was even more rugged and handsome than normal. It made me wonder what she could do for me if I ever sat in her chair. Next, she styled his hair with a lot of products to help it stay in place when they used a wind machine.

Only once she was done did he open his eyes and smile over at me. "What do you think?"

"You look beyond handsome. You're gorgeous, but then again you always are. Elise did a great job with you. It was really cool to see her add in the contours that make you look so devastatingly handsome." A slight blush tinted his cheeks at my compliment. "Any woman who sees this commercial is going to buy whatever it is you're selling. Shit, I don't even know what this commercial is about."

Elise and Luke laughed as she fixed an out-of-place hair. "It's for a Scandinavian cologne. A buddy of mine asked if I'd help him out at the last minute. It was one of the things I was working on yesterday." He answered as he stood and shook hands with Elise. I noticed her cheeks redden as he smiled down at her. I was happy to know that it wasn't only me he had that effect on.

She had made Luke look the best that he could look, and all I wanted to do was get him alone in a room and do very bad things to him until they were ready.

I mentally shook my head to bring me out of my hormone induced haze. "That's very sweet of you."

"I do what I can for my friends. They were all supportive of me while I struggled. Now's my chance to help them out." He stood and waited until I was out of my chair before he ushered me to the door.

"Even sweeter." I hugged him for only a moment before I remembered his makeup and hoped I hadn't ruined it. I gasped with my hand over my mouth, looking up at him for smears on his shirt.

"No worries, shorty."

"I guess there are times when it's good to be short."

"I think you're the perfect height. The perfect fit." Luke leaned down to growl in my ear. "If you need me to show you later I can."

"Yes, please." My answer was breathy and unlike anything that had ever come from me before.

"I'll show you to wardrobe." Elise led us out of the room and down the hallway. The house we were in was huge and if we tried to find our own way we were sure to get lost. Luke had informed me on the way that it was common to rent a house to shoot commercials, music videos, and even magazine shoots.

"Have fun today. It was good to meet you both." Elise said as she left us.

"You too." We both answered at the same time.

"Excuse me, Mr. Sandström? We're ready when you are." A skinny man with red framed glasses peaked out into the hallway at us. He had brown hair that was in a mohawk, large brown eyes, and thin lips. We followed him into the room to a rack full of men's clothing. I watched as he started pulling clothes off a rack and holding them up to Luke dismissing them all.

"Bring in the next rack," he shouted causing me to jump.

Slowly, I started to walk backwards until the back of my legs hit a chair. "Are you okay?" Luke asked, one brow cocked.

"Yeah, I just wanted to get out of the way."

"I think we can make this work." The guy shook his head as he walked over to a bag. "Lars didn't mention your size. It's not easy to dress a man as large as you are."

My thought was that he was lucky to get to dress Luke and he should be grateful that he got to put his hands on him.

Luke's head turned to look at the man who I assumed was in charge of wardrobe. "It was last minute. Um… if you need me to I have my suitcase in the car. Did you have an idea on what you wanted me to wear?"

"Robbie." A tan man with bright blue eyes and pale blond hair sneered as he walked in. "Are you still bitching? Luke here shouldn't be offering up his own clothes to make your life easier."

"Lars, it's not a problem." Luke strode over and hugged him. Lars wrapped him in a big bear hug and then clapped him on the back.

"Hey, buddy. I've fucking missed you, and I only get you for a few hours? Not fucking fair." He turned toward the wardrobe man with a piercing look. "I want him in a suit for the first half and then some tight as shit jeans with a t-shirt and a button down over it for the other. I plan for the button down to come off at some point. Can you manage that and do it in a timely fashion?"

"Yes, Mr. Olsen," Robbie stammered out before turning back to the rack of clothes.

"I know you've got a plane to catch so we'll try to do this as fast as possible. Lana is a bit dramatic, but I've informed her we have to do everything in one take so hopefully that will keep the drama to a minimum. Let's sit while we wait. Where did you say you're going again? I haven't been able to keep anything straight trying to get this commercial taped by the end of the year."

"Not a problem. We're headed to Mexico with some friends." Luke started toward me as Lars went to the other side of the room to sit on what looked to be the most uncomfortable couch on the planet. It was all hard edges and not one spot looked to be cushioned. "Lars, I'd like you to meet my girlfriend, Alex. Alex, as you already know, this is Lars, my friend from back home in Sweden."

"Girlfriend?" Lars stood and came over to us. "You've been holding out on me! God, she's gorgeous." His hands wrapped around my upper arms, and he stood back eying me. "You did always get the best-looking girls."

I said nothing as I watched him appraise me. His eyes traveled from head to toe more than once until Luke cleared his throat.

"Lars, don't make her uncomfortable." The slight growl in his voice was filled with a possession that caused butterflies to take flight in my stomach.

He made a dismissive sound in the back of his throat. "She's not uncomfortable. Every woman likes to hear that they look good. Let's hear what she has to say."

Two sets of eyes locked on me. One with concern and the

other amusement. I didn't know what to say. Anything I said in that moment would seem inconsequential.

Luke's hand slipped in mine, lacing our fingers together. "Seriously, man, let's get the show on the road, or don't you remember that we've got a flight to catch later this afternoon?"

"Chill. What's up your ass?" Turning to look down at me, Lars asked. "Has he been this way all morning?"

Squeezing Luke's hand, I smiled. "No, you seem to bring it out in him."

"Very well. Robbie get this man dressed so Mr. Sandström can get to Mexico!" Lars stalked out of the room without looking back.

Turning quickly, I looked up at Luke. "Shit! Is he mad?"

His eyes went to the door before coming back to mine, he let out a sigh. "No, he's just being melodramatic. Don't worry about him, he's stressed about trying to get the filming done today. Normally we'd shoot for two or three days and knowing it all has to be done today is making *him* cranky."

"If you're sure. I feel like I got off on the wrong foot with him."

Leaning down he brushed his lips against mine before pulling back enough to look into my eyes. "I'm sure. I wouldn't lie to you."

"I know," I whispered against his lips.

"Alright then let's get you dressed per Lars orders," Robbie said, clapping his hands obnoxiously.

We separated, and I quietly sat back in a chair and watched as Robbie fitted Luke first in jeans that were so tight you could literally see *everything*. I wasn't sure how Luke could stand to wear them, but he never said a word or showed any discomfort. Robbie moved almost franticly as he made adjustments and flitted around the room.

"All done," he sing-songed as he placed the jeans back on the rack for Luke to wear later. "I'll let Mr. Olsen know that you're ready. He'll send someone to come get you in a moment."

"Thanks," Luke murmured before he made his way toward me looking mouth wateringly delicious in a black suit with a dark gray shirt underneath.

The moment he was in reach my hands were on him. I couldn't help myself. "You look hot." My eyes roamed over every inch as my hands got their fill until we could be alone.

"I'm glad you approve." Grabbing my hands in his, he stopped me from getting too frisky. "I won't be able to live it down if I walk out of here and I'm hard."

"I'm sorry." I couldn't hide my smile as I looked up at him making him arch his brows. "Okay, I'm not sorry. You're in trouble. I simply can't get enough of you."

"That's one problem that I don't think I'll mind having." He winked, his mouth close to caressing mine until a high-pitched squeak filled our ears and he pulled back.

"I'm so sorry to interrupt, but Mr. Olsen is ready for you."

"Don't worry about it." He called out loudly as he smirked down at me. Then for only me to hear, he spoke with his lips brushing against the shell of my ear. "Later."

Following behind and keeping my hands to myself, I tried to keep my mouth from hanging open at the lavishness of the house as we passed by room after room. It was opulent on top of posh. I'd never seen anything like it on TV nor in any magazine, but I tried the best I could to hide my awe and not look like the small-town girl I was and embarrass Luke.

My awe was instantly gone the moment I saw who Luke would be working with for the day. Even from afar it was obvious that she was a model with her willowy frame, confident stance, and graceful movements. She was everything I was not.

Elise came out to do a little retouching on both Luke and the model before Lars introduced them to each other. She hadn't even looked at either one of us when we walked into the room with her superior attitude, but once she caught sight of Luke, she couldn't stop touching him. It was little touches to his arm, chest or hand. Her smile was blinding, and her laugh was fake. I hated her, and it was only the beginning of the day.

"Alright, everyone quiet. Okay guys, here's what I want from you for this scene. Lana, you're going to be at the mirror applying your lipstick and looking like you're getting ready, and Luke, I want you sitting in this chair watching her." Lars turned to Luke, giving him a knowing look. "Look sexy as fuck while you gaze at her then when I give you the signal, I want you to get up and strut into the bathroom where you'll then push up against her and run your hands across her body."

Did Luke know about this? Did he think I'd want to watch him put his hands all over another woman?

"Places everyone!" Lars shouted as he moved off the set to stand behind a monitor.

Luke moved to the chair he was supposed to sit in. I watched Lana, the supermodel, take off her robe where she was only wearing a pair of barely there black lace panties and bra.

Her body was perfect.

Mine was not.

Why the fuck was Luke with me when he could have someone like her?

"I'm going to turn on some music to get you in the mood. Move with the beat. Got it?" Lars looked first to Lana who nodded her head, that sat on her long elegant neck, and then to Luke, who gave him a thumbs up.

"Radioactive" by Imagine Dragons started to play over the speaker system that ran throughout the house.

Music filled the air as Lana stood in front of the mirror. Even though I hated to admit it, she knew what she was doing as she primped in front of the mirror while somehow looking provocative at the same time.

Lars signaled for Luke to move in and I held my breath as he moved toward her, each step was met by the beat of the song in perfect harmony. When his hands started to slip up her thighs, I closed my eyes.

"Cut! Start again." The music stopped, and my eyes snapped open at Lars directive. "Luke, you need to look like your turned on by her not like you wouldn't touch her with a ten-foot pole. Be sexy. Smolder for the camera. You know all that shit that you do."

"Got it." Luke gritted out before looking over at me with an apology in his eyes.

"Do you want to get out of here, so you can go on your little vacation with your girlfriend? If so, then get your head in the game."

Lana's eyes searched the room until they landed on me, her lips curling up in an ugly sneer.

Lars caught the tail end of her sneer before she could right her face into an innocent pout. He looked to Luke and said something in what I assumed was Swedish. They went back and forth for a couple of minutes until they were laughing so hard that Lars had to wipe a tear from his eye.

"Okay, okay, places everyone," Lars said, humor still in his voice.

Over and over again, I watched as Luke put his hands on Lana and each time his hands moved across her bare flesh my hackles rose. Luke was playing his part, but each time Lana would mess up causing them to do the scene repeatedly. I wanted to scream and claw her eyes out. I had a feeling that she was doing it on purpose, but I stayed quiet and silently fumed from my spot in the back.

"Stop!" Lars called out with annoyance for what seemed like the hundredth time. "We're done here. I told you one shot for each scene. I'll work with what we got. We still have to do the next part with a wardrobe change. Let's take a short break to have a quick bite to eat and get set up. Lana, can I talk to you for a minute?"

"Of course," she purred as she made her way over walking as if she was on a catwalk. She looked ridiculous.

Luke stalked over to me, grabbed my hand, and guided me out the door. I was sure he didn't know where he was going, but I wasn't going to say anything. He'd become highly annoyed by Lana's antics about twenty takes ago and I wasn't sure what would happen if I spoke.

The one thing I did know was that Decker would have

railed on me and took all of his frustrations out on me, and I didn't want to be in the same scenario with Luke.

Keeping quiet, I rubbed my thumb over the back of Luke's hand as he stalked through the house bypassing people left and right until he found a room where we'd be alone. Instead of talking, he grabbed me by my hips and lifted me in the air, planting my butt on the bar. Pulling a stool in front of me, Luke sat, wrapped his arms around my waist and buried his face into my stomach, before he placed a soft kiss and turned his head, hugging me.

Before I'd wanted to say something about how I wasn't sure if I could handle being in a relationship with Luke if there were more days like today, and I knew there would be many more days like this in his and my future. But when his face hit my stomach and he squeezed me tight, all thoughts of not being able to handle it flew out the window. Touching Lana had been hard for him and her continuing to fuck up must have grated on his nerves. Was it hard because I had been there and had to watch?

Running my fingers through his thick hair, I took a shuttering breath. This would be our life if Luke and I worked out. I would have to watch him touch other women for his roles and women would throw themselves at him wherever we went, especially as he became more well known. *Would I be able to handle it?* I knew that if I became jealous like I had today that it would drive a wedge between us. Not once had Luke acted as if he took pleasure in what he had to do.

Luke's arms squeezed me tighter, and he turned once again to kiss my stomach. His voice was anguished when he spoke. "I know today was hard for you to watch. I could see it in your eyes, and I want you to know that was not my intention when I asked you to come with me today."

I needed him to see my face when we talked so that he could see that I truly understood. I slid off the counter and straddled Luke's lap, wrapping my arms around his neck. "I know it wasn't. I'm not going to lie to you and say that it wasn't hard because it was. I hated every moment that you touched her, but…"

"Tell me." He frowned.

I blew out my cheeks. "It was more because she was enjoying my discomfort. She wanted to make me jealous, and it worked. Big time."

"If it makes you feel any better, I think that Lars is chewing her out right now. He's not stupid. He caught onto her game and he'll make sure she doesn't pull that shit anymore, or she'll be known in the industry as a trouble maker. She wants to make the move from model to actress and this is her big chance. She's not going to want to mess that up just so she can make you jealous."

Laying my head on his shoulder, I asked against his neck. "Do you wish you hadn't asked me to come?"

"No?" he questioned then gave a small chuckle. "I want you to see what I do. I want you to be a part of my life, but I also don't want you to run away because of it."

Sitting up, I cupped his cheeks as I gazed into his cerulean eyes. "I was so excited to see you at work. If I would have known… I'm not normally a jealous kind of girl."

Resting his forehead on mine, Luke looked into my eyes for a long moment. "You know she's jealous of you, right?"

I huffed out a laugh. "Jealous of me? Right?"

"Oh girlie, girl." Lars called out from the doorway causing us to break apart. He started walking toward us with an evil grin on his face. "You have no clue, do you? You're gorgeous and I may be wrong, but she was probably planning on trying to advance her career today with her leading man, if you know what I'm saying."

My teeth gritted at the thought. "That makes me hate her all the more because he's mine."

"Oh, possessive. I like that. For once I don't think Luke minds someone claiming him."

Luke's arms wrapped tighter around me, but he said nothing as he watched his friend come closer.

"I've had a word and I've been assured that Lana will no longer have any more problems on her end, so if you're set to get changed we can hopefully finish with enough time for you to catch your flight."

"It doesn't matter if we are done or not, we'll be making our flight."

"I'm only joking, my friend. I know this is important to you and now I can see why." Lars winked at me. "You did good, my friend. You did good."

18

"HAVE YOU EVER BEEN TO MEXICO?" I ASKED LUKE AS WE RODE in the back of a town car the resort had sent for us. Everyone else had arrived the previous day, so we were alone for the time being.

He rolled his head against the headrest. "No, not Mexico. Have you?"

"When I was a child I came twice, but that was back when you didn't need a passport to enter the country. I relied on my blonde hair and blue eyes as my way to get out."

"What?" Luke asked with a laugh. His brow furrowed in confusion as he looked at me.

"I was young, probably around nine or ten, when I went with my grandparents and of course because I was so young I had no identification. When we were coming back across the border the people acted as if they weren't going to let me back in the country, so my grandfather told me to flash my pretty blue eyes at them. All I knew was that I didn't want to get stuck in Mexico, so I batted my eyes, and everyone laughed at me." A smile tipped my lips thinking back. "They let me right through."

Luke laughed again, his head thrown back against the headrest. "I want to see pictures of you back then. I bet you were cute."

"Oh, no. I don't think so." I shook my head at him as I cringed internally. "I was so not cute."

"Everyone thinks they weren't cute when they were young unless they're full of themselves and with how beautiful you are now, I know that you were cute, very cute."

"Well, you are very sweet, but you are also very wrong. I know the truth."

Pulling me closer, Luke swept his lips across my cheek until they greeted the shell of my ear where he vowed. "Baby, I'm going to tell you every day that you are beautiful until you believe me. Even if it takes until the end of my days."

Fuck, I loved him. Could he be any more perfect for me?

I interlaced our fingers and then brought them to my mouth, kissing the back of his hand. "Seriously where have you been all my life?"

Leaning down, he rested the side of his head against mine and spoke softly. "Waiting to meet you in that restaurant."

"You're going to make me cry." I started to turn my head to look out my window, but Luke stopped me.

The warmth that emanated from his eyes melted me and made me lean into his touch once again. "I won't make you cry and even if you do, it's okay." His eyes searched my face, but whatever he was looking for he didn't find. I hated disappointing him, but there was nothing I could do in that instance. "You don't have to hide from me. I'll never find you lacking. *That* I can promise you."

"I know and I'm trying. It's easier to believe the bad especially when you've heard it for so long." I let out a frustrated breath. "It's been engrained in me for so damn long that I don't know any other way, but for you I'm trying my hardest. You might have to remind me a few or a thousand times."

We both let out a laugh, but it was cut off abruptly as we stared into each other's eyes and I had an epiphany.

I had found him. The one man on the planet that was perfect for me. I was sure of it and I would not let anyone, or anything fuck it up for me. I would fight heaven and hell to keep him.

Almost like we could read each other's minds, our lips crashed in a wave of emotion too great to name. It was sweet and desperate at the same time, full of so much want and need that I was sure that if we didn't reach the resort soon, we'd get arrested for public indecency to say the least.

Luckily for us the car pulled to a stop in front of the resort before any clothes were removed. Unfortunately, we wouldn't be alone for a while because the second after we were checked in and escorted to our villa, our group was waiting for us. Even though I'd missed Anna, I was desperate for just a little more time with Luke.

"Alex," Anna called excitedly and waved from a lounger that sat outside the living area, overlooking the ocean. The view was gorgeous, and I could hear the waves crashing even from inside. It was heaven and I couldn't wait to spend the next few days basking in the sun, enjoying the pool, friends, food, and especially Luke.

"Hey!" I waved back and took in the small group of people

that were hanging out in the shade. Luckily, I'd met them all when I'd visited Anna for the fourth of July, so I wasn't too uncomfortable around them. They were all celebrities or with celebrities, but they were also just people who made insane paychecks.

Before we could make it to her lounger, Anna had sat her drink and sunglasses down on a small table and stood in greeting. Wrapping her arms around me, she hugged me tight. "I'm so happy you guys are finally here. I didn't want you to show up and everyone be gone. Plus, I don't want to overdo it in the sun. I'm not getting any younger," she said brightly, with a genuine smile that would put anyone immediately at ease.

Anna was older than I was by almost ten years, but she could easily pass for my age if not younger. She had nothing to worry about with ageing. I needed to find out her secrets and start now so I could look as good as her.

I didn't have time to respond. She quickly turned and gave Luke a small hug and then stood back with her head tilted to see him better.

"Luke, I'm so happy you could make it. I know Alex would've been sad if she only had the likes of us to hang out with."

"That's not true." I proclaimed until Anna turned toward me with her hands on her hips, her brows raised with a knowing look on her face. "Well, I would have been sad if Luke had to miss the trip because I would miss him, but I would've been happy to be with you."

"I know, honey. I was just kidding around with you. You guys are in the honeymoon phase where you can't get enough of each other."

Wrapping my arms around Luke, I rested my head on his chest and smiled at Anna. "I wouldn't quite call it the honeymoon stage, but I can definitely attest to the fact that I can't get enough of him."

"I bet you guys are married or at least engaged by this time next year."

What?!

Both Luke and I turned abruptly to Ruby, Anna's best friend for the last ten years or so. I wasn't sure of the look on his face, but I knew my mouth was gaping and that my eyes had gone wide with shock.

"Everyone knows it." Ruby said over her shoulder as she stood to walk down to the beach. "It's only a matter of time. Don't try to fight it."

Fight it? I wouldn't fight it, but I hadn't even told Luke I loved him yet nor he, I. She was putting the cart before the horse, but I had no doubt that she was right.

"Come on." Ruby angrily looked back once more. "They're here, we waited, and now I want to go to the beach."

Well, shit. It looked like I hadn't made a friend in Ruby. Was she mad that Anna had invited us on their annual vacation? My head tipped up to see Luke looking down at me with a surprised look on his face. Shrugging my shoulders, I looked back to Ruby's retreating form before my gaze went to Anna.

She watched Ruby with a frown and only turned to us once Ruby had thrown something down on a chair and took the one next to it.

"I'm sorry. I had no idea she was going to do that. Her boyfriend broke up with her right before Christmas so she's not really feeling the love, and I think she's a little jealous of you two."

I couldn't help but look back to where Ruby was sitting down on the beach by herself. "If I would've known she was going to be upset by us coming, I wouldn't have come."

"Fuck her!" Cyndi answered back as she stood and started to collect her stuff. "She'll get over it. Don't let her ruin your vacation. I know I'm not going to let her ruin mine. Besides, young love is sweet and hot." She gave us a wink before she headed to the beach to join Ruby.

"I agree," Grace said quietly as she too started to put her towel and suntan lotion in a beach bag.

I'd only met Anna's friends the one time I'd gone to visit her, but I liked them. Well, maybe not Ruby, but I liked the rest of them. They were each so different from each other but complimented each at the same time. Ruby was a bitch while Cyndi was fun and outspoken to Grace's quietness. Anna, I felt, held them all together.

Luke shifted in my hold and tightened a hand around my hip. "Maybe we should give you all some time alone before we join you."

"No," Anna answered, shaking her head. "Don't let her win. Don't let her see any defeat. Go put your stuff away if you want, change, and then join us. You deserve to be here just as much as she does. Okay?"

I nodded because what else could I do. I didn't come all this way for someone to ruin my time with Luke and Anna. I felt Luke nod too before I started to turn and head back inside.

WE'D BEEN DOWN AT THE BEACH FOR A COUPLE OF HOURS. THE girls all laid out on loungers until we got too hot and had to take a dip in the water, and the guys played volleyball with another group of men they'd found on the beach.

Ruby had kept quiet the whole time and pouted when I took my seat next to Anna, but I paid her no mind. Instead of focusing on the negative, I watched Luke and Colton with their shirts off, their muscles rippling with each movement as they got hot and sweaty. It was hard to take my eyes off Luke and his body. He was getting me hotter than the sun.

I wasn't sure when everyone else had ate, but I'd barely eaten anything since we'd gotten up early for Luke to shoot his commercial. I leaned over to Anna touching her bronzed arm.

"Hey, I'm going to go see if Luke wants to go get something to eat with me. I'm starved. I got up too early to eat much. If you need us, text me. I should have my phone on me."

Anna leaned closer to me to the point it looked like she might fall off her lounger with a worried look on her face. "Are you sure there's nothing else?" Her eyes darted toward Ruby in a silent question.

"I'm sure. I really am hungry, that's all. Do I like that she's upset with me for some unknown reason? No, but there's nothing I can do about it and I'm not letting her ruin my time here."

"Good." Her hand reached over and squeezed mine. "Don't eat to heavily. The only bad thing about coming here this time of year is the sun sets pretty early. Typically, once it starts to set, we start getting ready and then head out to dinner. I have a really cool place planned for tonight since you've never been." Her eyes gleamed with excitement causing me to smile at her.

"I look forward to it, just let me know when we should be ready." I leaned closer so that I could whisper, and she would still be able to hear me. "Who else is staying in our villa?"

"Cyndi," Anna answered with a knowing look.

Standing I looked down at Anna and waved. "Great!" After making eye contact with everyone but Ruby and giving them a wave, I made my way over to where Luke and Colton had played volleyball. Now they were all sitting around talking and drinking.

The moment Luke saw me coming their way a smile broke out across his face and he stood. It made me beyond happy to see his reaction. It felt wonderful and unbelievable, and I was going to bask in it every opportunity I had. I also didn't mind the hungry look that crossed his face as he took me in from head to toe. I had on a simple bikini that was an ombre of turquoise colors that went well with what little tan I had left from the summer.

"Hey, beautiful." He wrapped an arm around my waist and brought me to him until our bodies were flush to one another. My hands slid up from his ripped abs to his glistening chest.

"Hey, handsome. I wanted to see if you wanted to go get something to eat with me."

His eyes half-lidded, he gazed at my mouth. "I'm sure I could be persuaded to eat with a lovely lady."

With my arms wrapped around his neck, I smiled up at him. "I could really use a shower before we go anywhere. Would you like to join me?"

A throat cleared behind us before the group chuckled.

I looked around Luke's arm to see Colton trying to fight his amusement. "Alex, you didn't introduce me to your man."

"Did you not introduce yourself?" I asked, shaking my head at him while he tried not to laugh. "Luke, this is Colton." I pointed to Colt. "And Colt, this is Luke."

"Her man." His voiced sounded proud to call himself mine and I loved it almost as much as I loved him.

"My man. Now, if you'll excuse us, I need to take a shower and get some food in me."

"Sure. Have fun you guys." Colt gave us a wink while his lips twitched.

Lacing our fingers together, we walked up to our villa. "Did you have fun with the girls?"

"I guess," I replied with a shrug of my shoulders. "Ruby kind of brought down the mood. Anna and I talked a little bit, and I relaxed, but that's about it. I'm sure it would've been different if Cyndi hadn't fallen asleep."

"I'm sure. She seems like she'd be pretty crazy."

"I don't really know them. I only met the girls the weekend I met you and I kind of ditched Anna to spend time with you."

"Well, I'm glad you did otherwise we might not be here right now." Leaning down until his lips found mine, Luke pinned me to the sliding glass door that led out to our balcony.

"Do we have time for a quickie" I asked against his lips.

"No quickies for you. You went your whole life without an orgasm before me. I want it to be good for you and for you to enjoy it. Every time."

"It's very good for me. Hell, I can't get enough of you and after I sat and watched you play volleyball, it's all I can do not to jump you out here where anyone could see us. Anyway, I'm sure I could still enjoy a quickie. You're very good at pleasing me."

A wicked grin tipped his lips. "I aim to please. Now, let's get inside so I can strip that tiny bikini off you. It's been driving me crazy since the moment you put it on."

"Really?" I asked, as I snaked an arm around to undo the tie at my neck.

Luke's eyes darkened as he stepped toward me, sweeping me off my feet and carrying me to the bathroom over his shoulder. I hadn't really taken our room in when we first arrived. We'd simply put on our swimsuits and headed down to the beach.

Lifting my head from his back with my hands on his hard ass, I squeezed each cheek while I envisioned biting them.

Luke slid me down his body and my feet touched the cool tile. The bathroom wasn't as big as I expected it to be. Maybe it had something to do with how big Luke was. His broad shoulders filled the room as he stepped inside the shower and turned on the water.

To the right of me was a bathtub with candles all around it, but sadly it wasn't big enough to fit the both of us. I'd never really thought of the size of bathtubs before meeting Luke since I was short and had no problem fitting in one, but now I was annoyed that we wouldn't have the opportunity to use it.

Warm hands smoothed down my sides pulling me against his chest. "Hey, what's with the frown?"

"This tub is too small for the both of us." My bottom lip popped out, and I knew it was childish, but seriously I wanted to use it with him.

His lips found my neck and trailed kisses down and across my collarbone. "Baby, we've got that hot tub right out there. I know it's not the same, but we can still enjoy it."

"You're right. I think right now we should enjoy the shower."

Without a word, Luke untied the strings from my bikini bottom and had my top off in record time as he walked me backwards into the shower spray. At the same time, my fingers tried to untie his shorts, but they were wet and hard to get undone. Instead I tried to push them down over is hips, but they wouldn't budge.

I gave one last tug with no results. "Damn it! I need you naked."

One hand slid up my neck to cup my jaw, our lips fused together in a hungry kiss. Our teeth clashed, and my tongue tasted him, causing me to moan.

My moan grew as I felt his erection spring free from his shorts and press against my stomach. Wrapping my leg around his hip, Luke's hands lifted me up until his tip could slide along my wet folds. My arms and legs wrapped around him as I held myself up. I licked up his neck and jaw until my lips found his mouth once again and I nibbled on his bottom lip.

Stilling, Luke positioned his hard cock at my opening and thrust deep inside, filling and stretching me all in one motion.

My back arched against the cold tile of the shower wall as my body accepted every inch.

Luke flexed his fingers and dug them into my hips, as I wrapped my legs and arms around him even tighter. It took everything I had in me to keep hold and not slip as our bodies moved together in a hypnotic dance, reaching a dizzying peak before relaxing into each other.

My hand trailed across his bare chest and down to hook around his side. Closing my eyes, I relished being in Luke's arms and that we were in no hurry. "That wasn't as easy as it was at your house." I laughed and felt Luke's body shake along with mine. "That step thing in your shower is definitely needed for us and our height difference. I think that was my work out for the week."

"It was a good workout and one that I look forward to again."

"I don't know how you did it. I mean, you did most of the work and I'm spent. If you hadn't carried me to the bed, I'd still be sitting in the shower."

Chuckling, he turned and wrapped both arms around me. "I'd never leave you in the shower. And for your information, I'm just as spent as you are."

"I don't want to get up. I was hungry before, but now I could stay here with you and take a nap."

Luke hummed as he shifted his leg in between mine. "Why don't we order room service? While we wait for it to arrive we can nap and then eat in bed if we want."

"That sounds like a great idea." I snuggled closer to his body and drifted off until I felt him move from underneath me. "What are you doing? I was so comfy."

"I know." He smiled and sat down next to me. "I could hear your stomach rumbling in your sleep, so I thought I'd find the room service menu and order us up some sustenance."

"That's probably a good idea." My fingertip traced down

his arm and along the vein in his hand. Turning his hand over, I linked our fingers together. "Even after all that Chinese food last night, I feel like I haven't eaten in days. You really worked up an appetite in me."

His response was to cup my cheek before placing a soft kiss to my lips. "You do my ego well."

"I'm only telling the truth. You may need another vacation after this one because I plan to ride you every chance I get."

"Good to know we're on the same page." With that parting shot, Luke winked and left.

19

I'D QUIETLY BEEN TAKING IN THE RESTAURANT THAT ANNA wanted us to try. It was unlike anything I'd ever experienced. It was in a cave and when I heard those words, I wasn't excited. My first thoughts were it was going to be cold, dark, and dirty, but it was nothing like I imagined.

Instead, it was amazing. The space wasn't large and with the low lighting it made each table intimate, with bright and fun colors that glowed on the walls from the floor. We had a table in the very back and I'd been seated where I could see the entire place. I sat back and drank one of the best margaritas that I'd ever had while taking it all.

"So, what did you two do the rest of the afternoon?" Anna had a knowing smile on her face as her eyes kept moving from Luke, to me, and back again.

"I was tired from all the traveling yesterday and today, so we ordered room service and stayed in bed."

"Bed being the operative word here." Colt elbowed Luke.

I could feel the pink rise from my chest and up my neck

until it reached the tip of my ears. Had someone heard us when we got back to our room?

Beside me, I felt Luke's body go rigid. "Do not shame her." Luke growled. "Are you not going to fuck your wife while you're here? Do you want everyone here to give you shit or knowing looks every time the two of you walk into a room?"

Colt's eyes widened as he stared back in shock. Luke was pissed, and it only seemed to escalate as the seconds went by.

"I'm sorry, dude. I meant no harm." Colt finally managed to speak, but I wasn't sure if it was enough for Luke.

"I don't understand you American's. You're always ashamed of your body or talking about sex, unless you're making fun of someone. Do not shame her. Alex has every right to express herself in any way she sees fit and sex is a part of that."

"Luke," I called, placing one hand on his bicep in the hope to calm him down.

When he turned to me all fury was gone and only what looked like love was in his eyes. It was possible I was mistaken and only read what I wanted to see, but in that moment I hoped I was right, because it would crush me if I was wrong. "You were embarrassed." He said softly for only me to hear.

"I was." I agreed feeling silly for something that was so good and right between us. "But you're right. We're both two consenting adults and I shouldn't let what others say bother me."

"Alex." Colt cut in. "I'm sorry. I was only having fun and never meant to embarrass you. I really am sorry."

"Thanks," I replied, briefly looking at him and then turning away to take a quick sip of my margarita.

There was no reason for me to be embarrassed. I was an adult and had done nothing wrong. For the first time in my life, I was enjoying sex and wanted it with a man that I was in a relationship with, and that man wanted me just as badly. A man that I loved and who had repeatedly told me that he was in it for the long haul.

"Not all of us are European, Luke," Cyndi called from further down the table. "I'm not saying that anyone here is ashamed of their body, but yes, we are all American's and didn't grow up showing everyone our bits. We all know you've got no problem showing the world your body."

"What?" I asked looking at everyone at the table. "We do?" I had no idea what Cyndi was talking about. Had Luke gone out and flashed them or something when I'd fallen asleep earlier?

"I have nothing to hide," Luke shot back.

"Yes, we all know," Ruby condescendingly replied.

"Am I missing something here?" I asked as I looked between Luke and Ruby.

"Oh, honey, I'm sure you haven't missed an inch of him," Ruby sneered.

Setting my glass down, I squared my shoulders as I looked down the table at everyone. "What the hell is going on? I don't know what your fucking problem is with me, but we'll get to that later," I said to Ruby. I was tired of her attitude, but she'd have to wait. "What I want to know is what's behind this insinuation about Luke?"

"Honey," Anna said softly with sadness in her eyes.

I was getting frustrated and wanted to leave before I blew up at everyone and made myself look like an idiot. Taking a deep breath in, I placed both palms on the table in an effort to calm down. "Just tell me. Someone tell me what she's talking about."

"It's nothing bad." Anna started and then turned to give Cyndi and Ruby a dirty look before looking back at me. "I don't even know if it's true. It was something Ruby mentioned once she found out that the two of you were coming." She gave me a sad smile and then looked to Luke. "Like I said it's nothing bad, there are rumors that when you have to do a scene where you're supposed to be nude that you don't wear a cock sock. You just let it all hang out."

"I don't wear anything. I don't see what the big deal is. Do you wear one, Colt?"

"Yes, I do." Colton answered like it was the most obvious thing in the world.

Were they saying that Luke was running around the set naked for all to see him?

"Look at her now," Ruby laughed evilly from her end of the table.

Seriously, what was wrong with her? I'd done nothing to Ruby and barely been around her.

"I don't see what the problem is?" Luke asked with genuine confusion. "Before I came to the United States, I'd never heard of this cock sock. When asked if I wanted one I declined. I'm not ashamed of my body, and no one has ever seemed to be uncomfortable with my nudity so, what's the point?"

"So, your cock isn't swinging in the breeze for all to see," Cyndi said a little too loudly causing the few people that were close to us to look over intently.

"Oh my God, Cyndi! Hush!" Anna gave her a stern look, but quickly looked back to me. "Alex, like I said it's not a big deal. You know Cyndi is just giving you shit like she always does, and as for Ruby, well, she's upset that I invited you without asking her. But she has no say in who I invite. Colt and I are the ones paying for the villas and I want to spend my vacation with my good friends. Pay no mind to her."

"It's hard not to when everyone seems to have a problem with us." Hearing the sadness in my voice, Luke hugged me to him and placed a kiss to the top of my head.

Our food was delivered and what started out as a fun night out with friends turned into a quiet, uncomfortable dinner. No one spoke until we were ready to leave and either head back to the hotel or find a bar or club to go to.

When everyone chose to hit the town and drink, Luke and I opted to go back to the resort. I didn't want the drama, and I wanted to talk to Luke. I wasn't comfortable with the thought of his nudity on set. I couldn't get the thought out of my head of a hundred or more people on every movie or television show he was on, saw what he was packing.

"Something's on your mind," Luke said as we walked back to our villa. No words had been spoken once we decided that we would not be joining the rest of the gang. I wasn't sure if Luke was bothered by what had been said at dinner or not. He certainly didn't act like it as he looked around at everything we passed while I was stuck inside my head.

"You're not wrong."

The arm that hadn't moved from around my shoulders gave me a long squeeze before it slipped down my back and settled at my hip.

"Do you want to talk about it?"

"I do, but I'm afraid it will turn into a fight," I answered as I looked up at him.

Luke stopped in his tracks, grabbing my hand, and caused me to be pulled back and look up at him. "A fight? Why would we fight?"

Putting my hand to his chest, I answered. "Because I feel very strongly about it and I think you do too."

"We'll never know if you don't talk to me about it. Do you want to wait until we're back in our room or talk along the way?"

Turning my head, I could see the resort further down the road. It wouldn't be long before we were back in our room, and I didn't want anyone to witness either one of us getting angry or shouting. All we needed was for our first fight to be posted on social media.

"Let's wait until we get back to our room."

"Maybe we can use the jacuzzi while everyone's away and talk there."

I couldn't help but smile even though I was upset. From the moment I saw the Jacuzzi in our room that overlooked the ocean I'd wanted to use it. I had a feeling it would be used many times by us during our stay.

"I like the sound of that." I started on ahead pulling him with me. "Come on, let's go." A chuckle came from behind me causing me to smile back at him. "What?"

"You don't seem as worried."

I shrugged and continued back to our room. We didn't talk the rest of the way, but I wasn't as worried for some reason. Luke had a way about him that seemed to melt all of my problems and worries away when he was with me, even if he was the problem. I wasn't sure if that was good or bad, but for the moment I wasn't going to worry about it.

After a few minutes of having my eyes closed as I relaxed in the hot water of the jacuzzi, Luke pulled on my foot and brought me to him on the other side. It was unnerving that the hot tub stuck out making it look like you could fall out and into the sand below, but I knew that I wouldn't.

Wrapping my arms around his neck, I sat straddling Luke as I took his face in. I watched as a drop of water trailed from his forehead, down his cheek and neck, all the way down his chest, and into the water. Every time I saw Luke without a shirt on, I wanted to jump him, or anytime really. The attraction I felt for him was insane and made me wonder how I got so lucky that he ever even looked at me. The other part was that Luke treated me better than anyone had ever treated me before. Not once was he an asshole to me, and his attentiveness and the way he cared about everything I said or did was an extreme turn on.

"Are you ready to talk yet?"

I hadn't been ready to talk. It was hard to think about anything except how gorgeous he was in the moonlight and all wet.

Moving off him and facing out toward the water, I rested my chin on my arms. "I think you're the only man in the world that ever wants to talk about this sort of stuff."

"Are you the only woman who doesn't?" he countered.

"It's not that I don't want to talk about it. Once we got in here, I only wanted to ogle you. I can easily get lost in you."

"I find it hard to control myself around you too, but I also know that our time is short." His finger trailed from my shoulder down my arm and back again. "I don't want anything left unsaid when we'll be apart for a few months, especially if it's something that's better said face to face."

Laying my cheek on my arm, I looked over at him with a smile. "You're too perfect."

A light rumbling chuckle filled the air. "Is that your complaint?"

"No, you being perfect is not a complaint. It's a wonder, but let's not get lost in that conversation. I feel like I could go on and on about how you're perfect for me."

Leaning down, Luke brushed his lips against mine. Once he pulled away he murmured. "I'm glad you think so."

"I'm not sure how to bring this up. I mean, you know that I don't like something, but…"

Running a hand down my arm, his voice rumbled from beside me. "Just spit it out. I won't interrupt you, just say what you need to say."

"Okay, here it goes." Taking a deep breath, I let it out and told him what was bothering me. "I don't like the idea of you being naked on set. I understand that with many, or almost *all*, of your roles they want you to show off what you've got, and I don't blame them. Do what sells, but the vast majority in the audience doesn't need to know that you held true to the scene and didn't cover yourself up."

Luke's full attention was on me. He wasn't looking out at the water or trying to avoid this. I had every bit of him. "Is there more?"

"I feel like your penis is mine." A laugh escaped, and I

slapped a hand over my mouth. "Oh my God! That sounds so bad."

Luke shook beside me and even wiped a tear away once he had calmed down some.

"I understand your views on American's and our attitude towards nudity and sexuality, but someone or many someone's seeing you fully naked while you're working... it doesn't sit well with me. I feel like I can't ask you to not do that because you wouldn't care if I walked out to the beach with everyone there and was naked for all to see."

"If you were comfortable with everyone seeing you naked, then no I wouldn't care, but I do know that *you* would care if anyone else saw you. I would care though, if you were doing it because you wanted to make another man attracted to you, or to make me jealous."

"To me your cock is a very private part of you and I don't like it that everyone on set gets to see you like that. To know every inch and vein. I know I'm not the only person in the world who has been intimate with you and knows your cock in detail, but for hundreds of people to see it. I don't like the thought of it."

I blew out a breath and shook my head before I looked back out to the ocean and the moonlight glinting off the waves.

I could feel his eyes on me as I stared out at the water. We were both quiet for a long time before Luke broke the silence. "It does upset you greatly, doesn't it?"

Letting out a deep breath, I nodded. "It does, and it makes me feel stupid."

Slipping his fingers under my chin, he turned my head, so

that I was looking straight into his eyes. "Why on earth would it make you feel stupid?"

"Because I know that it's going to continue to bother me and it won't matter."

"Hey, what you think does matter." Furrowing his brows, his eyes penetrated mine. "Especially to me. If you want me to wear one of those flesh colored socks, then I will. It's not worth you being upset or it coming between us. I should clarify that no one is close enough to know every inch or vein, not even the actress I'm with, and when there's a sex scene the crew is very minimal." His lips twitched at the last part and I was sure mine did too. I knew it was ridiculous, but I think it helped get my point across.

"You'd really do that for me?"

"Beautiful, you'd be surprised by what I'd do for you." He leaned forward until our foreheads touched, and we were gazing into each other's eyes.

"Would you so willingly show your cock if it was small?"

Instead of answering me, he blinked as if in shock.

"Come on now, you know that your cock is big. The first time we had sex I wasn't sure how all of you would fit in me. If I hadn't been so turned on I would have been scared you were going to break me."

"We fit perfectly together. In every way." His was voice full of conviction.

"I have to agree."

God, I loved this man. I wanted to cry with how much he meant to me and that he so easily gave in to what I wanted. I somewhat understood his view on nudity even though I didn't feel the same way, but I was so happy that I wouldn't obsess over it and have it become a problem.

I leapt from where I'd been sitting, wrapping my arms around his neck and crushing my mouth to his. Our teeth clashed together before my tongue swept in searching for his. He tasted of Luke and the beer and tequila he had at dinner. He tasted perfect.

Pulling my mouth from his, I wrapped my hand around his neck as my thumb stroked behind his ear. "I have something I want to say, and I hope it's not too soon, but I can't hold it in any longer or I might burst." I smiled nervously at him and bit the inside of my lip. "Every day it becomes harder and harder not to tell you." His eyes glowed in the moonlight, staring deep into my soul, giving me the promise that he might just love me back. Taking the leap, I brushed my lips to his. "I love you, Luke."

I wasn't sure what I was expecting when I finally told him, but what he did next was definitely not it. Luke wrapped his arms around me as he stood from the water and carried me to bed without a word. I stared up at him, leaning back until my flushed skin was cooled by the satiny blanket.

One hand slid up the side of his torso to his neck and into his silky hair. I pressed my chest into his until every inch of me was touching every inch of him that I could manage.

His warm hands cupped my jaw, thumbs fanned out and caressing my cheeks as he looked down at me, eyes bright and at the same time dark with hunger.

I felt his warm breath on my lips, my eyes took them in; full, pink and parted. Perfect.

"Tell me you mean those words," he demanded, his voice rough and husky.

"I would never say them if I didn't mean them. I promise you, Luke. I love you."

His eyes moved over me, taking me in as a slow smile spread across his gorgeous face. I desperately wanted to know what he was thinking and before I could ask, he surged inside of me with one thrust.

"Oh God, Luke!" I moaned so loud I was sure that it could be heard from miles away, but in that moment, I didn't care. Luke was my sole focus as he slowly pulled out and pushed back in again and again so tantalizingly slow, I thought I might lose my mind from pleasure and the intensity of his gaze.

One hand took mine and laced our fingers together above my head while the other continued to cup the side of my face with his forearm in the bed.

Wrapping my legs tight around his sides, I followed the rhythm he had set. It was slow and sweet and unlike anything that I'd ever experienced. My head turned as I felt the tears prick my eyes and my nose start to burn.

"Alex, baby, look at me," he breathed against the hot skin of my neck right before he licked a path down and across my collarbone.

I complied instantly and got his dazzling smile in return. He rubbed his nose along mine then rested his forehead to mine. All the while he kept up the slow motion of in and out that was building me higher and higher.

His blue-green eyes, burning with intense swirling emotion, locked onto mine as he whispered against my lips. "I love you, Alex."

At his declaration my back arched, and my head flew back as a blinding wave of pleasure hit me. I wasn't sure how long it lasted. It felt like hours while at the same time only seconds. When I came down, Luke had shifted his ass to his heels with me in his lap, arms tight around me as he continued moving slowly.

Once my head cleared, I threw my arms around his neck and started to ride him, picking up the pace. What was once sweet had turned heated. Luke was mine, and I was claiming him. Just like he was claiming me.

He pulled me down with each thrust of his hips, hitting me in just the right place each and every time, causing me to moan and tighten around him once more. My body tingled and heated as a new wave of pleasure started to envelop me.

Moaning my name, Luke stilled and buried his face in the crook of my neck before letting out a long, deep groan that sent tingles down my spine. My arms held Luke close as he lowered us down to the bed.

With my eyes closed in pure happiness, I felt his body shift off and to the side of me. His hand cupped my face once again as his thumb traced my lower lip.

I opened my eyes just in time to see him bend close and brush his lips to mine. His eyes never leaving mine, he spoke softly against my lips. "It wasn't too soon."

Shifting to my side, I wrapped an arm around his waist as I nudged a leg between his. Leaning down, I placed a kiss over his heart. "I didn't want to scare you off."

"Beautiful," he dipped his head until our eyes met. "There's nothing you can do to scare me away. I've been trying to tell you that." He kissed my forehead and ran his fingers through my hair. "You've got me and you're never getting rid of me."

"I hope you're right," I replied quietly. "It would break me."

"I'll never break you. Only build you up stronger, into the woman you were always meant to be. My Alex."

"Luke," I moaned his name as I buried my face in his chest. "You're going to make me cry."

"Because you're happy?" he questioned, smoothing a hand down my hair.

"Happier than I've ever been." I said, muffled by my face still in his chest.

"Then you cry if you want to cry." He shifted out from under me. "I'll be right back. Let me get something to clean you up with."

I watched as he slid out of bed. His muscles rippled with each move and I couldn't take my eyes off his long, muscular body, his cut stomach and arms, his tight ass, and powerful thighs. My sex spasmed, I already wanted him again.

Luke was my walking, talking aphrodisiac.

I watched him again as he came back into the room with a warm, damp washcloth in his hand while I grew wetter with each movement. My eyes never left him, and I didn't care if he caught me.

He kneeled on the bed and ran the warm washcloth between my legs and it felt heavenly. My eyes closed as I let out a low moan and smiled. No one had ever taken care of me the way Luke did. Every day that passed he made me feel more treasured and precious.

A second later, I heard the washcloth hit the floor somewhere near the bathroom right before he pulled me into his arms.

"Sleep," Luke said as he kissed the top of my head.

With the drama of the day, getting very little sleep the night before, and the amazing sex we'd had, I was wiped and fell asleep feeling happy and loved.

20

"From what you've told me," I said, as I looked out the balcony doors toward the ocean. "I'd say Astrid is using you. She doesn't seem genuine in what she wants from you. I don't know if it's possible, but if I was you I wouldn't tell anyone your last name when you first meet. I don't know how common Sandström is there. If it is common, then don't say who your brothers are. That way a girl can get to know you for you, and once you know she likes you for you, then you can tell her who your brothers are."

A deep sigh filtered through the phone from the other end. "You make it sound so easy." Leo muttered in a sad tone.

"Yeah, easier said than done. I get you wanting to be yourself and not hiding anything, but people are assholes, and you've got to do what you have to, to make sure you're happy."

"I'm happy my brother found you."

"Thank you, Leo. That means a lot that you think so."

"I've never heard my brother talk about a girl he was dating like he talks about you. You're special."

I couldn't help, but smile. Leo spoke quietly, as if what he was telling me was a secret. And perhaps it was, or so he thought. Either way I already loved Leo. There was something about him that I immediately clicked with. Maybe it was a family trait and I wouldn't know until I met more of his family. I knew that Leo felt the same way since it took him all of ten minutes to start telling me about his situation with a girl and asking my advice.

"Well, I think your brother is special, and I can't wait to meet you in person."

"I'm going to come to California this summer if not sooner. I'm not sure I'll be able to with school, but if I have the opportunity, I plan to come see Luke."

"That's very sweet. I know he misses his family and I feel bad that I invited him to come on this trip when he could have gone home."

"Don't feel bad. I don't think he would have come home unless you came with him." Leo assured me all the way from Sweden.

"Really? I felt really bad because of how much he talks about missing you guys."

"I'm positive. So where did my brother run off to while he let us talk?"

"He's outside on the terrace talking to Colton." I answered, looking out at them in deep conversation.

Leo laughed down the line.

"What's so funny?" I questioned. His laughter made no sense, but it put a smile to my face none the less.

"My brother who's an actual movie star meets a girl from a small town in Missouri, and she's introducing him to one of Hollywood's golden couples. When he told me who you guys were going to Mexico with I didn't believe him at first."

"It is surreal. I never intended or thought this would be my life."

"It's funny because Luke doesn't care about the Hollywood lifestyle. He only wants to enjoy his time on set and spend time with his friends and family. He's never going to kiss Hollywood's ass for a part or to make a name for himself."

"He doesn't have to," I interrupted. "When anyone meets him, they instantly feel what a good person he is. He's so sweet and caring. Not to mention funny."

"You love my brother," Leo quietly announced with pure confidence.

"I do, but even if I didn't I'd say the exact same thing. If Luke wasn't my boyfriend, I would still want him in my life at least as my friend."

Calling Luke my boyfriend felt insignificant, juvenile and silly, but I sure as hell wasn't going to call him my lover to his brother.

"But you're glad he's not just your friend, right?" Leo laughed.

"Very glad, but I'd take him anyway I could get him. He's that great of a guy."

"Fuck, I'm glad he found you."

Tears burned at the back of my eyes from the sincerity in his voice. I wasn't sure if it was because Luke had been lonely or because his past girlfriends had been train wrecks. Either way, I was happy I was now Leo approved.

"Me too," I said, managing to keep the croak out of my voice as I swallowed it down.

"Well, I should let you go. I don't want my brother to say I monopolized all your time." It was easy to hear the smile in his voice and his love for Luke. I loved how close they were.

"I doubt that would happen, but I should probably go. There's a girl here who seems to have a problem with me and I don't want her to think I'm hiding from her."

"Do I need to come and kick her ass?"

"No, she's not happy that I was invited. I'm the new girl." I tried to explain when I didn't really understand it myself.

"It shouldn't matter if you're new or not."

"It shouldn't, but it's the only explanation except that she just doesn't like me. I've only been around her once before and she was fine then, so I don't know what it is."

"Maybe she's just a bitch."

A bark of laughter escaped causing both Luke and Colt to glance at me from outside. "Maybe, but I'm trying not to let it bother me."

"Good luck with that. I hope the rest of your vacation goes well. Tell Luke that I'll talk to him once you guys get back."

"I will, and it was so good to talk to you, Leo. I can't wait to meet you."

"You, too." He replied before hanging up.

I was sad to let Leo go, but I wanted to enjoy my time with Luke, Anna, Colt, and the Mexico sun. I knew when I got back to Missouri it was going to feel like it was subarctic in comparison.

Grabbing my book, I started out to where Luke and Colt

were sitting until I heard what they were saying and stopped dead in my tracks.

"I'm afraid of what's going to happen once her ex finds out who I am. He already makes her life miserable, she doesn't need this." Luke said softly, but not quite enough to where I couldn't hear what he'd said. His head turned to look back out at the beach and water.

"I hope you're not thinking of doing something stupid like breaking up with her so that he won't cause any problems." Colt took a large drag of his beer.

"Fuck no! I'm just trying to figure out what I can do in some preventative measure in case he becomes a problem and I'm almost two thousand miles away. If anything happened to her or Mason because of her involvement with me, I would never forgive myself," Luke uttered, his voice broken at the thought.

This time I couldn't hold back the tears that stung my eyes, and I didn't want to. My chest burned at the emotion in his voice. I didn't care if Luke or Colt saw my tears. I wanted Luke to know how much what he just said meant to me, even though he didn't know I heard him.

Without thought, my feet took me to stand beside the lounger that Luke had been sitting in since he left me to talk to his brother.

The moment he looked up at me in surprise, a lone tear escaped, traveled down to my chin and fell to the ground. The look of surprise instantly vanished, and concern was etched on his face as he took me in.

"Alex, what's happened? Is Mason okay?"

Instead of answering, I threw myself into his lap, wrapped my arms around him, and shoved my head in the crook of his neck. Luke only paused for a moment before he hugged me back, and murmuring what could only be something in Swedish because I had no idea what he was saying and one peek at Colton said that he had no clue either.

"I love you." There was nothing else I could say; my heart and body were so filled with love and happiness.

"I love you too, but that doesn't explain why you came out here crying." He answered back, looking confused and more gorgeous than I'd ever seen him. His brow furrowed with concern and confusion, and his soul gazing eyes did me in. They led right to his pure heart that I had somehow worked my way into.

"I was crying because I love you so much I literally felt like I was going to burst. I heard you talking to Colt just now."

Luke continued to look at me with confusion not understanding. Hell, I couldn't understand why I had such an intense emotional response to what he said either, but since meeting him that had been the new norm.

Clearing his throat, Colt laughed when we pulled away looking shocked to see him still sitting there. "I don't mean to break up the love fest, but I might have a solution for you."

Luke sat up straighter, with me still in his lap, giving Colt his full attention. "I'm open to suggestions."

"Anna mentioned a while back that you've been looking and saving for a new house. One that's actually in Mason's school district."

"I have, but it's been hard to find one and have a substantial enough down payment. Houses in that area go very quickly. Do you know of one that's not crazy ass expensive?"

I had no idea why I asked Colton Patrick if *he* knew of a house in Fairlane that was for sale or affordable for me. I mean, why would he? I was sure he had better things to do than watch the housing market in his hometown and even if he did, it would be way out of my price range.

"As a matter of fact, I do. Do you remember where my house was when you were there?" I felt Luke's body tense as Colt continued to talk. "There's a house in the neighborhood and it's not too far away from the elementary school that Mason goes to. I'm not sure if it's in that school zone, but since he's already going there, it shouldn't matter."

"Colt, I can't afford any of the houses in that neighborhood. Maybe if one had a pool house it would be doable." I gave a bitter laugh at the thought. Wouldn't that be lovely to live in the backyard of some rich person?

"I think you can afford it. I actually know you can, because I own every house in the neighborhood. The only people who live there are friends and family and before you say you can't afford it again, hear me out. No one who lives there has paid full price on those homes except for me. My family and friends who live there don't have the money it would take to buy the house they are in without it taking a serious chunk of change out of their pockets, and I don't want that." His eyes moved from me to Luke. "I wanted to provide the houses that I thought my family deserved to live in when they wouldn't take my money to buy one for them outright. So, I bought a huge piece of land and developed a gated community where I knew my family would be safe from people trying to find me or use them. Right now, there are three houses that are vacant, and no one has ever lived in them. I'd like to offer you one at a reasonable price."

I looked to Luke to see that he had a blank look on his face. It seemed he'd be no help. Why was he acting strange all of a sudden? Was he only acting this way, so he wouldn't influence me?

"I don't know. It feels like charity to me and although it might take me longer than I want it to, I'll eventually move."

Colt sighed and looked to Luke for what looked like help, but Luke continued to sit like a statue. "Would you feel better if I told you the price I had everyone else pay for their houses? I promise you it wasn't a dollar either. They all felt the same as you do right now."

"At least they're your family."

"I have friends who live there too. And you're my friend, Alex. I want to help you out. I know that if you could you'd probably be moving to LA, and if Luke wasn't so busy he'd be in Fairlane."

"Can I think about it?"

"Sure, why don't I give you two some time and we'll talk before we have to leave. Sound good?"

"Yeah, sounds good."

As Colt started to walk away, Luke called out to him. "How much did your friends and family pay?"

Colt's smile grew in the few steps he took as he walked back to us. "Fifty thousand dollars."

It was too much and not enough all at the same time. I knew those houses would sell for at least half a million in our little town. It was a steal (literally) and I didn't have that much money saved up.

The second Colt was out of ear shot, I moved over onto his lounger facing Luke. I wanted to know what had happened with him. Why had he remained quiet until the very end and why was he so stiff?

"What was that?" I asked after a few moments of silence.

"What was what?" Luke looked away from watching Colt to me.

"You playing statue," I replied, annoyance clear in my tone. He knew exactly what I was talking about.

"For a moment, I was jealous and wasn't thinking." Shaking his head, Luke turned to sit facing me on his lounger. "I forgot everything I knew for a split second. I don't know why, and in that second I thought maybe something had happened between the two of you."

"What?!" I nearly shrieked. "How did you forget that he's married to Anna? Did you think he cheated? That I would do that?"

"No, no! It was stupid, I know. Like I said, it was a momentary lapse in thinking." Taking my hand in his large one, he started to rub his thumb nervously over the back of my hand. "Fuck, Alex, don't be mad at me. Please." His eyes deepened into a dark storm, begging for me to let this go.

"Tell me why you didn't relax when he continued on. Why did you sit there like that the entire time, making me wonder what the hell was going on with you?"

"Because I'm human and stupid," he answered back, looking sadder by the second. "I didn't know what he was going to say, but I didn't want to influence your decision, so I stayed quiet."

"You didn't want to influence my decision? Do you know what one of the first things I thought of was when Colt was telling me about the house?"

Eyes on me, they never wavered. "No."

"It was that I wanted to talk to you and see what you thought because for some crazy reason, I thought if you were going to be in my life that I should discuss things of that magnitude with you. Obviously, I was wrong. I at least wanted to talk it out with you and get your advice."

Resting his elbows on his knees, Luke kept hold of my hand, while leaning forward and bowing his head until it was almost between his knees.

"I'm sorry I fucked up. It never crossed my mind that you'd done something with him. It was…" he took a deep breath and lifted his head until we were eye to eye. "I thought maybe he tried to hit on you or something of that nature. It was an irrational thought, and I was jealous. I'm not normally a jealous man and I hate that I was in that moment. It seems we bring it out in each other."

"I… I don't even know what to say. Do you trust me? That I would never cheat? Or be a part of someone else's cheating?" I tried to pull my hand away but Luke only held tighter, until he saw the hurt etched on my face.

"I don't know how to make this right. I wish I could go back in time and not have that reaction. Please, tell me what I can do." His eyes begged.

I had no idea what he could do to make this better so instead of answering him we sat in silence.

"I can't fucking believe this," Luke murmured. I wasn't sure if he meant for me to hear him, but I had.

"What is it?" I asked wanting to run back into our room so that I could be alone and think.

"Five minutes ago, you were crying because you loved me and now you don't even want to be in the same space as I am."

"I still love you, Luke. That hasn't changed."

"But something has?" The lost look in his eyes made me want to cry and hug him to me, but I needed time to cool off, so I didn't do or say something we'd both regret.

"Only the fact that I was bursting with love a few minutes ago and now I'm upset. I need some time to cool off." I held my hand up in a stop motion at the look on Luke's face. He wanted to say something or talk it out right now. Either way, I needed to wait. "Please give me some time."

"I don't have much of a choice." His Adam's apple bobbed as he swallowed. "I'll be here when you're ready to talk. I'm sorry, Alex."

"I know. I'm sorry, too. I'm going to go down with the girls and chill out while I think. You don't have to stay up here. You could hang out with Colt."

"Maybe later, but right now, I wouldn't be very good company." He sat looking up at me with his eyes glistening. It took everything in me not to curl up in his lap and try to make him feel better.

Halfway down to the beach I looked back to see Luke still sitting where I left him. Instead of looking gorgeous and sexy with his skin bronzed from the sun, his chest bear with his swim trunks riding low on his hips, I could only think about how sad he looked. Even from afar, I could see that he was miserable.

How was I going to fix this?

Are you dying to find out what Alex is going to do?
Find out today with Hollywood Fairytale.

21

MISERABLY I DRUG MYSELF DOWN TO THE BEACH. I'D LEFT MY heart with Luke, but I needed this time to breathe and think. I was too upset to talk rationally and I knew that my old defenses would come into play if I stayed and tried to talk.

About halfway down, I looked back to find him missing from the balcony. How badly had I fucked things up with the best thing that had ever happened to me?

Luke didn't deserve anything but the best of me. Not the irrational side that would yell and likely say something I'd regret. The look on his face when I walked away nearly killed me.

I needed to remember that taking this time would be for the best.

Sitting down on a lounger next to Anna, I looked out at the water. I loved hearing the sound of the waves crashing, but even they couldn't stop my heart from aching.

"Is everything okay?" I wasn't sure how long I'd been

sitting there not saying a word. Maybe they thought it was because of Ruby that I was keeping quiet.

"No," I shook my head and continued to look out at the water.

"Do you want to talk about it?"

"I don't know." I answered truthfully.

"Why don't we go up to the pool and talk? We don't have to talk about what's bothering you if you don't want to," Anna said as she stood gathering a few of her things. "Where's Luke?"

Looking to where I'd left him, Luke was nowhere in sight. "He's back in our room."

Since I'd forgotten everything I was planning on taking down to the beach, I waited for Anna to tell everyone that we'd be back before I followed her up to the pool at our villa.

We waded in silently and didn't stop until we were each at the edge with our arms crossed on the ledge, looking out at the ocean once again.

Anna didn't pressure me to talk. Instead she seemed content to stare out at the ocean and wait until I decided if I wanted to talk.

"I don't normally open up to people about my problems," I confessed after we'd been there for quite some time.

"Most people are like that, but when someone is your friend, you should be able to talk to her and hopefully she can help you. If not, the least she can do is listen."

I thought about what she said for a minute and realized she was right. I did want to talk to her and see what she thought about the house and what Luke had thought. I told her everything. From Luke buying a house, hearing Luke talking to

Colt, to how I needed some time because I didn't want to over-react or say something I'd regret.

"That's an awful lot to take in." She finally said with a sympathetic glance. "It was probably wise that you gave you and Luke a little space even if it hurt you both."

"He looked so sad," I responded, my chin quivering.

"Because I truly believe he was sorry. It was a knee jerk reaction. At least he told you the truth when you asked him. We're all human and we're going to make mistakes. You're going to fight every once in a while, honey."

"I know it's normal, but it brought back the horrible feelings of being with Decker. All the fighting and the way he changed almost instantly when we moved in together. I told Luke I loved him last night, and he loves me back. I don't want to ruin what we have."

"Of course, he does. I've known it since the moment I saw the both of you when you got here."

"I never thought I'd feel love again in that way or that I'd find a good man who'd want me. He's perfect for *me*, but I need to realize that not everything is going to be perfect for *us*. Being with Luke here has been wonderful and to know that he loves me now… I already knew the next few months were going to be tough, but now I don't know how I'm going to cope with missing him."

"I can tell you it's not easy and it will test your relationship. It's hard enough when you're in the same time zone but with the time difference it will make it harder."

"I've had a little taste and the time difference definitely made it difficult. I know that Luke's going to have long hours and we'll just have to make time for each other. It'll be a lot harder this time."

"Well, you know that if you want to talk, I'm here for you. I've been through it all and had my share of failed relationships because of what you're going to go through. And with the Ashlyn bullshit you know that you can't believe everything people or the media say. You know you can trust Luke."

"I know I can. He could have easily lied to me earlier."

"Exactly. It would have been easy for him to do that, but he told you the truth even though it hurt you both.

"Someday Ashlyn is going to mess up and get caught. Until that day happens, you have to continue to document the things you know about. She's crazy, and you have to watch out for her."

"I don't worry about her too much. I know everything she says is a lie and that Luke's telling me the truth. I don't doubt him. If it was anyone else I would, but not him. That probably sounds stupid."

"No," she answered back with a sweet smile. "I don't think it's stupid. My advice is to talk to Luke. *Always*. Tell him how you're feeling. Don't let it come between you."

"I know. I didn't want to ruin our trip, but I'll talk to him."

"Good. Now about the house."

Groaning, I ran my hands through the water. "Yeah, about the house."

"What Colt said is true. Everyone who lives there paid a fraction of the cost of what their houses are worth."

"It still doesn't feel right, but I also know I'll never get another offer like this. I'm going to talk to Luke about it."

"You're thinking like a couple and that's always a good thing."

"Yeah, that's one thing I learned from Decker. It was always about him, and I don't want to follow those same foot-steps. I would've happily discussed matters with Decker if he'd been willing."

"You won't sweetie. There will be times when it'll be hard, but you know what you need to do. Just talk to Luke like you want to now."

Smiling sadly over at her, I spoke. "I'm glad you have such faith in me. Now let's talk about something else." I laughed and looked back out at the ocean.

Anna laughed her soft laugh and put her wet hand on my arm. "Maybe later. Right now, I think you should go talk to Luke. You're both hurting and only you have the ability to stop it. Do what you need to do, and I'll be here when it's all over. Well, not right here because I'd be a shriveled up, pruny mess, but I'll be around."

Turning, I gave her a hug before I started to make my way back across the pool. "Thank you, Anna." I called over my shoulder.

"Anytime and don't hurry back." She gave me her girl next door smile and winked at me ruining the innocence in her smile.

22

LUKE'S EYES LIT UP THE MOMENT I WALKED INTO OUR ROOM. HE sat up moving to the edge of the bed. "Are we okay?"

Tears burned my eyes as I made my way over to him and by the time I was standing in front of him, one lone tear was trekking down my cheek.

"Baby," Luke choked out, wrapping his arms around me and laying his head against my chest.

"It's okay," I whispered into the top of his head. My fingers threaded through his hair while my other hand cupped the side of his neck. "We're okay."

Pulling his head away, he looked up at me devastated. "I'm sorry."

"I'm sorry, too. I should've stayed and talked to you, but I was afraid of what would be said and my old behaviors from dealing with Decker would come out. I don't want to fight with you, but I realized that we're going to. We're not going to agree on everything, but we need to talk through it and not let it get in the way of *us*."

"You came to that realization while you were at the beach?" he smirked at me.

"Kind of, Anna and I went to the pool and talked, but it was more like she was telling me what I already knew. I... I've always thought you're perfect for me and in my head, I thought we wouldn't fight. Now I know that even though you're perfect for me, we're going to fight if we're together. Its life. I was scared that if we fought, we'd somehow turn into Decker and me."

Pulling me closer, he shook his head. "No, baby. We'll never be anything like you and Decker. I promise you."

"I hope you're right." I laid my head on top of his. "I don't want my baggage to ruin this." I let out a deep breath that felt like I'd been holding it since we walked down to the beach. "We need to talk."

"We are talking." He shot back.

"I know." I laughed out. "But I want to talk to you about Colton's offer. About us."

Tilting his head to the side, Luke had a look of confusion on his face. "What about us?"

"After shooting this season of Night Shadows, you'll still have two more years left on your contract. They might even want you for more, you never know."

Moving back further on the bed, he patted the space beside him. Crawling onto the bed, I looked over at him. "What does that have to do with us?"

"I guess I want to know where I fit in. As much as I want to be with you, I live in Missouri and there's no way in hell that Decker is ever going to let me move away with Mason. Night

Shadows takes up a quarter of the year and then you film a movie or two before filming the next season."

"I don't have anything set to film after this season. Nothing has felt right, and I want to spend time with you and Mason."

Taking another deep breath, I tried again to get out what I wanted to say even though I was afraid of what his answer might be.

"Okay, I guess what I'm saying is I don't want to be apart any more than we have to be. You bought a house for me to stay in LA which is amazing. You know I love the house and I can't wait to spend more time in it with you."

"Do you think I don't want the same thing? Christ, Alex, it already hurts knowing how much I'm going to miss you while we're apart."

"I know you do, but when? I don't want to wait two more years. You tell me you're never going to let me go and that you miss me, but living long distance for years is not ideal. I heard a little of what you said to Colt and I'm seriously thinking of taking him up on his offer to buy a house in that neighborhood, but I want to talk to you first. I guess what I'm asking is where do you see this going?"

He chuckled and knocked his shoulder into mine. "Now you're being the girl wanting to talk about feelings and all that." He joked, his face becoming serious before taking my hand in his. We both looked down at my small hand dwarfed by his large one. "I was going to talk to you about all this once I had some answers, but I see that we need to do it now before you drive yourself crazy wondering. First, I was waiting until you told me you loved me. Now that I'm one hundred percent positive you feel about me the way I feel about you, not that I was really questioning it, I want to talk to H@T and the director to see if they'll change the filming schedule to start in the summer. That way you and Mason can be in LA with me while I shoot most of it.

"Once the season is finished filming, I can come to Fairlane, if you want me to. Tell me if I'm wrong."

"You're not wrong. I want you there, but I'm worried that Fairlane isn't exciting enough for you."

"Fairlane has you. We'll make our own excitement." He countered. "I don't know if I can promise you that they'll change the shooting schedule for Night Shadows, but I'm going to try my hardest and I hope that they'll understand."

"Understand what?"

"That I fell in love with you and it will kill me to be apart from you."

"Luke." Kneeling on the bed, I brushed my lips across each of his eyes, his nose, chin, and finally across his soft lips.

"In a year we'll be married and maybe one day we'll have a baby." His lips brushed mine with each word.

Oh my! That was more than unexpected.

"Are you proposing?" I squeaked out, my eyes wide with excitement and surprise.

He shook his head with a lop-sided grin on his face. "You'll know when I propose and now is not it."

"But you're going to propose?" I asked with what I knew was a silly smile on my face.

"One day, but you won't know when. I know you've said that there's a possibility that you'd never get married again unless you found the right man…"

He wanted to know if he was the right man and if I'd say

yes. There was no doubt in my mind that he was the right man for me and I would most definitely say yes. I would scream it from the rooftops and the highest mountain.

"I found him. I don't think you've got anything to worry about."

"That's good news." His smile reached his eyes lighting up his face and my soul. "So, you're thinking of taking Colt up on his offer?"

Talk about a subject change. Did he not want me to ask questions?

"Thinking about it. I know I'll never get offered a house that's worth that much for only fifty-thousand dollars. It's too good of an opportunity to pass up."

"But?" he asked, his smile fading.

"It feels like charity and like I'm taking advantage of him at the same time. But I think it's the right move. I don't need any crazies coming up to my house and scaring Mason, and it should keep Decker away at least for a little while. Once he knows that I moved though, he'll be giving me lots of shit, but I can handle it."

"He won't be able to get through the gates. I don't know this neighborhood, but that's why gates are there. Although there are ways to get around them. Hopefully, he isn't that smart."

"Hopefully, but I won't underestimate him and his need to make my life miserable."

"I won't let that happen." Wrapping an arm around my shoulders, Luke pulled me into his side. "So," he drew out the word nervously. "I'd like to help you pay for the house."

"I can't let you do that," I replied instantly.

His brows furrowed. "Why not?"

"Because until recently you didn't even own a house and now you're going to buy two?"

"The house in Fairlane is the price of a car. It's not going to break the bank and it will be worth it. You and Mason will be safer and in a bigger house. A house that I plan to live in with both of you. I want to do this. I want to help."

Shaking my head, I looked to him. "I don't like this. I've been saving to buy a house since I left Decker. It means something to me."

"I know it does and I'm not trying to belittle you, or what you want. Let me ask you a question. If we were married would you have a problem with me buying the house for us?"

"No, I guess it wouldn't. Would you have a problem with me buying the house?"

His eyes widened. "No, why do you say that?"

"Because I was going to buy it. I've been saving and you saying you'll buy it makes me feel like what I've been doing is insignificant."

"That was not my intention at all. Alex, I want to help. I want you to keep your money and keep saving if you want. Those tickets that you bought me to Hawaii weren't cheap. I… I don't know how to say this without you taking offense so please know I'm saying it with the best intentions. You work hard. In my opinion too hard sometimes, and I want you to be able to live easier and not worry about saving money to buy a house and feeling like you can't buy Mason something he wants. I know you deprive yourself. I want you to live easier that's all. Think if our roles were reversed. You can understand that can't you?"

I did understand, and I knew that if the shoe were on the other foot, I'd want the same thing he did.

"Yeah, I understand that, and I appreciate it more than you know. I'm not poor. I mean compared to you and everyone out there." I pointed out to the beach. "I'm poor. I don't have hundreds of thousands of dollars, let alone millions, but I do have some money."

"Baby," Luke laughed. "I'm poor compared to everyone out there. Don't feel bad or like you have to compete. If you do, it will only make you miserable. Just be you and be happy with yourself."

"Yeah," I hugged him and kissed the dimple in his chin.

"Now, if we're done talking about how we're going to try to live the rest of our lives together, I'd like to get to the makeup sex."

A laugh escaped, my eyes wide. "I've heard it can be quite good."

"I think we should find out." Luke husked out as he leaned into me with a lascivious smile on his lips. We descended until he was flush against me, his legs tangled in mine, and our hands intertwined above my head.

23

LUKE

"IS EVERYTHING OKAY NOW BETWEEN THE TWO OF YOU?" ANNA asked as I took my place on the lounger next to hers.

I nodded and let out a deep breath. "Thanks for talking to her."

"Honey, she would have come to the same conclusion whether I talked to her or not. The only thing I did was maybe speed up the process."

"Either way, I'm still thankful. I don't know how much longer I could've taken not knowing. For a little while there I thought she might be done with me. Decker fucked her up in so many ways that still affect her."

"Exes will do that to you and when it's made public it's even worse."

Internally I flinched. From what Alex had told me about her ex when he found out about us it wasn't going to be good. I could easily imagine him going to a tabloid and selling his story with lies he could dream up that would wreck her the most. He'd do anything to hurt her and I'd do anything to protect her.

"I don't see good things happening when he finds out about us."

Anna looked at me with sadness. "You're worried."

"I am. That's what I was speaking to Colton about when he offered her the house. Hence the fight. Well…"

Giving a grimace, she turned to look out at the water. "It's complicated. Let's leave it at that."

"Alex told you?"

Knowing how much Alex liked Anna, I hoped that Anna, and by extension Colt, wouldn't hold my stupid thought against me.

"Hey," she called quietly, placing her hand on my arm. "Don't worry about it. You don't know Colt and sadly we know how things are in this business. Rarely are couples faithful with long distances keeping them apart, thinking they can get away with it, the egos that are involved, and in your and Colt's case having women throwing themselves at you all the time. But I know that Colt's one hundred percent faithful." She drew in a breath and then a mischievous smile spread across her face. "If he wasn't, he knows that I'd chop off his balls."

Anna and her ex-husband Kevin's divorce was very public. The media wouldn't leave them alone, especially when the world found out that Kevin had been cheating on Anna on just about every film set he'd been on since they'd met. "Yeah, the ex and public."

"Kevin made it hard for me to trust again, and after what Decker put Alex through and then Matt, she's got baggage. It's hard for her to trust anyone with her heart. We've all got baggage, but what I am certain of is that she trusts you not to be them. It would hurt for you not to trust her."

Did Alex think that I didn't trust her? I needed to make sure she knew that I trusted her implicitly.

"I trust her. I trust her with my life. With my heart. With my soul."

A smile lit up her face. "You love her."

"More than anything."

"I'm sorry about Ruby." Her change of subject so abruptly caught me off guard. "Normally there's not this much drama. It's all drinking and lying on the beach soaking up the sun."

"How were you to know?"

Anna shrugged, shaking her head. "I don't know, but I don't think either one of you will want to come next year." She gave a bitter laugh looking over at the other girls. "You should go be with Alex. Enjoy this beautiful place and each other."

"I will. We will. I left her so that she could talk to Mason and not feel rushed. She won't say anything, but she misses him and worries about him when he's with his father."

"Go be with her and tell her that you love her. Don't worry about us. I promise that Colt and I won't hold it against you."

"How much do I owe you?" Humor laced my words.

"Oh you!" She swatted her hands at me. "Don't be silly. Just go be happy."

I stood towering over her thankful for her therapy sessions with both Alex and me.

~

"CAN YOU RUB THIS ON MY BACK? I DON'T WANT TO GET burned." Alex held out her sunblock. My gaze had been transfixed as she rubbed the lotion on her legs, and across her chest. I was hard as I moved behind her, nudging my erection in her back.

Squeezing a glob out, I rubbed my hands together to warm the cool lotion before I placed them on her sun kissed skin. Slowly I massaged her back making sure every inch was coated. She hadn't done her arms, so I leisurely started at her shoulder and worked my way down to the tips of her fingers. She moaned making me harder. We needed to get into the water before someone caught a photo of me dry humping her from behind.

Wrapping my arms around her, my voice was rough at her ear. "Hey, beautiful, how about we get into the water?"

Looking back at me over her shoulder, she smiled softly. It struck me then how much I'd missed her smile and having her in my arms in the month we'd been apart. I didn't want to think about how hard it was going to be the next couple of months with my busy schedule.

"Let's go, handsome. Even in December it's hot here."

With her arms wrapped around my neck and her legs around my hips, Alex leaned her head back into the water. Her hair fanned out all around her like a blonde halo making her look like an angel. Her smile was radiant as she looked up at me with love in her eyes.

Closing her eyes, she spoke quietly as she came up out of the water. "I love the water and the sound of the waves. This is perfect. The best of both worlds. No sharks, but still the smell, the gorgeous water out in front of us, the sounds, and best of all, you."

Kissing her forehead, I murmured against it. "I'm glad you think so."

Placing her head on my shoulder, she spoke against my neck. With each word her warm breath tickled my skin causing my cock to ache. I desperately wanted to take her again even though it had only been a couple of hours since I last had her, but there were too many people around.

"Thank you for coming here with me. For giving up going somewhere cold so I could have this."

"It's not a hardship, Alex." I let out a small chuckle. "I know I said I like the cold, but it's not as if I'm going to melt."

She laughed, squeezing me tighter.

Turning, I kissed the top of her head as I ran a hand down her back until it cupped her ass cheek. We both groaned as I pushed her into my aching erection.

I would never figure out what her fucking ex's problem was because when I touched Alex, she lit up like a firework and was so responsive. I thought it would take me weeks or maybe even months for her to open up to me sexually after what she told me she'd been through with Decker. Instead she instantly blossomed at my touch. How could he ridicule her for the things he asked her to do? How could he not give her the same pleasure he expected from her?

Now we were like two teenagers who couldn't get enough of each other.

"How are we going to work out?" She asked out of nowhere.

Where the fuck had that come from?

"What?" I choked out unsure if I hid the hysteria that was rising inside of me.

Her fingers tangled with the hair at the nape of my neck calming me some, but not enough to take me off edge. "Someday I want to live on the beach and you want to live in Antarctica." Her grip on me loosened as she yawned.

"My beautiful girl, I don't want to live in Antarctica." I couldn't help the chuckle that escaped at her crazy statement. "I simply want to spend time in my homeland and visit a place or two that are not beaches and are mildly cold. If one day you want to live on the beach, then one day we will live on a beach, and maybe one day you'll agree to vacation somewhere that's not tropical."

"You're too good to me and of course I'd go wherever you wanted to go. Within reason."

I couldn't help but laugh. One of the reasons I loved her was how often Alex made me laugh. "Of course, within reason."

Alex responded, but her voice faded out when I caught sight of a flash of light in the bushes that surrounded the outer edge of the pool area. Had it been a camera?

I moved so that my back was to the wall of the infinity pool that way Alex could look out at the ocean and I could keep my eye on those around us. We were in the big pool area so that we could take advantage of the bar that was in the pool itself. Alex thought it was fun and who was I to deny her. But it meant we were not alone, and anyone could be watching us or taking pictures.

I didn't want to alarm Alex if I didn't have to. She knew that there was always a possibility that our picture could be taken, but she was always in the now. Always acting as if it was only her and I, and I loved that about her. I didn't think she minded the pictures, but I didn't want the world to scrutinize our relationship.

Alex was the first person that I'd dated that didn't care that I was an actor. In all truth, being an actor probably didn't help, and I worried that one day something would happen that would make her think twice about being with me and possibly leave.

The bushes moved by where we'd laid our towels out on a couple of loungers. A hand snaked out to the table only to then withdraw quickly back into the shrubbery.

What the hell! Had someone took something of ours?

It wouldn't be the first or probably the last time if someone had stolen something from me. That was why I usually never left anything out in the open, making me wonder what the hand I'd spotted had been doing?

Alex's worried face popped into my vision. Her hand rested on my cheek as her eyes took me in.

"What's wrong?" Her mouth turned down as I shook my head and let my eyes sweep the area once more. Her hand pressed against my chest making me stop and look down at her. She had been sleepy, but now she was worried and for some reason sad. "Luke don't lie to me. If you want me to trust you, you have to trust me. It's a two-way street."

My throat dried up so much that I could feel my Adam's Apple bob with each swallow. Turning away I looked down at her and saw that she was hurt. I'd done that to her by trying to protect her, and I knew that I needed to tell her the truth or eventually I'd lose her.

"I do trust you. I only wanted to protect you."

Her brows knit together as she looked over my shoulder. "From?"

"I thought I saw a flash from a camera."

"Oh," her mouth stayed in the 'O' as she looked around and then started to squirm out of my grasp. "I didn't know that we were still hiding what we are." She swallowed what looked like a rock in her throat before she placed her hands on my chest and started to push. Tears welled up in her eyes.

"Alex, baby. No," I shook my head. How had she mistaken me so badly? "We are not hiding anything. Never again will I hide who you are to me and what you mean to me."

"I don't understand then."

"I wasn't trying to hide that we're together. I... I don't know if I saw anything or not, but I worry that one day it's all going to be too much for you and you're going to leave me."

Her arms tightened around me, her face warring with emotion before she closed her eyes for a brief moment. When she opened them again, they were clear and resolved.

"I trust you. That should be no surprise to you with all the shit that Ashlyn Jade has been spewing about you." She sputtered but continued with fire in her eyes. "Never once did I think what she said was true." With her voice rising, she vehemently cried. "Not once. Do you understand me, Luke Sandström?"

"Yes." I didn't get another word in before she kept going.

"You've got to have faith in me that I know whether or not I can live your life with you. You are worth whatever stands in our way unless *you* do something to fuck this up. If I thought for one minute that I wouldn't be able to handle the stress of being with you then I wouldn't be here. I would never lead you on like that. I would never have let Mason meet and become attached to you."

She meant every last word, and it rocked me to my core.

"Fuck, Alex," I growled deep and low. My lips only an inch from hers. "I want to be inside of you so badly right now."

"What's stopping you?" She asked her voice turning breathy in an instant, her hands ran up my chest to my shoulders.

"The fact that we're out in public and I don't want to be arrested in Mexico."

"Mmhmm," she purred against my ear. "You make a fine point. This was nice and all, but I think we need to go back to our room now." She said the last as she ground her hips with mine. "Can you walk out of here?"

"Not if you keep rubbing against me like that." Even then I would be sporting some sort of wood, but that seemed to be the case anytime Alex was near. There weren't that many people around, so no one should notice in the short amount of time it would take to wrap a towel around my hips and get up to our room as quickly as possible.

"Maybe you should put me down then." She flashed me a smile as I released her only to then grab her hand as we made our way out of the pool and over to what little stuff we'd brought down.

My steps faltered when I saw on the table a note in bold marker with the word, 'CHEATER' on it. I only stopped for a second before I grabbed the note and crushed it in my hand, all the while looking around the area. Who had left this here?

I could feel Alex's breath against my arm as she clutched it with her free hand, but she didn't say a word as I picked up our towels and started to make our way back to our suite.

There was no worry about my erection as we made our way through the crowd at the intersection that took you from the pool to either the main hotel, the outdoor restaurant, or the private houses that we were staying in. The moment I saw that note it was gone, and only left fury in its place.

Just as we made it passed the crowd and down the path to our place, I spotted a woman who was way too skinny to be healthy, with medium length brown hair and brown eyes looking back at me with a smirk on her face. It wasn't just any woman. It was Ashlyn.

This woman was trying to ruin the best thing that had ever happened to me and I had no clue why. I'd only met her a couple of times and spoken just as many words to her. My vision went red and my feet started moving against the hot concrete. I felt nothing but my rage. The only thing on my mind was to stop her from spreading her lies, trying to ruin me, and what I had with Alex.

"Luke! STOP!" Alex appeared in front of me, her hands on my chest pushing me backwards. "You can't do whatever's going through your head right now. This is what she wants." Her eyes widened as if she knew what I wanted to do. "Think of what will happen. Please!" She begged, pushing with all of her might to stop me in my tracks.

I kept moving forward, my only agenda to stop Ashlyn until I heard Alex squeal and start to fall. Without thought, I swept Alex into my arms as if she were my bride, turning in the direction of where we were staying. I no longer cared about what Ashlyn was trying to do and only wanted to make sure Alex was unharmed.

"Luke! What the hell is going on?" she whisper-yelled, looking alarmed.

Instead of answering, since I'd already drawn enough attention, I focused on getting us back and keeping my cool.

Once we were in our room, I sat Alex down on her feet and then quickly closed the door and all the curtains and blinds.

Walking back, Alex watched me with unblinking eyes. "Will you please tell me what's going on? You're scaring me."

Kneeling down in front of her, I took her small hands in mine. "I'm sorry, baby. I never meant to scare you. I lost my head there for a minute and I wanted to regroup and make sure no one could see or hear us."

"But why? One moment we were coming back here to jump each other and the next thing I know, you…"

"I lost it. You know how I was telling you about how I thought I saw a camera flash?"

"Yeah, of course, I remember."

"I had my eyes on the area and I saw a hand reach out from the shrubbery next to the table that was between our two chairs. It was there one-second and gone the next. I got distracted with your gorgeous body against mine and your words, but when we got to our stuff, there was a note on the table."

"Okay? This started you acting weird?" She asked with a small amount of uncertainty in her voice.

"It was Ashlyn Jade. When we were coming back here, I saw her in the crowd watching us with a smirk on her face, and I knew that it was her that put the note on the table. God knows what else she's done since she found us. There's a good chance that she posted more pictures on the internet of her with me in the background, and possibly you too. There's got to be something to make her stop. I'm going to contact my publicist to see if there's anything that can be done, or if I should put out a statement."

"There's got to be something we can do. Its slander against your character." Her sweet face became red, her eyebrows drawn in anger. "Maybe you need to set up your own social media account and post some pictures of your own, showing you're not with her and that she's lying. Hell, I don't know. Up until recently, my life has been pretty boring, so I haven't had anything to post. I only have a Facebook account."

"I'll talk to Sarah and see what she says, but she's been trying to get me to open up at least one account for years, so she'll most definitely be on board with me posting pictures. Will you do it with me? If I'm going to start, I want you to be a part of this with me."

She blinked up at me a few times before speaking, unsure of what I wanted. I didn't even know what I wanted since I hadn't been a part of the social media world. "Of course."

She was with me no matter what. Even if she didn't know what I wanted. Even if I didn't know what I was asking.

24

WE WERE BACK IN LA, IN LUKE'S NEW HOUSE, A NEW BED, AND IN the morning, I'd be headed back to Missouri where I wouldn't see Luke again until March. I already missed him, and he wasn't even out of my sight yet. I didn't know how I was going to get through the next couple of months.

My head rested on his shoulder, my arm draped around his waist. "I don't want to go home tomorrow." There was no hiding the sadness in my voice, but I was determined not to ruin our last night together by being miserable. "I want to stay in this bed with you forever."

Luke's arms squeezed me tight as he threw a heavy leg over my hip, cocooning me in his embrace. I was plastered to his body and if I got any closer, we'd be fused together.

One.

Maybe that was the point. Either way, I liked it and cherished being in his arms during those last moments before we were separated.

His chest rose as he took in a deep breath. "I know. I wish

time could stand still even for a little while so that I could have more time with you."

I knew that being away from each other wouldn't only be hard on me. Luke would miss me, and with the way he was clutching me and the sadness in his tone, he was feeling it too. I rubbed up and down his back as I nestled my head between his pecs. "I wish you could come home with me. I'm not ready to give you up yet."

We were both quiet for a few moments. I stared at the ceiling, watching the shadows from the pool dance while I continued to rub Luke's back, when he broke the silence.

"I could go back with you."

"What?" I asked jerking my head back to look up at him almost clipping him in the chin.

"Filming doesn't start until the third week of the month. We can look at the house together and I can be there if Decker tries to cause a problem. While you're working, I could be learning my lines or visiting the gym." He stopped, a thoughtful look took on his gorgeous face. "I could work from there. It would give us another week together. It wouldn't be long enough, but it's more time."

Sitting up on the bed, I bounced with excitement maybe pulling out of his arms to get a better look at him. "Are you serious? Don't joke with me. Not about this."

"Hey." His voice was as serious as a heart attack as he took in my face. "I would never joke about spending time with you."

"And no one will care that you're not here?" I asked with excitement, but trying not to get my hopes up.

"I'm sure there will be people who won't be happy about

it. That's why I can only go for a week so that I can do what I need to do here before filming starts."

"If you need to stay here I understand. I would never ask…"

"You didn't ask. I offered. I know that if you could stay here you would. I have no doubt in my mind, but you need to get home to Mason and back to work. We can be together for a little while longer, but in all honesty while it might make things easier right now." He stopped, and his gaze traced over my face before he took my hand in his. "It might be easier now, but I think it will make things harder in the long run."

"You think?"

"Yeah, beautiful, I do," he answered solemnly, nodding his head. "I hope I'm wrong though. After our fight the other day," Luke chewed the inside of his cheek and looked down at our joined hands. His shoulders rose and fell with each deep breath he took. "I thought there was a good chance that I'd lost you. I wasn't sure if we were going to get passed me being stupid."

"Luke, stop beating yourself up about it. I was never going to break up with you. I only wanted a little time to cool off and think about everything. It's as much my fault…"

"Don't. Let's not travel down this path. It's over and I'd like to think we're in a better place now that we came out the other side." He squeezed my hand with a soft smile. "I don't want to let you go, but if I want to go with you tomorrow, then I should probably book my flight."

"What if there are no more tickets left?" I panicked, jumping out of bed.

"Alex," Luke laughed grabbing me by the hips, stopping

me before I tugged on the t-shirt he was wearing earlier. "I don't think it's a high demand flight."

"I know it's not, but now that we can spend another week together I've got my hopes up. If you couldn't make the flight…"

"Shh," Luke whispered, one finger against my lips. "If I can't get on that flight there are other flights. Now instead of us going over this again and again, how about I go get my laptop and check the flight. I may be low maintenance, but I'll still need to pack."

"Is there anything I can help with?"

"No, I've got it. Why don't you relax, and I'll be back in a few minutes?" Getting up from the bed, Luke leaned down and gave me a short, wet kiss.

I fished my Kindle out of my purse so that I could read while I waited. Luke would know pretty quickly whether or not the flight was available, but as the minutes ticked by with me in his bed and his enticing smell enveloping me, my eyelids grew heavier with each word I read.

My eyes fluttered open as the bed dipped down and Luke pulled me flush against him. Wrapping me in his arms, his breath fanned against the back of my neck.

With a large yawn, I asked. "Did you manage to get a ticket?"

Giving me a squeeze, he answered with a velvety caress that caused my eyes to droop just from his words. "Yeah, baby, I did. I came up here earlier to tell you, but you were already asleep."

"I'm sorry. I didn't mean to fall asleep on you." Trying to turn to look at Luke, I stopped as he held me in place.

"It's okay. Go back to sleep. We have to get up early to catch our flight."

"I'm so happy you're coming home with me." I yawned the last few words out making it almost impossible to understand me. Luke laced our fingers together over my stomach. "I love you."

Placing a soft kiss on my shoulder, he spoke against my skin causing shivers to run down my spine. "I love you too, beautiful."

With a smile on my face it didn't take me long to drift off to sleep.

"LADIES AND GENTLEMEN, WE ARE ON SCHEDULE TO LAND AT 11:00 a.m. Central standard time. I hope you enjoy your flight."

My head turned, my eyes bleary from the early morning hour. "I don't like it when a three-hour flight takes five hours because of the time change. Otherwise, I would have took a later flight."

Luke's brows furrowed as he looked down at me. "You do know it still takes the same amount of time, right?"

"I do, but I wasn't thinking clearly when I booked the flight. I looked at when I'd be landing not taking off. I think I was too excited to notice."

Wrapping his arm around my shoulders, he gently pulled me down until I was leaning against him and my head was on his shoulder. "You'll be happy once you're back in Fairlane and home with Mason."

"I know I will." I snuggled deeper into him and wrapped

my arm around his middle. "The best part is you're coming home with me."

"Are you sure Mason won't be upset having to share you?"

"Why would he? Mason loves being around you."

"Maybe he doesn't want to share his mama with the man she's been with for the last few days, especially when he'll have to go back to school the next day."

"It's very sweet of you to think of him, but I don't think he'll mind. He'll be ecstatic to see you."

"Leo can't wait to meet you." He added, shocking me. His fingers ran through my hair making my eyes close. The feel of his touch was comforting and loving. "He's already said he's going to try to come in March when you come visit."

"Right now, I love that idea, but when the time comes when physically I haven't been with you in two months, I might feel differently." I confessed.

"I have a feeling that we'll both be feeling that way, but Leo will understand that we'll want some alone time."

I'd meant to sleep during our flight, but I couldn't stop thinking about how hard it was going to be to not see him until March.

Turning my head, I kissed his shirt right above his heart. "I'm going to miss you so damn much."

Squeezing my shoulder, bringing me closer to him, Luke spoke just above a whisper. "My beautiful girl, I'm going to miss you too. More than I can express."

Tilting my head up, I peered up at him only to see the underside of his jaw. "I thought you were asleep."

His fingers had long since stopped moving through my hair but had remained tangled in the strands.

"I could say the same for you."

"That was the plan, but sleep didn't find me."

"What found you then?"

"You," I breathed out in a deep sigh. "I've decided now that I got to spend a real amount of time with you that I'm spoiled."

"A real amount of time?" he questioned, pulling me back so that his eyes locked on mine.

"This is the most time we've spent together and now that I've had time to think about it, I think you're right that it will be harder. Every time we have to part it gets harder and harder to say goodbye."

"I feel the same way and that's why I want to talk to the director of Night Shadows and maybe the executives of H@T about changing the schedule. It's never been done, but we won't know until I try."

"What will we do if they won't?" I hated to ask, but if Luke was shooting in LA for five months out of the year for Night Shadows and wanted to do a movie or two, I wasn't sure how we'd ever see each other.

"We'll figure something out, but let's not worry about it until we know for sure. I'll try to explain the situation and make them see reason."

"I'll try not to worry."

25

"CAN I ASK YOU SOMETHING?" LUKE ASKED THE SECOND I SAT down on the couch after putting Mason to bed.

"Of course, you can ask me anything." I answered, turning my body toward him.

"I know you said in time you'd open up and I don't want to rush you." His eyes were wide as he watched me. "If you don't want to answer something then don't feel you have to, but I want to know everything about you. The good and the bad."

"Well, now you're starting to scare me." Yes, there were things I hadn't told Luke, but only because I never spoke of them. To anyone. I was sure there were things that I didn't know about him too. Even though Luke knew me better than almost anyone after spending so much time getting to know one another via the phone and emails, there was only so much you could say in the amount of time we'd known each other.

"Nothing to be scared of. I promise that nothing you say can or will ever make me leave you."

When I said nothing, he smiled at me, pulling my feet into his lap and started to massage one beginning at my heel and working up to dig his thumb into my arch.

"Why don't you ever talk about your parents?" he asked, not knowing that the question would break my heart.

Tears instantly filled my eyes and even though I knew it would be hard to talk about my parents, I knew now was the time to tell Luke about them.

"My mother hasn't been a part of my life since I was a small child. When my mom and dad first separated, I lived with her, but she had an abusive boyfriend who did very bad things to me and once my dad found out, I was taken away from her."

"Fuck, Alex, what did he do?" Luke asked, abandoning my foot massage to pull me onto his lap and wrapping his strong arms around me. "You don't have to talk about this if you don't want to. I… I never thought it would be anything like this. I thought maybe it was a fight or something. Never…" He choked on his words and squeezed me tighter against him. "I never…"

My face had been stuffed into the crook of his neck until his words cut off, but I had to look at him when I heard the pain in his voice. I wasn't prepared to see the agony etched across every inch of his sad but handsome face.

"Hey!" Sitting up straighter in his lap and cupping his cheek, I tried to smile but knew that I failed. Talking about my parents would be hard, but I had to be strong. "It was a long time ago. I'm fine now."

His eyes were so sad and beseeching it made me want to

cry, but I needed to show him that I was okay and had been for a long time.

"Are you really?" he didn't believe me.

"It's just something I don't like to talk about."

"I can understand that. Did Decker know?"

Tilting my head to the side, I wondered where he was going with this. "Yes," I answered hesitantly.

He looked over my shoulder, his mouth opened and closed until he clenched his jaw. The muscle twitched once before his gaze came back to me. Was he upset that Decker knew? "I need to know…" he swallowed once heavily and then continued. "I don't want this to be difficult for you, and we never have to talk about it again after this night, but I need to know if you were… what kind of bad things?" His eyes darted to the side, but just as quickly came back to me. His next words were spoken in an agonizing whisper. "Did someone touch you?"

The moment those words came out of his mouth, Luke squeezed his eyes shut. I hated that even for a moment he thought something so terrible had happened to me. If it had I couldn't imagine who I'd have turned out to be. I wouldn't let him think that had been my fate for even a second longer.

Rubbing my thumbs over his stubbled cheeks, I looked him square in the eye to make sure he could tell that I was telling him the truth. "No, Luke, no! Nothing as horrendous as that. I was neglected and beaten, but never that. I believe that's the reason I hate crying in front of others. When I would cry about something that's when he'd take out his frustration out on me."

Shaking his head, Luke's eyes finally opened looking bleak. "You were still only a little girl. No one should ever go through what you went through especially when they are so young. I'm so sorry that happened to you and I understand why you wouldn't want to talk about it. Thank you for trusting me with that."

"I trust you with my life." I answered honestly.

Hugging me to him once again, Luke spoke against the top of my head. "Can you talk about your father? If it's too much I understand, but I'd like to know about him someday."

"It's okay. I want you to know, but it's hard to talk about him and you know my aversion to crying in front of others." I closed my eyes and blew out a deep breath. "I'm getting better though. At least I think I am."

His arms tightened to protect me from my past as he rested his cheek on the top of my head. "I think so too."

"It was hard for my dad to raise me, a little girl, on his own. He didn't have a great job, but he did his best. If it weren't for my grandparents giving him money for school clothes and supplies I don't know how he would have managed. He never married or dated or anything at all that I know of. He worked hard and when he was home he spent every moment with me. I don't know if he was waiting until I was out of high school or what for him to move on with his life, but he never did." Hanging my head, I continued. "I was so ashamed when I found out that I was pregnant and had to tell him. That's why when he said that I had to marry Decker, I did.

"After we got married, I hardly saw my dad. He was still working all the time and Decker had changed. I didn't want to do anything that would set him off, and for some reason every time I saw my dad he would lose his shit for days. I think it was because he was afraid that my dad would say I didn't have to stay married to him anymore. Especially if he found out the way Decker was treating me. Ten years ago, he was killed in a drunk driving accident." Taking in a stunted breath, I finished. "It had been months since I'd last seen him."

There was no holding back the tears as I thought back to all those years ago. Instead I let loose all the sadness I'd been holding in since my father's death. Sobs wracked my body even as Luke held me tight against his strong frame. My body shook and bucked as I let out years' worth of regret and sadness. I hiccupped out how much I missed my dad over and over again.

Standing from the couch, Luke walked us into my bedroom, closing the door before crawling on to the bed with me still in his arms. Once he had us settled, each on our sides and my face tucked safely against his shoulder, he wrapped his entire body around mine. Cocooning me in, making me feel safer than ever before.

"Fuck, Alex, I had no idea. No wonder you didn't want to talk about them. I should have known it wasn't something trivial when you've been so open with me about everything else. I'm such a dick for making you talk. All I wanted was to be able to ask your father for your hand in marriage, but I should have known something was amiss when you never spoke of him."

One hand rubbed up and down the side of my body while he ran his fingers through my hair with the other. It wasn't until he started to lightly murmur Swedish that I started to calm down. I had no idea what he was saying, but it was soothing. Once I finally let everything out and had thoroughly soaked Luke's shirt with my tears, my body and mind were weary as if I'd ran a marathon instead of crying for who knew how long in Luke's arms.

I'd folded myself into him, as if I could escape inside of him, while Luke continued to soothed me anyway he knew how, not once caring about his shirt or that he was uncomfortable.

Even though all I wanted to do was fall asleep in his arms, I sat up and looked down at his surprised face and started to pull his shirt up the strong planes of his stomach. He sat up without word, letting me take off his wet shirt. Once I'd thrown his shirt to the floor, Luke's arms were around me once again and pulling me back down onto the bed and into the cocoon he had created earlier.

We were quiet for long moments before I decided that no matter how hard it was to talk about, I still wanted Luke to know everything.

"I haven't talked or seen my mom since I was thirteen. Ever since I could remember, I knew that I was never a priority in her life. She has four other kids. Two with the man who abused me, and two more she had with the husband after that."

His body tensed, and he held his breath for almost a minute before he spoke, anger laced in every word. "She married the man who abused you?"

"Not only did she marry him, but for years she denied anything ever happened. I don't know when I realized it, but at some point, I figured out that I only visited her when it was convenient for her. She had no rights to me, but my dad let me visit her when I wanted, and if she was available.

"She sounds like a bitch who doesn't know what she's missing by not being in your life."

"It is what it is. I'm used to it, but I wanted you to know in case she tries to come back into my life, if she learns about you or tries to contact you in anyway."

Kissing the top of my head, his voice was filled with gravel when he spoke. His body still held some of the tension from earlier. "I hate that happened to you and I wish I could take it away, but we both know that I can't. It explains why you're such a strong, independent woman. Thank you for telling me and opening up to me."

Tilting my head up, I kissed the bottom of his jaw.

"We should get some sleep since we have that appointment in the morning and you've got to be drained after tonight."

"I am tired." I answered with a long yawn. As my eyes drifted closed, I mumbled. "Just keep holding me."

"Always."

26

AFTER WORKING FOR A COUPLE HOURS, I DECIDED TO STOP AND take advantage of the fact that Luke and I were alone for a few more hours. Luke had urged me to get the work I needed done while he went to the gym and start going over his lines for Night Shadows.

My steps faltered when I found Luke reclined on my couch with bare feet, ankles crossed in low slung grey sweatpants, and a tight white t-shirt stretched across his biceps and chest. As mouthwatering as all that was, it was the thick, black framed glasses perched upon his nose that stopped me and had me almost drooling. At any given time, Luke was hot, but with those glasses on he was scorching. If a lady could have a boner, I got one in that moment seeing Luke.

How had I not known he wore glasses?

Dear God, he needed to wear them at all times. No, then the women that threw themselves at him would be relentless. On second thought, he should only wear them in the house around me.

I was pulled from my thoughts when Luke cleared his throat. "Alex, are you okay? You've been standing there for a good two minutes."

Starting toward him, my body heat increased with every step. "Never better." Settling on the edge of the couch by his side, I couldn't take my eyes off his glasses or stop from fingering the side of them. Not that I ever had a hard time looking at Luke.

"Do you like the glasses?" he asked cocking his head.

I was sure that he thought I'd gone crazy, but I only nodded as I leaned down and brushed my lips against his before I licked along the seam.

"Oh, you do like them." His voice had grown husky and his blue eyes turned as dark as a storm.

"I really do. How have I never seen these?"

With a small smile gracing his face, he answered. "I only where them when I'm reading for long periods of time."

"You can't wear those out in public," I blurted out.

Face lighting up with amusement, he only looked hotter. "Why do you say that?"

"Because I don't want to go to prison for having to kill all the women that will throw themselves at you when they see you wearing those glasses."

"Feeling possessive?" he smiled slyly, pulling me closer.

"You are mine."

Wrapping his hand around the back of my neck, Luke smiled up at me as he took in my fixed gaze. "Very much so."

"I really love those glasses on you. It makes me want to jump you, lick you, and do many more bad things to you."

Throwing his script on the table, Luke grasped my hips

and pulled me on top of him. He growled out. "Nothing you want to do to me is bad. Especially in bed."

Leaning down, I kissed and nipped up his neck. "Even if I want to tie you up and never let you go?"

His eyes flared and then he shot up from the couch holding me to him. "Is that an option?" he asked as he stalked toward my bedroom. Wrapping my legs around his waist, I squeezed him tighter.

"With you anything is possible." I responded as I licked up the column of his neck.

"Fuck, baby, you surprise me in the most unbelievable ways."

With my hands tied above my head, Luke leaned in and gave me a soft kiss on one corner of my mouth and then the other. Going from throwing me down and tying me up in a frenzy, to being sweet and gentle made my lips curl up before his tongue swept across them and plunged deep.

"This can be whatever you desire. Don't be afraid to voice what you like and dislike."

"No spanking. As for everything else, I don't know," I shrugged as best I could, starting to feel slightly uncomfortable. Before I was in the moment, but now I was reliving my past. "Decker always got pissed off at me because I didn't like the spanking."

Luke's eyes immediately flooded with understanding and tenderness. "No spanking or anything else of that nature. That's not really my thing anyways." He smiled down at me with his nose scrunched up. I watched as his smile slid away and his eyes heated once again. "I want to drive you wild with want. I want to push you until you can't take it any longer. Are you ready?"

"Yes," I answered breathlessly. He'd brought me back to the here and now and those sexy glasses that I hadn't known about got me revved up again.

Luke stood from the bed and slowly took off his clothes, giving me my very own personal striptease. The throb between my legs pulsed harder and my body wanted to move to relieve the dull ache, but I was only to be able to shift slightly from the bindings at my wrists and ankles.

As he slipped out of his sweatpants and boxer briefs, his cock bobbed up and down until it finally landed on his chiseled abs. Moving to the end of the bed, he kneeled, and wrapped his long fingers around my foot. He blew on the arch of my foot, tickling me, but with the bindings and his hold I was immobile.

"Luke, I want you. I need you inside of me." I moaned.

He chuckled as he nibbled up my calf. "All in good time."

He continued, as if he had all the time in the world, as if he wasn't aching for me just as badly as I wanted him. I watched his erection bob and twitch as he moved up my body sucking, licking, and kissing up one side until he met the juncture of my legs. He was so close to where I needed him only for him to smile mischievously up at me and start on the other side.

"The point is to drive you wild with want, beautiful. You'll soon be rewarded."

"You always drive me wild. I always want you," I panted and squirmed as much as my bindings allowed.

Time was not on my side. I was starting to think this wasn't a good idea. I didn't like that I couldn't touch him. I wanted to drive my fingers through his hair, kiss him desperately, and feel him slide into me.

"I want to touch you. Please, this is torture." I begged. My body desperately tried to touch him anyway it could as I arched and attempted to curl a leg against him.

"Soon, I promise. You're doing so good. Let me have my way with you just a little bit longer."

"A little longer," I answered breathlessly as his tongue licked from my stomach to my aching breasts.

His cock rubbed against my leg as his tongue swirled around my nipple, driving me mad.

"Luke," I moaned, arching so that every inch of me that could, touched his long, toned body.

My breast popped out of his mouth and he ran his tongue up the column of my neck. "Where's your vibrator?"

"What?" His question shocked and embarrassed me. He knew that I owned more than one because I'd used them a few times while we Face Timed, but it was still embarrassing.

"Your vibrator. I want to use it on you while I taste you." He growled, nipping at the shell of my ear.

"In the top drawer. Push down on the bottom and it will lift up."

"A secret compartment?" he smiled down at me deviously.

"So, Mason doesn't find them."

"Smart and beautiful."

Pulling out my simplest vibrator, Luke moved down my body. His lips glided over every inch of me until they met where I wanted him most. My back arched off the bed the instant his tongue swirled around my already swollen clit and he pumped my vibrator in and out of me to the same rhythm as his tongue.

"Luke," I moaned and continued to chant his name over and over again as his magical tongue and mouth, along with my vibrator sent me over the edge until my body was languid and spent.

Kissing up my frame, Luke untied my hands and they immediately delved into his hair, pulling him to me.

"That was amazing," I breathed heavily still trying to catch my breath.

"So, you'll let me do it again sometime?" he asked, licking and biting on my bottom lip.

"Definitely if you wear those glasses. Will you let me tie you up sometime?"

"I think that can be arranged." He winked at me with those sexy as fuck glasses on.

27

STANDING IN FRONT OF MY BATHROOM MIRROR, I STRAIGHTENED another section of hair. "Are you sure you want to do this?"

Even from my bathroom, I could hear him chuckle as he reclined on my bed reading over something. I wasn't sure what he'd been going over since he finished getting ready. All I knew was that Luke didn't have on his glasses. For that I was thankful because if he did, we would have been late or not have made it at all to Mason's school Sock Hop.

"Am I going to be a part of your and Mason's lives?" he asked from the doorway. I hadn't heard him move from the bed.

Looking at him through the mirror, I answered. "I hope so."

"I sure as hell hope so. If I'm not working, then I want to be wherever you are. I know right now things are kind of in the air until I talk to H@T about the shooting schedule, but if we can be together whether it's here or there, I want to be with you and Mason. Part of being in your lives is going to Mason's activities."

He stopped long enough that I sat my straightener down and turned to see him looking uncertain.

"What is it?" I asked as I took the two steps to reach him. My hands instinctively went to rest on his firm pecs.

"Do you not want me there?"

"Oh, Luke." I wrapped my arms around his middle and hugged him with all my might. When his arms squeezed me against him, I rested my head against his chest and breathed him in.

How could he think I didn't want him there?

"I want you there and to be with you every second that I can. I'm worried about all the attention you'll get. I don't want you uncomfortable."

"They'll get used to it and stop paying attention eventually. Are you going to be uncomfortable?" he asked looking down at me, his hand running along my back.

"Yes, but not because of you."

His brows furrowed. "Then why?"

Letting out a deep breath, I broke his hold and went back to getting ready. All the while, I tried to keep eye contact with him in the mirror.

"Whenever I've been to the school functions I've always felt like an outsider. I only know a few of the parents." I shrugged as I finished the last strand of hair. "I'm always uncomfortable when I go, especially with Taylor gone. Luckily, Mason doesn't feel the same way."

"Why'd you volunteer if you knew you'd be uncomfortable?"

"Because I want to be a part of all aspects in Mason's life. I want to help, and I know it takes time to make friends."

"Are you sure you're not just waiting for Taylor to come back?"

Turning to face him, I leaned against the counter. "Maybe a little. I know she'll be back. I just don't know when."

Luke turned to look out of the bedroom before he looked back with a smile. "You should probably finish getting ready. I can hear Mason pacing."

I couldn't help but smile. "He's excited."

"As he should be. It's fun being his age."

The moment the car stopped, Mason was unbuckling his seatbelt, ready to dart out of the car. My mouth opened to yell at him because in his excitement, Mason wasn't thinking and was about ready to cross the parking lot without looking. Instead Luke called out to him.

"Hey, little man, hold up."

Mason stopped in his tracks and waited until Luke and I caught up at the tail end of the car.

"Sorry." Mason said looking from me then to Luke and back again to me.

Looking down at Mason, he said. "Just be careful. We don't want you to get hurt."

"Sorry," Mason muttered looking down at his feet.

What he did next made my heart melt and heal in ways I never knew possible. Mason reached up and placed his hand in Luke's. I watched as Luke's big hand engulfed my little man's hand and I wanted to cry it was so sweet, but instead I followed behind them so that I could witness it for as long as possible.

It didn't last long. Once Mason set foot in the gym, he took off toward his friends who were huddled in a corner. He wasn't there more than a few seconds before he had the group out on the floor dancing. It was the cutest thing seeing all those little boys dancing without a care in the world.

Luke bent down, his lips brushing my ear. "So, what are you supposed to do?"

"I'm supposed to check in with someone named Kim to see where they're putting me."

My only problem was that I had no idea who Kim was. I decided I would go over to the table where they were selling food and drinks to see if they knew where I was supposed to go or who Kim was.

Lifting up on my tippy-toes, my hands-on Luke's shoulders, I spoke in his ear. "I'm going to go over there." I pulled back and pointed over to the table. "And see if they know what I'm supposed to do."

"Okay, I'm going to watch Mason and his friends."

Half an hour later, I'd finished my shift of selling glow-in-the-dark necklaces and bracelets and was on my way back over to Luke to supervise the kids. So far, from what I'd seen, none of the kids had caused any problems and I didn't think they would. If we were on the other side of the school with the third to fifth graders, then we might have had some problems.

I found Luke leaning against the far wall talking to a few of the dads, and shook my head as I took in at least a dozen women who were hanging on Luke's every word.

The moment he saw me trying to cut through the crowd, his eyes lit up and a smile spread across his handsome face.

Reaching his arm out through the surrounding crowd he had amassed, he brought me to his side.

"Hey!" he greeted me with a kiss on the cheek.

"Alex, this is Jay, Doug, and Corey." He pointed to each and they all smiled and waved back. "This is Alex, my girlfriend."

"Hi, nice to meet you all." I greeted them with a wave.

I noticed that Luke hadn't introduced any of the women. Two of the guys were gossiping about some other guy having a mid-life crisis. Cheating on his wife, changing his wardrobe, and buying a flashy new sports car.

"This is for all the helpers and chaperone's here tonight." The DJ announced.

From the time we arrived all the songs that had been played were fast paced and were played a dozen times a day on the radio. The kids loved the music if their non-stop dancing was any indication.

Lacing our fingers together, Luke pulled us out to the center of the dance floor in the middle of all the kids. He didn't say a word as he smiled down at me. Not until the first strands of "Iris" by the Goo Goo Dolls started to play over the speakers.

"May I have this dance?" Luke gave me his lop-sided grin that always cause butterflies to take flight in my stomach.

"Yes," I answered as the first words were sung.

We didn't dance fancy or anything like that. Instead we held each other and swayed to the music.

My eyes watered as I looked up at Luke. We were dancing for the first time and it was to my favorite song. Everything was perfect in that moment.

"Did you do this?"

He leaned down, resting his cheek at the side of my head so that I could hear him. Our height difference was at a definite disadvantage right then. "I may have requested he play the song."

"How'd you know?"

"Yesterday when I came home from working out, you were playing it with this amazing smile on your face and I figured it meant the song was special to you. I knew we were coming here and I planned to see if they'd play it for you."

Home.

Luke had said he had come home. I was so happy I wanted to cry, but I didn't want to ruin the perfect moment.

"You guessed right. I love this song and even though I never planned to marry again, I've always wanted this to be my wedding song." I gazed up at him my heart full of love. Luke had no idea how much more special he'd made my favorite song. "I love you."

He kissed the side of my head and murmured. "Deep down you're a romantic at heart."

A smile tipped my lips. "You think?" I certainly never thought so.

"I do. You just never had anyone who would reciprocate those feelings until now."

"This *is* pretty romantic, Mr. Sandström." I patted his chest above his heart. "Thank you for this. If we weren't in a room full of impressionable children I would kiss you so hard right now."

"You can pay me back when we get home."

There it was again. Luke had called my house home and I loved it.

"And if I could, I'd climb you because God you seem extra tall tonight. I should've worn heels." I placed my hand on his stubbly cheek. "I'm sorry you've always got to bend down so far to reach me."

Threading his fingers through my hair, Luke kept swaying to the music with me. "Not a hardship in anyway."

"I want to dance with you every day that we're together."

"You've got a date."

"Did you know you're the best boyfriend ever?" I placed my cheek against his chest and with one ear listened to my favorite song and the other listened to my favorite sound. Luke's heartbeat.

"No, but I'm glad you think so." Luke twirled me out and back into his embrace before his lips caressed the shell of my ear. "I love you too, beautiful."

28

Opening my eyes, I was greeted with a worried face instantly making me go on alert. "Sweetheart, what is it? Are you okay?"

"Momma?" Mason shakily spoke from the side of the bed. "Miss Prue is yelling at a man in her front yard. They woke me up." It had to be early if they woke Mason up and that wasn't a good sign.

The bed dipped as an arm wrapped around me. "Are they still yelling?" Luke asked his voice rough first thing in the morning.

Mason nodded stilled worried, his bottom lip trembled. "I don't like it. Miss Prue is always nice to everyone."

"I'm on it, buddy," Luke knifed up out of bed and started to head to the door.

"Luke! You need some shoes and a coat. It's freezing outside." I called as I watched him walk down the hall barefoot with only sleep pants on. A pair that we bought so that he could sleep in bed with me and Mason wouldn't get any surprises in the morning if he came in. Luke liked to sleep naked, but that wasn't always plausible with a seven-year-old in the house who could come in any minute.

Lifting the blankets from the bed, I patted next to me for Mason to get in. I held him tight as I heard shouting coming from next door and then the front door closed.

"Are you okay, sweetie?"

"Yeah, Luke will fix it." He calmly told me. He was right. Luke wouldn't let some man yell at a woman.

"Get the hell off my property, Holden! You are not welcome here!" Prue shrieked.

A deep rumble came after, but I couldn't make out what was said.

"You have no right to be here! I don't want to talk to you or see you ever again! Leave like you did before, Holden. Leave!"

I could hear Luke and the other man's voices, but they were further away so it was impossible to understand what they were saying. It was several more minutes before Mason and I heard the front door close again and saw Luke coming back into the bedroom.

Releasing my lip from between my teeth, I asked. "Is everything okay?"

"If you mean that the guy left then yes. If you mean your neighbor, then no she's not okay. I guess her father passed away and the guy, Holden, showed up out of nowhere."

"Prue's dad died?" I asked in shock.

Luke sat down next to us on the bed. Even though he didn't know Prue, he looked saddened by the thought of her father dying. "Yeah, baby. He died and that… a-hole decided now was the time to talk to her when she's already upset."

"I should go over there and talk to her. See if she needs anything. Will you guys be okay if I'm gone for a little while?"

Mason sat up and gave me a quick hug before he hopped down from the bed. "I'll be fine, mamma. Luke, will you make me pancakes?"

A small grin grew on Luke's face. "Yeah, buddy. I'll make you pancakes. Do you want chocolate chips?"

His eyes grew wide. "Do you like pancakes with chocolate chips too?" Mason asked excitedly.

"Is there any other way to have them?" he asked back, knowing that chocolate chip pancakes were Mason's favorite. I knew Luke would only eat them for Mason because you didn't eat pancakes and have a body like his.

Mason darted out of the room and I was sure he was headed to the kitchen. I couldn't help but smile.

"Go. We'll be fine here. If we need anything you're right next door."

"Thanks, handsome." I gave him a quick kiss and rubbed my thumb over his stubbled cheek. "I'll be back as soon as I can."

"No rush. Take care of your friend. While you're gone I'll pack up some more boxes so that we'll be ready to move your stuff tomorrow."

"It's going to be weird for the house not to have any of your things in it. How will it seem like it's your house too? Maybe we should wait."

"You're not waiting." Looking down at me sternly, he took in a deep breath and gritted his teeth. His jaw ticked twice before his face changed back to my sweet Luke. "Your ex-husband is going to find out about us eventually, along with others. I want to know that you and Mason are going to be safe and being in a gated neighborhood and a house with a security system will ease my mind. I *need* to know that your safe when I'm across the country. Please do this for me." His eyes pleaded with me.

Even though I wasn't ready for the change without Luke, I gave in. I didn't want to cause him undue worry. "Of course, I'll do it for you. I don't want you to be worried about us and I know Decker will eventually find out. He's going to blow up even though he has no right to."

Pulling me into a hug, Luke kissed the top of my head. "All the more reason for you to be somewhere safe so that he can't get to you."

"Someday he'll find me and confront me." The thought made my heart race knowing it would be ugly. Before I could think on that any longer or get lost in Luke, I stood to get ready. "Go make Mason some pancakes and I'll check on Prue."

KNOCKING ON PRUE'S DOOR, I LOOKED BACK OVER TO MY HOUSE. I could see Luke's tall form through the kitchen window as he let Mason help make breakfast.

The front door opened and my head turned to catch Prue's tear-stricken face. When she saw it was me, she opened the door further and started to walk away. Staying silent, I followed her back to her bedroom and sat down next to her prone form after she laid down and curled up into a ball.

"Prue, sweetie. Are you okay? Is there anything I can do for you? Luke told me about your dad." I said the last barely above a whisper.

"Can you bring him back, cancer free?" She asked brokenly.

"I wish I could." Picking up her hand, I held it as I watched her cry silently. "I'm so sorry, Prue. He was such a great man and I'm going to miss him. Can I make you a cup of tea or anything?"

"No, I don't want anything, but to be left to mourn my father in peace." She said quietly into her pillow.

"Who was that guy who was here earlier? Do we need to be worried about him?" I asked curiously.

She turned her face into her pillow and cried out. I rubbed up and down her back trying to soothe her as best I could. "What is it, sweetie?"

"It's Holden," she sobbed. "He's back for some reason and showed up here demanding to speak to me. Saying he was already here and heard about my dad."

"Who is he to you?"

He had to be special enough to cause her so much heartache.

"The man who broke my heart." She sobbed. "I don't want to talk about him though. I don't want to remember what he did to me."

"Do I need to be worried that he'll come back?"

Turning her wet eyes to me, she spoke with conviction. "He's not violent if that's what you're thinking."

"I wasn't sure what to think." Holding her, I let her cry until she seemed to be all cried out for the moment. I hated that after tomorrow I'd no longer be her neighbor. "Um... I hate to bring this up now, but I haven't had a chance to talk to you since I got back from Mexico, but I'm moving."

"What? Really? Where? When?" She giggled, and it made me smile. "Oh, gosh, listen to me and all my questions."

"Don't worry about it. I'd have the same one's if you were moving. I'm moving tomorrow, but it's still in town so we can see each other whenever. The deal was too amazing to pass up and eventually Luke will move in too."

Prue sat up against her headboard wide eyed. "Wow. Things are really serious between the two of you. I guess Mexico was a hit."

A smile came over my face as I thought of our time in Mexico. "It was amazing and so is Luke. Every day I wake up and have to pinch myself to make sure I'm not dreaming. How am I living this life? How did I get so lucky to have such an incredible man find me and get along with Mason so well? It's wonderful and sad at the same time to see. Mason's father has never given him the time of day and Luke listens to every word he has to say. Right now, they're making pancakes together." Happy tears filled my eyes and so did Prue's.

"Oh, Alex, I'm so happy for you. You and Mason." Leaping forward, she wrapped her arms around me in a hug.

"Thank you! I didn't mean to make this about me, but I didn't want you to find out I was moving when you saw the truck show up in the morning. We won't be far, and you can come over anytime or call if you need me. Please, it's going to be so weird at first being in a new house. I need someone to help me pick out furniture because I can't decorate to save my life."

"I'd be happy to help. Just tell me when you need me. It'll help keep my mind off of my dad and Holden."

Pulling back from our hug, I let her know I'd help her anyway if I could. "If you need a place to get away or hide from Holden just say the word. I'd be happy to help. If you're sure you don't need anything I should probably get home to help pack. I have no clue how he packs, and I'd like to know where all my stuff is since he'll be leaving me to do all the unpacking, and I won't be able to ask him where everything is every time I can't find something."

"Thank you for coming by to make sure I was okay. I really appreciate it. I'm going to miss you and our talks even as infrequent as they were."

"Call me if you need anything. I mean it." Giving her a knowing look. Prue was like me in that she rarely if ever asked for help. "Day or night I'm here for you, and I'll miss you, too."

"I will, I promise."

We hugged once more before I left to head home. A little life shined through Prue's eyes as she waved goodbye.

It was time to pack up my old life and start my new life with Luke and Mason. I was finally getting my happily ever after.

29

STANDING IN MY NEW KITCHEN, I WAS TRYING TO FIGURE OUT HOW I was going to organize everything. I had way more space than ever before and yet I still couldn't figure out where to put everything.

When my phone rang, and Taylor's picture showed up on my screen, I was happy to stop and talk to her.

"Hey you!" I answered as I sat down on a stool at the kitchen island.

"Hey!" Taylor called back. "How's the new house? I wasn't sure if you'd answer."

"The house is a beautiful mess. I'm trying to put as much stuff away as possible while Luke's gone."

"Did he leave already?" Taylor asked confused.

"No, he leaves the day after tomorrow." My mood instantly shifted thinking about Luke leaving. "God, Taylor, I'm going to miss him so much."

"I know honey. I'm sorry. I wish there was something I could do."

"Its life." I sighed so loudly into the phone it reverberated back. "Once Decker finds out about Luke shit is really going to hit the fan. At least now that we've moved he can't get passed the gates."

"You let me know if he causes you any problems."

Letting out a sigh, I looked out the window. "We know he will."

"I know. Is there a house in that neighborhood for us to move into when we move back?"

"I'm not sure, but it would be awesome. I'd love it if we lived that close."

"Me too. Have you met your neighbors?"

"Not yet. Colt said he would introduce me to them when he and Anna came later in the month."

"Your life is so crazy now I can't believe it, and I'm missing all of it being all the way in Florida."

"When are you moving back?" I asked sadly.

"I wish I knew. Ben cried so hard the other night because he misses Mason so much. I'm going to try and come visit when he has a couple of days off from school. Hopefully our spring break doesn't coincide with yours or we'll probably miss you."

"Mason would be very upset to know that he missed a visit from Ben."

"If Decker wasn't a problem would you and Mason move to LA?"

"Yeah, I probably would. It's going to suck to only see Luke for a week out of five months." I didn't even try to hide my sadness. "It doesn't matter though because Decker will never let that happen."

"You're right he won't. He loves being an asshole, especially to you. So," she drew out the word. "I never got to hear about how it went at the sock hop the other night."

"Oh, you should have seen the women swarm around Luke and then act like they were interested in whatever he was talking about. It was pitiful."

"What else? I know you're holding something back. I can hear it in your voice."

"Damn you know me too well." Looking up at the ceiling, I felt tears burn the backs of my eyes. I took a deep fortifying breath and told her what I'd been holding in since that night. Luke didn't even know. "I overheard some of the moms saying they didn't know what Luke saw in me, that I was ugly, and he could do so much better than me."

"Oh honey," Taylor said sympathetically. "You know that's not true. They're just jealous bitches. Don't listen to a single word they say. Luke loves you and I believe with all my heart that he's the man that you're meant to be with for the rest of your life."

"But am I who he's meant to be with?" I asked hesitantly. Taylor was the sweetest, bestest friend in the whole world and I knew she'd tell me the truth.

"Without a doubt. Don't you dare start doubting your relationship because if you do then it will not withstand your time apart and with that crazy ass Ashlyn, you've got to be on your toes and strong."

"Taylor," I whispered her name as my chin trembled. "It really hurt to hear them say that. I even dressed up and did my hair and makeup to the best of my ability. I looked my best without professional help, and they still talked behind my back."

"Because they are so fucking jealous that you snagged one of the hottest men in the world, who's also becoming a big name in Hollywood, but also because he's the sweetest, funniest, most loving man to you and it's easy to see just by the way he looks at you."

"Stop. You're going to make me cry." I sniffed but held back.

"It's okay to cry sweetie. Cry because you're sad about what those stupid women said about you and cry because Luke loves you and what you've found is so damn special."

"Every day I wake up and have to pinch myself because I think - how can this be my life? For so many years I was miserable and felt so unloved, and now just thinking about Luke makes me want to burst with happiness." I laughed. "It's really quite sickening."

"If it was anyone but you I would think so too, but you deserve to be happy and feel loved."

"We all do, but that doesn't mean we get it."

"Unfortunately, not. Now back to happier topics, I kind of can't believe that you bought a house in a neighborhood I didn't even know existed and that Luke is pretty much going to be living with you when he's not working."

"I didn't know it existed either until I met Colton. It's very private, I can give you that. I wonder how long it will take Decker to find it. It's not like he ever brings Mason home."

Taylor huffed into her phone. "He'll probably follow you once he figures out you don't live at your old house."

"Probably." I sighed. It wasn't going to be fun I knew that. I was thankful to have an alarm system and the security gates. I needed to change the topic away from Decker. I didn't want thoughts of him to bring me down. "How's that baby doing?"

"Draining the ever-loving life out of me, but besides that she's doing great. Growing and kicking me at all hours of the day and night. I barely get any sleep. I'm going to be in a world of trouble when she's born if she keeps going like this."

"I wish I could help. Jack needs to get his ass in gear so you can move back here."

"You're telling me. I keep threatening to move back since he's always working, and I could at least be with you and closer to family, but he's not going for it."

"Well, now that I've got this big house you can stay if you need it. You guys were good sports staying in my tiny house."

"I may take you up on staying with you again if Ben's spring break isn't the same time you're gone to LA. Does Mason know?"

"No," I laughed and shook my head even though she couldn't see it. "If he knew, Mason would pack today and ask me every day when we were leaving."

"Aww, it's so sweet how much he likes Luke. I love that for him."

A smile stretched across my face. "I love it too. Luke's so good with him and it's genuine. Something Mason's always been missing in his life."

The door coming from the garage beeped letting me know that Luke and Mason were back. "Hey, Luke and Mason just got home. Can I call you in a couple of days?"

"Of course, you can sweetie. We'll eat ice cream over the phone and cry."

"You're on. Don't be surprised if I'm a blubbering mess. I'm going to miss him so damn much especially after I keep him locked in the bedroom all day tomorrow while Mason's at school." I whispered the last as I watched Mason and Luke walk into the kitchen. Mason had a happy smile on his face and Luke looked about ready to explode.

"You go girl! Get some for me." Taylor chirped happily. "Um... do you know that you and Luke have been outed?"

"Outed? What do you mean?" I watched as my face scrunched up in the reflection of the kitchen window.

"It's everywhere!"

"What's everywhere?" I asked confused.

"That you and Luke are definitely a couple. There are pictures of you two together at LAX and then in Mexico. I haven't looked in a few days, but I'd bet one of those bitches posted pictures of the Sock Hop too."

"I had no clue, but I knew it was going to happen sooner or later. My only worry is Decker. Maybe I should tell him I'm seriously dating someone, so he doesn't find out through gossip or online."

"Maybe." She didn't sound convinced. "Either way it won't be good. Hey, I'll let you go. I wanted you to know since I know you stay off those sites. Talk to you in a few days." I hung up and walked directly to Luke, who had stopped to look outside, and wrapped my arms around his waist, my chin to his back.

"Is everything okay?" I asked quietly. "Did Mason do something?"

He took in a deep breath that I could feel inflate him as I continued to hug him from behind. "Mason was perfect."

"Okay, I'm not sure what's going on then. Can you please talk to me?" I squeezed him once more and started to move around him so that I could see his face, and possibly get a read on him, but Luke extended his arm to stop me. With my head tipped back, I looked up at him questioningly.

"Can you get Mason settled doing something and then I'll tell you in private?"

My eyes widened. *In private? What the hell was going on?*

"Yeah, I can do that." My body started to shake as nerves wracked through me. What could Luke possibly have to tell me that had to be done in private. Nothing good, that was for sure.

Leaning down Luke kissed my forehead and tried to smile in reassurance, but it was barely more than a tip of his lips and didn't meet his eyes.

It wasn't hard to find Mason something to do. The house was a mess of boxes with almost everything still packed, and it wouldn't be long until he'd want to play with his toys. I set him up in what would be his play room to put away all his toys with the promise that tonight he could pick whatever movie he wanted for us to watch. Not that I normally denied him, but he was excited so that was all that mattered. That and getting back to Luke as quickly as possible as I tried to come up with some reason as to why he was so angry when he got home.

Luke's gaze followed me as I walked back into the kitchen and over to him, biting my bottom lip. The moment I was within reaching distance, he wrapped my hand in his and held it to his chest, his heart thumped wildly.

"Is Mason good? He didn't say anything did he?" he asked with a tick of his jaw.

"Not a thing. Why? What happened?"

He barked out a dark laugh. "I bought an SUV and afterwards I thought you might be unhappy."

He bought a car?

"But? I can tell that's not what's upsetting you."

"I took Mason to get some ice cream at a place that was near the dealership. He saw a toy store in the shopping center and wanted to look through the window. I saw no harm in letting him look since it's warmer today." He paused looking down at me with a mixture of anger and sadness.

"That's fine, Luke. It's a nice day today and I'm glad he got to enjoy it a little. Is that it?" Surely it wasn't, but I was hopeful.

He hung his head his eyes on his shoes. "On our way back, I received a call from my publicists. I pulled over in a parking lot to take the call. You know after the incident in Mexico, I informed her that if anything came up with Ashlyn about either of us I wanted to know."

"What shit is she spouting this time?" I growled out. If I ever was in the same vicinity as this bitch and knew it, I was going to kick her ass. I was over her lying about Luke.

Luke's Adam's apple bobbed as he swallowed nervously and squeezed my hand in his. "She took a picture of Mason and I and posted it on Instagram. I haven't looked at it yet, but Sarah is contacting her people to get it taken down immediately."

I stood frozen as I blinked at Luke. That crazy bitch was in Fairlane and posted a picture of Mason on the Internet! Pulling away, it was my turn to look outside. I may have been standing at the window, but I saw nothing but red. My mind and body were in a state of shock, rage, and sadness all at the same time. I wanted to run out and murder that crazy bitch. We knew that she was crazy, but now she'd taken her game too far. How were we going to stop her?

From behind me Luke spoke in a rush. "I know Mason didn't sign on for this and neither did you. I'll do everything within my power to keep Mason out of the press, and to keep you both safe."

Was it possible that she knew where we lived? Would she be waiting for us when we left? I was already grateful to be behind the gates of our new neighborhood and the security system that had been upgraded yesterday morning.

"Please don't leave me," Luke heartbreakingly whispered from behind me.

When I turned back to look at him, my heart cracked at the heart break in his eyes. They were pleading with me to stay. What he didn't know was that I'd never let him go.

My eyes closed as tears burned the backs of my eyes, I needed to be strong in this moment for Luke. Yes, I was undeniably pissed about what Ashlyn had done, but I knew that Luke had no part of it. I knew that at some point there would be a chance Mason would be around paparazzi and get his picture taken, but had also hoped that we could appeal to their sensibilities and they'd leave him out of pictures. It was easy to see the draw - people wanted to know what celebrity's children looked like, but they were still innocent children that should have their privacy protected.

Taking a deep cleansing breath, I let it out and opened my

eyes to find Luke's worried gazed locked on me. Moving toward the island, I patted a stool with a small smile. "Come sit."

Luke eyed the stool warily but did as I'd asked. I jumped up onto the island next to him and looked down at his face. The sadness and fear in his eyes made me sick. Luke was the kindest, sweetest man I knew he deserved to always be happy, and one photo from Ashlyn had rocked his world.

"There is nothing in this stratosphere that could ever make me leave you," I pledged with our eyes locked. I wanted him to not only hear it, but to see it in my eyes. I wanted Luke to have no doubt in his mind.

His big hands gripped my hips and dragged me until I was seated in front of him. Wrapping his arms around my waist, Luke leaned down to rest his head on my stomach holding me tightly.

For a moment, I was taken aback by his actions realizing how truly scared he'd been. Running my fingers through his hair, I spoke to my sweet man. "Thank you for taking care of the picture. I knew it might someday be a possibility, but I never thought it would happen while we're here in Fairlane. Do I want Mason's picture out there for the world to see? No, I don't, but it's something I can live with if I need to. I can't accept that crazy bitch being the one to spread his face around. She had no right! What's her game?" Luke shook his head against me and kissed me through my shirt. "Does she want the public to hate you? Me? Does she think that I'll believe her pictures and dump you? I don't know how she's not in a mental institution. How are we going to get her to leave us alone?" I cried out, resting my head against the top of his.

Shaking his head, Luke looked up at me bleakly, "I don't have any answers for you except that she's crazy. Sarah's looking into what we can do, but she's not hopeful. Ashlyn hasn't done anything physical toward either of us or made a threat."

"If I ever see her anywhere near any of us, I promise you here and now that I'm going to kick her ass. She's gone too far. Mason's an innocent little boy."

Pulling me tightly against him, Luke murmured. "I know, baby. I'm so sorry this happened. I thought we were safe here." Dejectedly he shook his head. "I wasn't thinking."

"Because you shouldn't have to. I thought we were safe too. Luke," I said tipping his chin up to me. "You have nothing to be sorry about."

"You didn't ask for this."

"I asked for you." His lopsided grin shined up at me after only a few words. "I knew what I was getting into when I decided to be with you. You're sweet to your fans when they come up to you, but you don't seek them out or the attention of Hollywood. Your privacy is very important to you, and you do what you do because you love the work. I believe it's what you were meant to do."

Eyes shining, Luke rested one hand against my racing heart. "Fuck, Alex, you know me down to my soul. What did I ever do to deserve you?"

Pressing my lips to his, I smiled. "I ask myself the same thing every day."

After breaking away from a soft, wet kiss, Luke engulfed me in his arms. "Thank you for not freaking out. I was... I thought it might be more than you could handle, but I was wrong. Never again will I underestimate your strength."

"Or my love for you. You've been permanently etched into my heart, Lucas Sandström. I can't imagine my life without you in it."

We sat quietly for a moment in a what I would normally describe as a disgusting love-sick haze, but since it pertained to me, I loved it as it made my heart swell in love and appreciation for the man in front of me. Then I remembered something that Luke had mentioned earlier.

"Wait, you bought a new car?" he nodded woodenly. "Where's my car?"

"In the driveway. I had the salesman drive it back. Don't worry."

"What the hell did you buy that they'd be willing to drive here?" Seriously it was at least thirty minutes to any dealership. No wonder they'd been gone for so long.

Luke tried to hide a smile by clamping his mouth shut but it didn't work. Instead they kept slipping out and quirking up. "Who knew buying an SUV would upset you more than a crazy stalker?"

"That's not funny, Luke. Why did you buy a new car? Mine's perfectly fine."

"Yes, it's perfectly fine for you, but I'm a big man and I need room. Plus, if it snows I want to know that when you and Mason are out that you're safe and now I've guaranteed it."

"Just because you've bought it doesn't mean that I'll drive it. You've already done too much with helping buy the house. Next thing I know you'll go all Fifty on me by putting money in my bank account."

Looking at me strangely, he shook his head. "I have no idea what you are talking about, but if you need money for anything in the house let me know and I'll happily give you the money."

"No! I don't want that!" I cried out. "Look, I don't want to yell at you or get upset, but I need to feel like I'm doing my part."

He let out a frustrated breath. "You *are* doing your part. You paid for half of this house." He motioned around the kitchen. "I'm not taking over, but I'm not going to let you spend every penny you have to fill this house and take care of it."

"I paid for half, but we both know that this house is worth way more than what we bought it for."

Pulling my body against his, he smiled down at me. "Did you hear yourself just then? You said *we* bought this house. This is my house too and I'm going to help."

"It's not going to feel like your house except that I could never afford this." I muttered.

Looking hurt, Luke asked quietly. "Why do you say that? I'll be here as much as I possibly can."

My fingers slid from his hair to brush against his stubble. "I didn't mean it in a bad a way. Please don't misunderstand, but all your stuff is in LA. Nothing of yours will be here."

"I beg to differ. You'll be here, and you are most definitely mine." That got a minute smile from me. "Is that what's bothering you? That I won't have anything here to claim my spot?"

Looking down at my lap, I bit my bottom lip. "It's stupid, I know, but it won't seem like you live here if you don't have anything in the closet or drawers."

"There's a SUV in the garage that's mine and I'll leave the keys in one of the kitchen drawers." He replied back, lifting his chin in satisfaction.

Looking down, I answered. "You know what I mean."

"I do, and I shouldn't take it lightly. I can leave everything I brought here if it will help. It's not much, but it's enough to put a few of my things in the closet and the drawers in the bathroom just like you want. Then when you come to LA, you and Mason can leave some of your stuff there too." After placing a kiss on my forehead, he continued. "With never living together and then me being in LA for the next five months, I can see your point. If I could live here, right now, I would, but we have to make the best out of the situation and see each other when we can. Right now, I can't give you dates, but if I ever have a weekend open know that I'll be on the first plane here."

Hugging him tight, I laid my head on his shoulder, my lips brushing his neck as I spoke. "I'm being a big baby. I know that you are doing the best that you can, and you'd be here if you could. If there's a weekend when I don't have Mason and you won't be working the entire time, I'll be there. You're not even gone, and I already miss you. Even with being chest to chest with you, I miss your touch. As your scent invades my senses, I long to smell you again. To be without feeling you inside me has me wanting to lock you away and have my way with you until we both can't move."

Skirting his hand up the front of my shirt, Luke pulled down the cup of my bra and pinched my nipple. His tongue made a path from the crook of my neck across the exposed skin of my shoulder. "Right now, I can't do anything to help your need for me to be inside of you, but I have a feeling that there won't be much unpacking tomorrow while Mason's at school. I'm going to wring every last orgasm out of you until you beg me to stop."

"Yes, please."

30

LUKE

"Beautiful." My lips pressed against the top of her head as she cried into my shirt, clutching me to her. "You're breaking my heart."

The moment Alex woke up and found me up on an elbow watching her sleep, her eyes instantly filled with tears. She'd held them back as I made love to her one last time before it was time to head to the airport, but after dropping Mason off at school she finally broke down and let them flow.

For months I'd encouraged Alex that she was safe to cry in front of me, but this time I was the cause. Not because a childhood friend had died, or she was telling me about her parents. It killed me to know that I was the root of her pain.

If it were up to me, I'd never leave her. I'd take her with me or stay in Fairlane, but I had obligations that I had to fulfill, and she had to stay here with Mason.

Fuck she was killing me with her endless tears and sobs.

With how upset she was, I wasn't sure if Alex would be able to drive herself home after dropping me off. If there would have been someone to drive her home I would have suggested it. Sadly, Ryan had stopped communication with her all together and Taylor was in Florida. I had a feeling she would need her friends over the next few months. At least Taylor would do her best to perform her best friend duties no matter how far away she was. Perhaps once I got inside, I'd send her a message to call Alex.

Running my hand over her hair and down back one last time, I nuzzled my face into the top of her head and breathed her in. She smelled like her coconut shampoo. Like the beach on our trip to Mexico. I may love the colder temperatures, but Alex had made me a beach lover because she always smelled of the coconuts and our amazing trip where she finally told me she loved me. It was sappy, but I didn't care. I'd been waiting to hear those words from her. Someday I'd take her to all the beaches she'd ever dreamed about and if I was lucky a few of them would be clothing optional.

"Hey, beautiful." Kissing her hair, I straightened up and pulled back. "Can you look at me?"

Big blue eyes, heavy with sadness and tears stared back at me causing my heart to painfully twist inside my chest. I'd wanted to be strong for her but separating from her was killing me just as much. I wasn't sure how much longer I could hold myself together.

"I hate to say this, but I have to go. Are you going to be okay?"

Her lips trembled until she sucked her lower lip in and bit down on it. "No." She choked out.

"Hey." I tried to comfort her as best I could in the small confines of the car. "We're still going to talk and FaceTime every day. Honey, this isn't goodbye. It'll be no time until you and Mason come to visit me for spring break." Cupping her face in both my hands, I swept her tears away with the pads of my thumbs. Even tear streaked she was beautiful. Leaning down, I brushed my lips across her soft mouth. My heart cracked a little bit more with the taste of her tears on her lips.

My eyes closed as I rested my forehead to hers. "I love you. More than you know. More than anything. We'll make it through this. I promise."

Even knowing that Alex loved me, I couldn't help but doubt that the long distance and months away from each other would create a rift between us. Time and distance were no friend to even the strongest of relationships and although we were strong, we were also new.

"I know," she murmured against my lips, her arms wrapping around me, holding me tighter. "I love you so fucking much it hurts."

"I know, Alex. I know." Because I felt it too.

Her hand drifted, cupping my neck, pulling me to her. It was possessive and desperate at the same time. Fuck, this was going to be much harder than I thought. But I knew I needed to be strong for her.

"I love you," I whispered into her mouth.

"I love you." She barely managed to sob out before her lips crashed into mine. Winding her arms around my neck, she pulled me even closer. When my tongue slipped inside for one last taste we both moaned, knowing it had to end.

Getting out, the cold January air sobered us up as we stood beside the SUV taking each other in for the last time. The next two months were going to be the longest of my life. Even knowing I'd be busy shooting, I knew missing Alex would be at the forefront of my mind each and every day.

Taking the one step that separated us, I pulled her into my arms for one last hug. Her arms wrapped around me so tightly, not wanting to let go. Neither did I. This was where I belonged. Alex was my home and I was leaving her. I couldn't fight the tears that blurred my vision any longer. Burying my head into her neck, I breathed in her coconut scent one last time before pulling away. It had to be now or never.

"I'll call you the moment I get home, okay?" My voice broke on the last word causing Alex's head to whip up in a look of shock. "This is just as hard on me as it is you. I'm going to miss you like crazy and I love you so much."

"So much." She barely got out before more tears started to stream down her already tear stained cheeks.

Taking a step back, I grabbed my luggage. "I gotta go."

Nodding her head, Alex watched me go from her spot on the sidewalk. It wasn't a big airport so there weren't any workers or overhead announcements saying she had to leave or that parking was for loading and unloading. Instead, everyone took their time as they said their goodbyes and moved inside.

"I love you!" Alex called out the moment the doors opened for me and a gust of warm air hit me. Turning to look at her, I let a tear break free as I saw her slumped against the car door watching me bleakly.

My mouth ran dry at seeing her pain, but I pushed past it to tell her how much I loved her too. Then without looking back, I strode into the airport before I said fuck it all and never left Alex's side.

31

PULLING UP IN FRONT OF DECKER'S HOUSE, THE HOUSE I'D LIVED in for over a decade, I took in a deep breath. With twenty minutes until I was supposed to pick up Mason at his grandparents' house, my ex-husband sent me a text informing me I was to pick up my son at his house instead.

Getting out of the car, I looked around and noticed that the yard looked neglected and there were no lights on in the house. I took in a deep breath and slowly let it out before I rang the doorbell. It had been awhile since I last laid eyes on my ex-husband. Usually I picked Mason up at his grandparents' house, which I preferred.

A long moment passed before I heard Decker pounding his way toward the door. It sounded as if an elephant was loose and trampling through the house. The door swung open and I sucked in a breath at the look in his eyes. If possible, his pitch-black eyes would have sliced through me as he glared down at me.

I wanted to take a step back, but knew I needed to stand

my ground. I couldn't show him any weakness. It was predator against prey around him at all times.

Lifting my chin, I prevailed against my instincts. "Where's Mason? I want to make sure he's had dinner and a bath before bed and it's getting late."

A grunt emanated from deep inside before answering. "At my parents."

Taking a calming breath, I tried not to lose my shit. He'd been the one to inform me I needed to pick up Mason at his house. "Why did you text me telling me to pick him up here then?" I asked as calmly as possible.

His eyes narrowed into slits. "Did you think I wouldn't find out?"

"About what?" I asked innocently. I could tell he was itching for a fight and I wasn't going to give him more than he already knew.

"Don't pull that bullshit on me." He demanded taking a step forward.

Still I held my ground. Not showing any weakness.

"You'll have to be more specific. We don't talk so I'm sure there are plenty of things you don't know about me."

"Oh, I know. I've got people and they tell me what you're up to."

Doubt it.

Still I kept quiet.

With his arms straight at his sides, Decker's fists clenched as he took me in. I knew I looked good. Better than I ever had while being married to him. I was toned from working out, my hair was down with fresh highlights, and I was dressed the way that made me feel good about myself. Not like the clothes

I'd previously worn so that he wouldn't think I was 'trying too hard'.

"Are you still with that..." he scrunched his nose in disgust.

"Luke." I finished for him.

"I don't know the assholes name. Are you?"

"Yes, as a matter of fact I am, and I don't see that changing."

Ever, I wanted to add but didn't.

"I wouldn't be too sure about that if I were you," he sneered.

"I'm not going to discuss my relationship with you. Now if you don't mind, I'm going to go pick up Mason."

"I found out who your boy toy is. Is that why you moved?" His jaw ticked as he ground his molars together.

Shaking my head, I stood firmly in my spot when what I really wanted to do was to get in my car and speed away. This was the moment I'd been dreading, and now more than ever did I wish Luke was with me.

"No, I moved because I got an amazing deal on a house and couldn't pass it up." I answered truthfully. Even if Luke wasn't in the picture, I would've bought the house. The only difference was that I wouldn't have been able to furnish it for the next ten to fifteen years like it was now.

"By whoring yourself out?" he spat.

"If that's what you want to think then that's fine. I know I'm not going to change your mind."

I knew once Decker got something in his head there was little anyone could do to change his mind and I didn't care or have the energy to try. I had no more shits to give concerning my ex-husband.

"That's what's going around town. That you whored your way into a new house." He smiled vilely down at me.

"And I can only guess who started that rumor." *Him.* "It makes no difference because I know the truth and that's all that matters."

"Really? What are you going to do when your boy toy's deported? Who's going to pay for that house of yours then?" he sneered.

A triumphant smile spread across his face and all I wanted to do in that moment was smack it right off. Instead, I put my hands in my jean pockets and rocked back on my heels.

"First off the house is paid for so nothing is ever going to happen to it and second, Luke isn't going anywhere."

"What makes you so sure? All it would take is one little call to the right office stating that he's threatened Mason or more, and he'll be out of the country lickety split. Visa revoked." His smile grew into an ugly menacing grin.

"Are you threatening me?" I asked, my jaw clinched.

"Me? I would never." Decker stated innocently.

The fuck he wouldn't.

"I think with all that money you seem to have come into there's no need for me to give you my hard-earned income every month. Now that you've got your sugar daddy, why should I have to pay child support for a kid I rarely see anyway?"

If it was possible, I was sure that smoke would've come out of my ears. It was Decker's decision not to see Mason. He was the one who always unloaded our son on his parent's or had them pick him up. It didn't matter. I wasn't the one who made him pay me child support every month - it was the state. If he wanted to stop paying that was fine by me, because maybe then he'd get his ass thrown in jail and if I was lucky I'd be awarded full custody.

Having full custody had been a dream since the moment the judge gave Decker any rights to Mason. If only they would have listened to what Mason wanted or how Decker had treated him all of his life, then maybe it would have gone my way, but the judge wouldn't hear a word saying that Mason was too young and didn't know what he wanted. That it was possible I'd been coaching him to say negative things about his father. I didn't need to coach Mason for him to say how Decker had neglected him all his young life.

"Cat got your tongue? I can see that you know I'm right. One day not too long from now, when everything crumbles around you, you'll wish you never left me. Mark my words."

There was nothing else I could do but gape at him. How was he so delusional? There was no way in hell I'd ever go back to him. Even if Luke broke up with me tomorrow leaving me broken hearted, I'd rather die than be with him again.

"Now you really should go pick up Mason. It's getting late and I'm sure my parents will need their rest after having Mason all weekend long. I know he wears the shit out of me when I have to spend any time with him."

With that he turned and slammed the door in my face.

What the fucking hell had just happened?

Did he really believe all the shit he spouted?

Fuck him and fuck that.

Not in a million years.

32

LUKE

ALEX WAS HUNCHED OVER HER MACBOOK, HER SMILING FACE greeting me as she answered our nightly FaceTime call.

"Hello, beautiful. How are you today?"

Placing her hands on her chest, Alex's eyes tried to focus on me, taking a little too long. "Have you been drinking?"

"What else am I supposed to do? Mason is at his dad's and you're all the way in California. I'm all alone." Her lower lip stuck out in a pout looking cuter than ever.

"If I could, I'd be there with you. I'd hold you, kiss you, and make love to you."

Closing her eyes, she smiled probably imagining all the things I'd just told her. "I know you would. Only one more week to go until I get to see your handsome face in person." She bit her bottom lip as if she had something else to say but was unsure. Uncertainty won out as she kept quiet and watched me get comfortable on my new couch.

During the little down time I had between shooting, sleeping, and working out, I'd been trying to finish furnishing the house I'd bought before Alex and Mason arrived. I wanted it to feel like a real home not just a pit stop for when they were here.

"Are you excited for Leo to be there in a couple of days?" She asked before taking a sip of her drink. Her glassy eyes focused back to me and smiled again.

A smile grew on my face. I missed my family so damn much and Face Timing with them wasn't nearly enough after not seeing any of them in over a year. Like it wasn't enough with Alex.

"Your smile says it all." She grinned back making me long to kiss her. "I can't wait to meet Leo. Even though I've only talked to him a few times I already love him."

"He loves you too." Boy did he ever. Never had my brother liked any of the women I'd dated before. Not even in high school, but Leo asked about her every time we talked.

"It's going to be hard to have sex with Mason and Leo around." She blurted out and her face flushed. "I miss sexy times with you."

"Leo won't care, and Mason's room is on the other side of the house, or you'll just have to be quiet." Alex was never quiet when we had sex. It was as if she was making up for all the years of never being able to make a noise during sex. As for me, I didn't care, but I knew she didn't want Mason or Leo to overhear us. I'd do whatever made her comfortable and to not have negative feelings about our sex life. Now that she wasn't in that tiny house we wouldn't have that problem. She could be as loud as she wanted, and I couldn't deny that I loved I was the only man that had ever brought her to orgasm.

Never would she go without again. If anyone was going to be denied it was me.

"We'll figure it out when we get there. I don't think Mason will have a problem being on the other side, but I want to make sure he'll be comfortable."

"I've been working on his room a little and I think he'll like it. Lots of Marvel movie posters on the walls, with bedding to match. I may have even bought him some action figures that he already has to keep here."

Alex sniffled as her lips tipped up in a sweet smile. "What did I ever do to deserve you? You're the absolute best. You're going to spoil him if you're not careful."

"There's nothing wrong with a little spoiling every now and then. I may want to spoil you too."

I watched as her face almost became alarmed. "No," she shook her head a little too fast. It was a wonder she didn't get dizzy from the movement. "You've already spoiled me too much. I don't need anything, but you. Just *you*, Luke."

"That's good to hear. Did you have something on your mind earlier?" I asked hoping that she'd tell me what was on her mind and off the thought of me spoiling her and Mason. It didn't help that I hated the thought that she was keeping something from me.

She shook her head no as her eyes flicked up and down the screen of her computer then nodded her head. "Maybe, but I don't want to ruin our talk or my buzz."

What could she possibly have on her mind that would ruin our talk? Was she having doubts? Everything up until that moment had seemed fine. I knew that she missed me, but she had seemed to be handling the long distance.

When her ex found out they had moved, and he couldn't get into the neighborhood, he tried to make her life a living hell with constant phone calls and texts. It got to the point that she had gotten a new phone and number and kept the other one only for her limited communication with Decker. To top it all off, he had found out that she was dating someone, but he didn't know who yet. It seemed he had forgotten about me from the day of the funeral. Maybe he thought I dumped her. It didn't matter.

"Okay," she almost shouted with her eyes closed. "I need to know. Are you going to have to move back to Sweden?"

"What?" I laughed, but quickly contained it at the look of worry on her face. "No, I don't plan to move back there any time in the near future. Maybe when we're old." I shrugged. I liked the idea of us living there once we were in our fifties or maybe older. "Who knows what we'll want to do?"

"Who knows? You do! Are you going to have to move back?"

"No," I shook my head reiterating what I'd said previously. "Why do you ask?"

"Someone put into my head that you might get deported or your visa might expire, and you'd have to go back."

"Who the hell put that in your head?" My tone rose to the point of shouting, but I managed to reign myself in before I lost control. This was what she was worried about and I needed to relieve Alex of her worries that I'd be taken from her. Perhaps her ex had figured out who she was dating and was trying to get into her head. Whoever it was, they were no friend of hers if they were talking shit they had no clue about. "I have dual citizenship, so I can choose to live whichever place I choose. I have an apartment that I keep in Stockholm now that most of my family lives there. We all have places very close to one another and they look after mine. I think most of the time Leo lives there because he's there every time we talk."

Tears filled her eyes as she watched me speak. Once I was finished, one lone tear escaped as she sat still staring at her screen. Talk about a complete one-eighty. Was this because she'd been drinking or something more?

"I'm sorry I'm keeping you away from your family." She frowned and took a large mouthful of her drink.

"Would you drink some water for me?" She nodded her head and produced her always present water bottle taking a big swallow. "Thank you. Now please listen to me. You are *not* keeping me from my family. The commitments that *I* made, and their schedules, are what's keeping us apart. Yes, I could have gone –"

I needed to choose my words carefully or they could be misconstrued especially in her drunken state. I wanted to say home but knew that those were the wrong words. Sweden had been my home for as long as I could remember until I met Alex. She was *now* my home and I wanted to be where she was.

"For Christmas, I could have gone to Sweden to spend some time with my family, but I wanted to be with *you*. I thought we needed that time for us to grow and spend more than a few days together at a time. In the long run, I have no doubt that there will be plenty of Christmas's, many other holidays, and vacations that we'll spend in Sweden or elsewhere with my family." I took a deep breath as I took in her face. "You need to remember that it's a two-way street and they can come to visit me as well. I don't begrudge them for being busy and they understand why it's been so long since I've seen them, and what's kept me away."

She blinked a couple of times before she spoke almost too quietly for me to hear. "Thank you for that, but I still feel guilty." Lips turned down, she twirled her ponytail around her finger. "I wish you didn't have to choose."

"Baby, its fine. Don't worry about it. One day you'll have full custody and you can go wherever and whenever you want with Mason. Until that day, we'll make the best of it. It's no hardship."

"It was Decker," she blurted out, face red.

"What about him?" I was confused. What had the asshole done now?

"He was the one that put the idea of you being deported into my head. He found out who you are and is so pissed. Not that it matters, he would've been irate no matter who I dated. Even if he was some short, bald man. The only thing that would make him happy was if I found some man who abused me or if you broke up with me."

"Not going to happen." I fumed. Now wasn't the first time I'd thought about paying him off to stay out of her and Mason's lives. It would be worth it so that he didn't pull anymore shit.

"He threatened to stop paying child support. Maybe then he'll get in trouble and I can get full custody of Mason. That would be a dream." She said the last wistfully.

"We'll figure something out. Maybe if he stops paying child support it will help your case. I can't say."

Her face softened. "You have no idea how much I love you. I can't wait to be in your arms again. I don't know if I'll be strong enough to leave you."

"I love you too, skön."

Her head tilted to the side in confusion. "What does that mean?"

"Beautiful."

An easy smile spread across her face until it reached her deep blue eyes. Alex was always beautiful even if she didn't believe it, but when she smiled she was gorgeous.

"I love it when you call me that." She yawned, quickly covering it up with her hand.

"Getting tired?" There was no doubt she was since she'd been drinking for who knew how long.

"A little bit. I shouldn't have drunk so much. I'm sorry. I guess no phone sex tonight."

"Nothing to be sorry about. You deserve to let loose. You know, I don't call you every night for phone sex. We aren't all about sex."

Closing her eyes, Alex tilted her head to the side. "I *do* know, but it makes me feel closer to you when I pretend it's you that's touching me." A tear slipped down her cheek as she bit her bottom lip.

"Baby," I cajoled.

A smile slowly formed on her beautiful face. "Do you remember the first time I tried to give you a blowjob? Oh my God, I'm so sorry for that."

My hand slipped down into my briefs, I squeezed my cock and let out a moan. "What I wouldn't give to have your lips wrapped around my cock right now."

"Your cock is beautiful. If I was there I'd blow you."

How drunk was she?

"It's perfect. I miss your cock."

"He misses you, and so do I."

"God, I miss you." A yawn escaped, and she quickly covered it with her hand.

"Before I let you go for the night I got some good news when I left the studio tonight."

I couldn't believe that I'd held it in for as long as I had, but I had to tell her before we got off the phone.

"What is it?" she asked hopeful, biting her bottom lip.

"From now on Night Shadows will start filming in June. They weren't sure if it was doable but understood how important it was for me to be with you as much as possible, plus the circumstances of why you can't be in LA during the school year." I watched as a smile slowly spread across her face with each word I spoke. "The bad news is that if they can get next season written by the end of filming season three then they want to start four almost right away. No one will know until close to the end of shooting."

"Oh my God, Luke!" She jumped up and all I could see was the lower half of her pink tank top. "Really! That's great news! I mean, I secretly hope they don't finish writing it in time so you won't have to film it until next summer, but it doesn't matter. I have so much more freedom in the summer. It will be a lot of traveling for when Mason has to see his dad, but it will be worth it. I can't believe they agreed!" I watched as she jumped up and down a few times. "I can't tell you how happy I am." She sat back down with her hand over her heart.

She didn't have to because the way her face brightened, the

happy tears in her eyes, and the perm-a-smile on her face told me all I needed to know. Along with all her jumping. It was as if I'd given her the moon and stars and all I'd done was given her more of myself.

Lifting her hand, Alex trailed her finger over her screen as she continued to smile.

"What are you doing?"

"Touching you. I don't know if I can wait a week to wrap myself around you."

A week would seem like a year until I had her in my arms, but in the end all of this would be worth it. "I promise it will pass in no time. The second I get you alone I'm going to taste every inch of you."

"I like the sound of that." Her face flushed with want.

"It's a date." I promised.

Leaning forward she pressed her pouty lips to her screen. "Until then. I love you, my sweet Luke."

"I love you, too, my beautiful Alex. Sweet dreams."

"Of you, always."

33

Unlike the last time I flew into LA, Mason and I didn't have to wait for Luke to pick us up. Instead he was waiting for us with a sign that read Alex and Mason. The moment Mason caught sight of Luke, he took off as fast as his little legs could take him and didn't stop until he hit Luke's arms as he picked him up for a big hug.

I couldn't help but smile at them. Mason had missed Luke since last seeing him in January. Although they talked on the phone some, they didn't talk nearly as much as Luke and I. Little boys don't have a lot to say on the phone or at least not for long. It was so sweet seeing them together and how happy Mason was when around Luke.

"Buddy, I'm going to put you down, so I can say hello to your mom. I need you to do me a favor okay. Can you do that?"

"Yeah." Mason smiled up at him.

Taking one of Mason's fingers, Luke looped it through one of his belt loops. "It's only for a minute while I say hi."

Nodding Mason said, "Mama missed you, so you should say hi."

"Thanks, buddy. I missed her too. Now hang on." Luke insisted.

Stepping to me, Luke pulled me into his arms squeezing me tight. It felt like home and safety. It had only been a second and I never wanted to leave. His arms left me for his hands to cup my face. "Hello, beautiful." He grinned his lop-sided smile. "Fuck FaceTime doesn't do you justice. You look too good. I can barely keep this PG." Giving me a kiss that was a little more than PG, he pulled back to murmur against my lips. "I missed you."

"I missed you too, handsome. I'm counting down the hours until we can be alone."

"It's a promise." Breaking away, his eyes scanned around us. "We should probably get out of here." Turning to his right, Luke signaled what had to be the biggest man I'd ever seen. He was taller than Luke and double in width. "This is Rome and he'll be helping us get your luggage and get out to the car. I'll carry Mason, and when we get outside I'm going to try to explain that we don't want any pictures of Mason taken, or at least not his face."

"Do you think it'll work?" Because I desperately wanted it to.

"I hope so otherwise life around LA will be much more difficult. Sarah plans to issue a statement afterward explaining that we want privacy for Mason and hopefully, because he's a minor, they'll respect our wishes."

Kneeling down until he was eye level with Mason (it was quite the feat with the incredible height difference between the two), he explained. "When we leave there will be lots of people and some may have cameras trying to take our picture. I'm going to carry you out to the car and I want you to keep your face hidden against my neck. If that's okay with you?"

"Will you and mama be okay?" Mason sweetly asked.

"Yeah, we'll be okay. We've got Rome here to help us if anyone gets out of line. Now's not the best place to talk about it, but when we get to the house I'll try to explain all this craziness." He made a silly face causing Mason to smile. "Sound good?"

Mason nodded and with that Luke stood with Mason in his arms. "Alex, make sure you've got a good hold on your purse. I want you to keep one hand at my elbow and if you can, loop a finger through my belt loop." He looked saddened for a moment before he started to head for baggage claim.

This was the price he had to pay to be an actor and I was sure in that moment he would have given it up just to be able to walk out of the airport with ease.

We were in luck and the area wasn't swamped with people waiting for their bags. When I spotted our bags, I only had to point, and Rome quickly grabbed each of them up and started to escort us out to the parking lot.

The moment we stepped outside, and the cameras started to swarm us, Luke lifted a hand and started to speak in an authoritative voice. The crowd quieted and listened intently. "Alex and I want to ask that you please respect her son's privacy and not take his picture especially his face. He's only a child and doesn't deserve to have his face splashed all over the internet. We want to make this experience positive for him so please respect our wishes. Thank you." He waved

360 | HOLLYWOOD REDEMPTION: LUKE AND ALEX

and started to move again with Rome pushing up behind me.

Amazingly enough the paparazzi stepped back a few steps giving us room to make our way to a black SUV where only a few took pictures. Luke placed Mason in the back with a booster seat already installed and waiting just for him. Rome put our luggage in the back of the car and shook Luke's hand before he disappeared off into the parking lot.

Once inside he picked up my hand, kissing my palm. "Are we ready?"

"Ready." Mason called from the back seat excitedly.

"Are you hungry? I thought we could pick up some lunch at In-N-Out Burger. It's a must have while in LA and I doubt my brother has eaten anything, so he'll be starved by the time we get back."

"I'm hungry! Can I get a Coke, mama?"

"We'll see about a Coke," I answered him. Turning to Luke, I couldn't help but smile as I took him in. "I really missed you. You have no idea how much." I palmed his cheek and let my thumb rub over his scruff and bottom lip.

His lips parted, eyes dilated. "I have a pretty good idea."

I couldn't wait for Luke to show me how much he'd missed me during our last two months a part, but that would have to wait until we were away from innocent eyes.

"Whose car is this? It looks exactly like the one you bought in Fairlane, but a different color."

Luke looked out the windshield sheepishly before side-eyeing me. "It's mine. There's a lot of things you can't do with a car and after buying yours—" My head whipped in his direction because the one in Missouri was not supposed to be mine.

He dismissed my look with a flick of his hand. "You know what I mean. If you think about it, I wouldn't have even been able to fit both you and Mason along with your luggage in the other car. This is more prudent, and it's helped a great deal as I worked on the house."

"Don't think I'm going to forget about your little slip," I warned.

"Never a doubt in my mind." He quipped back with a big smile.

"Luke," I sighed heavily. We hadn't even been in LA an hour and I was already worried and frustrated. "You've lived here almost five years while you stayed with friends and only a single car in your name and now you've bought two houses along with two more cars all within a few months. It's not that I don't appreciate everything that you've done because I do, but I don't like that you've spent all this money."

He placed his hand on my leg and let it spread out engulfing my thigh. My words stalled as I enjoyed the warmth of his touch. "If you're worried that I'm spending all my money there's no need. Yes, what you said is true. I stayed with friends and only had my car because I was so busy that I saw no point in owning a house where I'd never be, but things have changed. My life has changed for the better. I have you and Mason now and I plan to be home as much as possible." His hand squeezed my thigh to reassure me. "As for the money, I have plenty of it. Staying with friends afforded me the opportunity to save on rent or a house payment. If it will make you feel better when we get home, I'll show you how much I have in my accounts."

Placing my hand on top of his, I laced our fingers together. "That won't be necessary. I trust you."

"I think it would put your mind at ease." He turned and smiled at me.

On our way to get lunch, Luke and Mason talked about In-N-Out Burger and what Mason had been doing at school. I loved the ease in which they talked. It was something Mason had never had with his father and it was obvious he craved a male figure that cared both about what he had to say and about him. It broke my heart that he'd lived this long without it, but if I hadn't been married to Decker, I never would've had him. A tear slipped down my cheek and I hastily wiped it away. I wouldn't think about Decker and his asshole ways while I was here with Luke.

"Hey, are you okay?" Luke asked softly with concern.

"Yeah." I leaned over to kiss him on the cheek and whispered in his ear. "Happy to have you in our lives."

"I feel the same, beautiful. I feel the exact same."

34

WHEN I IMAGINED MEETING LUKE'S YOUNGER BROTHER FOR THE first time, it was nothing like what happened in real life. The moment the garage door started to go up, he bounded out of the house and was sweeping my door open before I could blink. Taking my hand, he pulled me out of the car and into his arms, squeezing me tight. Not quite as tall as his brother, Leo was still well over six-foot-tall with me cradled in his arms, rocking me back and forth.

Murmuring into his shirt, I spoke unsure if anyone could hear me. "I think he likes me."

"Mama?" Mason asked hesitantly in a small voice.

Pulling away, I turned to find Mason standing beside Luke, holding his hand with worried eyes. "Hey, sweetie. It's okay. This is Luke's brother, Leo. He's just excited to meet us. He's not scary. I promise."

Leo moved from behind me and slowly walked over to Mason where he got down on his knees, holding out his hand for Mason to shake. "I'm sorry if I scared you, buddy. Like your mom said, I was excited to finally meet you both. I've talked to your mom on the phone a couple of times, and every time I talk to my brother he talks about you and your mom." Every word was spoken quietly as he tried to ease Mason's fears.

Leo eyed Luke in what looked as if he hoped he wasn't scaring Mason further. It was an odd situation since Mason had never had that kind of reaction to anyone before. It wouldn't be good if he was scared of Luke's brother for our entire trip.

Luke smiled at his brother and nodded his head. "Hey, little man. How about we let Leo bring your bags in and I'll show you to your room. I've been working on it and I think you're going to like it."

"You have a room just for me?" Mason's eyes were wide and eager.

"One all for you."

Mason smiled brightly. You would have thought he had received every Christmas present he'd ever asked for in that moment. "Let's go!"

We watched as Luke took him inside the house and a few seconds later we heard Mason exclaim. "You've got a pool! Awesome!"

Leo rested a hand on my shoulder. "I really am sorry about scaring him. It seemed like Luke was gone forever and I was excited."

"Don't worry about it. Mason's tired and hungry and wasn't expecting to have a huge man come bounding out of the house. It's sweet you were so excited to meet us."

"How could I not be? The whole family is so happy that Luke met you."

"What do you mean?" I asked as we walked into the kitchen.

"We were all worried about him. He's been here in the states working almost nonstop with only a few friends and then all of a sudden, he's calling home talking about this woman he met and her little boy." Leo stopped at the counter and leaned against it. "It was obvious from the first phone call that he was enamored with you. I've never seen him this way about a girl. It's great to see him find love and settling down."

"You need to stop or you're going to make me cry. I'm not going to lie and say I wasn't worried about what your family would think about me, a divorced, single mother."

"Don't talk like that. Luke hasn't told us much, but it sounds like you're better off not being married and Mason is adorable. You shouldn't worry, my family already loves you and once they meet you you'll be part of the family."

Wrapping my arms around him, I hugged Leo as relief flowed through me. "Thank you."

"Is everything okay?" Luke asked with Mason by his side. He watched, concerned, as I stepped back from Leo.

"Sweetness must run in the family. Leo almost made me cry."

"Only telling her the truth, bro. Please tell me that you got me some burgers." Leo eyed the bags full of food.

Luke laughed as he started to remove everyone's lunch. "I told you he wouldn't have eaten yet."

We sat at a small table that was in the kitchen area eating our lunch. I took in the changes that had been made since I was here in January. Not much had been done since Luke had only just bought the house, but now I could see all the small touches he'd added. There were candles and a few knick-knacks here and there. I hadn't ventured into much of the house, but now it looked lived in. It was a home instead of just a house.

"Mama did you know that there's a pool? Luke said I could swim in it, but only if someone is out there with me."

Reaching over, I squeezed Luke's arm that rested on the table. "He's right you have to have someone out there. I bet we'll get to swim a few times while we're here, especially if the pools heated."

"For you, it's heated. I haven't had a chance to use the pool yet, but I knew you'd want to hang outside and use the pool."

"Hey, Leo," Mason called animatedly. "Did you know that I have a new house where we live, and it has a pool too? We haven't been able to go swimming because it's too cold there."

"A new house with a pool? That's cool. I know all about the cold. I live in Sweden and it's been cold and dark for months. I may never want to leave the LA sunshine."

Mason tilted his head with furrowed brows. "Where's Sweden? Is it close to Missouri?"

"No, it's very far away." Leo's face softened. "Sweden isn't in the United States. It's in Europe. Do you know where that is?"

"Mmhmm, no," Mason shook his head. "I think I've heard of it."

"After lunch we'll get on the computer and I'll show you where it is if you want."

"Have you seen my room yet? Mama my room is so cool! You have to see it. Can I show you after we eat?"

"Yeah," Leo answered. "You can show us and then I'll show you where Sweden is while Luke shows your mom what he's done to the house." He winked at Luke, but quickly turned his attention back to Mason.

After lunch was finished, we all let Mason lead us to his room where he showed Leo and me the room Luke had made for him. It was amazing all the work that he'd put into making Mason a space of his own.

Crooking my finger, I beckoned Luke to me. He gave me a small smile as he slowly walked to me. Once he was in arm's reach, I wrapped my arms around his neck, giving him a hug and kiss. "Thank you. I can't remember the last time he was so happy. This means a lot to the both of us."

Pulling my body flush against his, Luke kissed my forehead. "I'd do anything for the two of you. Get used to it."

"Where's your room, mama? My bed's so big you can share with me if you want."

Biting my bottom lip, I was unsure what to say. Luckily Luke saved me. "When you're here your mom and I will share my bedroom and when I'm in Fairlane, your mom will share her bedroom with me."

Mason looked confused for a moment and I got worried that he wasn't ready for this step in our lives. If that was the case, I was going to be heartbroken. I couldn't imagine spending another night not in Luke's arms.

"If that's alright with you. We should've had a sit down with you and asked how you'd feel about me moving in with the both of you and sharing a bedroom with your mom."

When Luke stayed the last time, he slept in my room, but maybe Mason hadn't paid much attention. I knew for a fact that he'd found us asleep in my bed together.

"You're moving in with us?" His little eyebrows furrowed in confusion. "But you live here."

"It *is* confusing and for that I'm sorry. My job requires that I be here to shoot the show that I'm on, but when I'm not shooting it or have another project, I would like to live with you and your mom. I would also like for you to consider this house yours too."

Mason's eyes grew large as he looked from Luke to me and then scanned his room before coming back to Luke again. "I'd have two houses?"

"You'd have two houses," Luke answered with a twitch of his lips.

"Can I come here whenever I want?"

"Most of the time. If you have to be with your dad or in school, then you have to stay in Fairlane."

Mason sat down heavily on his bed and his little bottom lip stuck out. I felt the same way, but there was nothing I could do since his father had joint custody and there was no way he'd let us live here because then our lives would be happy without him.

Sitting down beside him, I hugged my sweet little boy to my side. "When you're not in school or with your dad we can be here with Luke. Would you like that?" Mason nodded his head but didn't say anything. "Do you not want Luke and I to share a room? Is that it?"

"You should share a room, so you can be happy. Maybe then you won't cry as much."

Shit. Obviously, I hadn't done a very good job at hiding my crying. With my head hung, I spoke quietly for only Mason to hear. "Baby, I'm sorry you heard me crying."

"Were you crying because of Luke?" he asked for everyone to hear.

Looking up, I saw that both Luke and Leo were watching us intently. I couldn't lie about why I'd been crying. "Yeah, baby, I was crying because I missed Luke and wanted to be with him."

"Sometimes when I'm with dad, I cry because I miss you and wish I was at home. Is that bad?"

Clutching him to my chest, I hugged him as tears began to build. "It's not bad. When you're gone I miss you too."

"Do you cry when I'm gone?"

Smiling sadly, I nodded. "Yeah, I do. I always miss you when you're gone."

"He can move in with us." He nodded resolutely. "I don't want you to be sad anymore and I like Luke. Are you going to get married?"

Clearing my throat of all the emotions that had built up, I still sounded a little hoarse when I spoke. "Someday. Maybe. He has to ask me."

This time it was Luke who cleared his throat from across the room. "I have it on good authority that your mom will say yes *when* I ask her to marry me."

Clapping his little hands, Mason beamed up at me. "I think he's going to ask."

"Hey, buddy. How about you and I go to the office and I show you where Sweden is while your mom and Luke talk?" Leo could barely keep his face straight as he led Mason out of the room, and to the office wherever the hell it was in the house.

"I don't even know where the office is." I stated as Luke pulled me from the room and down the hall.

"It looks over the pool. I thought you'd like that. It's relaxing."

"You're really going to have to give me another tour after we *talk*. I hardly know where anything is."

"Yes, after we talk." He turned on me, locked the bedroom door, and looked serious instead of ready for me to jump him.

My hands turned clammy and shook from the look on his face. "What's going on?" I asked suddenly nervous.

"Why did you say maybe we'd get married?" The hurt was evident in his eyes.

My heart broke seeing how sad my words had made him. Pulling him to the bed, we sat down, and I kept hold of his hand. "I said maybe because even though I truly believe that one day we'll get married, there's no guarantees in life. If for some reason we didn't get married and I told him we were, it would break his heart." I took in a shuddering breathe. "I don't want him to think that I lied to him. He's already lived a hard-enough life because of his father."

Luke didn't understand, and I'd unintentionally hurt him. I watched his pained face look outside and I fought desperately not to cry. I needed to stay clear headed and not break down.

"In theory I understand." He stated as he continued to look away. "If I asked you to marry me today would you tell him we're getting married?"

"*If* we were engaged I'd tell him, but this isn't a scheme to get you to ask me to marry you. Hell, he just found out today that we're living together."

"Why didn't you tell him?" he asked, hurt again.

Fuck me. I was really falling down on the job at being a mother and girlfriend.

"If I'd told Mason that we were living together he wouldn't have understood why you weren't there. He's only seven. Even after all this time he's still getting his head wrapped around the idea that his parents no longer live together, and that he has to go be with his dad every other weekend when he doesn't want to." Rubbing my thumb over the back of his hand, I felt tears prick at the back of my eyes. "I promise you that I didn't do it to hide or hurt you. It's killing me to know that I hurt you. I'm so sorry, Luke. I hope that you know that I'd never intentionally hurt you."

Smiling sadly at me, he pulled me onto his lap. "Maybe I'm overreacting. I never thought of any of it from your point of view. I've been shouting it from the rooftops that when I finish filming that we're going to be together and living in Fairlane."

Straddling him, I brought my lips to his, my arms around his neck as I spoke. "This isn't how I planned our reunion. I was going to jump you the minute we got in here. Now, I feel like I've let you down and I'm a failure."

Resting his forehead to mine, he sighed. "If anyone's a failure here it's me. Not once did I think about Mason and what he'd make of our relationship. We slept in the same bed when I was there last." He shook his head. "I never thought that he wasn't ready or might have a problem."

"I don't blame you and as you saw earlier he doesn't have

any problems. He really loves you. Every day for the last two weeks he's been asking when we were leaving to come here. He missed you."

Holding me tighter, he rested his head against mine. "Sounds like he wasn't the only one."

"I never denied that I missed you." Closing my eyes, I soaked in his body heat, his smell, and the fact that I was in his arms once again.

"No, you told me, but not that you were crying." Kissing the side of my head, he rearranged us until we were laying down on the bed with me cocooned by his body.

"You knew I cried some, but no, I didn't tell you every time because what was the point. It would only make you feel worse and I didn't want that." I closed my eyes as a tear escaped and dropped to his shoulder. "It was much harder than I thought it would be, even talking every day. There were so many times where I wished I could kiss you or even hold your hand. I just wanted your touch. To feel your presence."

"We have a whole week together, but I promise we'll do better this time around. I'll try to get a work schedule while you're here and we'll make plans and book plane tickets. At least once a month, we'll either be here or in Fairlane. Deal?"

"Deal. Now, how long do you think Leo can entertain Mason?" I asked looking up at him through my lashes.

"I think he can handle him for a little while longer. Why? What were you thinking?" he smiled mischievously.

"I'm thinking I need you inside of me. I want you in my mouth and for you to stop the need that's been building since you left. Having the real thing is so much better."

Sliding down, I unzipped his pants, taking him in my mouth, and finally letting Luke sate me for the first time in two long months.

35

THE BED DIPPED ON MY SIDE, SLOWLY ROUSING ME FROM A DEEP sleep. A soft brush of lips woke me even further. "I'll be back as soon as possible. Leo's coming with me today and maybe tomorrow you can visit."

"I'd like that," I whispered, closing my eyes as I started to fall back to sleep. "Love you."

Luke brushed the strands of hair from my face. "I love you, too, beautiful."

The next thing I knew, I sat upright as a shrill alarm woke me. *What the hell was going on?*

Mason's little feet pounded down the hall along with him crying.

Jumping out of bed, I ran to meet him and swooped him up in my arms. I had no idea what time it was, but it had to be early because Mason never slept late, and the sky was barely beginning to show a small amount of light through the down-stairs windows.

Luke had installed blackout curtains in his bedroom, so it

was impossible to tell what time it was in there without a clock.

Closing and locking the door to the bedroom, I raced to the security panel by the bed to turn off the alarm. I could barely think from the shrill noise and I hoped that once it stopped Mason would calm down.

My phone rang, and I scrambled to pick it up once I saw it was Luke calling. "Hello? Luke?"

"Alex," he said my name in a calm but tense tone.

"I'm here! The alarm's going off. It's so loud I can't even remember the code. Can you walk me through it, please?"

"Is Mason with you?" he asked with a strained but composed voice.

"Yes, we were still asleep, but we're in your bedroom now and he's crying."

"Okay. Great. I want you to do everything I tell you. Take Mason into the closet with you and close the door. Go now and tell me when you're in the closet."

Gathering Mason in my arms, I followed Luke's instructions and told him when we were in the closet. Up until that point, I'd thought the alarm going off was a mistake, but there was no reason for us to be in the closet if it was a false alarm.

"Good. Now I need you to look behind the clothes on my side. Feel along the wall until you find a rectangle like indentation. When you find it, I want you to push in on it. Okay?"

"Okay," I answered shakily. My hands searched every inch behind his clothes, going over and over it, and not finding what I was supposed to find. I was ready to give up and cry when my fingers hit an indentation. "I found it!"

"Push on it." I heard some other voices that sounded like

they were talking to Luke, but I ignored them. My sole focus was on his voice.

Pushing on the wall a hiss sounded as a door opened into a separate room that I had no idea existed. "There's another room," I stated the obvious.

"Yes, grab Mason and close the door. Once you're inside and press the red button on the panel no one can get in from the outside. One thing before you close the door. Your cell phone will cut out, so I want you to call me on the phone in the room. Can you do that?"

"I think so," I answered as I looked at what looked like a bunker inside a house. It wasn't fancy, but there was a cot to sleep on and a chair to sit on along with a small refrigerator in the corner. Along one wall were monitors showing the security cameras. Taking the phone from the wall, I realized I didn't know Luke's phone number.

"I don't know your number. I'm going to pull it up on my phone and call you." I sagged onto the cot with Mason on my lap, my hands shaking.

"Call me back," he demanded. "I love you, Alex. Everything's going to be fine. You're both safe."

"I want you to know that I love you so much." It took everything in me not to say that I didn't want to die. I didn't want Mason to be scared more and I didn't want to admit to myself that there was a possibility we were in that kind of danger, but what other danger made you hide in a secret room.

Hanging up, I pulled up Luke's contact information and quickly dialed his phone. "Alex," he sighed in relief. "Now hit the red button to lock yourselves in."

Standing up on shaky legs, I moved in front of the panel

and slammed my hand against the red button as if hitting it hard would make the door close quicker. I watched as it slowly closed with a hiss letting me know that we were now sealed in. Sliding to the floor, I looked up to find Mason watching me with wide eyes. He was scared and so was I.

I got up so that I could comfort him and be able to see what was going on with the monitors. I sat down once again, holding Mason tight and scanning the screens.

"Alex! Alex!" Luke screamed through the phone that I'd placed down when I went to shut the door.

Picking it up, I tried to look for what had set the alarm off and not cry into the phone. "I'm here."

"Thank God! You went silent and I didn't know what happened. Did you get the door closed?" I thought I heard tires screech in the background.

"It's closed. I'm looking at the monitors trying to find what set the alarm off." As I tried to see if someone was in the yard or inside, I saw a large rock thrown through one of the floor to ceiling windows that were in the living room overlooking the pool. I gasped, "Oh my God! Luke!"

Someone was trying to get into the house and whoever it was meant business. Didn't they hear the alarm? Luckily now that we were in the hidden room, we couldn't hear the alarm, but it was still going off when I closed the door and that person had to have heard it.

"What?" He asked, worry strong in this voice. "I swear I'm going to have a heart attack before I make it there."

"You're coming? Please be safe. I couldn't bare it if something happened to you. Someone just threw a rock through one of the windows by the pool."

"I'm on my way and so are the police. They should be there any minute now. Remember no one can get to you in there. You and Mason are both safe. I promise."

A lone body slipped from the broken window into the house with a baseball bat over his or her shoulder. I watched the person slowly creep up the stairs heading straight toward the bedroom. How did this person know where to look for us?

"Someone's coming," I whispered into the phone as I held Mason tighter.

"Where is he?"

I couldn't answer as the figure tried the handle but got nowhere since I'd locked it. Raising the bat to knock on the door, the figure stopped short and turned its head to listen.

Sirens?

Up until now the figure had kept its head down so I couldn't tell who it was except whoever it was, was skinny and short. Now I got a good look at her face as she turned to the camera and it was Ashlyn Jade.

Ashlyn was in Luke's house.

She had broken in.

Did she know that Luke was gone or was she hoping he was here? Did she know that I was here? She had to, because why else would she have brought the bat?

"Luke." In that one word, I was telling him that I was scared, that I didn't want us to die, and I wanted him here with us.

A flurry of fast spoken Swedish came down the line both from Luke and Leo.

On the monitor, her head swung from the door that she wanted to get into and down the hall. Was she hearing sirens?

Could she hear them over the shrill noise coming from the alarm? I wasn't sure, but if it would make her leave I was all for it.

"Luke," I gasped out. "It's Ashlyn."

My heart pounded in my ears so much that I couldn't hear what Luke was saying. It was almost deafening. Mason sat in my arms hugging me back just as tightly as I held him. Keeping his head down so that he wouldn't see something that he could never unsee. Somewhere deep within me, I knew that we were safe but seeing her out there overrode that thought process.

"The police should be there in one minute. You're doing great. Just a little while longer and it will all be over. Do you hear me?" he asked when I didn't respond.

"Yes," I managed to say faintly.

Ashlyn turned with an evil grin on her face and knocked on the door twice with the bat. Her body weight going with every hit. She meant business. When nothing happened, she turned around in a circle with her head thrown back, her mouth wide open. She was yelling. Even though I couldn't hear it, I knew she'd been screaming. The question was, who was she after?

Stopping abruptly, she swung one last time before racing down the hallway and out the window she previously broke.

"She's gone," I choked out. "She went out the way she came in."

"Stay on the line with me, Alex. I'll be there in less than five minutes. Are they there yet?"

"Who?" I asked confused.

"They're pulling up now," I heard in the background.

"The police. I was asking Leo, he's on the phone with dispatch." He answered back distractedly. "They should be there. Sit tight and don't come out until you see me on the other side of the door. The code is 0525."

"My birthday is the code," I stated. A sob catching in my throat.

Now that Ashlyn was gone my adrenaline crashed, making me a shaky, crying mess. Mason held my trembling hand with his eyes aimed at the monitor now that I wasn't keeping him from looking. I hated that I was breaking down in front of him, but I had no control over my emotions any longer.

"Mama, I see police outside."

"That's good. They're supposed to be here." Squeezing his little hand, I brought it up to my cheek and held it there. Oh God, he was never going to want to come to California again. My heart broke a little at the thought, helping to calm me down some from my spiraling emotions.

Taking us over to the chair, we sat watching the monitors waiting for Luke. Police were all over the yard and in the house, but I didn't want to leave the room and have to talk to them. I only wanted to be in Luke's arms.

My breath caught as I saw Luke's car pull into the driveway and he jumped out of the car. He took off running toward the house but got caught by one of the police officers. It looked like he was pulling at his hair. After a few moments, he was let go and running into the house and straight upstairs.

I stood with Mason in my arms as we waited to see Luke's face on the monitor, but he was stopped by the locked bedroom door. How was he going to get in? He took in the damage created by the bat and then rammed the door with his shoulder trying to get in. I didn't know what to do. Should we stay in the panic room or should we let Luke in the bedroom?

"What do we do?" I asked Mason. "I don't want him to get hurt."

There was a good possibility he might, unless he had the police knock it down. After all this I wasn't sure what we should do, but I didn't want Luke to injure himself or for anymore damage.

"Let's go let him in." Putting Mason on my hip, I keyed in the code and waited for the door to hiss open. Once it was open I ran to the bedroom door.

"Luke," I cried out as we reached the door and heard a loud thud.

"Alex?" he yelled, frantic.

My hand shook as I tried to unlock the door. It took a couple of tries before I swung open the door and Mason and I were both enveloped in Luke's strong arms. He sank to the floor with us. All of us were hugging and crying.

"We're okay. We're okay." I kept repeating trying to reassure myself, but also Luke and Mason.

A few feet away an officer stepped forward, causing me to tense. "Mr. Sandström, we need to talk to your girlfriend for a few minutes. Can you please come down stairs?"

I felt Luke nod his head as he tried to stand with us in his arms.

"Does Mason need to be there for the questioning?" Leo asked from down the hall.

"I don't see any need to question him." The officer answered as he took a step back.

"Hey," Leo said quietly as he helped us all stand in one big group. "How about I take Mason into his room and we watch a movie or something? Can I do that?" Leo asked, eyes on me.

"Do you want to go with Leo for a little while?" I asked unsure what to do.

Mason hugged me tighter. "Will you stay with mama?" he asked Luke, his big blue eyes filled with concern.

"I won't leave her side." Luke vowed as he hugged Mason closer.

"We were really scared," Mason whispered, his chin trembled.

"I know you were, but you're safe now, and I promise I won't let anything hurt you. Do you want to go with Leo? You can stay with your mom if you want. We're going to go downstairs and talk to the police and tell them everything we know." Luke explained to Mason in a calm voice, but I knew he wasn't calm. The hand that held my hip continued to shake as he spoke.

"Can someone make me breakfast and then we watch a movie?"

We all let out a chuckle at Mason's ease of getting over the situation. I had a feeling it would be a long while before the rest of us felt as at ease as he did in that moment.

Leo stepped forward, taking Mason from my arms. "How about you and I make you and your mom some breakfast? We can have it ready for her to eat once she's done talking to the police."

Mason nodded, still looking worried. Luke noticed and tried to reassure him. "If you get scared or worried at any time, you can come sit with us."

Wrapping an arm around my shoulders, Luke kept me

close as we went down to the living room and sat waiting for an officer to question us. Unable to avoid looking at the window Ashlyn had broken, I gasped at the evidence of her insanity. The entire floor was littered with little pieces of glass.

A tall man with salt and pepper hair, in a brown suit that did nothing for him, sat across from us introducing himself as Detective Simmons.

"I understand this is a difficult time for you, but it's best to do this while it's still fresh. If you can walk me through the events that would be most helpful."

I proceeded to tell him what had happened from the time I woke to the alarm going off, up to the point where I saw Ashlyn Jade flee. Luke took it from there explaining that she'd been posting pictures of Luke and myself or him by himself in the background of her pictures, proclaiming that Luke was cheating on me, to seeing her in Mexico, and her taking a picture of Luke and Mason in our hometown and posting it.

"I'm sorry we couldn't do anything until it came to this, but with your statement and the video footage she *will* be arrested. I suggest you both get restraining orders both here in California and Missouri. That way if she posts any pictures, or comes into contact with you, you can call the police and she'll be arrested. If you think of anything else, you have my card, and can call me anytime."

Standing up in a daze, the morning's events caught up to me, I shook Detective Simmons hand and told him I'd let him know if I thought of anything else. I had no idea what I'd told him. The entire conversation was a complete blur as I watched Luke walk over to where the other officers were taking pictures of the evidence downstairs. They had already finished with the upstairs.

Now that I wasn't scared out of my mind all I wanted to do was have Luke and Mason in my arms and sleep. I knew being tired was a result of my adrenaline crashing and hoped that a cup or two of coffee would wake me up. I wasn't sure what the plan was now after everything that had happened. Luke needed to be at work and we couldn't possibly stay at his house.

Walking into the kitchen, I found Mason and Leo eating pancakes at the table smiling and laughing. I loved that Leo was so sweet to Mason and had taken to him as much as his brother had. Somehow, he was making Mason smile and laugh after the morning we'd had.

"We made pancakes!" Mason exclaimed, waving his syrupy fork in the air.

"Yay," I answered back with a yawn. "Is there coffee?"

"From earlier." Leo stood and poured me a cup.

"Can you bring the creamer? I need an unhealthy amount to tolerate the taste of coffee." Leo chuckled and brought the creamer along with my coffee. "I'm surprised there were ingredients to make pancakes, let alone chocolate chip pancakes."

Sitting back down to finishing eating, Leo smiled over at me. "There wasn't until two days ago. We went grocery shopping and Luke bought everything he thought you two would want to eat."

"Really?" My eyes welled up with tears and I closed them with a smile on my face. My heart swelled once more at another thing that Luke had done to make our stay more comfortable. He'd turned the house that he bought back in December into a home for all of us.

Arms wrapped around me from behind, the smell of ocean and sandalwood calming me and making me melt into his strong arms. "You okay?"

"Never better," I answered, turning to see him over my shoulder.

Slipping into the chair beside me, Luke kept one arm around me. "I find that hard to believe. You were..." His eyes squeezed shut and his throat bobbed with emotion. "Terrorized this morning." It physically pained him to say those words.

Turning toward him with my legs between his, I took both his hands in mine. "This morning was scary. I'm not going to lie, but what you've done to make this a home for us..." Bringing his hands to my mouth, I kissed the back of each one. "It takes away the scary and the crazy of the morning. I'm looking on the positive side of things. I can't explain what it means to me. How much I appreciate all that you've done. Your fridge has done a transformation from the barely here and I only eat crazy healthy to well, I guess the best term for it is kid friendly."

"It was a little too healthy, bro."

Luke side-eyed his brother. "I wish it was that simple, but I have to eat healthy and workout. You don't think I want to eat whatever I want when I want?"

"Hey," I called to get his attention back to me. He was still feeling Ashlyn's break in. "I wish I was as dedicated as you are, and I thought it was sweet that you bought the ingredients to make Mason's pancakes along with everything else you've done for us. Thank you, Luke." Leaning forward, I pressed a chaste kiss to his lips wishing that I could linger longer, but we had company and I knew how easy it was to get lost in him.

"Dude, I'm just giving you shit. You know that."

"I was a little worried about what we'd eat," I admitted to both of them. "While I admire your dedication, I'm not sure if I can eat that way one hundred percent of the time." Wrapping my hands around my warm coffee cup, I stood and looked to Luke. "Can you help me with something upstairs?"

"Of course." His answer was immediate as he took my hand and walked with me to the stairs. "What do you need help with?"

"Let's go to the bedroom or your office. I want to talk to you."

Tilting his head, his eyes scanned over me once before nodding.

Letting me lead, I brought us to the bedroom and sat on the side of the bed, bringing Luke down with me. He looked worried and I didn't want him to think anything was wrong. I was sure his train of thought had gone to a bad place since I asked him up here. To help ease his mind, I crawled onto his lap, wrapped my arms around him, and rested my head on his shoulder.

Hugging me back, he kissed the side of my head and murmured. "Talk to me."

"What are we going to do? We can't stay here with the broken window and Ashlyn on the loose. It's not safe."

"I've got an idea. Pack up."

36

STARING OUT THE WINDOW, I WATCHED FOR THE FIRST SIGN OF water. I was beyond excited that Luke was taking us to a friend's house in Malibu so that we could enjoy the beach and get away until the window was fixed, and the security system upgraded. They were out of town and offered the use of their house and private beach so that the paparazzi were less likely to find us.

The thought of seeing the ocean kept my mind off Ashlyn breaking in and what she might do if she wasn't found. What had happened to make her so delusional? So obsessed? Shaking my head to rid my thoughts of her, I focused on the side of the road and my first glimpse of the Pacific Ocean in almost twenty years.

Reaching across the center console, Luke picked up my hand and brought it to his lips, kissing each fingertip. Speaking low enough that only I could hear him, he asked. "Are you okay over there?"

"Yeah, focusing on seeing the water. Finding the good in the crazy."

"It shouldn't be much longer. At least traffic isn't as bad as it could be, otherwise it might take hours to get there."

"Today, I don't think I could handle being in the car for hours." In all truth, I was starting to lose my battle with not thinking about earlier.

"I know, Alex, but I promise we'll be there soon."

A sudden thought came to me and I turned in my seat looking at Luke's tense form. "You're supposed to be shooting today. Don't you need to go back?"

He shook his head then looked over at me with a slight smile that didn't meet his eyes. "They gave me a couple of days off to handle everything and then I arranged for all of you to come to set with me for the rest of the week. My trailer's nothing glamorous, but it does its job."

I let my gaze travel over his rigid jaw that ticked every few minutes along with his death grip on the steering wheel. His eyes laser focused on the road. I had no idea how to get him to relax or if it was even possible after this morning.

"Would it be better for us to go home early? I don't want to cause any problems for you."

Furious eyes landed on me causing me to shrink back against the window as he yelled. "Are you fucking shitting me, right now?"

"Luke, calm down." Leo scolded from the backseat where Mason stared wide eyed. It wasn't that he'd never heard any swear words or yelling. He had. Plenty of times from me and his father, but what was startling was Luke had never once raised his voice in the amount of time I knew him. I understood that he was upset, and it was a normal reaction, but I didn't want Mason to think Luke was anything like his father.

"I'm sorry." He turned and locked eyes with Mason and gave him a sad smile. "I'm sorry, buddy. Please forgive me. I didn't mean to scare you or yell."

"It's okay. I'm kind of used to it." Mason answered back softly, eyes still wide.

"Well, you shouldn't be. Neither of you should, and I'm so happy that you got away from that and chose to have me in your lives." Lifting my hand, he placed a soft kiss against my knuckles and held it to his chest as he drove. "Again, I'm sorry and *you* are not causing me any problems. None whatsoever. If you feel unsafe here then I won't stop you from going home, but I don't want you to leave." His voice desperately pleaded with me as his sad eyes shifted back and forth from the road to me and back again.

Leaning over, I kissed his cheek and hugged him as best as I could in the car and spoke quietly only for him. "We'll stay. I don't want to leave you and I'm sorry, too."

"You've got nothing to be sorry about, beautiful. I know you were just trying to help."

"Look! Water!" Mason yelled excitedly from the back seat. All thoughts of Ashlyn, and Luke's reaction, evaporated as we all turned to see the ocean.

Standing at the floor to ceiling windows that looked out onto the beach, I listened to the waves as they crashed against the shore. Luke had taken our bags to our room and showed

Mason and Leo where they would be staying as well.

"Hey, you want to head outside to enjoy the beach?" Luke murmured as he wrapped his hands around my waist pulling me back against him.

"That sounds nice." My eyes closed as I leaned back against him. "Thank you for planning this even if it didn't go according to design, and make sure to thank your friend for letting us crash at their place for a couple of days."

"I'm upgrading both houses with the best security systems. What happened today will *never* happen again. Fuck, Alex." He sighed against the back of my neck causing me to twirl around in his arms. His eyes were closed, and his face etched in pain. "If anything would have happened to either one of you, I don't know what I would have done." He shook his head and squeezed his eyes together tightly. "Hearing how scared you were on the phone, and poor Mason's little face when I got there."

Burrowing my head in his chest, I inhaled Luke's scent of ocean and sandalwood letting it calm me. "I won't lie. It was fucking scary, and as soon as they find her I'll feel a hell of a lot better, but I'm not going to let that crazy bitch ruin our time together. That's what she's wanted from the beginning."

"We won't let her win and with the LAPD out searching for her it won't be long before she's behind bars. How about we all get our swimsuits on and head down to the beach?"

It didn't take much to convince Mason out onto the beach. He was mesmerized by the ocean and hurried me to put his sunscreen on as fast as I could. The moment we stepped outside the doors of the house, Leo grabbed Mason up and promptly ran into the ocean with him. There was a huge lounger that was the size of a small bed out on the deck, Luke and I stretched out on it as we watched Leo and Mason play in the waves.

Curling up to Luke, I rested my head on his chest. "I hope Leo doesn't think that he's here to be a babysitter?"

"No, he's enjoying hanging out with Mason. Trust me, he would say something, but I also think he's trying to give us time together. He's a good little brother."

"He is. It's obvious how much he loves and misses you."

Wrapping his arms around me tighter, Luke spoke into the top of my head. "Yeah, I missed him too. All of them, really. I was hoping me, you, and Mason could all go visit them for Christmas. My parents are dying to meet you, and it would be nice for it to be before the wedding."

Turning my head to look up at him, I arched a brow. "Wedding? Mr. Sandström, you do remember that you have to ask me to marry you first, don't you?"

Smiling down at me, he ran his hand up my thigh. "I very much remember, and I promise you it will happen. After today it's taking everything in me not to ask you, but I want it to be special, not brought on by circumstance."

"Really?" I knew that my face was glowing, and I couldn't wait for our special moment. He nodded, leaning down with his own bright smile. His warm lips met mine in a reverent dance.

"Keep it PG up there," Leo yelled from the water's edge.

"Later," he sighed against my mouth. Giving him one last

kiss, I pulled away, and looked out to see Leo burying Mason in the sand. We were so lucky that everything worked out for us and Luke had the foresight to set up the panic room. Mason seemed unaffected as he played in the sand and ocean, his entire face lit up by his smile.

My eyes burned with tears as I crawled on top of Luke, hugging and straddling him, wanting to be as close to him as I possibly could.

Holding tight, Luke kissed the side of my head. "Hey, what's going on here? Are you okay?"

"Today was so scary and Mason somehow seems fine."

"I think he is. He was scared, but you held yourself together pretty well given the circumstances."

"I didn't even know you had a panic room, but if you hadn't set a new alarm code or had the phone activated, I don't want to think about what might have happened."

"When I first bought the house, I had no idea what the room was until I described it to someone on set. I figured it might be good in an earthquake, so I set it up just in case. Whoever lived there before was probably paranoid, but I'm glad they were because I can't even bear to think of what might have happened if you weren't in that room. If she'd broken down the door and gotten to you two."

"What set her off? Why go after you?" The rhythm of his steady heartbeat soothed me as I continued to rest my head on his chest.

"Your guess is as good as mine. I only ever spoke a few words to her when I met her, and it was so long ago it makes no sense."

I closed my eyes and let Luke rock me back and forth as I

listened to the waves crash. My eyes drifted shut. "I love you so much."

Right before the waves carried me off to sleep, Luke leaned back and held me tighter. "I love you more than you know, beautiful."

37

TWO MONTHS LATER

DRIVING BACK FROM TAKING MASON TO SCHOOL MY PHONE RANG through the car system announcing Luke was calling. I promptly hit to answer his unexpected call.

"Good morning, handsome. How are you this morning?" I asked, excited to talk to him so early in the day.

"Morning beautiful. I'm good, and you?"

"Good. I'm on my way to the grocery store before I head home and start working. Where are you?"

His early morning voice was a little gravelly as it came through the speakers. "We're shooting on location today and taking a break while some things get set up. I wanted to share some news with you if you have the time."

"I always have time for you. What did you want to tell me? Wait. Give me a second. I'm almost to the store and I want to FaceTime you."

It only took another minute to pull into the parking lot, park, and to FaceTime with him.

"You know how I couldn't come home last weekend

because I had to do a photo shoot and that was the only time available with my schedule?"

"Yes."

How could I forget? I'd been so disappointed that I wouldn't see him. Since Mason and I had visited in March, we'd been back to LA a few times when he wasn't supposed to be at his dads and Luke wouldn't be too busy to see us. Luke came every chance he had and although he wasn't in Fairlane often, it did feel like he lived here. Each time he brought more with him to leave and fill his space. It wouldn't be long until he finished shooting.

"Well, it was for *People Magazine* and their Sexiest Man Alive issue. I was told there would be fifty men in the magazine, but not what category I would be featured in. Today I found out and I thought I should give you some warning."

It took my brain a minute to comprehend what Luke said to me. My boyfriend was going to be in the Sexiest Man Alive issue! "Okay?" I thought this was a good thing. Maybe they had cut him, but it didn't sound as if that was the case.

With a slight smile, he answered humbly. "I am this year's *People Magazine's* 'Sexiest Man Alive'."

"Oh my God," I cried out in excitement. "Of course, you are. Congratulations, Luke. I'm so proud of you."

He chuckled looking away, his cheeks pink. I didn't believe that Luke thought he was ugly, but he seemed to have no idea how good looking he was.

"When is the issue coming out? I'm going to buy every magazine I find. Can I get a big picture of your cover to put up in the office?"

His head shook, but he was smiling. "I'll see what I can do."

"Why did you think you needed to warn me?"

"Warning probably isn't the best word for it, but I wanted you to know before anyone else."

"Aww, my man is the sexiest. Thank you for telling me, Luke. Can I tell Taylor, or do I need to wait?" I wanted to shout it from the rooftops.

"You can tell her. There's an interview also where I confirmed that you're my girlfriend, but I didn't say much just that yes, we are together and it's serious. I told them I wanted to keep my personal life as private as I can."

"Which is understandable. After the whole Ashlyn debacle, I'm sure everyone understands."

He leaned forward resting his chin on his steepled fingers. "Most will, but there are always some that expect that our lives should be an open book. By the way, the director loved your cameo and wants you to do another one next season. They love the idea of you being one of my donors at least once a season."

"Are you kidding me? I only did it because the extra didn't show up and I wanted to help. You can't even tell it's me under all that makeup and hair."

"You liked doing it, didn't you? They're excited by this new idea. Instead of me ending up with the main girl I've been pursuing the entire series, or so it seems, I'm going to end up with one of my donors, who they will find out has been the same person all along. It's a little twist that will leave the fans happy for Nikolai."

"I liked doing it. It was incredible being on set with you

and seeing you in your element, and I *do* want your character to have a happily ever after. Everyone but the villain should get a happy ending, even though I know that's not always how shows work."

"If they are alive I'm sure they will, but I don't know who lives or dies, and I won't until the very end. I'm sure the ending will change a time or two between now and then too."

"Well, your character *must* have a happy ending and if I can provide that for you then I'm happy to help."

Even through the phone I could see his eyes soften and warm as he spoke next. "You *are* my perfect ending."

"You're the fairytale that I never knew existed let alone hoped for."

His face softened, with his lop-sided smile filling the screen. I loved that smile. It always made my whole body fill with warmth.

"God you are too sweet and perfect. Sometimes I wonder what I ever did to deserve you. I can't wait until you come home. I'm counting down the days."

"Me too. Listen, I only have a few minutes before I have to be back on set, but I wanted to discuss something with you." He paused, running a hand through his hair. "I got an email this morning which I'm going to forward to you once we're off the phone. I've been asked to shoot a movie this summer in Hawaii. I'll only do it if you and Mason can come. I know he won't be able to stay the whole time since he'll be with his dad and grandparents on vacation for some of it. Do you think since he'll be with his dad for two weeks that he'd give up a couple of his weekends?"

"Doubtful, especially when he finds out it's so that we can

spend the summer in Hawaii. Fuck that would be a long flight to have to make back and forth every two weeks."

I watched as his face fell for only a brief second before he wiped it away. I hated to see the disappointment on his face. "I know, but I wanted to ask."

"Thank you for asking. I've always wanted to go to Hawaii. Fuck! Why does Decker have to be such an asshole?" I leaned my head back against the headrest with my eyes closed. "I'll talk to him and see what I can do, but I can't make any promises. Send me the info. Is it always like this with last minute casting?"

"No," he shook his head and then looked off for a moment. "I've got to go, but to answer your question, no. They heard that Night Shadows wouldn't be shooting until next summer and wanted me for the part. I'll call you tonight during my break. Love you and see you soon."

"I love you too. I'll be the one with the big smile on her face."

"I couldn't miss you for the world."

Blowing him a kiss, I sat back after disconnecting. How the hell was I going to convince Decker to give up his weekends with Mason? He wouldn't give in, just so he could hurt me. He was still raging about finding out that Luke was still my boyfriend and an actor. He hated that he was handsome and good to me and Mason.

He would especially hate that we were going to spend the summer in Hawaii. The place I had always wanted to go while we were married, but he was unable to take me.

My work was cut out for me.

38

TURNING OVER, I TRIED TO GET COMFORTABLE, BUT IT WAS impossible. It was day two of being sick, and I was miserable. Luckily Mason was at his grandparents for the weekend, so I didn't have to feel bad about neglecting him while I stayed in bed.

My eyes drifted closed as I wondered what Mason had done that day. The Nyquil was doing its job of pulling me back to sleep when I felt the bed dip. I shot up, looking around in the dark. My heart felt as if it was going to beat out of my chest. I started to turn on the lamp by the bed when strong arms encased me. As I started to fight out of the hold, I registered the smell of ocean and sandalwood.

Luke.

"Alex, it's only me. I'm sorry to scare you." He rasped in my ear.

Pulling out of his hold, I turned to launch myself back at him. Wrapping my entire body around his, I kissed his neck as I felt his arms tighten around me.

"What are you doing here? You're a week early." I murmured hoarsely against his warm skin.

"You're sick so I wrapped up everything early that way I could come home to take care of you. I wasn't sure if I would be here tonight or not, so I decided not to tell you since I knew you wouldn't get any rest waiting on me."

"How did you get here?"

"Airplane." He chuckled, kissing my temple. "How sick are you?"

"Pfft, not that sick. I meant from the airport, smarty-pants."

"I called Josh to pick me up." He rumbled in my ear.

"I would have picked you up," I pouted, as one hand rubbed up and down his back. He felt so good and so right. In my arms was where Luke was meant to be.

"I know you would have, but then it wouldn't be a surprise." He nuzzled into my hair placing kisses and inhaling every once in a while. "How are you feeling? Good enough to come downstairs?"

"I feel a hundred percent better now that you're here. What's downstairs?"

"Something I set up." He answered as he pulled me up off the bed. His hand caressed my cheek as he took me in in the soft moonlight that escaped through the crack of the curtains. "I missed your pretty face."

"I missed your everything. Your smell. Your heat. Your eyes and that kissable mouth. I don't want to let you go." Tears welled in my eyes at the reminder of how hard it had been to be separated from him for so long.

"You don't have to let me go. I'm right here and I'll do everything in my power to make sure we're never apart again like we were these last few months. Now come downstairs with me so I can show you something."

I let Luke lead the way with our fingers intertwined and what I was sure was a big stupid grin on my face, but I didn't care because Luke was here and nothing else mattered. When we got to the landing, he swept me up into his arms and made me promise that I wouldn't look until he told me to open my eyes. Nuzzling my face into his chest, I had no problem keeping my eyes closed. I would have kept them closed forever if it meant I could stay in his arms.

The first thing I noticed the moment he stepped off the final stair was the amazing scent of flowers. It filled the whole downstairs area and I knew that it was something Luke had done.

Sitting me down on my feet, Luke kept his hands on my waist as I got my footing. With my eyes still closed, I waited as a few moments of silence passed. Luke hadn't moved from his spot in front of me, but he also hadn't told me that I could open my eyes yet. Were we waiting on something?

One hand after the other let go of my waist for him to take my hand, squeeze, and place a kiss on it. "You can open your eyes now."

Cracking one eye open and then the other, I saw candles lit everywhere my eyes could see. Even outside on the deck. But what I noticed most was that the most gorgeous man in the world, my Luke, was down on one knee in front of me.

Tears instantly sprang to my eyes as I took him in. It was finally here. The moment I'd been waiting for, but never knew when it would happen.

He let out an amused breath, smiling up at me. "I wanted

this moment to be perfect. To find the perfect time and setting, but I realized yesterday when we were talking on the phone and I heard how miserable you sounded, along with how much I missed you, and all the opportunities that I'd let pass me by, I didn't want to wait for the perfect moment any longer. I'm sorry that you're sick, but I want it now." His face grew serious. "No, I need it now. I want to marry you as soon as possible and the longer I wait to ask you, the longer I have to wait for you to be my wife." His eyes glittered up at me, filled with tears of his own. "I wasn't sure if I was ever going to find 'the one', especially in Hollywood, but there you were, shining like a beacon in that restaurant, and I didn't know what to do with you at first." Luke let out a chuckle. "I wasn't sure if you would take a chance on me or want to be subjected to everything that is involved when dating a celebrity, but you were always so strong. The moment we kissed in New York, I knew you were it. You are 'the one'. My everything. My soulmate. The woman I want to spend the rest of my life with." His Adam's apple bobbed as he pulled out a jewelry box and gazed up at me with all his love for me shining back at me.

Nestled inside the box was an emerald cut, pink diamond ring, with two smaller stones on each side, blinding me even in the candlelight. He kissed the ring and then the back of my hand. "Alexandra Scarlett Sloane, will you please do me the honor of becoming my wife?"

The last time I was engaged I never got a proposal. The engagement was a weekend long formality before we were married. From the first time Luke had mentioned marriage, I never imagined what he would say when he asked, and nothing I could ever have thought of would have been anywhere near as perfect as what he said tonight.

Happy tears swept down my cheeks as the biggest smile I'd ever worn prevented me from speaking. I couldn't stop smiling or looking at his perfect face until his eyes dropped for a moment, breaking our contact.

"Yes! I would be honored to marry you and be your wife." Falling down onto him, I wrapped my arms around his strong shoulders and placed kisses all over his face until I reached his kissable lips. "I love you so much, Luke. I still can't believe you're here. This feels like a dream. I'm going to be so mad if I wake up in the morning and you're in LA, and there's no ring on my finger all because of some Nyquil induced dream."

He laughed against my lips, sweeping me into his arms once again and placing us on the couch with him above me. "I love you and I can promise you this is not a dream."

Cupping his cheeks in my hands, my thumbs swept along his stubble. "This is all so perfect. I don't care that I'm sick or whatever else you were waiting for. You made it perfect. Thank you." I nearly sobbed out.

"Anything for you."

He kissed the juncture of my neck and shoulder as his hands slid up the camisole I wore breaking the kiss only to remove it. Taking his time removing each piece of clothing left me panting with need.

Peering down at me, Luke asked with concern. "Are you up for this? If not, I can take you up to bed."

"Don't you dare." I threatened. My body felt as if it would combust if he stopped. "I want you to make love to me. We need to consummate our engagement." Holding my hand up, I wiggled my fingers, watching the diamonds flash in the candlelight. It would take a while before this didn't feel like a dream. Sitting up, I pulled Luke's shirt off over his head and ran my hands down his chest. His warm skin over tight muscles rippled at my touch.

"I believe we're supposed to consummate the marriage not the engagement, but I'm not going to argue with you. I'll happily consummate anything you want." He wiggled his eyebrows at me causing me to laugh.

"I missed you so damn much. I can't explain to you how happy I am that I get to fall asleep with you by my side."

"I think I have some idea," he murmured as he trailed kisses down my neck.

My hands delved underneath his waistband to meet his smooth, taut ass. Grinding myself against the ridge of his jeans, I wanted his pants off and to have the real thing. I was desperate for him. To feel his skin against mine. For him to stretch and fill me.

"Luke," I panted in his ear. "I need you inside of me now." I tugged on his jeans to no avail. "You have too many clothes on."

He stood, taking his body heat away, but in that moment I didn't care. I watched as he quickly undid the button on his jeans and slowly slid the zipper down. Taking his cock in his hand, he stroked a few times, moaning with each rotation. "Is this what you want?"

"I want all of you." I writhed as he nudged my opening.

"Ask and ye shall receive."

Luke pushed in and I thought he was going to slam into me. That our joining was going to be fast and hard after being apart, but instead he took his time filling me inch by inch. One hand found mine and laced our fingers together over my head as the other pulled one leg high up on his back for a deeper angle.

In and out he filled me, never taking his eyes off mine. He didn't speak, but his eyes said everything.

I love you.

I'm home.

You're mine and I'm yours.

Forever.

39

IN HIS ARMS.

In *our* house.

My head rested on Luke's chest and as I listened to his heartbeat, falling asleep, I knew what I wanted. "I want to get married this summer while we're in Hawaii."

"I'd marry you tomorrow if I could, but can you plan the wedding of your dreams in such a short amount of time?"

"It's not a lot of time, I know, but I don't want anything too crazy. I just want to marry you with our friends and family there. I can find a planner who can do the rest. I have a few things I'd like, but they're easy. We can do it right after filming wraps, that way we can go on our honeymoon and not have to wait."

Leaning down he kissed the top of my head. "Whatever you want."

"What do *you* want?" I didn't want this to be all about me.

"I want to see you walking down the aisle to me, and for you to be my wife. For my family and friends to be there." He half laughed to himself. "I wanted you to meet them first, but I know they'll love you and I don't want to wait."

"Well, I'm sure I can meet them at least a couple of days beforehand. Does that count?" I laughed out and squeezed my arm around his middle.

"Not exactly what I had in mind, but I guess it counts." His voice rumbled through his chest, one of my favorite sounds. "Leo already loves you and has been singing your praises since he went back home. My mom is dying to meet you now."

"I'd say for her to come visit when we first get to Hawaii, but it's a lot to ask of her to come back in a couple of months. If Mason wasn't in school we could visit them, but we leave the day after he gets out. Maybe we can Skype or something like that. It's better than nothing." Letting out a sigh, I apologized. "I'm sorry it's so difficult to find time to see your family."

Holding me closer, Luke nuzzled my hair. "Don't worry about it. We'll figure something out, and we're going to visit them for Christmas." He smiled at the thought. "We need to decide a date so that we can make sure that everyone has time to make arrangements. If anyone can't afford to come let me know and we'll help them out."

"If we wait until after your movie wraps up that puts the wedding at the beginning of August or maybe late July. Do you want our wedding date and subsequent anniversaries so close to your birthday?"

His chest moved as he shrugged his shoulders. Not an easy task while lying in bed and with me on top of him. "I don't mind. It could be on my birthday and I'd be happy. That would make the day even better."

"Tomorrow let's look at your shooting schedule and try to find a date that we think will work. Right now, I want to fall asleep in your arms and spend all of tomorrow in bed with you."

Angling his head to look down at me, Luke locked eyes with me and I knew instantly I wouldn't get what I wanted. "Spending the day in bed sounds fantastic, but I have a feeling that you're not talking about resting. I'm not sure if an all-day sexathon is really what's best for you right now. You need rest to get better."

"I'm already better now that you're here." I mumbled into his chest. "Besides it will be a long time before we'll have another day to stay in bed. I want to cuddle, have as much sex as possible, dance, and eat all day. It sounds like the perfect day with you."

"Hey," he softly spoke as his index finger lifted my chin to meet his gaze. "I'm here now and not leaving once the weekend is over. We'll have all the days that Mason's in school until we leave for Hawaii to spend in bed and do all the things that you want to do."

Closing my eyes, I took in his words. Slowly I opened them back up to see a sated and serene look on Luke's face. "I can't believe you're really here."

Luke pulled me up until we were face to face. "I'm really here. No more being apart. I may not go to bed with you every night, and I may not be there when you wake up every morning, but I promise you that every night we will sleep together no matter where we are."

I spoke, brushing my lips against his with each word I spoke. "I want you to promise me that if you have to leave me in the morning, no matter how early it is, I want you to wake me up so that I can at least tell you goodbye." I smiled down at him. "And I want you to wake me up when you get home so that I can say goodnight."

An amused smile teased his lips. "Are you sure you know what you're asking? I know how much you love your sleep. I could have to leave at four in the morning or get home at two or three. You never know, especially on a tight shoot."

"I love you more than sleep so yes, I'm sure. Promise me."

This time his smile was blindingly happy. "I promise, but if you ever change your mind let me know. Now seriously let's get some sleep. Goodnight my beautiful girl. I love you." He pressed a long kiss to my forehead.

Scooting down and off to the side, I placed a kiss over his heart, and nuzzled into his side. "Good night, my handsome fiancé. I love you."

I SAT OUT ON THE PATIO, ENJOYING THE MORNING WEATHER, looking out at the pool waiting for Taylor to call me back. I'd left her a message almost an hour ago, and I couldn't wait to share the news that Luke had asked me to marry him last night.

My phone rang and instead of it being Taylor to my surprise it was Reeves. It had been a long time since I'd last talked to him. He'd been out of the country filming and with the time difference it was about impossible to talk on the phone. We'd managed to text a little bit here and there, but I'd sorely missed my friend.

"Hey, stranger!" I answered, a big smile on my face. Luke looked up from the book he was reading with a questioning look on his face. I mouthed Reeves name and he gave me a happy smile before going back to reading.

"Hey, back! How are you?" He answered back.

"I'm unbelievably happy. How are you?"

"Shit, but we'll get into that later. Is the reason you're so happy have anything to do with the rumors that Night Shadows isn't going to be filming until next summer and changing their airing schedule?"

"That's part of it, but not the main reason." I answered vaguely, about to burst with my news.

"I take it things are still going well with you and Luke. When is he supposed to be back in Fairlane?"

"He's already here. He arrived last night." A big smile spread across my face as I thought back to Luke surprising me last night.

"Okay?" he drew out the word. "What aren't you telling me?"

Coughing, I waited until I could speak. "Sorry, I've been sick. That's why Luke came home early, but it's what he did when he arrived that has me unbelievably happy."

"You do sound a little congested. What did he do? Wait," he shouted. "Do I want to know?" he asked laughing.

"I wouldn't tell you that." I laughed along with him. "But yes, that did happen." I couldn't help but crack up at his groan.

"I don't want to hear about your sex life. You're like my sister. It's just wrong."

"Aww, Jenner. That's so sweet."

"Only the truth."

Making a happy noise, I smiled over at Luke who was still reading.

"Okay, shorty. The suspense is killing me. Tell me what's going on."

Looking down at my ring, I wiggled my finger for probably the hundredth time that morning. "I'm engaged." I may have yelled into the phone with my excitement.

Luke reached over to pull my left hand to his lips and kissed my finger right above my ring. He smiled, and mouthed 'I love you,' and went back to reading.

"Congratulations! It's about time."

"About time? We haven't even known each other for a year."

"Doesn't matter. That man has wanted to marry you since you were here right after Christmas. I'm sure it's been killing him to wait."

"You think?" I asked, squeezing Luke's hand.

"I don't think, I know."

"You're done filming, right? I want you to come to the wedding."

"I'd be happy to be there. Do you already have a date?"

"We do. You know how we're going to Hawaii for two months for Luke to shoot his movie?"

He laughed which in turned made me smile. "Even over text I could tell how excited you were to go." Now I was even more excited to go to Hawaii.

"I really was and still am. Even more so now. So, we're getting married on August twelfth. That's two weeks after the movie's supposed to wrap up so that gives us some extra time in case it goes over."

Jenner made a strange noise before he quietly laughed. "You do know that it could go longer than even two weeks, right?"

"Of course we do, and we're going to tell our plans to everyone so hopefully everyone will work hard not to create any overages."

This time Jenner couldn't hide his laugh. "Good luck with that. At least Ashlyn's in jail and it doesn't look like she'll be getting out anytime soon. If she was still on the loose, I could assure you she'd fuck it up."

"I have no doubt in my mind that she would. I'm not sure if I'd be able to sleep at night knowing she's on the loose. Anyway, on a lighter note, we'll also be keeping this quiet. Only friends and family are invited and hopefully they'll keep their mouths shut about the date."

"You won't have anything to worry about until you're seen with a rock on your finger. I don't know how you feel about it, but maybe while you're in Hawaii don't wear your ring until after the wedding. There's no doubt in my mind that it'll be leaked that you two got married."

"Ugh! Why are people so noisy? I don't want to hide it, but you're probably right if we don't want to be hounded until they finally see a wedding band, and then there will be all that hubbub."

Jenner cracked up laughing and didn't stop for a full minute. I had no idea what he was laughing about. "Is that what they're calling it these days? Hubbub?"

"Hubbub is the nice way of saying it. I get it I do, but we

shouldn't have to put out a statement every time something happens with us."

"I hate to say this," Jenner stated quietly, causing my stomach to drop. "I know you love Luke, but if you can't handle this life already then you need to back out now. It's only going to get worse. Everything will get worse." The tone in his voice made me pause. I knew that he was talking about Luke and me, but I had a feeling he was talking more about himself and Poppy.

"I love Luke and I'm not going to let anyone ruin this for us." I stated vehemently.

"Okay, I believe you, but I needed to put it out there."

"You did and now it's done." My tone may have been a little too harsh from the way Luke looked at me with his brows furrowed. I gave him a small smile and decided to get to the bottom of Jenner's life. "Now that we're done talking about me, let's get back to why your life's shit."

Letting out a sigh, he swore underneath his breath. "Do we really have to? Let's not ruin your wonderful news."

"I must insist that you tell me what's going on. We haven't talked in forever. Hey! I have an idea, but don't get too excited because it's not going to get you out of talking to me now, but we're going to stay a day or two in LA before we head to Hawaii. Maybe we can get together during that time."

"I should be free and if I'm not I'll make sure I am." He was quiet for a few moments before he spoke again sounding defeated. "So, I came home a couple of days ago and when I walked into the house pretty much everything was gone."

Shooting to my feet, I gasped in shock. "Oh my God! Were you robbed? Wait don't you have an alarm system?"

"Yes, I do. Stupidly I told my wife when I'd be arriving home and she cleaned out the house to furnish her new house with her new boyfriend." Even through the phone I could feel how furious he was.

"Fuck, Jenner, I'm so sorry. I knew things weren't good, but that's…" I didn't even know how to finish that sentence. It had been some time since Jenner has spoken to me about Poppy. Making my way inside to the kitchen, I got a drink and took a long sip.

"What it is, is fucked up, and it gets better. After repeatedly trying to call her to no avail, yesterday I got served divorce papers."

I wanted to tell him it was for the best, but I knew he didn't want to hear it, so I kept my comment to myself. "I'm sorry. Is there anything I can do?"

He laughed bitterly. "Nothing anyone can do. I've known it was over for a while, but I didn't want to admit it to myself or anybody else."

"Anyone who knows you knows that this is not your fault. You have nothing to feel ashamed about. I'm not saying you do, but I know that was a big motivating factor in why I waited so long to get divorced. I wish I'd done it sooner, but there's nothing I can do about it now, and I'm happier than I've ever been in my life, so I can't complain." I drew in a breath unsure if I should say how I felt. "I believe there's someone out there for you, you just haven't met her yet. Process how your feeling and be ready and open when the time comes."

"Wow. All that because you have Luke now." His laugh

was still a little bitter, but I knew he didn't mean it toward me, but his situation.

"It's all because I have Luke." Looking out the window to Luke, I couldn't help but smile. It sounded gushy and lovey dovey, but I couldn't help it because it was the truth and it was impossible to hide. I didn't want to have to hide my feelings for Luke from Jenner or anyone else for that matter, and I shouldn't have to.

"I know and I'm happy for you. It may not sound like it, but I really am. No matter all the hard feelings you may still have toward Matt, you've got to be thankful for all the people he brought into your life."

"I am. He brought me you, Anna, and most importantly Luke, and for that I'll forever be grateful. Although it was Colton that brought Matt here so maybe I should be more thankful for him."

"Maybe," he laughed. "Shit someone's at my door so I should let you go. Who knows who it is. Hopefully I'm not getting served papers again."

"I doubt it. I'll talk to you soon, and I'll text you what day we'll be there. I really hope we get to see you."

"Me too. Talk later."

Sitting down in the lounger beside Luke, I picked up my book and went back to reading. I was hooked into the world of the Luxen that Jennifer L. Armentrout had created and was on my fourth book in the series. I was already dreading the end and anticipating a book hangover.

"How's Jenner?" Luke asked after I got settled down in my seat.

Frowning, I turned on my side to him. "Not good. He got

home a couple of days ago and Poppy cleaned him out and yesterday he was served with divorce papers."

"It's not a surprise, but that sucks for him. He really did try everything he could to keep them together. She checked out long ago."

"I know, but I still feel sorry for him. I told him we'd try to go see him on our way to Hawaii since we'll be in LA."

"We can do that. How are you feeling?"

"Rested." I answered blandly.

Throwing his head back, he laughed full out in a deep rumble. "Any day this week we can have a full on sexathon if you want, but first I want you better."

Sticking my lower lip out, I pouted half-jokingly. "I under-stand, but I missed you and like snuggling with you in bed, amongst other things."

"I would happily stay snuggled up in bed with you, but we both know it wouldn't stay that way. What time will Mason be home tonight?"

My half pout turned into a full-on frown. "Eight o'clock was the deal I made with Decker."

Luke's lips followed the same path mine had. "I wish I would have been here when you talked to him."

"I don't know if that would have helped. He may have requested that I pay him child support instead of demanding that he no longer pay his. In some ways I understand why he doesn't want to see me with you. I wouldn't want to see him with a woman that was better than me in any way."

Scooting his lounger closer to mine, he wrapped an arm around my shoulders. "First of all, we both know that he's never going to find anyone anywhere near as good as you. He might be able to hide who he is for a short while, but I doubt he'd be able to hide his ways for long even if he did find someone."

"And second?" I asked, curious.

"Him not paying child support will work in our favor. You asked for permission from him to take Mason out of the state for two months, but it's the state that decides if and how much he should pay for child support. Before we leave I want to talk to my attorney about filing a request for full custody in August, after our wedding and honeymoon."

"Where are we going on our honeymoon?"

He smiled slyly at me and bopped me on the nose with the tip of his finger. "It's a surprise."

Resting my cheek on his shoulder, I looked up at him. "I'm not a big fan of surprises. How will I know what to pack?"

His sly smile grew wicked. "The least amount of clothing possible. A dress, a few bikinis, and maybe a coverup." He screwed his face up for a moment. "That should cover it. I don't plan for either one of us to be clothed for much of the time, but I might take you out to dinner, hence the dress."

"I like the way you think. I trust you to pick someplace that we'll both like. Have you been there before?"

Hand running up my arm, he answered. "It will be new to us both."

"Nice, I doubt that'll happen very often."

"There are plenty of places I haven't been, but for work I normally end up in the same places."

"I do approve of the location for Riptide." Pulling closer, he smiled down at me. He knew I loved the location. "I do feel bad though, for changing your shooting schedule on Night Shadows. If you want to do any movies…"

"Don't feel bad. You never know the circumstances or timing, and if we get full custody of Mason life will be a lot easier. Don't worry about it now. We'll take each offer as they come and look at it then."

"Smart." I wanted to say more, but his mouth was on mine in the next instant. The moment he turned into me our loungers split and he fell to the floor in a hard drop. Peering over the edge of my chair, I tried my hardest not to laugh. "Shit. Are you okay?"

"I'm fine," he answered with a laugh as he got up.

"We need to get one of those big lounger bed things like what we used in Malibu. That way we can both be comfortable and have plenty of room."

Rubbing his hip where he landed, he grimaced as he stretched out on top of me. "I'll order one later tonight."

"Perfect. Now, where were we?"

Before Luke could answer my phone rang, breaking us out of our haze.

To answer or not to answer.

It rang again and when I looked it was Taylor.

"It's Taylor, hold that thought." Sweeping in, I kissed him quickly before answering.

40

"HEY MAMACITA. HOW ARE YOU?" I ANSWERED TAYLOR'S PHONE call.

"Tired and irritated. How about you?" she answered back without her usual chipper tone.

"I'm great. What's going on with you? You don't sound like yourself." I asked, worried. There were very few times in the years I'd known Taylor that she wasn't happy.

"I just spent all morning grocery shopping. It was insane since it's the weekend and then on Friday, I spent three hours at the doctor's office. We all know that babies come at unpredictable times, but if the doctor's out of the office with a difficult delivery they really should reschedule you instead of making you waste your whole morning in their stupid office. My whole weekend feels ruined."

"It *is* annoying. I remember being pregnant with Mason and being on bedrest. Having to sit in their office for hours almost every time, but heaven forbid I get out of bed and try to make myself something to eat or want to take a shower. As for going to the grocery store on the weekend, I never go. I don't have the patience for it. I totally feel you your pain."

"I know you do. This is it though. I'm making Jack get fixed after the baby's born. I'm not doing this again and the worst part is he's never around and when he is, he's either asleep or I need him to watch Ben, so I can spend the morning at the grocery store."

"I know honey and I'm sorry, but it'll be over soon and then you can move back here. Hopefully in time for the new school year."

"If he's not done by the time school starts I don't care, I'll move back without him. Do you have a room Ben and I can stay in until we find a house?"

"You know you can always stay here anytime and for as long as you want. You're family."

"Thank you, sweetie. You know I think of you as family too. Enough about me, you sounded so excited when you left your message. What's going on?"

"I wish I was there to tell you, but this will have to do. I'm engaged." I shrieked into the phone.

"Oh my God, I wish I was there to see your ring. Take a picture and send it to me. I want to see it." Taylor squealed loudly in excitement.

"I will. I promise." Staring down at my ring finger, I breathed out. "It's gorgeous."

"Oh my, you just let out some love-sick noise." She cackled into the phone.

"Probably, it still feels like a dream. I can't believe he surprised me by coming back early and proposing."

"Hi, Taylor," Luke called from beside me.

"Hi, Luke." She called loud enough I was sure he heard her. "You deserve this sweetie and it isn't a dream. This is your life now. I'm so happy for you." Taylor let out a happy sigh.

"Thank you, Taylor. That means a lot. I want you to be my Maid of Honor. It's kind of short notice, but we plan to get married August twelfth.

"Aww, of course, I will. I'd be honored. You do know that it's an inferno in Missouri in August don't you."

"Yes, but we aren't getting married in Missouri. We're getting married in Hawaii after Luke's movie is finished filming."

"Perfect! Wait. How are you going to plan a wedding in a couple of months?"

I couldn't help but laugh. "Good question. I'm going to start looking online at where I'd want to get married and try to find a wedding planner on the island to help me. That's the only way I'll be able to do it. It's not going to be big, or at least I don't think so. We're only inviting friends and family. Once I know more you'll be the first to know. And let me know if you have any problems coming so we can help you out."

"You don't have to do that. The only problem I can see is that Jack might not be able to attend."

"I know that might be a possibility, but I'm hoping he can. This week I'm going to find the perfect place, figure out the guest list, and let everyone know when and where to make sure they can come. The only problem is that we don't plan on letting the media or public know until after we're married. I don't know how to say don't tell anyone or we'll kill you nicely."

Taylor laughed, making me smile. "I can see how they

could be a problem. You don't want them hounding you all the time. You do know that once you get married they'll be on baby watch, right?"

"I hadn't thought about it, but I'm sure they will. It's crazy to think that we have to release a statement for things that everyone else does and no one cares."

"But they do care. At least they love you and don't write horrible things about how they wish Luke would break up with you all the time."

"Some do," I said sadly. I couldn't expect everyone to like me though.

"They hate you because they want your man and if they had any idea how great he is and how sweet, they'd be a hell of a lot worse."

Side-eyeing Luke, I knew he could hear me and wasn't sure how he'd feel about what I had to say next. "I know, and I definitely don't want them crazier than they already are. Jenner suggested that I don't wear my engagement ring until after we're married, but I hate the idea of not being able to wear it."

"He's right. They'll spot it, but you do what you have to do. Talk to Luke about it."

"I will. I'm sorry I told Jenner before you. I wanted you to be the first I told, but I did call you with the news first. He just happened to call me now that he's done with his movie."

"How's he doing?" Taylor asked. She had grown fond of Jenner from our conversations and what a good friend he'd been after the accident.

"Not good. He got served divorce papers yesterday and Poppy cleared out the house before he got back."

"What a bitch. I hope he finds a sweet girl someday that's nothing like her."

"He will. I know, because he deserves it. He's too much of a good guy to have her stain his life."

"Speaking of stains. How do you think Decker is going to take your news?"

"Amazingly I haven't thought about it, but I'm sure he'll be an asshole. Maybe I won't tell him. He can find out once he and Mason get back from their vacation."

"I'm still surprised he didn't throw more of a fit when you asked if you could take Mason to Hawaii for two months."

I coughed out a bitter laugh. "Me too," I frowned. "It was a little too easy if you ask me. I'm afraid of what he's planning."

"He doesn't have the code to your gate or anything does he?"

"Oh hell no, and that's never going to happen. I don't want him to be able to get in anytime he wants. Dealing with him is so annoying. Luke thinks we can get full custody since he said he wouldn't pay child support anymore."

"It's a possibility, but don't get your hopes up until you've talked to a lawyer and even then."

Looking out at the pool and away from Luke, I shifted in my seat. "I know. It's weird, I was thinking the other day about how different I am, like I'd lost a part of myself."

"What do you mean?"

"I used to be so independent and now… I don't know how I'd describe myself. I'm lost when Luke's not around. I missed him so badly I ached these last few months, and now I feel like I'm relying so much on him. I've never been this way before and, in some ways, it scares me."

"How does it scare you?" She asked in a quiet concerned voice.

I hadn't noticed Luke get up, so I was startled when he slipped in behind me and wrapped his arms around me, resting his chin on the top of my head.

"I can't imagine my life without him in it. If something happened…"

Interrupting, Taylor vehemently stopped my line of thinking as Luke held me tighter. "You can't think that way. It will only drive you crazy. Are you different? Yes, you are, but in a good way. You're still independent, but you are also in love with a man that will never ask you to be anything other than who you are. It's okay to want him around. That's how you're supposed to feel about the man you're with. You still have your job and that may change or evolve in time, but I don't think you'll ever get lost again. I won't let that happen and I know for damn sure that Luke won't let that happen either."

Leaning down until his lips brushed my ear, Luke spoke so that only I could hear. "You have nothing to worry about."

I turned to look over my shoulder to my now fiancé. What I said next was for the both of them. "Thank you, I really needed that."

"That's what friends are for. How many times have you talked me off the ledge from leaving Jack because I'm so miserable here? You remind me that it's only temporary and when we're back in Fairlane everything will be back to the way it was or even better."

"Monthly," I joked. It wasn't even close to that much, but

the further along she got into her pregnancy the more she hated to be stuck there with Jack rarely around.

"See, I owed you one." She laughed, breaking the tension. "I wish school was over, so I could see you before you left. I won't even see you for your birthday."

"I know, but they need all the time they can get to film this movie. It's going to be tight. They've already started without him, doing all the scenes that they can before he arrives."

"What are you going to do while he's filming?"

"I don't know. I haven't thought about it yet. I guess, when I'm not planning a wedding, I hope to watch them film the movie, see the sights with Mason, and enjoy the beach and ocean. Hopefully, Luke will be able to join us some."

"Sounds like the perfect way to spend summer," Taylor sighed wistfully.

"I hope so."

"I hate to let you go, but Jack just walked down stairs and it would be nice to spend a little time with my husband before he has to go back to work."

"Don't worry about it. I understand. Send my love to Jack and Ben, and I'll keep you updated on the wedding plans."

"Talk to you soon."

"Talk to you soon." I answered back.

She made a kissing sound into the phone before disconnecting.

After I got off the phone, Luke and I were quiet for a few minutes. I leaned against his chest with my head resting back on his shoulder, looking out over the pool area. His arms were still around me, hugging me to him.

Breaking the silence, he cleared his throat. "It sounded like you had a good talk."

"We did and I'm sorry."

Moving me to the side so that we could see each other better, he asked with his brows drawn. "What are you sorry for?"

"I should've talked to you about how I was feeling. I was sick and I just… I don't know how many times I've been sick and alone, but this time I wanted so badly to be with you. I'm not used to feeling that way."

"Alex," he pulled me closer, kissing my forehead. "There's nothing wrong with wanting me here. Do you think I'm weak for coming early because I wanted to take care of you?"

My brows pulled together, forehead scrunched tight. "Of course not. I think it's sweet."

Luke dipped his chin, looking down at me seriously. "It's right for you to want me here, with or without you being sick. I know it's not something you're accustomed to, but in time you'll learn that its normal. Never have I hidden how much I missed you while we were apart. I was stuck in LA far away from you, but at least you had Mason here with you almost every day. No one is going to think you're weak."

Nuzzling my head underneath his chin, I laced our fingers together. "Most will think I'm a gold digger or a witch that put a spell on you to make you fall for me."

"It doesn't matter what they say as long as we know the truth. There's always going to be someone out there spouting ugly things about me, you, or our relationship. That's not going to stop, but we can't let what they say get to us otherwise we'll always be miserable, and doubt will start to surface."

"What about my engagement ring?" I asked as my thumb rubbed over the diamond.

"I think for now you should wear it. Maybe if you're at the store or feel someone's eyes on you turn it so they only see the band. On flights, you should probably take it off. I love seeing that ring on your finger." He laughed to himself, his lopsided grin appearing as his thumb followed mine over the diamond. "I bought that ring the first day I had free when I got back after Mexico, and I've been waiting ever since to find the perfect time to propose. I don't want our special moment to be ruined by the paparazzi or a noisy fan, so as much as I hate to say it, maybe leave it here when we go to Hawaii or only wear it around the hotel room."

Staring down at my gorgeous ring, I thought of how much it sucked I couldn't wear it because of crazy fans and paparazzi, but I had Luke and he was worth all the shit they put us through. "Does it ever make you want to stop acting and live a normal life?"

"Hey," he called, tipping my chin up to look at him again. "I do have a normal life here with you and Mason. It's just that I have an abnormal job for someone living in the Midwest." He grinned, and my heart swelled in my chest. "But to answer your question, yes, there are days when it doesn't seem worth it. When I couldn't leave a hotel without security unless I wanted to be mobbed. It's strange that now I don't have to worry about it so much. I've been around and made my stance known that I want my life to be as private as possible, but I have no problem taking a selfie or signing an autograph for a fan if they respect me and my space. Unfortunately, Liam never put those ground rules out there, and he gets mobbed when he goes out unless he's very careful."

A shiver racked my body thinking of a crowd of people trying to get to Luke. "That's scary."

"It is, but I promise you that you and Mason will never be put into a situation like that. If I even remotely think that the public or paparazzi will be a problem, then I'll make sure you have security. I think that the statement we put out about not wanting Mason's picture to be taken or posted on the internet was received well. We have more to worry about from the people here than Hollywood taking his picture and posting it."

Giving Luke a knowing look, I frowned. "Yeah, you are going to be a hot commodity around here for quite some time. I can't even count the number of women who decided that they wanted to be my friend after seeing you at the sock hop. As long as you don't wear those glasses out of the house we should be fine."

Licking his lips, Luke's eyes became hooded. "I feel some eye strain coming on."

Running my hand up his sculpted chest, I kissed the dimple on his chin. "We can't have that now can we. You should put your glasses on before it gets too bad."

41

For the last half hour, I nervously waited until Mason arrived home. Decker demanded that he bring Mason home and up to the door no matter what I came up with for why he shouldn't. I knew I couldn't keep him away forever, but it had been a nice run. He even threatened to not let Mason go with us to Hawaii if he didn't see that Mason was living in a suitable home. We knew that was bullshit because you could see some of the houses in our small neighborhood from the gate and they were all spectacular.

Decker was always unpredictable, and I knew he would blow his top once he saw the house that Mason and I now lived in. What I wasn't sure of was if he would internalize it and wait until an opportune moment to lash out at me, or if he wouldn't be able to hide his displeasure that we were living better than we ever had when he provided for us.

In truth, even when we lived in our much smaller home before I met Luke, we were living better only Decker didn't know it. We may not have had the money to do or buy everything we wanted, but we were happier living out from under his shadow.

When the phone rang to let him through the gate, I jumped up from the couch and bolted to the front door with Luke hot on my heels. Wrapping his large hand around mine, his thumb rubbed back and forth across my wrist in a soothing motion.

"Nothing bad is going to happen. He can try all he wants to ruin this for you, but *you* have the power not to let him."

Wrapping my arms around him with my face buried in his chest, I answered with as much conviction as I could, but my voice still came out wobbly. "I know." Going by the tight squeeze Luke gave me, I wasn't fooling him.

Even before the doorbell rang, we could hear Mason running up to the door. The sound of his footsteps put a brief smile on my face until I came face to face with my ex-husband where it promptly slid right off.

Mason ran in, first hugging me and then Luke. With his big blue eyes trained up at me, he asked. "Can I show dad the pool? I told him we had one, but he didn't believe me."

"If he has time. It's getting late." I replied hoping he wouldn't want to take a look around.

"Oh, I have time to finally see where my son is living." Decker answered with a glint in his eyes as he pushed through the door and into the entry way.

Mason looked from his dad to me, his smile slipping. I put on a bright smile as I led them through the kitchen and out onto the deck. Luke trailed behind quietly.

Arm extended out toward the pool, Mason exclaimed proudly. "See, I told you!"

Decker's dark eyes narrowed as he took in the backyard

and patio. It was our own private oasis set in Fairlane. I planned to spend a lot of time out here, so I'd set up what looked like an entire living room's worth of furniture underneath the deck along with a grill, bar, and sink. Out around the pool there were two different areas with chairs, tables, and loungers. While Luke had been shooting in LA, I'd been busy trying to make our house a home for when he'd finally be able to stay. At first, I didn't know that we would be spending the summer in Hawaii, so I wanted to make our backyard as nice as possible for the summer months. It didn't matter though. We were already enjoying it and I knew we would when we got back at the end of summer.

"Hey, why don't you show me your room before I have to leave?" Decker said placing his hand on top of Mason's head and directing him toward the house.

Mason turned his head underneath his hand. "I wish you could see my room at Luke's house. He decorated it so cool. It has posters and bedding from all my favorite Marvel characters."

"I'm sure it's great," Decker gritted out, giving Luke a dirty look as they passed by to go into the house.

There was no way I was letting Decker walk around anywhere he wanted in the house. I didn't trust him. If there was a way to ruin something or make me upset, he was sure to do it.

This time Luke took my hand as we went back inside and made our way upstairs to stand out in the hall looking in as Decker stalked around Mason's room inspecting every little thing. His room was spotless, but that was only because he had a playroom downstairs with all his toys. That room was a disaster since before he had gone to his dads for the weekend. I was sick, and hadn't asked him to pick up before he left.

Once Decker was finished looking over every inch he squatted down in front of Mason, his face unreadable. "I'll see you when you get back from your trip with your mom and then me, grandma and grandpa are going to take you on a real vacation." Standing he left the room without another word. I looked to Luke for him to follow Decker, I'd be right behind.

Happy that Decker was leaving, and that Mason was home, I hugged him, swaying back and forth. "It's about time for bed so why don't you get into some PJ's and brush your teeth and I'll be right back to tuck you in, okay?"

"Will Luke tuck me in too?" he asked nonchalantly as he went to his dresser to pick out a pair of superhero PJ's.

With a small smile, I answered. "If you want him to I'm sure he will." Luke would love to hear that he'd been asked to tuck Mason in. I couldn't ever remember a time when Mason had asked Decker to tuck him in. "I'll be back in a few minutes."

Hurrying downstairs, I found Luke and Decker in a heated discussion close to the front door. Decker's face was bright red by the time I came to stand next to Luke.

"I don't know who you think you are, telling me what to do." Decker growled, stepping toward Luke, trying to intimidate him. It didn't work since Luke had almost a good five inches on him.

Luke straightened to his full height, looking down on Decker. "This is my house. I'm your ex-wife's… boyfriend." I knew he wanted to say fiancé, but we didn't want to risk him going to the press. We were lucky he hadn't already gone to some gossip magazine and made up some story. If he knew we were getting married he would do everything in his power to ruin it.

"Decker you got what you wanted so please leave." I begged quietly, hoping Mason wouldn't hear. I didn't have it in me to fight him tonight.

"How on Earth do you think I got what I wanted?" His arms flailed around as his face got redder with each word. "Here you are with some new boy toy who's flashing his money all over town, buying a new house, a car, and everything in between, while everyone talks behind my back about my wife leaving me. It makes me look bad," He yelled, face turning purple. "But do you know who's going to look bad in the end? It's going to be you, you stupid bitch, once he leaves you and you have no place to go." He laughed maniacally, eyes trained on me.

"That's enough," Luke growled. "I've already kindly asked you to leave my house, but I will *not* have you talking to Alex that way. The only person who's going to look bad is you and you want to know why?"

Decker crossed his arms over his chest as he glared daggers at Luke. He shook his head as his eyes mocked Luke, saying, 'yes, tell me why.'

"You did all of this to yourself by treating her like shit for years. If you could've been nice or treated her better, she'd still be in your house, in your bed, but she's not and I'm not stupid enough to do anything to jeopardize what I have with her."

"Whatever! You can have her. She's a dumb slut anyway. Maybe at least for you she'll suck your cock." Decker spat out.

I never understood how he could ridicule me and say I was

a slut when in the next second he'd complain about me being a prude and not giving him blowjobs.

"Every day and twice on Sunday's so you better get going." Luke shot back as we stood at the front door to make sure he left.

"This isn't the end," Decker shouted from the sidewalk. His arms straight, fists clenched.

"It never is," I replied as I leaned against Luke's side. We watched him get into his truck, slam the door and drive away. His tires peeled out, leaving skid marks on the street.

Closing the door and setting the alarm, Luke hugged me to him. "Hopefully he won't want to bring Mason home anymore now that he's got that out of his system." I thought about it then added. "At least for a little while."

"Is that what it was like every time he used to bring Mason home?" he asked, his chin resting on the top of my head.

"No, this was actually low key for him if you can believe it. That was him being loving toward Mason. Normally he ignores him which is better than the alternative of lashing out and being mean. On a brighter note, Mason asked that you come with me to tuck him in."

"Yeah?" His lopsided grin slowly made an appearance as he gazed down at me.

"He likes you and wasn't expecting you to be here." My hands slid up his chest to rest on his pecs. "I'm just thankful he's been so easy going about me and you."

Leaning down, he kissed my forehead. "I believe it's easy because he sees how different our relationship is compared to yours and Decker's. He's a smart kid that has good judgement."

Taking his hand, I led him up the stairs giggling. "You're only saying that because he likes you." I joked. "Which admittedly isn't hard to do." Tilting my head side to side, I said. "Although it's possible he wouldn't like you as much if you didn't like his favorite superheroes."

He laughed, trailing behind me up the stairs. "I'm pretty likable."

Looking over my shoulder, I winked at him before opening Mason's door. "I'll show you just how likable you are once we get Mason to bed."

Sitting up straighter and clapping his hands when we walked in the door, Mason's smile beamed at us. "You came!"

Luke sat down beside him, putting his hand on Mason's shoulder. "If I'm home and you want me to I'll always tuck you in."

Looking down at the floor, Mason dejectedly said, "My dad never tucks me in."

Tears instantly stung the back of my eyes hearing his heartbreaking words and the sadness in his voice. In the blink of an eye, I was down on my knees and hugging him to me. "You're going to have to beg me to stop tucking you in and one day you probably will, but I hope that'll be a long time from now, like after you've gone to college."

Luke's hand rubbed up and down my back, calming me as if he knew I was seconds away from crying. "What do you do before bedtime?"

Pulling back, I smiled at him for breaking the sadness in the air. "He brushes his teeth, most nights he takes a bath, puts on his pajamas, and then I read to him. We've been reading Harry Potter and we're on the fifth book. It's been taking us quite a while since we're lucky to read half a chapter a night."

"I've never read the books." His mouth turned down, but quickly turned back into a smile. "I've watched all the movies."

"The movies are good, but the books are much better."

Seeing the books on Mason's shelf, Luke went over and picked out the first one. "I'll have to read them then. It's a good thing I'm a fast reader since you're on book five."

Mason's eyes lit up that Luke wanted to be a part of our nightly routine and read the books. I hated that Decker never tried to connect with him.

"I've got some news to share with you," I said excitedly. I couldn't hold back any longer. My smile was stretched so wide at the thought that I was afraid I might scare Mason with my Joker smile.

Mason's eyes darted toward Luke, but quickly came back to me. I stood by Luke and held his hand. We were a team and I wanted him to be as much of a part of this as he wanted. "As you can see Luke came home early last night because I wasn't feeling good." Mason frowned. "I'm feeling much better now," I quickly reassured him. "But that's not the news. The news is that last night Luke asked me to marry him." Mason's eyes widen almost comically, and his mouth fell open. "And I said yes."

"Does that mean you're going to be my daddy now?" he asked so sweet and innocently. I felt the tears sliding down my cheeks before I could stop them.

"Well," Luke started and then cleared his throat. "We'll be

family. I'll be your step-dad, but I can never replace your dad. My family will be your family."

"Do I have to call you dad?"

"No," Luke shook his head as he knelt down. "You can call me whatever you want."

Looking serious, Mason nodded and then stated. "This will be good."

"It will." Luke and I both replied as we watched Mason grab his book off the shelf. Looking up at Luke, I smiled. "I guess that's it." His eyes followed Mason before agreeing.

Now that Mason had a much bigger bedroom, I'd upgraded his bed to a full size, so it was much more comfortable to read to him at night. With all three of us on it I was thinking maybe I should have gotten him a queen or even a king. Mason climbed underneath his blankets and I tucked him in just the way he liked. It was close to the point he couldn't move while sleeping, but he had a little wiggle room. I couldn't imagine sleeping like that, but Mason didn't sleep well unless he was thoroughly tucked in.

After getting him just right, Luke and I climbed onto his bed. I laid down beside him to pick up where we left off reading before his weekend with his dad, and Luke sat taking up a good portion at the bottom of the bed. Mason lasted a little longer than he normally did from the excitement of having Luke there with us.

Quietly we got up, I turned off the lamp, and kissed Mason's cheek. I was looking forward to having Luke as a part of our nightly ritual and I knew Mason was too.

Now it was time for me to show Luke just how likable he was. Maybe I'd even ask him to put on his glasses.

42

Taylor's eyes traced over the patio that overlooked the pool where we were having dinner. All of our friends and family were with us in Hawaii for our wedding. To keep the wedding private, Luke rented out the entire place for the rest of the week. Everyone was feeling free with the entire resort being ours.

"Wow, I still can't believe you guys booked the whole place, but I get it. I think I've finally picked my jaw up off the floor after seeing Anna, Colton, and Reeves walking around earlier. They were very sweet about by my star-struckness."

"Is star-struckness a real word?" I laughed at her.

"It is now, and it might be my perpetual state being friends with you and Luke if celebrities will be dropping by for holidays and birthdays."

I could only shake my head. "I seriously doubt any will be dropping by, but after you've been around them for a little while you realize that they're just like us. They're normal people with normal problems."

Side-eying me, she spoke out of the corner of her mouth. "Except that they have an abnormal amount of money."

"Afraid they might hear you?" I whispered back with a smile.

"I don't want to offend anyone."

"You realize now that you're back in Fairlane that you'll be around Luke and he's one of them, don't you?"

"Luke is so normal except for his hotness."

We both burst out laughing at her statement. I had to agree. Luke was pretty normal aside from how sweet and amazing of a man he was. There was a possibility that I was biased.

Biting her lip with a sad look in her eye, Taylor asked. "Did you invite Ryan?"

Letting a sigh out, I looked at everyone taking their seats. "Even though I hadn't talked to him in months, I thought that maybe he'd finally see that Luke is the guy for me and that all the shit Ashlyn posted was a lie, but he didn't even respond to the invite."

Taylor's face fell. "I'm so sorry. I know that you're disappointed that he hasn't come around."

Wetness sprang to my eyes, and I bit my bottom lip. "I miss him. Ryan was there for me after the divorce and we got close again. He was my go-to-guy for when things went wrong with the house and they went wrong a lot."

Wrapping her arm around my shoulders, Taylor pulled me in for a side hug. "Well, you don't need him anymore. You've got a new house and in a couple of days you'll have a new husband that adores you."

"Can you believe it? Two years ago, I never would have thought I'd ever get married again. Hell, I didn't think I'd ever date again and now I'm marrying the most amazing man in the world." I closed my eyes and smiled. "One day I'm going to have his baby and I *know* that we're going to live happily ever after. My life became a fairytale." Taylor looked over at me her eyes wide and her mouth parted. "What?"

"Are you really planning on having a baby?" she asked in a hushed voice.

"How could I not want to make a baby with him? To make another person that's a part of him?"

Luke dipped down from behind me, kissing my cheek. My gasp then smile caused his lips to tip up as he sat down beside me. "What prompted your dreamy eyed look?"

"You," I answered truthfully. "How much my life has changed in the last two years and how great it is now."

Leaning in, Luke cupped my face and gave me the most tender kiss of my life. We didn't care that everyone in the room was probably looking at us. His thumb caressed my cheek as his lips swept against mine one last time.

While I had a dreamy look before, I knew then that I had a starry-eyed gaze now. Luke had a tendency to do that to me and I hoped that it would never go away.

He kissed the tip of my nose and then my forehead. "You're not the only one with a great life, beautiful."

I could only smile at him.

"Are you ready for tonight?"

Luke shrugged as he brought a shrimp to his mouth. "I could take it or leave it, but I'm happy to spend more time with my dad and brothers."

Chewing on the inside of my cheek, I worried if Liam and Leo had planned to take Luke to a strip club. Surely they would try to keep it low-key, so the media wouldn't find them. I wasn't worried Luke would cheat or even touch a girl, but what a girl would try to do and might make up to make a little money. Since we'd been in Hawaii for a little over two months, it was known that Luke was shooting a movie and that Mason and I had joined him. Luckily for us there weren't any paparazzi here, but there were still plenty of people that had taken pictures and posted them online.

"Do you know what the guys have planned?"

Turning to look at me with an assuring smile, he wrapped his hand around mine. "They wouldn't tell me but promised not to get me in trouble. What about you? Do you know what Taylor and Anna planned?"

"Nope." I gave Taylor the stink eye, but she was talking to my high school friend, Josh, so she didn't see. "Only not to get me so drunk that I'd have a hangover tomorrow."

He hummed to himself as he looked at the people at our table before turning back to me. "I think I have more to worry about than you do."

"I don't know how that's possible. The men definitely outnumber the women and I know how much trouble Josh, Mark, Jason, and Jack can get into."

"So, you do admit that you're worried," he stated with amusement.

"No. Well, yes, I'm worried, but not for the reasons you might think I am."

"What reason is that?" he asked before shoving an entire shrimp in his mouth.

"I'm worried about someone trying to make it look as if something happened with all you guys out. Maybe some girl will think we broke up and will try something, and when you reject her she'll be mad." I shrugged. "It could happen."

"Hey," he murmured against my ear as he pulled me close. "I'm not trying to trivialize what you're feeling, but I don't think you have anything to worry about. It's something I'm always conscious of," he stopped and frowned. "Sadly, now you are too."

"I don't want ugly rumors right before we get married. I want it to be perfect."

"I want it to be perfect too and it will be. No one's going to find out until we release a statement, and by then we'll be safely tucked away in Fairlane."

"You don't think people will speculate why Anna, Colton, and Jenner are all in the same place as we are with our friends and family? I'm surprised they aren't already."

"They can speculate all they want, and we knew it would happen if we invited everyone here. Now I want you to sit back, relax, and enjoy yourself."

My lips met his in a brief kiss until Jason groaned about having to watch us. Still, I smiled as I rested my forehead to his. "Thank you for making me feel better."

I watched as his eyes crinkled up as he smiled.

"That's my job."

I didn't care that everyone was watching us. And that I'd only just met most of Luke's family. This was the man that I loved and always would. I knew he'd never let me down.

"I love you so damn much," I whispered and then kissed him with everything that I had to show him how much I loved him in that moment.

"Oh, come on! We know that you're in love and all, but

seriously dude, you're making the rest of us look bad." Jason groaned.

"Too bad," I answered back before I threaded my fingers through Luke's hair and pulled him into a kiss.

Hot, wet, and deep.

Everything faded away.

No friends or family.

Only me and Luke.

43

LUKE STRODE INTO THE BATHROOM AS I WAS PUTTING ON MY FINAL swipe of blush. I'd gone all out with my makeup for the night. No one would tell me exactly what the plans were, and it was making me slightly nervous. Standing beside me I watched him put some gel in his hair that was getting a little longer and wanted to flop into his eyes. I loved it longer and wanted to run my fingers through it, but I knew our time was running short. Soon Taylor and Anna would be here for our night out.

"What's wrong?" he asked, washing his hands of the gel.

Jumping onto the counter, I sat with my legs splayed so that Luke could stand between them which he promptly moved to do. My dress slid up my thighs, and Luke's hands followed the fabric. His thumbs swept the inside of my thighs making my core start to thrum with want.

"Besides that, we have to spend the night apart?" I huffed and stuck out my lower lip. "Stupid traditions."

A small smile spread across his face as he looked down at

me. "Did I not please you enough today?" he chuckled knowing what he was doing to me.

Luke wore a pair of dark jeans that fit him perfectly, molding against his ass and thighs, along with a pair of black boots and a dark grey button-down shirt that he hadn't bothered to button yet.

My hands skated across the ridges of his abs up to his pecs where they rested naturally as I looked up at him.

"Not now with what your fingers are doing to me," I answered breathless, my hunger for him evident. "Along with the thought that I can't have you later. There will be drinking tonight, I'm going to get horny, and you won't be there to help me." Scrunching my face up as I realized something. "In fact, I won't even be able to pleasure myself with Taylor in the room."

His blue eyes turned stormy at my words. "Do you need one last orgasm for tonight?"

"Yes," I answered, my hands falling down to his belt to start unbuckling, only for him to stop me.

"Hey, we don't have time for that. Let me help you."

Without giving me a chance to answer, Luke's hand caressed down to my calf, kissed the arch in my foot, and rested my foot against his shoulder.

"You wore panties." His voice deep and gravelly made me instantly wet.

"I thought it would be smart if I was drinking and wearing a dress. I don't want to flash anyone and have it all over the internet." I moaned as he moved them aside and pressed his thumb firmly to my clit.

"Smart girl."

Lifting my other foot to the edge of the counter, I splayed my legs wider giving him more access. One hand grasped his bicep while the other stayed firmly planted.

Sliding two fingers inside, he pumped in and out with a slow tempo as his thumb rubbed circles over my bundle of nerves. I'd already had three orgasms since I woke up, and one less than an hour before, but that didn't stop me from wanting Luke or being ready to go off almost the moment he started to touch me.

"Luke," I moaned low in the back of my throat. "More."

Faster and harder Luke's fingers pumped as his tongue swept into my mouth like a summer storm. It was intense, strong, and short. Tasting and nipping my lips before leaving me gasping for air.

Reaching up to bring him back to my mouth, I stopped when he knelt to the ground and brought his mouth to my aching core. His tongue felt divine. Soft and smooth compared to his thumb. Circling and sucking, his fingers curled, hitting my magic spot and sending me soaring.

"Oh, God. Luke," I moaned. My legs shook as they clamped around his wide shoulders. My fingers fisted his gelled hair.

Leaning back against the mirror, I sighed out. "God why can't we do that all night?"

Dipping down, Luke sucked on my bottom lip before murmuring, "Beautiful, we've got an entire week of doing that day and night. In a little more than twenty-four hours I'll ravage you from sun up to sun down."

"That sounds like a plan. What about you though?" I asked eying the erection pushing at the zipper of his jeans.

Adjusting himself, he grimaced. "I'll be fine."

My fingers traced along the denim. "You don't look fine." Peering up at his messy hair, I bit my lip. "I messed up your hair. Let me fix it."

Looking at himself in the mirror, he smirked down at me. "You don't like the just fucked hairstyle?"

"Personally, I love it, but I'm not so sure I like it when you're going out without me."

Closing my eyes, slowly I tilted my head side to side. "My legs feel like jelly. I don't think I can even put my shoes on."

Without saying a word, Luke left and came back with the heels that I'd set out to wear for the night. They were black and sparkly just like my dress. Instead of kneeling, he raised my leg to place on his shoulder, leisurely slipping my shoe on.

"You're the best," I declared as I wrapped my arms around his neck and kissed the dimple in his chin. "Tomorrow you'll be my husband." I couldn't help but smile.

His eyes sparkled as his full lips curved up into a smile. "And tomorrow you'll be my wife."

Looking down, I started to button up his shirt. "Does it bother you that I've been married before? That you're not going to be my first husband?"

Stopping me from buttoning any further, Luke wrapped his fingers around my wrists. "Maybe if you had married him out of love, but no, it doesn't bother me." Letting go he used one finger to tilt my chin up to look at him. "I think it bothers you. You wish I was your first."

Tears instantly sprang to my eyes, my chin trembled as I spoke. "It isn't fair. You deserve to be someone's first husband, the father of their first child. Your special and I want you to feel how special you are. Not…"

His lips pressed to mine as his arms wrapped tight around me. It wasn't a passionate kiss, but one of comfort. Our lips rested against the others, eyes closed. "What we have is special. Don't ever think differently. I don't care that you've been married before because I know that we're going to stay married until the day that one of us dies and forever after that."

With everything in me, I held myself together. I couldn't cry. Not now when I was supposed to leave in only a few minutes and my makeup would be ruined. Opening my eyes, I was met by Luke's Caribbean blue's staring back at me. "You can't say such sweet things to me and not expect me to cry."

Looking down at me the love he held for me swam in his eyes as a soft smile tipped his lips. "But do you feel better?"

"I feel better." I answered. He had made me feel better, but I was still an emotional wreck. Tomorrow Luke would be my husband and I couldn't wait. I felt as if I'd waited my entire life for him. "I love you."

His eyes softened at my words. Something I noticed they did every time I told him I loved him. Sometimes it was still hard for me to believe that he was just as affected by me as I was him. "And I love you, beautiful."

We heard footsteps only a second before Taylor appeared in the doorway. She bit her lip, trying to hide a smile. "Hey, I thought you'd be ready."

I couldn't stop my smile. It was likely she knew exactly what we'd been up to.

"Almost. Luke is putting on my shoes and then I'll be

ready." Dangling my other shoe by my fingertip, Luke shook his head, but took it none the less.

"What are you guys up to tonight?"

Hiking my leg on his shoulder, Luke ran his hand up from just above my knee to the arch of my foot. "Don't know. They wouldn't tell me."

Taylor laughed, her voice tinkling. "Sounds familiar."

"Indeed."

My head moved back and forth between them, my hands resting on Luke's chest for balance. It made me beyond happy that they got along so well. If they hadn't, I didn't know what I would've done because I desperately needed them both in my life.

"Are you sure your mom's okay with watching all the kids?"

Turning his head in Taylor's direction, Luke slipped my heel on. "Positive, she loves kids and wants to get to know Mason. She's tired of waiting for us to have kids and is ready to take on her grandmother role. I think she's hoping Alex will get pregnant while on our honeymoon."

A choking sound came out of me, but both Luke and Taylor ignored it.

"So…" Taylor bit her bottom lip, clasped her hands behind her back while looking at anything but us. She was nervous for some reason. She took a deep breath and met both our stares. "I wanted to give you a heads up for tonight."

Luke growled a foreign curse under his breath, his arm wrapped around my shoulder.

My brows furrowed. I didn't like or understand the tone

the room had changed to. "What is it?" My voice shook. Luke's hand squeezed my shoulder.

"It's got nothing to do with the parties." Taylor blurted out and then spun around where she stood, stopping to look hesitantly back at us. "I don't want to cause any problems, but Luke, I wanted to warn you that Jack will probably try to persuade you to change your mind about the prenup."

Pulling away, he stood rigid in front of us both. His tight jaw ticked every few seconds while he kept his eyes closed.

Sliding off the counter, I stepped toward him and wrapped my arms around him. For one-second, I was afraid he'd reject me, but his arms instantly wrapped around me as he buried his face in my hair. I stood rubbing my hands up and down his back as he slowly relaxed in my arms.

One last squeeze and he took a step back. "It'll be fine. He's made his opinion clear on what he thinks I should do, but don't let it ruin your night. I'll politely let him know that I'm not going to change my mind."

"Luke, maybe…"

"Not going to happen." He interrupted, eyes blazing. "Now give me one last kiss before you become my wife."

"You like saying that word," I mumbled as I stood on tiptoe to kiss him.

"Very much so. Now kiss me, my soon to be Mrs. Sandström."

"I'll give you guys a minute. I'll be out in the hall."

I kissed along his jaw until Luke picked me up, bringing me level with him. Wrapping my legs around his waist, I placed a chaste kiss to his lips and smiled.

"Don't tease me," he growled playfully.

One hand slipped into his hair as the other cupped his cheek. His eyes darkened with lust as I smoothed my tongue across his bottom lip. He opened for me. Our tongues moved against each other's in a sinful dance. It was always so easy to get lost when I was in Luke's arms and his mouth on mine.

"Um..." Taylor interrupted sounding embarrassed. "I'm sorry to interrupt, but it's been five minutes and we really need to get going."

"Right," Luke smiled devilishly at me. Giving me one last kiss, he put me down. "I'll see you tomorrow. I'll be the one waiting for you at the end of the aisle."

I couldn't help but reach up to give him one last kiss on the dimple of his chin. "I can't wait."

"Okay, I hate to be the bad guy, but we've really got to get moving." Turning to Luke, Taylor spoke as she pulled me out the door. "I'll take good care of her."

"I love you!" I called from outside the bathroom door. "Don't have too much fun!"

Stepping out of the bathroom, he replied, leaning against the door frame as he watched us, lips tipped up. "I love you too, beautiful."

"I can't believe you've been in Hawaii for over two months and haven't been to a luau until now," Taylor whispered from her spot beside me.

My eyes were glued to the men juggling fire sticks and dancing. I couldn't believe that I hadn't been either. Mason would've loved it. I'd have to make sure we all came to one when we visited again.

Leaning toward her, I kept watching. "Luke was too busy filming otherwise we would have. I'm kind of bummed that Mason didn't get to see one."

"Honey, you're marrying a movie star. If you want to come back once a year or hell even more, you can. You're not going to be stuck in Missouri. You're going to travel to places all over the world and you might even find one you like better than Hawaii."

Maybe.

Sipping my drink, I eyed our surroundings. "This is pretty tame for a bachelorette party. Not that I'm complaining."

Anna looked from her place across the table at me with a knowing glint in her eye. "Do you think this is all we have planned?"

"How am I supposed to know when everything was kept so hush-hush?" I whisper-yelled.

"We don't have anything planned too crazy in case someone takes pictures or videos. We're keeping it all private, but we thought we should at least feed you first." Anna winked, turning back to watch the show.

"Do you know what the plan is?" I asked Taylor.

Without taking her eyes from the ladies whose hip action I was instantly jealous of, she answered me. "Of course, I helped plan it."

"And?"

"And you've got nothing to worry about. Now finish your drink and relax."

Down the table from us, Stella, Luke's sister, yawned. Our

party consisted of Anna, Taylor, Stella, Gabi, and Jessica Kelly. Jessica played Luke's vampire daughter on his show, Night Shadows. I'd met her when I visited the set and loved her instantly. It was easy to see how close she and Luke were. He got along with the other actors, but for some reason they were a little standoffish when I was there. All except Jessica.

Where I only had five people in my party, Luke had almost three times the amount of people I did. While we had Anna, I had a feeling that if anyone was followed, or filmed it would be Luke's party since they had Colton, Reeves, Liam and Luke.

I stopped questioning them and enjoyed the show, food and drinks. They were all amazing. I could have sat there all night watching and drinking and been perfectly content, but Anna and Taylor pulled me from my seat and to our waiting car.

The moment we pulled up in front of the resort, I looked around the car to see knowing smiles on each of their faces. Since I didn't want to annoy them by me continuing to ask questions, I kept quiet. These were my friends, and I was going to trust them.

Taylor draped her arm around my shoulders as she guided me into the resort's bar. A small band was playing, but the only people besides them were the bartender and us. Without saying a word, the bartender started to pour us each a drink. I had no idea what it was, but it was tailor made for me. It was sweet, with some rum and had a slice of orange and cherry on top.

The band played all my favorite songs from Imagine Dragons to The Chainsmokers, The Lumineers to Maroon 5. By then I'd drank enough that I didn't care what we were doing. I sang loud along with the band, but my jaw dropped when Gabi walked over and took the microphone. At that same moment the bartender pulled out a bunch of penis straws placing them in all our drinks. His cheeks flushed pink, and I couldn't help but laugh. Taylor took that as her opportunity to place a crown on my head that lit up.

"I'm honored to be here to celebrate Alex's last night as a Sloane," Gabi said from up on the stage. "I met Alex a few months ago when I was doing a guest spot on Luke's show and we hit it off right from the start."

"I love you, Gabi!" I pointed at her and yelled, swaying on my seat.

"I love you too, Alex. Bartender get her another drink! Get everyone another drink!"

The bartender already had a pitcher of whatever he made for us and filled each of our glasses to the brim. I took a sip of my drink through my penis straw as did everyone else, each of us laughing at the absurdity.

"The day I met Luke and Alex, I was walking back from makeup when I spotted them dancing outside the studio. A song was drifting out from another sound lot, but you would have thought they were playing it just for them. They didn't even notice me as I walked by. They were in their own little world.

"When Luke asked me if I'd sing at their wedding, of course I said yes. He told me the song that Alex had been dreaming of hearing at her wedding. He also told me that every day they're together they dance to at least one song. How fucking sweet is that?"

"Go ahead and swoon, ladies. I got a good one." I bowed, nearly falling off my stool.

Everyone yelled back different versions of the same thing. "Yeah, you did. And Hell, yeah."

"I'm not going to sing your dream song, but I wanted to sing one of your favorites." Gabi whispered to the band and they started Maroon 5's *She Will Be Loved.*

It was one of my favorites songs and I knew Luke had told her. I wanted to tell him how much I loved him and that it was so sweet of him to tell Gabi about our dancing.

"Ladies," Stella called, as she stood from her stool when the song was over. "I need to go powder my nose. Who's going to join me?"

"I shouldn't," I groaned, standing up. "Once you start, you can't stop, but I need to relieve my bladder."

After asking the bartender where the bathroom was, we all stumbled to the bathroom each taking a stall.

After washing my hands, I swiped on another layer of gloss. I watched as each girl came out. Stella wrinkled her nose, lifting her arm to smell.

"I hate to be rude, but we stink like… I don't know. The luau maybe?"

Gina narrowed her eyes at Stella but didn't say anything.

"I've got some perfume in my purse. Maybe if I spray it around the bathroom…"

Gina interrupted her with a firm shake of her head. "Not happening, I'll be waiting out here." She thumbed towards the bar.

"What's her deal?" Stella asked as she dug in her purse trying to find her perfume.

Jessica applied her red lipstick with perfection in front of the mirror. "Maybe she's offended that you said she stinks."

Stella's mouth hung open for a moment. "I didn't say *she* stinks. I said we all do."

"It's still offensive," Jessica deadpanned.

"Well, we'll all smell like roses and she'll smell like a dead pig," Stella sneered before a big smile came over her face as she cheered. "Here it is."

Before any of us could say anything, Stella started to spray her perfume throughout the room. I knew something was wrong the instant my eyes started to burn and water profusely. Darting for the door, I heard the others start to cough and gag.

"What the fuck?" Gabi questioned as I stumbled out the door. "Why are you crying?"

"Stella," I coughed out. "Oh my God that wasn't perfume. I think it was pepper spray." I tried to look around to find a chair to sit but couldn't see. "I need something to wipe my eyes." I croaked out as one after the other they came spilling out of the bathroom.

"Stella are you trying to fuck us?" Jessica shrieked.

Someone bumped into me causing me to trip and almost fall, but Gabi grabbed onto me and waited until I was steady.

"Oh my God, I think it's coming out here," Gabi coughed. "Are you okay?"

"I think so. Can we get some towels to wipe our faces? I don't know what to do? Do they need to be wet?" My shoulders dropped in defeat as I tried to clear my watery eyes with my arm. "What they hell are we supposed to do?"

"I think we need to wash our faces and anything else that the spray's on with soap."

What a pain in the ass.

"Gabi," I felt around until I caught an arm hoping it was hers. "Can you take us back to our rooms so that we can get cleaned up? And maybe call it a night."

"A little pepper spray is not ending our night," Taylor laughed then let out a hacking cough. "We'll just move the party to your room. The night's not over yet."

"We can't even see," I whined. "How is the night not already over?"

"Because we got you a stripper, and he's not here yet. We can't get our deposit back."

"I'll pay you back if that's what you're worried about."

"Honey," Taylor called from somewhere close by. "Trust me when I say you'll want *this* stripper."

"Why would I want a stripper when I'm about to marry the hottest guy in the world tomorrow?" I asked exasperated.

"You just do." She chuckled, looking over at Anna. "Now, let's go get cleaned up before he gets here. Hey, bartender? Can you tell the stripper that we're up in the room when he gets here and send up another pitcher of those drinks?"

"Um… sure." He replied as we started to walk out of the bar.

44

"Why are we still doing this? I didn't want some stripper to begin with and now I look all blotchy from scrubbing my face free of pepper spray." I whined to Gabi walking out of the bathroom.

"Fuck if I know. You'd think the rest of them had never seen a naked man before with how badly they want that stripper to show up."

It was weird. I mean, Anna had her very own heartthrob with an amazing body.

I spoke quietly as I watched Taylor and Anna walk in, so they wouldn't hear me. "Maybe I'll push the stripper off on them when he gets here."

"Do you think Luke will care that you have a stripper?" Gina asked out the side of her mouth.

"He wouldn't care unless something happened."

"Would you care if the guys got him one?"

Would I? A feeling of jealousy surged through my body.

"Kind of." I shrugged. "I don't think he'd do anything, but

I don't know how to explain it. It makes no sense when he has to be intimate with some of the most beautiful women, but it does."

Gina rolled her head toward me with a slight frown. "You can't help what you feel."

"Why are you in your yoga pants?" Anna asked with a laugh, plopping down in a chair across from me.

"Because I had to take a shower to get all the damn pepper spray off me. I didn't think we were planning to go out again. Are we?" I looked from Taylor to Anna, and then to Gina sitting beside me on the couch.

"No, we're staying here, but I thought you might want to look nice for the stripper." She bit her lips in an attempt not to smile.

"I hate to burst your bubble, but I don't care about the stripper," I replied bluntly.

"Look who I found out in the hall. The stripper," Jessica laughed maniacally as she stepped into the room. In truth it scared me a little.

"Unless you got me Superman or Thor, I don't care. I hate to be a party pooper, but my eyes are still burning, and I just want to chill."

"What's this about Superman?" A familiar voice asked.

Luke stepped into the room with the rest of the guys trailing behind him. Colt had a boombox that he placed on the table.

A smile stretched across my face. "What are you doing here?"

He smiled back at me devilishly. "I'm your stripper."

My eyebrows rose. "Really?" I asked excitedly.

"She said she didn't want a stripper," Gina crowed from her spot on the couch.

"Oh, I'll take this one." I held out my arms, but Luke shook his head at me.

"All good things come to those who wait."

"Is sex included in this strip-tease? Because I am not waiting until tomorrow night if I have to sit here and watch you strip for me."

"She just said that out loud," Jason barked out.

"Do you have underwear on? You can't be stripping in front of everyone if you don't have underwear on." No way in hell were they all seeing the goods.

"Oh... my... God." Jenner laughed and shook his head.

Luke headed to the radio, looking over his shoulder at me. "I have underwear on. Do you?"

"No," I laughed, shaking my head. "I've got yoga pants on."

His brow furrowed. "I noticed. What happened? You all changed."

"What happened?" I laughed out. "Your sister sprayed the bathroom with pepper spray and we all almost died."

"You didn't almost die," Stella retorted.

Luke started to head back to me, his eyes turned worried. "Shit are you okay?"

I heard in the background Anna, Taylor, and Jessica all answer their husband's that they were fine.

"I'm fine. My eyes are just a little irritated. I told them I wasn't going to get dressed back up for a stripper I didn't want, but now I'm thinking I should have."

His eyes softened. "You look beautiful. I'll strip for you no matter what you wear."

"I have a feeling this isn't the first time." One of the guys murmured.

"Are you really going to do this?"

A wicked smile grew across his handsome face. "Of course, I need to make your bachelorette party memorable."

A rush of warmth fell over me. "You already make my life memorable, but I'll happily take a strip tease from you as long as touching is allowed."

His eyes crinkled as he smiled. "I'll make an exception just for you."

Colt stood from his spot beside Anna making his way over to the boombox and hit play.

My eyes widened as Luke took his first step toward me. It wasn't his usual long stride. Each step he made dripped sex. I couldn't believe they'd planned this, and Luke went along with it.

A sexy smirk graced his lips as he stalked toward me. With every step, he swiveled his hips in a movement that I was all too acquainted with. Stopping before me, he turned and shook his delectable ass in my face. My hands had a mind of their own as they reached out and squeezed each firm ass cheek before smacking one side.

Luke jumped away, turned, and started to slowly unbutton his shirt. Each button undone with the beat of the song.

"I can't believe he's doing this." Jack grumbled from the other side of the room.

Josh laughed into his hand. "I don't know why not? If I wasn't pudgy around the middle I'd do it too."

"No one wants to see you strip, not even your own girl-friend," Cory retorted.

"Shut up." I looked around Luke to scowl at them. "You're ruining my strip tease."

"I think she's enjoying it." One of the guys said with a laugh.

"I'm enjoying it." Both Gina and Taylor said at the same time and started laughing. Taylor fell into her husband and continued to giggle into his shoulder. I had a feeling she was taking advantage of finally being able to drink and was beyond a little tipsy.

Luke grinned as he slowly slid his shirt from his sculpted torso.

Each thrust of his hips brought him closer and closer to my chair until he stood directly in front of me. I ran my hands up his thighs until I reached the edge of his jeans. I was ready to unbuckle his belt and take him into the other room, but Luke had other plans.

Turning around, he slowly lowered himself until he was grinding the tops of my legs.

"Take it off," Gina catcalled.

"Is that what you want, Alex?" Luke asked from over his shoulder, his voice low and gruff, and sexy as hell.

"Yes," I answered breathlessly.

He gyrated his hips one more time before he stood in front of me and made slow work of undoing his button and zipper, driving me mad with want.

He knew what he was doing to me and I didn't care that I was ready to jump him in front of all our friends.

Slowly he dragged each leg of his dark jeans down his legs

and stepped out of them to be left in only a pair of male teal bikini briefs.

Stella said something in what I assumed was Swedish before she left the room with her hand over her eyes.

Leaning forward, each hand took hold of his ass as I pulled him to me. "Where did you get those?"

Lifting an eyebrow, he asked. "Do you like?"

I eyed his package that was already at half-mast. Definitely not appropriate for our audience. "I prefer you without, but I do like them."

He bent down until his lips caressed the shell of my ear with each word. "I made a pit stop on my way back to the hotel after the guys asked me to do this impromptu strip tease." He bit the shell of my ear. "I think it's time we take this somewhere private."

"I agree." I motioned him to move closer. "Don't mind us, but we're taking this party into the other room."

Wrapping my legs around his waist. Luke stood with me, grinding against my core.

"Oh, shit this is where it stops being PG."

"And that's when all the fun begins," Jason whooped.

"Don't be pervs and listen. It's time for you to all go back to your own rooms," I hollered back at them before I squeezed my legs tighter around Luke's waist and crashed my lips to his.

45

WITH PURPOSE I WALKED DOWN THE ROSE PATH THAT LED TO MY destiny. I briefly glimpsed at our friends and family, but I couldn't stop taking in the man who waited for me.

Dressed in white linen and barefoot, Luke smiled softly at me. Each step, I felt my smile grow until I reached him, beaming up at him.

Taking a step closer, Luke grasped my hands, smiling down at me.

"Welcome everyone. Lukas Theo Sandström and Alexandra Scarlett Sloane have chosen you, those special and important to them, to witness and celebrate the beginning of their life together. Today, as they join in marriage, they also create a new bond and a new sense of family - one that will undoubtedly include all who are present here today."

I had no idea what the officiant said after that as we stood there lost in each other's eyes. My only thought was that I was marrying the man of my dreams. I had never known love that transcended all else. Luke's thumbs rubbed back and forth across the tops of my hands in a loving and soothing manner.

My thoughts were interrupted as the officiant said. "Luke and Alex have both written vows to each other. Luke you may start."

"Alex, I promise that every day for the rest of our lives I'm going to make you feel beautiful.

To make you smile and laugh.

To dance whenever and wherever the song takes us.

To be there to lift you up every time you fall and wipe away the tears.

To love Mason as if he were my own.

To fall more in love with you each day that I have with you.

I love you, Alex. Forever and always."

Luke

WIPING THE FEW TEARS THAT TRAILED DOWN HER CHEEK WITH MY thumb, I gave her an encouraging nod. With each word of my vows, I watched as her eyes brimmed with tears and eventually slip down her golden cheeks.

I couldn't believe that in only a few short minutes she'd be my wife. Clearing her throat, she gazed up at me with so much love in her eyes, my entire body pulsed with emotion.

"Long ago I gave up the little girl's dream of her fairytale life until you walked into my life.

You've given me everything that I never knew I wanted and more.

You've shown me what love really is.

That it's okay to let your guard down.

To trust.

To cry.

And to love.

Every day, I promise to show you how much you're loved.

How honored I am that out of everyone you chose me, love me, and never fail to make me feel treasured.

You are my forever. I love you, Luke."

Every word she spoke from her heart. Her love shining bright and true through her eyes. I had never loved her more than in that moment.

"Do you Lukas Sandström, accept Alexandra Sloane as your life mate and one true love, promising to share in all that life offers and suffers, to be there for her in times of plenty, as well as times of need, to soothe her in times of pain, and to support her in all endeavors, big and small, for as long as you both shall live?"

"I do," I vowed proudly.

Never taking my eyes off Alex, nothing else existed but her. For the next week she was all mine, and I was going to ravish and spoil her. After our honeymoon, she'd never have a doubt in her mind how special she was to me.

"Luke, I give you this ring as a symbol of my love. As it encircles your finger, may it remind you always that you are surrounded by my enduring love. "

"And now, by the power vested in me by the State of

Hawaii, I hereby pronounce you husband and wife. You may now kiss your bride."

Everyone cheered and clapped. I only had eyes for my bride as I swept her up in my arms and our lips melded together. Her mouth opened as I dipped her, my tongue stroked against hers. It was easy to get lost in Alex, but I had to keep some composure and not ravish her in front of everyone.

Standing up, I stood her on her feet. Her eyes glazed over in lust and love. "Let's do this."

~

Alex

"THIS IS BEAUTIFUL. YOU AND THE WEDDING PLANNER DID A great job with everything." Luke murmured against my ear. The hand resting on my shoulder pulled me closer to his side.

We were outside with fairy lights twinkling and candles lit everywhere as we overlooked the ocean. Off to the side we could see the gauzy material that made up the tent our guests sat under during the ceremony at sunset as we said our vows.

"Have I told you how absolutely stunning you look tonight?"

My ever-present smile stretched further as I nuzzled his neck. "Only half a dozen times or so."

"Have I told you how hot you look with that ring on your finger?" I wasn't sure what it was, but I couldn't keep my eyes off his left hand. His long tan fingers curling around his champagne flute or the way they brushed across my skin, his ring glinting in the light. Seeing Luke with a wedding band on made me want to do dirty things to him.

"How much longer do we have to stay here?"

Maybe he had the same idea I did.

"Eager to leave?" I whispered into his neck. His only response was a playful growl.

"I'd like to say goodbye to everyone, but after that…" Luke stood and pulled me up with him causing me to laugh. "Okay, let's go say goodbye."

Pulling me to a stop in the middle of the dance floor, Luke beamed down at me. "Aren't you forgetting something?"

"I thought we were getting out of here?" I whisper-yelled as I took in the crowd that had started to surround us.

"We will, I promise, but first we have to dance as husband and wife. One last dream fulfilled."

"What?" Tears filled my eyes as I watched Gabi step onto the stage and take the microphone in hand.

Wrapping his arm around my waist, Luke leaned down. "You'll find out in just a moment."

"Hello, everyone. I'm Gabi, Luke and Alex's friend. It's been an honor getting to know them in the short amount of time since we met back in March." Turning to look at us, Gabi smiled sweetly. "Unfortunately, we couldn't get the original band so I'm going to sing. I hope I do your song justice and make this part of your night as special as the two of you are. Watching the two of you, I dream to one day find a love like yours. Ladies and gentlemen, Luke and Alex Sandström dancing their first dance as husband and wife."

The intro of *Iris* by The Goo Goo Dolls started and Luke

wrapping me tightly in his arms. "You didn't want to miss this did you?"

I could only shake my head as I fought the tears that threatened to spill. Resting my head on his shoulder, I took in a shuddering breath as I tried to contain the emotions that were swirling inside me. Luke cupped my head with one hand, his other on the small of my back as we swayed to the beat.

For as long as I could remember I'd loved this song. There were times when it would put a smile on my face and make me happy, and other times when I wasn't in a good place that it would make the tears flow in sadness. Even when I was down, I loved it no matter what.

Over the last few months, Luke and I had danced to it numerous times. He never cared what song we danced to or where we were when we danced. Sometimes I stood on top of the table so that I could be eye level with him and other times, I'd jump up and wrapped my legs around him as he swayed us around the room. Other times we'd be at the park or on the beach. It didn't matter where. Never once did Luke complain and each and every time we danced, I fell for him a little bit more.

Only once I'd mentioned I wanted to dance to *Iris* when I got married, and he'd made that happen. We were discussing the food and music of the reception, when Luke smiled his lop-sided smile and told me he had it covered. Never in my wildest dream did I think he'd try to get The Goo Goo Dolls or Gabi to sing it. He made my dream come true. A moment that I'd never forget until the end of my days.

By the end of the song, I couldn't fight the tears from falling any longer. The shoulder of Luke's shirt was drenched with tears as I pulled back to look up at him, my chin trembling.

"Did I do good?" he asked, face soft as his thumbs wiped away my tears.

"Good doesn't even come close to how I'm feeling right now. You, Luke Sandström made the entire experience perfect. It's beyond perfect. It's *everything*."

I NEEDED HIM. IT HAD BEEN LESS THAN TWENTY-FOUR HOURS SINCE my last orgasm, but this would be my first as Mrs. Sandström. The heated look in his eyes for the last hour hadn't helped matters any.

Luke bent me over the bed that was now covered in rose petals and slipped inside of me.

"I can't hold back." He panted in my ear. "Next time, I'll be gentle, but I need you too much right now."

I thrust back against him and ground my ass against the area above his cock.

He plastered his front to my back and plunged his tongue deep inside my awaiting mouth.

My thighs trembled as I started to come apart. My body clenched around his throbbing cock only for him to pull out and flip me on my back before pushing inside once again.

Reaching up, I ran my hands up his chiseled abs, around his broad shoulders, and pulled him down for a fierce kiss. Our teeth clashed together. Our tongues dueled.

My muscles twitched, and my core tightened as my nails dug into his back.

Luke stilled, his eyes opened as he watched me fall apart underneath him.

I erupted into Earth shattering pleasure.

"I love you," he moaned as he started pumping in and out in a frenzied tempo.

The love that reflected in his eyes, and each strategically placed thrust, had me falling all over again right along with him.

Rolling off to the side, Luke held me tight in his arms. We melted into each other as husband and wife. From that day forward, we would always be one.

"Was today everything you ever dreamed of, Mrs. Sandström?" he asked as I started to drift off in his arms.

The entire day had been perfect. A fairytale come to life. My Hollywood redemption.

"Everything and more."

EPILOGUE
3 YEARS LATER

"Are you going to tell me where we're going?" I asked when I spotted Luke crossing into the closet through the mirror.

"To that Japanese restaurant that you like," he called from inside.

That sounded good, only I hoped that he wouldn't be suspicious when I didn't order any sushi.

"Did your meeting go well?"

"Yeah, I'll tell you about it later." He sounded distracted as he shuffled and banged about.

Curling my last piece of hair, I asked. "What are you doing in there?"

"Just grabbing a few things I want to take back before I forget."

Walking to the closet, I stopped at the door. "If you would have told me what you wanted I'd have packed them for you."

Luke looked up at me while he shoved something into his

bag. He still traveled light wherever he went and had gotten me to reduce what I packed, but that was only when we were going from one house to the other. Otherwise it looked like I was moving every time we traveled anywhere.

Placing his bag on the floor by the door, Luke leaned down to kiss my cheek. "I know you would've, but it was something I thought of on the way home. If you're ready we should leave. We skipped lunch to finish up and I'm starved."

"I only need to put my shoes on and I'll be ready."

It was early November and in Fairlane I'd already started wearing jeans and long sleeves. Half the time with a jacket, but in LA the weather was warm and gorgeous so I was wearing a fun gold dress.

I placed my hand on Luke's arm as I eased first one shoe on and then the other. "Are you sure you're okay?"

He kissed the top of my head before taking my hand. "I'm sure," he smiled, but it didn't reach his eyes. "It's been a long few days."

"We can stay in if you'd like. I'd happily stay home and curl up on the couch with you."

He smiled again and this time it reached his eyes. "I know you would, but we've got no food in the fridge and I promised I'd feed you."

"We could order in. I don't mind. You know I like to have you all to myself."

I could see the war going on behind his eyes, but eventually being tired won out. "Alright, take those shoes back off and let's call in a pizza. I'll meet you downstairs."

Promptly, I took off my heels before my feet could start

hurting and took the stairs two at a time, to get to Luke as quickly as I could. I desperately wanted to know how his meeting had gone and to tell him my news.

When I found him, he was sprawled out on the couch with his eyes closed, but the moment he heard my footsteps his eyes popped open.

Turning on his side, he patted the spot he'd cleared for me. "Come snuggle up next to me, my beautiful wife."

Happily.

With my head resting on his chest, I could hear his heart racing. Luke was nervous, but I had no idea what there was for him to be anxious about.

Instead of talking, he ran his fingers through my hair. If he didn't start speaking soon I'd likely fall asleep. The last couple of weeks I'd been dead tired, but we'd been busy. Luke had finished taping the series finale of Night Shadows, while I planned a party for the cast and crew, entertained Mason, and packed up what stuff we were taking back to Fairlane. The day after the party we flew back to Missouri and Mason went to stay with his dad and grandparents for two weeks. Two days later we were back in LA for Luke to meet with a director and movie producer who wanted him to be the male lead in a book trilogy they were making. We'd been there for a week and were set to fly back to Fairlane tomorrow.

I woke to the doorbell and Luke sliding out from behind me to answer the door. Blinking the sleep away, I watched his retreating form. After three years, I was still hot for my husband. Probably even more so. Our friends liked to joke with us about how sickeningly sweet we were together and how I always wanted to jump Luke.

I licked my lips as I watched him come back with two pizza boxes that smelled heavenly.

"Was that for me or the pizza?" he smirked as he set the boxes down.

"Most definitely you. You left this morning without waking me up." My bottom lip stuck out in a fake pout for only a second before it quickly changed into a smile.

"I'm starved." I moaned around a mouthful of my pizza.

"Me too," he said around his slice. "You wanted your chicken supreme, right?"

I nodded as I finished chewing a bite. "I can't believe we almost left without having it. I'm going to miss the food here. Maybe we should open up a restaurant or three in Fairlane, so we have more options."

Eyes wide, Luke stared at me as he opened and closed his mouth a few times.

I couldn't help but laugh. "I'm only kidding. Although it would be nice if there were more restaurants by us."

He nodded but kept quiet as he ate, which wasn't normal for him. For every minute that went by, my anxiety started to increase at what could possibly be keeping him quiet. His eyes followed as my knee bounced up and down. From the moment I met Luke, we always had something to talk about. I couldn't take another second of silence.

"I know you were hungry, but you've got to start talking because I'm over here about ready to lose my mind on what could possibly be wrong."

"There's nothing wrong." He wiped his hand off on a napkin only to then run his hand through his hair. "I didn't sign on to do the movies." He shook his head as it was his turn to watch me gape. "From the beginning I've always told you I'd do anything for love and family."

Sitting my pizza down, I made my way to his side of the couch and straddled him. "You have, but surely there's got to be some way for you to do the movie. I know how badly you wanted to do them."

His hands moved to my hips, his thumbs brushing against my lower back. "They want to film the movies back to back all in Canada." His eyes shut for a moment as he took in a deep breath and I wanted to cry. He wanted that role more than any other and now he was hurting. When he opened his eyes, I only saw resolve reflecting back at me. "When I told them I only film during the summer months it was all they could do not to laugh at me."

"Then they're assholes." I wanted to yell, but I knew it wouldn't help matters any. I needed to keep calm for Luke.

His lips tipped up into a small smile. "Not really, and they did try to work with me. They offered to do the first movie next summer, and then the other two starting the summer after that."

"I'm sorry, Luke." I cupped his cheeks and pressed a light kiss to his full lips. "I'm sure there's some way we can make it work if you really want the part."

Wrapping his arms around me, he pulled me flush against him. "I want the part, but if I do these movies it will change our lives forever. Yes, we'll be set for life with money, and my career will skyrocket."

"But?"

"The sex scenes are not what you've seen me do before. I did put in for you to be there for all the scenes, not that it matters now. The book fans will either love it or hate it and if they love it…"

"You'll be known everywhere you go and it will be hard to maintain the level of privacy we have now." I finished for him.

"I like what we have now." He leaned his head back on the couch and looked up. "It's a lot to put up with. If you're still okay with it knowing what you know now, and you think you can get Decker to agree with Mason being gone that long, I'll call them back. They said they'd give me until the end of the week to decide before they offered it to someone else. What do you think?"

I didn't have an answer. I couldn't until Luke knew. This wasn't exactly how I planned on telling him, but it would have to do.

"Do you think we could do it with a baby in tow?" I asked with a smile I was sure would break my face in two.

"I… well… um… a baby?" His eyes widened, mouth parted. "Are you sure? A baby? Our baby?"

"Who else's?" I laughed.

"Alex." His eyes softened as his hands rounded to my stomach and gazed down. His voice was barely above a whisper when he spoke. "We're going to have a baby."

I nodded as I swallowed the lump in my throat. After we decided to try, I cancelled my appointment at the doctor's office to get my shot. We were told that it might take me up to a year to get my period back and at least eighteen months to get pregnant.

He gazed up at me in wonder. "I thought it would take at least a year for you to get pregnant."

Warmth radiated throughout my entire body as I took in

the smile on his face. His eyes glittered with happiness and I knew mine reflected the same. This time would be different. This time was already different than the last. We cried from happiness, not from sadness at being stuck with each other for the rest of our lives.

"I love you so much." Luke repeated over and over again as he peppered kisses all over my face.

Tears streaked down my cheeks. "I love you too." A sob broke out. "We made a baby."

"It only took two months for you to get pregnant. It's a miracle."

"Thank you for giving me this."

His brows furrowed. "When are you due?"

"I don't know. I have an appointment with my doctor when we get back." I tried to do the math in my head but wasn't sure if I was right or not. "My guess is sometime the beginning of May."

"I know you're an amazing woman and mother, but do you really think you'll want to uproot your life and live in Canada for three months right after you have a baby? I won't be around to help you like I want to."

Wrapping my arms around his shoulders, I rested my fore-head to his. "I hate to be the reason you turn it down."

"There will be other movie roles, and if not then I'm okay with that, but I'm not okay with missing out on my child growing up. I haven't missed one of Mason's soccer games, a sleepover, or a skinned knee since I came into his life. I'm not going to start missing all the important stuff now, and I promised you that I'd be there to help you." He brushed his lips to mine before resting our foreheads together. I stared into his cerulean eyes that shined with happiness. "I can't do that being on set for fourteen-hour days. This is the right decision for us."

My heart melted with all the love I had for him. Each day I fell more and more in love. Luke Sandström was the perfect husband and father, who just proved it in spades.

"I love you more than words can ever express. I'm going to do everything in my power to show you each and every day."

He cupped the side of my neck, eyes full of adoration. "You already do." Our lips met in a soft brush. I kissed the corners of his mouth before nibbling on his bottom lip.

Lying me down on the couch, Luke rested to the side of me with one leg thrown over mine. Lifting the edge of my shirt up until it reached my breast that had already started to grow in size, he placed soft kisses over my still flat stomach. I couldn't wait to see it pop out with proof of our baby.

Looking down at me with his hand rubbing circles across my belly a tear slipped from his eye. "Thank you for giving me this. For giving me you and Mason, and your love."

"What else could I give you? You've already given me a fairytale life and I can't wait to see what's in store for the next chapter in our lives."

Want more Luke and Alex? Sign up for my newsletter and immediately get a bonus scene.

Luke and Alex Bonus Sign-Up

Want more of Fairlane?

Remember Prue, Alex's neighbor? She's got her own book, a second chance, military romance in Unsteady in Love.

Did you enjoy Hollywood Redemption? If so, please consider leaving a review on Goodreads, Amazon, and BookBub. Reviews mean the world to authors especially to authors who are starting out. Your review could be the deciding factor or whether or not someone else buys my book.

To stay up to date on all my releases subscribe to my newsletter. http://bit.ly/HarlowLayneNL

UNSTEADY IN LOVE - PROLOGUE

PRUE

The Day After High School Graduation

My toes skimmed across the worn wood of the porch as I tried for the hundredth time that day to reach Holden. We were supposed to go to Chicago to try to find ourselves an apartment for the fall, but Holden had failed to pick me up when he was supposed to. At first, I thought nothing of it and only thought he was late, but as time ticked by with no word, I started to get worried. This wasn't like my boyfriend of three years. Holden always called when he was going to be late, which wasn't very often. Hours later and I was a mess, grasping at straws as to where he was and why he wasn't answering any of my phone calls or text messages.

"Any word?" my dad asked out the screen door, worry etched on his strong but tired face.

"No." I hung my head as tears started to build for the millionth time that day.

"Why don't you drive on over to his house? Maybe his parents know where he is. I think leaving the front porch will do you some good anyhow." He gave me a weary smile that did nothing to ease my worries.

"Maybe I should. Sitting here isn't getting me anywhere," I strangled out, worried about what could have happened to Holden to prevent him from picking up his phone.

"That's my girl. I'm sure it's some big misunderstanding." He gave me a wan smile.

"You think?" My head popped up, hopeful.

"Baby girl, Holden loves you more than life itself. Nothing could keep him away."

He did. Holden loved me just as much as I loved him. My dad was right. Long ago, my dad had accepted that Holden would be around for the long haul. Not that Holden was bad news or anything. Only the fact that my dad thought I was too young to find the man I was going to spend the rest of my life with.

This all had to have been some kind of misunderstanding. Holden had probably left his phone somewhere and couldn't hear it the hundred times I'd called. That had to be it.

"You're right, Dad. Thanks. I'm going to see what's going on. Don't wait up for me." I hopped off the porch swing and dashed inside for my car keys. On my way out, I popped up on my toes and gave my dad's smooth cheek a kiss. So excited to see Holden, I tripped going down the stairs. Looking back up at my dad, he stood shaking his head and waved.

The entire way to Holden's house, I had the windows

down and let the wind blow through my hair. There was something about the feeling of the night air on my skin and my hair tickling along my back and arms that soothed me. By the time I made it to Holden's house, I almost felt like myself again.

As I pulled up into his driveway, I noticed there were no lights on in the house which was odd. There were always lights on at night from the timer they always set. Stacy and Bruce Montgomery didn't want their son to ever come home to a dark house. This was the first time in years I'd seen it pitch black inside. The worry from earlier reared its ugly head as I hoped a light would miraculously turn on.

Still, I parked and made my way up to the ornate front door. I tried to peek inside through the frosted windows to no avail. I knew there was no point, but I was desperate. It was eerie how quiet the house was. Not even a cricket was chirping in the yard.

Taking a deep breath, I rang the doorbell with the hope that this was all some sort of silly prank and waited patiently for someone to answer the door. After a few minutes with no one in sight, I decided to try my luck at the doorknob. If Holden knew I was coming over, he made sure that the front door was unlocked for me to come in. We'd been together for so long, I was part of the family. This time, though, I was met with the resistance of a locked door.

Where were they?

Fighting back the tears that were threatening to build, I slipped my phone out of my back pocket and punched in Holden's number one last time. By that time, I expected it to ring and go straight to voicemail or for it to be dead after all the times I'd called and texted throughout the day. I never expected the message that shattered my heart into a million pieces.

"We're sorry. You have reached a number that has been disconnected or is no longer in service. If you feel you have reached this recording in error, please check the number and try your call again."

Falling to my knees, my entire world crumbled around me.

Holden was gone.

And I was alone.

Read more of Holden and Prue's story today in Unsteady in Love.

ACKNOWLEDGMENTS

To my husband and sons who gave up their time with me so that I could accomplish my dream. You mean the world to me.

To my girls- Cris, Heather, and Michele. You were my first true tribe and I'll love you girls forever.

My KB 101 Tribe - Alyne, Molly, Kelsey, Kara, Syd, Jessa, Grahame, Catherine, Emma, Tracy, Richelle and Clare- fate brought us together to make a wonderful group. From day one, we instantly clicked. Thank you for all your support with answering all my questions and listening to my problems.

Alessandra Torre for make the Inkers group and giving us all your wisdom and time. To all the Inkers who I've gotten to know and all your help and advise.

Thank you to everyone else who shared and helped me through this amazing journey.

And to you the reader for taking a chance on a new author.

ABOUT HARLOW

Harlow Layne is known for her contemporary romance style of beautiful slow-burn, sweet, sexy and swoon-worthy alphas, and fast pace, super-steamy romance in her Love is Blind series.

Indie Author. Romance Writer. Reader. Mom. Wife. Dog Lover. Addicted to all things Happily Ever After and Amazon.

Harlow wrote fanfiction for years before she decided to try her hand at a story that had been swimming in her head for years.

When Harlow's not writing you'll find her online shopping on Amazon, Facebook, or Instagram, reading, or hanging out with her family and two dogs.

ALSO BY HARLOW LAYNE

<u>Fairlane Series - Small Town Romance</u>

With Love, Alex

Unsteady in Love - Second chance, military

Kiss Me - Holiday, Insta-love

Fearless to Love - Insta-love

Affinity - enemies-to-lovers, fake marriage

<u>Love is Blind Series - Reverse Age Gap</u>

Intern - office

The Model - office

The Bosun - military, first responder - Spring 2021

<u>Hidden Oasis Series - Romantic Suspense</u>

Walk the Line -first responder

Secret Admirer - stalker, insta-love, damsel in distress

<u>Willow Bay Series - Dark Forbidden Series</u>

Away Game - MM, bully (February 4, 2021)

<u>Worlds</u>

Cocky Suit - office, interracial

Risk: forbidden, sports

<u>Anthologies</u>

Spiced Holiday Kisses

Risking Everything: A Steamy First Responder Anthology

Heard It In a Love Song

https://www.harlowlayne.com

To stay up to date on all of Harlow's releases subscribe to her
newsletter: http://bit.ly/HarlowLayneNL

Made in United States
North Haven, CT
23 July 2023

39411063R00270